PRIZE CATCH

Alan Carter was born in Sunderland, UK. He immigrated to Australia in 1991 and now lives in splendid semi-rural semi-isolation south of Hobart, Tasmania. In his spare time he follows the black line up and down the local swimming pool, or drags on his wetsuit and braves the icy waters of the D'Entrecasteaux Channel. He is the author of seven previous novels: the Fremantle-set DS Cato Kwong series *Prime Cut* (winner of the Ned Kelly Award for Best First Fiction), *Getting Warmer, Bad Seed, Heaven Sent* and *Crocodile Tears*; and the New Zealand-set *Marlborough Man* and *Doom Creek*, featuring Sergeant Nick Chester, which won the Ngaio Marsh Award for Best Crime Novel.

ALAN CARTER

PRIZE CATCH

 FREMANTLE PRESS

For Kath, tireless adventurer.

PRELUDE

There always seems to be more roadkill just after the weekend. Makes sense. People are out and about more on Saturday and Sunday nights. Pub. Dinner. Family and friends. Innocent pastimes and lethal consequences. A wallaby lies brained across the cycle path and she veers further out onto the road to avoid it. The traffic is building but it's still early enough for drivers not to get too impatient. A crisp, sharp autumn morning with a dusting of snow on kunanyi/Mt Wellington and the North West Bay jerry mist spilling over the Channel. She's glad she opted for the thicker riding gloves today; even with them her fingers feel frozen. Hardly a breeze but there's an iciness at her core, which she puts down to the approach of winter.

Left onto Sandfly Road for the climb past the white weatherboard church. This isn't the steepest or longest hill on the ride, but it's the first and always seems the toughest. The sun breaches the eastern cloudbank and her last view of kunanyi is of a pink glow cast across the Organ Pipes. On now past the alpacas in the paddock, her breath steadying, legs warming up. The sharp twisting incline to the Nandroya Vineyard ahead of the blessed flat stretch towards Allens Rivulet. A tradie in his black muscle ute decides the one-and-a-half metre safety margin is not for the giving and she feels his sidewind. She gives him the finger but doubts he ever checks his rear-view mirror. Every ride there's at least one fuckwit. The ute disappears into the distance: good riddance. The long climb now towards Allens Rivulet Two, as it is designated on her Strava app, the last nasty hill until beyond the Longley Hotel up to Riverbend Road. A twenty-two K round trip before getting on with her day.

At times like this she's glad they made the move to Tasmania. It hadn't been an easy decision; she was Fremantle born and bred – a beach baby. The idea of moving somewhere not just cool but so fucking cold that swimming gave you a headache seemed mad. She didn't mind the Western Australian heat so much, but the evidence was before them – the summers were getting longer and hotter – and there's no point staying on if one of you is suffering. And Ros really was suffering: the relentless heat made her irritable, she slept badly, lost her energy, her joie de vivre. They'd moved to Tassie three years ago, contributed to the local housing affordability crisis by outbidding and outcashing the competition, and now here they were in semi-rural splendour. It was growing on her too. She'd given in, bought herself a swimming wetsuit and joined the local open-water nutters – at least during the warmer months anyway. Even Ros seemed to be almost back to her old self, the woman she'd fallen in love with. Yes, the move has been the right decision.

The Allens Rivulet sign has been partially blacked out by some graffiti, renaming it Aliens Rivulet. She smiles every time she sees it. A simple and effective commentary on the rural Tasmanian underbelly – or just a silly joke? The sun is well and truly up now, warming her back, and it's going to be another stunning day. She picks up pace for the downhill run to the Huon Highway. Head down for the sprint, click those gears into high.

It's already too late when she sees the vehicle that cleans her up and dumps her in the ditch like just another piece of roadkill.

1

'Got your lunch? Thermos?'

'Yes, Mum.'

'Don't you "Mum" me.' Kaz slips her tongue between his lips, gives his crotch a stroke. 'From here on, you're on your own, buster.'

Sam pulls her closer. 'Thank you.'

'What for?'

'For sticking by me, through all … this.'

'On your way. Don't want to be late on your first day.' Kaz scoops Ollie up from the rug and hands him over. 'Kiss your son and hit the road. See you tonight.'

Out the door. Sam checks everything is secured in the ute tray, chucks his holdall in the back seat and hops in. Gives Kaz and the bub a last wave and reverses out onto the road. Sparrow fart and hardly anyone around. It's a long haul from Claremont down the Brooker Highway through to the Channel, but leaving this early he hopes to beat the work traffic. Today and tomorrow are induction days – a straight nine-to-five before he's allocated his shift pattern of ten on, four off.

A job. At last.

He just needs to hold on to this one. That's all.

As he passes the Tasman Bridge to his left, the jerry mist is thinning out over the gunmetal Derwent. To his right, the city with the mountain rearing behind. The summit cocooned by cloud but some glimpses of early-season snow. A helicopter landing on the roof of Royal Hobart Hospital, somebody being medivaced. A road smash maybe. He feels the familiar tightening in his chest and throat, breathes slowly to calm it. Past the fishing boat dock and the old Hobart sandstones where the money and power reside. On the Southern Outlet now, up over Tolmans Hill and the transition to rolling countryside hemmed by dolerite ridges. The farm paddocks outside Kingston churned over for new houses: Blue Wren Estate. Maybe, in time, they'd be able to save up and buy one of those fuckers. May as well have a mortgage with rents the way they are, through the damn roof. He realises his fingers are gripping the wheel over-tight. Loosens them off.

New job. In these Covidy times too. He'd known the old skills and networks would come in useful one day. Catches the 7 am news on the radio: Covid blah-blah, anti-lockdown, anti-vaxxer demos over the weekend, cops scanning CCTV and ready to come knocking. Senate estimates, pollies' snouts in the trough again. A bomb somewhere in the Middle East. Weather set to be nice for the rest of the day. Beautiful.

A whole succession of small Channel towns on the way through. He'll never be able to afford to live in any of them. Cashed-up boomers from the mainland are buying up big time. Tree-changers. Climate 'refugees'. First-world fucking worries. To his left, glimpses of the water. Be nice to have a place here, though, looking out on that. All peaceful like.

Through the gate past the picket line of scruffy hippie protesters.

Yeah, fuck 'em.

—

She's going to be late but she keeps getting lost, every corner she turns is a dead end. She should know her way by now, for goodness' sake. She'll be late and he'll give her that look, break her down bone by bone, pore by pore. Fill her with shame and self-disgust. Looking down, she sees she's forgotten to dress appropriately again. Her mother's soiled slippers and dressing gown, that sour ashtray stench. Another corner and he's right there in front of her, blocking the path. Criticising everything about her. Nothing is, or ever will be, good enough.

Ros wakes with a start. Slides her hand across the bed, feels the residual warmth where Niamh has been. Opens an eye to survey the empty space. She supposes she should get up, have a pot of coffee waiting for when Niamh gets back from her ride. Sip and admire her while she does her stretches. Maybe make a list for the day to keep everything on track: coffee, breakfast, medication, piano practice, job application, anxiety attack, medication, nap and repeat ad nauseam.

Snap out of it, you're on your way back! Out of bed, trackies and t-shirt.

Uggs. Cardie. In the kitchen, Ros flicks the kettle on and opens a tin of cat food for Monica who's curling around her ankles and mewing.

'Okay, okay. Here.'

Cat sorted, she pours boiling water into the plunger. Seven-thirty. Niamh is usually back around now. Out the window to the north, the mountain is dappled by patches of light and shade from the scudding clouds. The wind seems to have bristled, even in the short time since she got out of bed. On the back lawn, the chooks have edged out of the hen house and peck the earth with a level of concentration she can only dream of. Medication. She knocks a couple back and feels the flattening out that makes life bearable these days.

Is this all there is?

It mustn't be. That's why they're here. To start again, to rebuild. To get better.

Yes. She can't and mustn't allow her life to be forever defined by that man and what he did to her. After all, she'd won, hadn't she? The compensation payout had helped them buy this house. And under the terms of the non-disclosure agreement there was a glowing job reference which they were obliged to honour. Water under the bridge.

Three years under the bridge and washed out to sea. Three years unable to land a new job. Glowing job reference dated and worthless. And him still on his upward trajectory after his campaign of bullying, belittling, isolating, gaslighting. Why? Because, like any predator, he'd spotted some weakness in her that triggered him. Nothing special about her except that she came into his line of sight and suited his purposes. Why did she let him get away with it? Was it disbelief and denial that this could happen to her? Some kind of shame she couldn't put a name to. That denial, in turn, translating into self-disgust. Feeding on itself. Unreal. Jeez, Niamh had been a saint putting up with this crippling, ugly, repulsive paralysis.

Come home, Niamh. Where are you?

Ros checks the time on the microwave. Nudging eight. Niamh is usually home by now, she has to be out by 8.30 am to get to her job. Shower, breakfast, everything before that. Where's Ros put her phone? She finds it on the couch in the lounge room, switched to silent. Swiping her screen back to life, she sees a number of missed calls and messages. None of them from Niamh.

Then she hears the knock at the front door.

–

He's clipped on his name badge, filled out a whole bunch of forms, had his photo taken for ID, been given his uniform: a polo shirt, fleece, beanie, baseball cap – all with the D'Entrecasteaux Salmon company logo. A fish leaping in the rapids, going against the flow. Protective and wet weather gear. Then some babe from marketing had shown them a video about the product. Who knew that farming fish could be so fascinating? Another from HR laid down the law about zero tolerance for this and that: drugs, alcohol, unions. Then they all signed the non-disclosure agreement.

Morning-tea time.

'Sam Willard. That right?' The woman holds out a hand for shaking. He juggles his cuppa and carrot cake into one paw, and they do the business. 'Kristin Baker. Call me Kris. Sustainable Business Team.' It's the marketing babe who showed them the flash video. On closer inspection she's not as young as he thought she was. But wearing well, that's for sure.

'G'day.'

'I was told to look out for you. Introduce myself.'

'Yeah?' He can't help the unease spreading across his face.

She laughs. 'Don't look so worried. We're all family here.'

Some of the other new guys are looking this way. The odd wink or grin. Wondering why she's singled him out. He's wondering the same. 'Great to meet you … Kris. Very happy to join the team.' He's stammering like he's sixteen and getting up the nerve to ask her out. He waves his carrot cake at the room. 'Great set-up. Impressive.'

Her eyes sparkle, she's enjoying his discomfort. 'You were in Afghanistan, I hear.'

Who from? He'd kept it off his CV. 'Yeah. While ago now.'

She nods. 'We look after our veterans.' Taps his name badge. 'Farm Attendant is just the start, Sam. I know you've got great potential.' She hands him her card. 'Welcome to the team.'

–

Could that really be Niamh there on the hospital trolley?

Ros glances at the detective and he nods for her to move forward, get a closer look. Yes, it's Niamh. Her face looks so peaceful. It's been cleaned up but there are grazes down the left side from temple to jaw, all swollen. Ros fights the urge to kiss Niamh, shake her awake. No touching, she's been told.

'Is that her?' The detective looks like he too is trying to hold it together.

She wonders if he has access to the same pills she's on, the ones that make things dreamlike. He's a handsome, sporty man. Ambitious too, she thinks. The kind of man her mother would have wanted her to marry. His name, what was his name? Ian Cavanagh. That's it.

'Ros,' says Ian, apologetically. 'Can you confirm …?'

'Yes, that's Niamh.'

He nods and the attendant covers Niamh's face as Ian guides Ros towards the door. Some paperwork changes hands, signatures required. Ros is passed over to a uniformed constable who will drive her home. Ian says he will be in touch soon. She slides into the back seat; the constable glances at her in the rear-view.

'Let's get you home, eh, Ros?'

'Yeah, thanks.' The pills are wearing off. The edges of her world dropping away like a landslip in torrential rain. How is she meant to go on without Niamh?

'The detective said it was a hit-and-run?'

'Did he?' The constable indicates, bolts through a break in the traffic. 'Got somebody to be with you at home, Ros?'

'No.'

'We can organise somebody.'

'No. I'll be fine.' I won't, she thinks. But a stranger would be worse, however sympathetic. Another tranche of her world slides down into the abyss. Soon it will just be her on a tiny tract of soil. Like a cow marooned in a monsoon flood. When can she next have some medication? Hours away yet. Hobart streets give way to bush as they climb over Tolmans Hill on the Southern Outlet. 'How could somebody do that? Run someone over and leave them for dead?'

The driver shakes her head. 'Probably horrified at what they've done. One minute you're looking at your phone, distracted, and next, bang.' Those big, young eyes in the rear-view. 'Sorry.' A shake of the head. 'The techs are up there examining the scene. If there's anything to find, they'll find it.'

And that still won't bring Niamh back.

—

'Hey Cav, take a look at this.'

Ian Cavanagh bins his coffee cup and heads for her desk. That look of having other, better, things to do. A fixture on his baby-smooth chops since he got his promotion last year. 'Jill?'

She points to one of the items on the morning traffic incident reports. 'This guy was clocked on the Huon Highway up at Vinces Saddle doing one twenty-five. Just after seven this morning. And blew point six on the breathalyser.'

'Early start or leftovers from last night?'

Why does Cav think that's relevant? 'Look at his address.'

'Margate.'

'He's on Sandfly Road, travelling in the same direction around the same time as our lady on the bike.' Jill does some clicks on the keyboard. 'Look at his history. He's a menace to other road users.' Indeed, he is. In the past five years his licence has been suspended more than it was in action: dangerous driving, speeding, DUI. 'There's more. The preliminary report from Traffic branch has black paint traces on the deceased's bike frame. Look what colour vehicle our speed demon drives.'

No prizes for guessing.

'Good stuff, Jill. Where is he now?'

'At his job in Huonville. The Traffic guys made him leave his car by the road and he caught an Uber. Here's his mobile.'

'Kieran McKay.' Ian gives Jill a nod of encouragement. 'A drive out to Bandit Country, Detective?'

'Sure.'

—

On the way out to Huonville, south-west of Hobart, Ian Cavanagh looks up their speed demon on social media. 'Ooh, our boy Kieran's warm for this. Listen to him on Facebook trolling cyclists. Quote: "Pay your road tax or keep out my way, fuckwit." Or this, a photo of the Tour de France peloton next to one of an Orc saying "Fresh meat". I think we've hit the jackpot, Jill.'

'Team effort, Sarge. As always.' Jill Wilkie can't disguise the ring of insincerity; she can't be arsed today. Another shit night's sleep. Hot flushes, fretting about Dad and where she's going to find the money to cover the hike in fees from his care-home provider. Fucking vultures. A sideways glance at Cavanagh. Just one rung above her in rank but completely at ease with his status, his destiny. Dresses like he means it. Sharp as. No kids yet, no aged and demented parents making demands of him, all the time in the world to realise his ambitions. Unless he gets cancer.

Cav makes a call to get the abandoned ute collected by Traffic.

Kieran McKay is a mechanic at a vehicle service and repair joint on the outskirts of town. The bloke's boss gives them all a filthy look when they step outside for a chat. Kieran lights up a smoke. 'What's this about?' Late twenties going on fifty. He's got a beer gut on him and one of those rural Tasmanian goatees that needs a tidy up but never receives it.

'How was the drive to work this morning?' Cavanagh waves the rogue cigarette smoke away and positions himself upwind. Jill is happy to let him run this while she studies Kieran's body language for fibs.

'You lot already know. I've been booked and I'll take whatever's coming.'

'Notice any cyclists when you were coming along Sandfly Road?'

'A couple, probably. There's always some. Never pay them much attention.'

'Tell us about the ones you saw. Where were they? What do you remember of them?'

He makes a show of thinking. 'One towards the Margate end, another up nearer the highway at Sandfly.'

'Male, female? Racer, mountain bike?'

A shrug. 'Can't remember. One had fluoros, one didn't. Has there been a complaint or something?'

'Why would there be?' asks Cav.

'You tell me.'

'There was an accident on Sandfly Road this morning. Cyclist got killed in a hit-and-run. Wondering if you saw anything, knew anything about it.'

'Not me, mate. Got the wrong bloke.'

'Have we?'

Kieran turns to head back to his job. 'Not going to pin that one on me, buddy. I'm finished here, work to do.'

Cav writes something on a pad, tears off the top sheet and hands it to Kieran. 'You'll need this.'

'What is it?'

'A receipt. We've impounded your car. If the paint on the victim's bike matches your paintwork, we'll be having another chat.'

'Fucken pathetic.'

'We'll pass on your sympathies,' says Jill.

'What?'

'To the family of the deceased cyclist.'

A snort. 'Don't fucken bother. One less on the road is fine by me. Best news I've had all day.'

—

By the end of the afternoon Sam pretty much has the gist of the job in hand. Dogsbody, at $36.25 per hour. A bit above Maccas pay rates but with plenty of fresh air. Who's he to complain, it's a job. At last. He just needs to keep this one. Not let his smart mouth and attitude get him booted. His capacity for insubordination. His propensity to self-destruct. The things he's seen and done which he can't unsee and undo. No, he's going to make this one work. Once the bub has gone down and they've had dinner, he excuses himself. Kaz was keen to hear about his day and he tried to make it sound fantastic.

'You'll be great,' she says, eyes shining. 'I just know you will.'

He's told her he wants to do some homework on his employers, be ahead of the game. It's partly true. He wants to look up Kris Baker. Only fair: if she's been researching him then he can repay the compliment. 'Won't be long.'

Kaz kisses him. 'Whatever you need, pumpkin.'

Type it in: Kristin Baker, D'Entrecasteaux Salmon. Lots of love on the first few pages of the search results: 'Tassie Fish Farm Company Lands Whopper', 'Rising Corporate Star', 'CEO-in-Waiting', 'Baker's Dozen – the Top 12 Aussie Companies Headhunting Ms Fix-it'. A puff profile piece in the weekend *Mercury*: 'From Duntroon to D'Entrecasteaux, Kristin Hears the Call of Nature'. So, she's ex-Army and a go-getter. Out of Duntroon and straight into Army Intelligence Corps, serving in Afghanistan a decade or so ahead of Sam.

'It was my job to identify threats and opportunities and to come up with ways to deal with them,' she is quoted, under a photo of her in fluoros staring into an aquatic Tassie distance. The camera loves her.

It no doubt serves her well in the corporate world. The profile raves about her creative, often risky, approach to corporate troubleshooting. Seeing off hostile takeover bids, outflanking rivals, clearing out deadwood, conquering new territories. But the inevitable question from the interviewer: what about the glass ceiling? A wicked smile in return, the journo notes.

'Glass ceiling? No such thing. It's just a thick layer of men.'

The article ends: Get ready to hear a whole lot more from the redoubtable Ms Baker.

Impressive, Sam thinks. But if she's so shit hot, with the multinational corporate world knocking at her door, what the fuck is she doing in this Tassie backwater?

And why has she chosen to home in on him?

—

'There's been a mistake. Niamh's going to be okay. She just needs a few days in hospital then she'll be coming home.'

Ros allows a tear to slip down her face. Her chest is full to bursting. Thank God. Oh, thank you, God. The nurse shares her tears, her relief. Begins plucking at a loose thread on Ros's jumper. Pulling. Miaowing. Somebody knocking at the door. Miaowing.

Ros wakes up. Then lets out a low animal moan, her face crumpling, reality punching her in the gut. The knocking persists. Go away. Just go away. Monica the tortoiseshell terror circling on the doona, plucking at it and mewing. Answer the door, says Monica, and give me some food. The mobile pings. A message from the cop, Ian. He's outside, is everything okay? Can he come in for a moment?

Shit.

Ros clambers out of bed. Nearly trips over the cat now twirling around her ankles. More knocking. Insistent. 'Okay! Coming!' Opens the door to a concerned and wet detective. It's dark behind him, and raining.

'Sorry to bother you so late.'

'I was asleep. What time is it?'

'Sorry. After nine. Sorry.'

'Has something happened?'

'Just a welfare check.' Ian steps inside before she can ask herself whether she even wants him to come in.

He insists on making her a cuppa: tea, coffee, herbal, anything. She relents and allows him to potter about in her kitchen. She hears him humming, opening and shutting drawers and cupboards. He returns with a tray: cups, saucers, milk jug, pot and cosy. She didn't even realise she owned a cosy. Maybe it was Niamh's. He found some leftover slice in a cake tin; Niamh must have made it. Does she mind, he enquires, it's been a long day. Then he tells her about Kieran, the cyclist-hating bogan and his black ute.

'Are you going to arrest him?'

'Mustn't get ahead of ourselves. We'll see what comes back from the labs.'

'It's murder. He murdered Niamh.'

Ian shakes his head. 'One step at a time, Ros. Whether it turns out to be Kieran or not, somebody has done the wrong thing. That could be anywhere on the spectrum from failing to report an accident, through reckless driving, to manslaughter or murder. We can't jump the gun.'

'Why did you need to tell me this now?'

'I was on my way home and I thought …'

'Home?'

'Kingston.'

'This is an extra ten Ks out of your way. More.'

'I needed to ask you some questions about Niamh.'

'Questions?'

'If this is foul play then we need to know if she had any enemies, anyone who might wish her harm.' Ian wipes some cake crumbs from his chest, takes another sip of tea.

'Okay.'

'Tell me about Niamh.'

Where would she start? Niamh's smile, maybe. Her smell. That glint in her eye when she's teasing. That fire when someone crosses her line. Once again, Ros finds it difficult to breathe, panic consuming her.

Ian places his hand on hers. 'We'll do everything we can to find the person who did this. I promise.'

She feels herself going under.

'Ros?' he says. 'You okay?'

2

Sam loves being out on the water in the early morning and watching the sun rise over the Channel. In the job a month now and so far, so good. Green hills dip down to the shore, cormorants duck and dive, now and again a fish leaps with a flash of silver. The maintenance barge is tied up between two salmon pens. The only sound is the low hum of the pump feeding the hose. It's a pity the guy he's been teamed with never bloody shuts up.

'Haven't seen a seal for a while. Shame. Love shooting the fuckers.'

Yeah, he's one of those types. Full of bravado, bit of sadism thrown in, don't need to dig too deep for the misogyny and racism either. He's a True-Blue Aussie.

'How long you been doing this, Jake?'

'Two years plus. Lovin' it.' He turns the high-pressure hose onto another stretch of netting and blasts away the jellyfish that come every day to cling. The jellyfish disintegrate in the jet of water but will reform and return in even greater numbers. 'Could do this all day.'

'You already do.'

Jake chuckles. A head shorter and ten kilos wider, he's taken a shine to Sam, to his rough humour, quiet ways. Happy to fill the many vacuums Sam leaves in the conversation. Something Sam picked up in the war zones – let the talkers do the talking.

'See that house over there on the peninsula?' Jake squints through the smoke from his ciggie. 'All the little coloured flags and shit.'

Tibetan prayer flags. 'Yeah.'

'Mad Cow, we call her. Some hippie artist. Always complaining about us to whoever'll listen.'

'What's her problem?'

Jake adopts a fey falsetto. 'The noise, the noise. The pollution. They're upsetting the balance of nature. I can't concentrate on my art!' He drops his voice an octave. 'Rich cow never done a day's work but wants to take our jobs from us. Stupid fucken bitch.'

'Anyone listening to her?'

'The ABC probably, journos, fucken bleeding hearts.'

Sam shrugs. 'Live and let live.'

'She won't though. She won't shut up until we're closed down and on the dole.'

'If nobody's listening, nobody's listening. Until then.'

Jake has gone still. 'You beauty.'

'What?'

He points to a dark shape breaking the surface of the water, shattering the orange reflection of the sunrise. 'Fucking seal.' He retrieves the shotgun from the steel cabinet. Ratchets it with a beanbag round. Sights and aims. 'This one's for you, Mad Cow.'

—

Ros is back home. All she knows is that she went to pieces that evening the cop, Ian, paid her a visit and she had to be checked into the Royal Hobart's mental health unit. Over the first two weeks they coaxed her through the crisis, counselled her, medicated her, reviewed and renewed her prescriptions. They believed she was ready to face the world again. They had to believe that because they were overflowing, overworked and needed her bed. Mental health has become a growth industry since Covid. Mental health this, mental health that. All that's needed is a commensurate growth in funding and resources.

Then came Niamh's cremation and funeral service and another breakdown. The ceremony passing in a medicated blur. Ros recalls hugs and handshakes from Niamh's work colleagues and her swim buddies. No-one to lean on during that time. With her father dead these ten years and her mum now sick and living with her sister in Vancouver, she had no family on hand. She's never been one to ask for their help anyway, they're a least-said, soonest-mended clan. Ros has no friends or colleagues here; she never worked or went out. How did she ever get through this so alone?

A short spell back in the mental health unit. More counselling. More prescriptions. A caseworker assigned. Last week Ros went through Niamh's things; she packed some into boxes now resting in the garage, others she left where they were. Not ready yet to slide open the door on a half-empty wardrobe or remove trinkets and traces of Niamh from their home. The funeral wasn't a proper goodbye. If and when, then maybe, but not yet.

So, according to the experts, she's fit and ready to face the new day.

Coffee first. Monica is pleased to have her home. Detective Ian had visited several times in hospital and reassured Ros that he was happy to call in every day or two and feed the cat and the chickens, collect any eggs. She knew it was above and beyond the call of duty but then again, she had no-one else, and so she'd thanked him from behind her veil of pills. In his own sweet way, he had helped her through this.

This morning the mountain is bathed in sun but dark clouds loom on the far side and there's a chill in the air. A distant siren sounds, triggering the alsatians next door into a frenzy of howling. Ros makes a mental note to replace the batteries in the anti-barking gizmo she aims at them whenever she's had enough.

She needs to get a list together. Clean and tidy the place, although it seems in remarkably good shape, better even than when she left it. Maybe Ian got out the vacuum cleaner while he was feeding the cat. Next, the bureaucracy surrounding Niamh's … parting. Insurance, super, the bank account, the property deeds, stuff like that. Niamh had been the primary breadwinner for the last few years, even if it had been Ros's compensation settlement that had set them up nicely. But there needs to be a plan, a way forward. The mental-health counsellor had been strong on that point – you must chart your own course now, Ros. Only you can do that.

It was all about road maps these days. Road map out of lockdown, road map out of crisis. Left at the traffic lights (assuming they're not stuck on red), slow down for the road works, avoid the pothole, fork right, and so on. Gardening. She needed to do some gardening. In the last month the weeds had taken a choking hold. Shopping. She needed to check supplies in the fridge, freezer and cupboards. Chart that fucking course, Ros.

After coffee.

The siren recedes and the neighbour's dogs resort to the occasional bark at God knows what. Does Ros want to stay here without Niamh? Where else would she go? What would Niamh want her to do? What would Niamh herself do?

–

There's been a stabbing down at the Salamanca pub strip over the weekend. A drive-by shooting on a house in West Hobart is likely a spillover from an ongoing turf war up north in Launceston. And one month on, the Sandfly hit-and-run remains unresolved. Ian Cavanagh is juggling three serious cases and has flicked most of his minor ones on to some flunkies. They already know who the perpetrators are in the first two thanks to a combination of snitches and CCTV rather than fine detecting. There's an action list and some doors likely to be kicked down in the next twenty-four hours. That leaves poor old Niamh Cassidy under 'any other business'. Jill senses an opportunity: any other business is her speciality and her favourite territory. Besides, she'd much prefer to work alone investigating the death of a woman who matters rather than waste her time on the same old ratbag gang skirmishes or boozed-up bogans.

Up front, gazing out over the throng, Cavanagh reiterates the lab findings. 'We now know that the black paintwork on Kieran McKay's ute doesn't match that on the victim's bike.'

Jill's been chasing the details from a lab technician. He only just came through after ignoring her calls for a fortnight. Apparently he was on holiday in Bali. 'The traces on the bike are a different chemical composition from the suspect ute.' Jill Wilkie squints at her iPad screen. 'So, the perp vehicle make remains unknown.'

Traffic investigators believe that the offending vehicle came from in front, at speed, veering into the victim to send the bike into the ditch. Niamh snapped her spine when she landed and hit the back of her head on a rock.

A voice from the back. 'If it was deliberate foul play, someone got lucky.'

One way of looking at it. 'We've commenced inquiries on the victim to see if she had any enemies.' Cavanagh brings up an image on the wall screen. 'A reminder. Our victim, Niamh Cassidy, age forty-four.' A second photo. 'Partner to Rosalyn Chen, age forty-two. Ms Cassidy was an architect. She designed eco-homes for a local bespoke builder.'

' "Bespoke", Sarge. Very fancy.' That same voice from the back.

'You're on fire today, Hughesy. Somebody get the extinguisher.' Cavanagh pastes on a smile, cricks his neck to loosen the tension he must be feeling. 'Ms Chen has been unemployed for nearly four years. Formerly worked as a lawyer in Perth but was involved in an unfair dismissal case at her workplace which resulted in a compensation payout and a series of mental breakdowns. The couple have been living in Margate the past three years or so. Ms Chen has been out of action most of this last month, more breakdowns, the funeral and such.'

'Lawyer?' says Hughesy. 'Bound to have a few enemies. What kind of law?'

'Corporate.'

'There you go.'

'Chen wasn't the target, Hughesy, if indeed this was targeted. It was Cassidy.'

'I'm with Hughesy on one thing at least.' Jill Wilkie stifles a yawn. 'Excuse me, bad night.' More hot flushes and fretting. 'But Hughesy's right: too lucky with the result for it to be targeted. I see this as reckless driving and leaving the scene. Manslaughter at a stretch. Misadventure.'

'But no witnesses, no leads, no forensics worth a damn.' Cavanagh can't hide his frustration.

It's destined for the distant backburner, nothing surer.

'I'm happy to keep it rolling along if you like, Sarge.' Jill gives him a smile. 'If you want to focus on stabbings and gangsters. Better for the clear-up stats, eh?'

He nods. 'Cheers, Jill.'

—

Sam is sickened by what Jake did to the seal but tries not to show it. He needs this job and knows what can happen if you don't play along.

'You'd have to be used to this shit, with the Muzzies and that, eh Sammy?'

The overfamiliarity is grating. 'They're a better shot than you, that's for fucken sure. You took the bastard's eye out and still didn't kill it. Where d'ya learn to shoot? The Royal Show?'

'Fuck off. The gun's shit. Needs a better balance.'

'Yeah, mate. Your turn to make the coffee.'

Jake goes down below and Sam is left up top, the barge rocking on the swell, rain coming in and the wind picking up. They've just about finished blasting the jellyfish off this cluster of nets, then they'll start all over again. But with the weather, nah. Maybe jag a dry-dock job for a while – net-mending or some such.

Jake hands him his coffee. 'White and none. Sweet enough already, Sammy?'

'Yep.' How many more 'Sammys' before he snaps the bloke's neck?

'So how was it over there?'

'Where?'

'Afghanistan, dick.'

Fishing for war stories. No bites from me, mate. 'Different. Boring, a lot of the time.' Shutters down.

Jake's disappointed, pissed off even. His face darkens. 'Fair enough.'

Knowing he needs to lighten the moment, Sam taps his nose and grins. 'If I tell you, I'll have to kill you.'

The levity works. 'Better mind my own business then, eh?'

Good plan. 'Ready to head back?'

'Sure. But first let's stir up Mad Cow.' They secure the barge and hop into the runabout. Jake over-revs the engines; if this was bitumen, he'd be doing doughnuts.

Up on the hill, under the Tibetan prayer flags, a woman gives them the finger and turns her back.

—

Ros has spent the morning pottering; the house didn't need much of a clean and the cupboards, fridge and freezer were well stocked. Some of the items were not the brands she or Niamh would have chosen but it's the thought that counts. She's sent Ian Cavanagh a thank-you text and a query as to any updates. A speedy reply asks where she is. Woolworths, she responds. Kingston. The Channel Court one. Give him half an hour, he says. Meet you in the café outside Woolies.

In the meantime she checks in, using the Covid app, and picks up the few items she wants. Nobody treats her like a new widow. Nobody has any idea the turn her life has taken. The new higher dosage medication is working well. She floats along in an artificially lit, temperature-controlled, muzak-soothed bubble. For now, that'll do nicely. Every so often, like in the soy-milk aisle, she'll catch a glimpse of somebody who might have been Niamh. Just a tiny stab when she realises her mistake. In the deli and dairy section, she suddenly has a craving for some of the things she hasn't had for ages. Picks herself out a few treats. She can have them now because Niamh isn't here to disapprove. Chokes back a sob at the realisation.

'Hi, Ros. Got here quicker than expected. Thought I'd come and find you. Coffee?'

He must have floored it all the way. 'My shout,' she says. 'I owe you.'

'No, mine. I insist.'

She relents. 'Okay. Flat white, if you're buying.'

Ian grins and, once she's cleared checkout, they adjourn to the café. 'How are you feeling? You seem in better shape than a week ago.'

'Good tablets.'

'Whatever it takes, eh?'

'Any developments? That guy with the ute?'

'Paintwork doesn't match. He's in the clear.'

Damn. 'Can't you lock him up anyway? Sounds like he needs it.'

'Would if I could but there's rules.' The coffees arrive. And as it's near lunchtime he's ordered their food as well. 'I got you focaccia. Hope you don't mind. I need to grab a bite whenever the moment presents.'

Presumptuous of him, but it tastes good. 'Are you married, Ian?'

'Engaged. Emily works in real estate. We'll get married in spring.' He scrolls through his phone and shows her a picture. A blonde woman, confident. Lovely.

'Congratulations.'

A smile. 'I'm lucky to have her.'

'So, what next with the investigation?'

A cloud blanks out the smile. 'We'll keep plugging away. There isn't much to go on so far but we'll keep at it.'

'Somebody had to have … I mean surely.'

His hand rests on her forearm. 'Somebody will pay, Ros. Trust me.'

But she doesn't believe they will. It's all around them, on the news every day. People do terrible things and there are no consequences. She has an urge to throw her plate and cup to the floor, to scream, to curl up. Everything closing in on her. Brittle. 'I need to go home.'

'Let me take you. I'll organise someone from the local station to drop your car back at the house. Give me the keys.'

She does. It's easy to let him take charge. Arms folded across her chest to hold everything in, she follows him down to the understorey car park while he makes the necessary phone calls. In no time at all they're back in Margate, she's taken more pills and he's tucking her up in bed. Does she imagine it or does it really happen? Just before she falls asleep, does he bend over and plant a delicate kiss on her forehead and go 'Shhhh'?

—

In the canteen there's all the salmon you can eat: salmon steaks, smoked salmon, salmon patties, salmon salads, salmon rolls, salmon bagels. All at discount prices. Trouble is, he now knows where it came from, how it got made, the soup of shit and chemicals the poor bastards swim in. Sam opts for a meat pie and Jake grabs a bowl of chips and a Mars bar. They join a mob of other blokes clustered around a table, a wall-mounted TV above them, muted, on the ABC News channel. Ribbons of breaking news, mainly Covid numbers across the bottom. A new strain is going through New South Wales like wildfire and governments, both state and federal, seem paralysed by indecision and ideology. Tasmania is lucky, so far, thinks Sam. The moat is a blessing but there's talk of lowering the drawbridge later this year.

'You guys met Sammy yet?' Jake does the introductions. Some have, some haven't, the turnover is high, different shifts and stuff. Hands shaken with those nearby, nods exchanged with those not.

'You believe in Covid, Sam?' Bloke at the other end of the table. Southern Cross on his left bicep. Half-empty Coke bottle in his mitt.

It's a bona fide virus, pal, not a random deity. 'Yeah, course I do.'

'Fucken bullshit. Scam-demic.'

Sam shrugs. 'Each to their own.'

'Brainwashed, whole fucken country. Sheep. Tell ya.'

Jake, bless him, changes the subject. A celebrity Aussie war hero no less, bravery-award recipient and author of the bestselling war memoir *Do or Die* is now a captain's pick by the PM for pre-selection for a plum government seat for next year's election. Noses out of joint, rumblings in the party room, an investigative journalist digging into his military service. Whispering allegations of war crimes. Fancy that.

'Fucking atrocious: the bloke's out there doing his duty, protecting our freedom, and the press want to rip him to shreds.' Jake gives Sam a look, like the speech is meant for him. 'Bastards need to show some respect.'

'Right on, brother,' says the Covid expert.

'What do you reckon, Sam?' asks Jake.

'War is hell, mate. That's what I reckon.' Sam can see he's rapidly losing

Jake. He knows he can't afford to have people turn on him but can't bring himself to play the game.

'I reckon Sammy-boy's what you call a fence-sitter.' Covid guru downs his Coke and stands to leave. 'Can't blame you, mate. It's not easy to keep the faith these days.'

Silence descends, people stop slouching. Someone at Sam's shoulder. He turns his head. Kristin Baker, rocking the work fluoros.

'How's it going, guys? All good?'

'Great,' says Jake, eyes shining. 'That right, Sammy?'

'All good,' he says, forking the last morsel of his pie.

Her hand rests lightly on his shoulder. 'Sam, have you got a moment? There's someone I'd like you to meet.'

'Sure.'

She leads him to a table in the far corner. A bloke sits waiting for them. Rises at their approach, hand outstretched. 'Dave,' he says.

'Hi, Dave.'

Dave is somewhere in his late forties. Early fifties even. Not wearing fluoros; he favours clean jeans, hiking boots, a long-sleeved t-shirt. Outdoors man personified, keeping himself in good shape. Does Sam detect some chemistry between Dave and Kristin? None of his business.

'This is Sam Willard, Dave. The guy I was talking about.'

They're talking about him? The jellyfish blaster on thirty-five bucks an hour?

'I could go another coffee,' says Dave. 'How about you, Sam?'

'Yeah, sure.'

And Kristin goes off to fetch them.

There's no name badge, no lanyard, no nothing. 'Sorry, Dave,' says Sam. 'Didn't catch which department you're from.'

'Why would you? It wasn't mentioned.'

He's got the smell of spook or spiv about him. Or ex at least. Probably an old comrade of Kristin's from her army days. That might explain the chemistry, the familiarity. These people. Sam can't be arsed, he really can't. 'So, what's your role?'

'This and that.' Some diversionary chat about the weather and the footy then Kristin returns with a tray of coffees.

'You blokes getting acquainted?'

'Starting to,' says Dave.

Sam stirs his coffee, dumps some of the froth in a spare saucer. The guys from his table are dispersing, casting glances his way, ranging from covetous to suspicious. They'll have him down as either a company snitch or golden boy in no time and then the shit will start up. Again.

'I was about to explain to Sam that I don't actually work for D'Entrecasteaux. I act in an advisory capacity.'

'Advisor?' says Sam. 'On what?'

'Strategies for risk management and minimisation.'

'Looking to buy a bigger jellyfish blaster? That'd be cool but the priority might be to manage the aquaculture more sustainably.'

Kristin grins, tucks a lock of hair behind her ear. 'Told you he was bright.'

'We're putting together a pilot project, Sam. And wondering if you'd like to be involved?'

'I'm a farm attendant, mate. I blast jellyfish with a hose. Shoot the odd seal. Mend nets. Not sure why you're even talking to me.'

'We've asked around. Heard good things about you,' says Kristin. 'We know you've had a rough trot the past few years. It's time somebody gave you a break.'

And so it begins, thinks Sam. 'This job's a break and I'm really happy to have it.'

'Are you?' says Dave. 'The pilot project pays well. What you make in a week right now, you'd make in a day if you're with us.'

And if you're not with us, then you must be against us. Don't do it, he's thinking. Not worth it. It stinks. Keep your head down, keep your life simple. He sees their gaze fixed on him. What if these people don't take no for an answer? Back on the dole at a click of the fingers. Maybe worse besides. Or maybe this so-called pilot project could fund a deposit on a house. He and Kaz and the bub, finally turning that corner. Maybe it's about time he reaped some reward for his gallant sacrifice on the battlefields.

'I'm listening.'

—

Ros wakes to noise coming from the kitchen. There's someone in her house. Niamh? No, she remembers. Not Niamh. The smell of cooking. She realises she is hungry. Goes to investigate.

'Good timing,' says Ian, drawing a casserole dish from the oven in a gust of steam and savoury aromas. 'Pull up a chair.'

She doesn't know whether to be enraged, scared or delighted. Or is this still a drug fever dream? Go with the flow. 'This is …'

'Lamb tagine.'

'"Weird" was the word I had in mind.'

'Weird?' He looks taken aback. Hurt even.

'I appreciate the TLC but it's above and beyond the call of duty. Way, way.'

'You're feeling better then?' He dishes up the food. It looks and smells glorious. 'My mum's recipe.'

'To die for,' she says, after a mouthful.

'Let's hope not.'

Dark outside. 'What time is it?' She glances at the clock on the oven door. 'Six-forty. I'm sorry. You didn't need to do this, Ian. You've got your own life. Surely.'

'Em's at CrossFit until seven-thirty. It's her night with the girls.' He studies Ros. 'Good to see you up and about again, Rosalyn. I think between us we'll make a good team.'

'What?'

'For Niamh. Find out the truth of what happened.'

She prods at the food. Wills her appetite to stay the course. These breakdowns are exhausting, she can't bear the thought of this being all there is. This paralysis, this utter collapse of all she thought she was. All that she used to be. 'Maybe it was nothing more than a stupid, sad accident. The sooner I move on, the better.'

'Hmmm.' Like he never heard her. 'What did Niamh do in her spare time, outside the architect job?'

'Swimming, cycling, bushwalks. Reading.' Being with me. Coaxing me through each day.

'Any volunteer work?'

'No, not enough hours in the day or days in the week.'

Ian smiles, helps himself to another ladle of stew. 'A real dynamo, eh?'

'Yes.' Absolutely.

'Not into causes or anything then?'

'Why do you ask?'

'Just trying to build a picture.' He holds the ladle her way. 'More?'

Enough. Time to draw a line under this. 'It's all very nice and considerate but, really, this is fucking weird. Wrong even.' Wonders if she's gone too far. 'I don't think I had lamb on the shopping list. I need to pay you for it. How much do I owe you?'

'Nothing, Ros. It's fine.'

'Really, I—'

'No.' Said cold enough to congeal the meat in its juices.

She stands and takes their plates to the sink. 'I'll let you get back to Emily.'

His mouth twists. 'There is no Emily. She left me six months ago.'

Uh-oh.

'I'm sorry to hear that, Ian.'

'Yeah.' He stands, slips on his jacket. Dredges up a smile but looks like he'd just as soon cry. 'I'll give you a call tomorrow. Got a few ideas percolating about Niamh.'

'I'm happy to let this drop if there's nothing to go on. Really.'

'I don't let things drop, Ros. It's not in my DNA.'

—

Sam has been allowed to go home two days early from his rostered schedule. A couple of days to think things over, they'd said. Kaz could be given the gist but not the detail. Hints had been dropped about the consequences if the pilot project wasn't successful – by that they meant if he didn't play ball – redundancies, they'd said regretfully. Last in, first out. That meant him. He found it hard to believe the 'special project' was warranted in the first place. He said so, there and then.

'If you've got the government, the main opposition, the key public servants and most of the media in your pockets, why do you need to be so nervous? You've already minimised the risk.'

'Officer material,' said Dave. 'My oath.'

Sam had bitten his tongue. Silence and discretion were always the better part of valour.

'The rogue elements sometimes come out of left field.' Kristin had changed out of the fluoros and back into corporate casual. 'Billionaires with consciences, activist shareholders, that's where the danger lies these days.'

Her office looked out onto the Channel. The sun had slipped behind the hills and rain spotted the window. The water had chopped up and Sam imagined Jake lobbing seal crackers into the waves to ease his boredom, fretting all the while as to why Sam was getting the special treatment.

'Where do I fit in?'

Dave had smiled. 'If this was *Apocalypse Now*, we'd be saying you're on a search-and-destroy mission, Sam. Terminate with extreme prejudice. All that shit.'

Jesus Christ. 'But we're not, mate. This is rural Tasmania and there are laws and regulations.'

'Sure, Sam, we'll go into the finer points all in good time. All we need to know is whether, in principle, you're on the team.'

He hadn't answered the question. 'Still trying to get a handle on where I fit in, Dave. Not trying to be difficult.'

But Sam could see that the bloke's patience was waning. 'I have it on good authority that you are decisive and good at following orders. In short, you're reliable.'

Where did he get that from? Not from the official record, for sure. 'Within limits.'

'Limits?'

'What's legal, what's not.'

'Leave that to us,' Kristin had said, with a dismissive smile. They'd all shaken hands and Sam climbed into his ute for the journey home, texting Kaz first to let her know he'd be back early. Question marks in reply. Worried. Had he blown it already? All good, he'd sent back to reassure her.

He sits for a moment, breathing evenly. As he reverses out of the car space, he sees the two of them looking out at him through Kristin's office window. Expressions hard to read. He gives them a nod. On the way back, passing the Kingston roundabout, he sees again the sign for the new housing development. Blue Wren Estate. Yeah, he thinks, we'll have a piece of that.

3

Wednesday morning, late May, and Jill Wilkie is wondering what cake to bring in for her birthday at the end of the week. Crap tradition. If it's her birthday they should be providing the cake, surely? Any time after Thursday she's eligible to retire from the job and start collecting her police pension. What would she do then? Maybe private security for one of the few big companies left in Tasmania. Insurance investigator, perhaps. Catch those malingerers claiming their workers comp for a bad back and clearly able to take the dog for a walk. Fuck that. Eligible to chuck it in or not, she can choose to stay until they drag her out, fingernails clutching the door jamb. Five years, ten, more. Maybe once Dad dies and the bills stop rolling in. Too early in the day to start feeling sorry for herself. The office is still empty, save for her and one of the civilian data wranglers who usually leaves early to pick up the kids from school. Carrot cake? Black Forest? Cheesecake? All of them will add unwelcome kilos, but that's no longer a concern when you're practically invisible.

Cheesecake it is.

'Morning, Jill. Bright and early?' Ian Cavanagh looks a bit ragged.

'Cav. G'day. Getting a tea, want something?'

'I'll make them. White, no sugar, right?'

'Well remembered.'

He glances toward the civvie then back down to Jill. 'Can I have a word?' Nods in the direction of the kitchen. 'Come and help me boil the kettle.'

She follows him, weaving between the desks and partitions. In the kitchen Cav squeezes some hand sanitiser onto his palms and rubs it in. Jill declines, she already had some earlier. 'Something up?'

'Where are you at with the hit-and-run?'

'I was going to follow up on the reports from the area doorknock. Put out another call on social media, including another dashcam request. See where that gets me.'

'Solid, Jill.'

Thanks. She accepts the mug of tea, jiggles the bag a little more before squeezing it into the compost bin. 'Anything else you think I should be doing?'

'The victim's ex. Mark Limace. He followed her down here from the mainland. Been living in Cygnet the last nine months. Funny thing, eh?'

'In what way?'

'Well, your wife runs off with another woman, might do something to your sense of self, you reckon?'

'Depends on your sense of self, I suppose.' Back out in the main office, the place is filling up. People shaking off rain droplets from their Gore-Tex and puffers. Checking phones. Amiable chitchat. 'I don't recall the ex featuring in the backgrounder. This is new?'

'Ros filled me in, last night. Said the break-up was pretty torrid.'

Ros? Last night? Please explain. 'You met up somewhere?'

'Long story.'

And that's all Jill's getting, obviously. 'She's never mentioned him before.'

'Traumatised, I expect. All those mental health issues. Besides, we were all focused on Kieran McKay. Alternative scenarios weren't on our radar.'

'Want me to take a look at this ex?'

A nod. 'I'll zap you the deets.'

'Sure, boss. No worries.'

—

Sam is enjoying the lie-in. Usually, he would have been up before dawn, hosing those pesky jellyfish away from the salmon nets. Kaz is stoked by the promotion and news of the extra money. She's daring to dream. He kept any doubts or misgivings to himself when he told her over dinner last night. Sex afterwards had been energetic, rewarding. A change after the months of newborn fatigue. She'd left him sleeping that morning to tend to Ollie. He can hear them now in the kitchen, toil and cooing intermingled. Beyond that the dull roar of the Brooker Highway. It was a foregone conclusion, but he sends Dave and Kristin the text confirming he's in. In reply, thumbs-up from one and smiley face from the other. As soon as he's signed the new contract, they can start the ball rolling on that Kingston house. Kaz is keen enough to arrange a tour of the display home today and perhaps flag things to the bank.

'Sure,' he'd said. 'Why not?'

A knock at the door. He hears Kaz go to answer it. Some murmuring. Footsteps. The bedroom door opens with an electric scrape on the synthetic carpet.

'Love?' She has the bub on her hip. Ollie is lively and wide-eyed at all the action. 'A woman at the door. A journalist?'

'What?'

'She's asking for you. She's from the ABC. Shall I let her in or …?'

'No, I'll be there in a second.' He throws back the covers and receives an admiring glance from Kaz.

'Maybe the word is out on you,' she says, smiling.

He grins. 'Maybe I should brush my teeth before I get too close to her?'

'She's ABC, hon. Too classy for you. Maybe if she'd been from the *Mercury*.'

The woman at the door looks in her mid to late twenties – jeans, expensive boots and a puffer jacket against the brisk weather. Her name is Larissa and she's wondering if he's got a moment.

'What's this about?'

She hands him a business card which says she is a content producer. 'We're putting together an investigative podcast series about war crimes allegations? Afghanistan?' She steps forward as if that will be enough to get her invited over the threshold. It isn't.

Afghanistan. Fuck. 'Yeah?'

'Your name has been suggested to us.'

'Who by?'

'Can't say right now, sorry.'

He shrugs. 'Can't help you right now, sorry.'

A frown. 'That's a pity.'

'Sorry,' he says again, mustering an apologetic smile.

'He seemed to think you weren't like the others. He hoped you'd do the right thing when the time comes. He said you'd promised him that you would.'

She doesn't have to say the name. Sam knows now.

—

Ros is meeting a lawyer. She's the same one they engaged to deal with Niamh's divorce and to tidy up outstanding matters on Ros's compensation claim. The office is in South Hobart on Davey Street just before it becomes Huon Road and starts climbing the mountain. The houses here are grand, a relic of old Hobart where the rich folk used to, and still do, live. But for all the fancy blue-blood trappings, Ros likes Jo Burke. The woman seems grounded and was able to fight the good fight when Niamh sought her help. The physique of a regular bushwalker, bedside manner of a no-nonsense angel.

'I'm so sorry about what happened to Niamh. It must be devastating.' She hands Ros a mug of coffee and they settle into the armchairs, looking out onto the huge backyard, mountain rearing above. 'What can I do to help?'

Straight to the point, Ros likes that about her. 'A whole bunch of administrative things – shared accounts, the property deeds, Niamh's super, even some utility bills, that kind of stuff. Simple enough, I suppose, but I just don't feel like ...' She feels herself tearing up yet again.

'I can take care of all that. You just need to give me power of attorney. At least temporarily. Then I can present whatever you need to sign all in one hit.'

Is she allowed to ask the next question? Jo was Niamh's lawyer primarily and Ros was granted a ringside seat. And, true, Jo is now Ros's lawyer. But was there a time in-between when Niamh confided in Jo? They were also cold-water swimming buddies, after all. Could Jo now share any such confidences with Ros?

'The answer is yes.' The woman had seemingly read her thoughts. 'Niamh came to see me about six, nearly seven weeks ago.'

'Why?'

'At the time I thought it was a touch melodramatic for Niamh. She was normally such a level-headed woman. Now, well, whatever the outcome of the police investigation, she was at least ... prescient.'

'Prescient?'

Fingers hooked in quotation marks. 'In the event of my death, that kind of thing.' Jo heads to the filing cabinet, takes a folder from the top that she must have had ready for their appointment. From the file she pulls a sealed and padded A4 envelope. 'For you. She asked that you open it in front of me so that I can bear witness.'

'Why?'

'Maybe in order to protect you?'

Or maybe to catch me when I fall. Ros opens the package. Outside, in the backyard, wrens skitter and hop. The rain has eased and the sun promises to puncture the veil of clouds. There are two USB drives, an A5-sized ring-bound notepad and another smaller envelope containing what feels like photographs. Plus, a handwritten note on paper that Ros recognises from their home.

My dearest love,

It breaks my heart that you are reading this. I hoped for such a thing never to happen. I hoped to be proven wrong. I hoped my imagination was playing tricks on me and that I would come to my senses, embarrassed at my stupidity. You always claimed to be the one who was the drama queen. I really don't know what I expect you to do with all this. The people this relates to, the matters it refers to, it's been public knowledge for years now. It changes nothing, these people are untouchable. I don't want this to be your burden – burn it, throw it in the bin, or pass it to someone who might have new ideas, new energy.

Ros, my heart, you must focus your entire energies on being well and on living. I am sorry I am not there with you. I so wanted us to grow old together. You brought sunshine into my life after the darkness of living with Mark. I will always be grateful for whatever time we have had and for the joy and love we shared. Be good to yourself, you so, so deserve the best.

All my love, Niamh xx

Ros's face is wet with tears, her stomach knotted in grief. Jo gives her a tissue and Ros mops herself with it. Hands Jo the note for reading. The lawyer seems to take an age.

'What do you want to do with all this?'

'You don't know what it's about? She didn't tell you?'

'No,' says Jo. 'She just came in with the package all ready. Said there was some strange stuff going on. Asked me to keep this safe and if anything happened to her to let you know about the package.'

'It's been over a month since she died.'

'I was made aware that you'd been in hospital. I intended to contact you by early June if I'd heard nothing.'

'Made aware by who?'

'The police.'

'Niamh told you she was in danger back then, what, six weeks ago? And you said nothing to me?'

'She never said in so many words—'

'She said, "If anything happens to me" didn't that give you a clue?' Ros knows this is unfair, that it's not Jo she should be angry with, but she needs to lash out at someone. Already she regrets it. Jo must know that Ros doesn't mean to be so hostile, that she's not in her right mind.

Calmly, Jo says, 'I'll print out the power of attorney for those other matters for you to sign before you leave. Maybe take time to digest this stuff Niamh left you, and if I can help in any way let me know.'

—

'What did she want?'

Sam slops milk onto his cereal, bends down to tickle his son's tummy and elicits a radiant smile. 'Nothing, Kaz. She's doing a story on some returned vets from Uruzgan. My name had been passed to her. I told her I wasn't interested.'

'Why not?'

'Old war stories. I've moved on.'

She gives him that 'since when' look but doesn't pursue the matter. 'Fair enough. So, if we're all moving on, how about we go and take a look at this display home in Kingston?'

'Good plan.' They pack up the car, strap bub into his seat, and set off down the Brooker. While Kaz scrolls through the website blurb for Blue Wren Estate on her phone, Sam drives and thinks about a routine morning patrol in a faraway land that ended in chaos and blood. All dutifully recorded on helmet-cam.

We gunna pop this fucker?

The question hadn't been addressed to him. He was a few paces behind and to the right.

We gunna pop this fucker?

He hadn't heard a reply, noticed any hand signal or nod, but the shots rang out immediately after. Three. Two in the head, one in the heart. They were all juiced on adrenalin, amygdala running riot. Sure, yeah, they wanted him to pop the fucker.

'Language, Sam. He might only be nine months old but they're like sponges.'

'What?'

'You said "pop the fucker". I don't know where your mind is but I can guess.' She presses her palm to the dashboard as he brakes late for the traffic lights. 'Maybe you should get it off your chest; talk to the journalist.'

A shake of the head. 'No need. She just brought a few memories back, that's all.' He puts a hand on her thigh and squeezes. Gives her his best smile. 'Tell me about Blue Wren Estate.'

'Home at last, it says here. Living the dream.'

On the dashboard bracket, his phone lights up with a message from Kristin. **MoA with you by end of day**. Smiley face.

Memorandum of Agreement? Not fully legally binding like a proper contract. Slightly more arms-length. Makes deniability easier.

—

Jill Wilkie finds Mark Limace at his weatherboard Cygnet cottage with its waterfront view and a little brown dog yapping in the side yard. She introduces herself and states her business.

'Shush, Maxie! Friend.' A glance at Jill. 'That's right, isn't it?'

Sure.

After a moment's deliberation she is invited over the threshold and offered coffee. Limace has gentle eyes and the demeanour of a thoughtful man. Around his walls are framed scenes, paintings and photographs of rural Tasmanian landscapes: the orange-tinted boulders of the east coast, misty dark rivers and giant ferns, towering dolerite outcrops. He works from home, he tells her, web designer. She says that must be fascinating. Pleasantries aside, steaming mugs at the kitchen table, sun bouncing off the pine floorboards. She starts in with her enquiry.

'You must have been shocked to hear about what happened to Niamh.'

'A bit, yeah. You wouldn't wish that on anybody.'

'How did you hear about it?'

'Once the name was released in the news, some mutual friends contacted me. Wanting to check whether I knew, and how I was going.'

'How are you going?'

A shrug. 'It's sad, sure, but I've moved on. Was there something you particularly wanted me to help you with?'

'Been in touch with Rosalyn Chen at all?'

He shakes his head. 'I don't think she'd want to hear from me. Top up?' The coffee pot is lifted in offer. She declines. 'When Niamh and I broke up it was … awkward. Messy. Luckily, we didn't have kids, could have been a nightmare. But it's all ancient history now.'

'You followed Niamh to Tassie from the mainland. Been here, what, a year?'

'Little less. I didn't specifically follow Niamh. I made my own lifestyle decision that Tasmania was where I wanted to be.' He turns his palms upwards, gives a smile. 'Just another bloody cashed-up climate refugee driving the property prices higher.'

'And ended up half an hour's drive away?'

'You make me sound like some kind of creepy stalker, but Cygnet has been on my radar since I came to the folk festival about twenty years ago. It's a pretty place. Who wouldn't want to live here?'

'You live alone, Mark?'

A nod and a twinkle of those gentle eyes. 'At the moment, just me and Maxie here. Still searching for Ms Right.'

'What was awkward and messy about it?'

'What?'

'The divorce. You described it as awkward and messy. With no kids in the frame, for two intelligent adults it would have been straightforward enough, no?'

A sudden glint of calculation crossing that soft face. 'I didn't see it coming, I must admit. Left of field. I thought it was all going well. I took it hard, at first.'

'In what way?'

'Hmmm?'

'How did that manifest?'

'I said and did some things I now regret.'

She's read the restraining order that was taken out against him. Threatening abusive phone calls and texts. 'Such as?'

An incredulous frown. 'Are you suggesting I had something to do with Niamh's accident?'

'Did you?'

He stands and starts clearing the table. 'If there's anything specific that you'd formally like to ask, let me know.'

Jill hands him her card. 'Do you have a business card, anything like that?'

He examines hers. 'Detective Senior Constable. Bit of a way to go to crack that glass ceiling, eh?' Yes, he has cards too and hands one over.

'Thanks,' she says. 'Enjoy your day.'

—

Ros lays the envelope on the table while she makes a cup of tea and a sandwich. Smoked salmon, cream cheese and capers on rye. An apple for afters. There are missed calls on her mobile. She ignores them all, and calls Jo Burke to apologise for losing it earlier. The response is cool but accepting.

'You're going through a tough time, Ros. I understand completely.'

'I forgot something I needed to sort out regarding Niamh.'

'Yes?'

'Her belongings: clothes, bike, phone, all that. I assume the hospital or police have them. Can I get them back at some point?'

'I'll follow it up.'

Where to begin with the package? Whatever is on the thumb drives will take up a block of time, she expects. The A5 ring-bound notebook. Flips through the pages. Scribbles, sketches, doodles. Meaningless. Maybe a skim of whatever is in that smaller envelope. She slits it open with her index finger. A small stack of colour photos, around a dozen in all. She flicks through them. Clears the table in front save for her tea and sandwich plate, takes a bite of food, then starts laying the pics out next to each other.

The first is of Niamh at Kingston Beach, in the background a wooded hill plunging steeply to the water, sun glinting silver off the flat surface. Niamh with the new ear hoops Ros bought her last Christmas. Niamh's arm around the waist of a younger man. They look happy, intimate. Like a couple on holiday, honeymoon maybe, smiling for the camera. A muscle clenches in her gut. She re-reads the personal note.

You brought such sunshine into my life after the darkness of living with Mark. I will always be grateful for whatever time we have had and for the joy and love we shared.

Is it that easy to deceive and that easy to believe? Who is this man? Date scribbled on the back, early February, three-plus months ago. She checks the calendar on the kitchen wall, it was a Saturday, Niamh's open-water swimming day. Yes, Ros sees now that her hair is still wet. They're fresh out of the water. He's from her swimming group. A friend. Nothing more.

And yet.

Next photo. Underwater – cloudy, yellow-grey-brown. Could be anything, anywhere. Next, a fish, on a marble kitchen benchtop. In fact, the next few photos are of the same fish from different angles then cut open. It's clear that it has deformities, like one side of it has developed normally and the other hasn't: fins, scales, eye all munted down one side. Cut open, the flesh is grey, and worms are visible within the entrails. Ros decides to leave the rest of her sandwich. There are two photos of outlet pipes into a river: one is a wide shot of signage showing it comes from a fish-breeding facility up in the Derwent Valley just beyond New Norfolk, the other is a close-up of what the pipe is spewing out. Now Ros wishes she'd skipped lunch altogether.

Okay, she thinks, Niamh got herself involved in yet another environmental cause – albeit one she hadn't thought to share with Ros. But why would she? Ros could barely function some days with her ongoing panic and anxiety attacks and her dependency on medication that flattened her out and made her boring to be with. No wonder Niamh wanted to go away and swim in icy water with six-pack Aqua Boy. Who wouldn't want to clasp that slim waist and muscly energetic bod?

Who the hell is he?

Ros opens up Facebook and looks for the page for the Kingston Beach Selkies open-water swimming group. There it is. So where is he, where is he?

There.

In memoriam. Zeb Meyer. Diving accident. February 14th.

—

Sam scans the draft MoA. In essence, he has been terminated by D'Entrecasteaux and seconded to Dave's consultancy, which goes under the innocuous name of DTS. The duration of the MoA is six months, to be extended by mutual agreement. During those six months, Sam will earn more than enough to put a cash deposit on a three-bedroom place in Blue Wren Estate. The display home was nothing special, a bit pokey to be honest, but the house would belong to them. There's a non-disclosure clause similar to that in his farm attendant contract, plus an indemnity clause clearing DTS of any responsibility should anything go pear-shaped.

Stuff that.

In red, he types into the draft 'unless as a result of carrying out directions of DTS Pty Ltd'. He knows his amendment is worthless but he's sending a message that he's nobody's fool. Non-disclosure agreements, indemnity clauses. Too many employers these days wanting to have their cake and fucking eat it. The rest of the contract, or rather the MoA, he can live with. He returns the email; he'll sign the paperwork when he gets back to work in the morning.

A hand on his neck. A soft kiss. 'You're heading back tomorrow?'

'Yeah, hon, more shiftwork, more time away. But a better gig.' He shows her the amount in the MoA. 'We can put our names down for Blue Wren, sign on the dotted line. What do you reckon?'

'I reckon you're my hero.' She slips her tongue between his lips.

They snog a while but the bub wakes just as things begin to heat up.

'Ollie sounds insistent.'

She smiles. 'He always is.' Brushes her hand across his lap. 'Hold that thought.'

He decides he may as well pack his bags now rather than leave it until the last minute. Undies and socks for a week. Some t-shirts. He's aware of that familiar tension and anticipation returning. A lightness fluttering in his guts. He used to get it every time before going out on patrol.

We gunna pop this fucker?

Thirty seconds after the shots had faded, more movements in the long grass. A second insurgent? Small hands appeared first, behind them a high voice.

Don't shoot, mister. Don't shoot.

The squad leader had the kid in his sights. He wasn't even going to wait for the nod.

'No!' Sam realises he's said it out loud.

The kid in the cornfield is the insurgent's eleven-year-old son. The 'insurgent' turns out to be an innocent farmer fingered by a local informant as payback for some historic slight. No matter, they'd planted a spare gun and radio on him and taken the trophy photographs for the official record.

The kid's name was Qadim, the father Imran. The boy would be in his twenties now. The patrol commander had crouched down in front of him, mimed the shushing of a closed mouth and the consequences if he didn't, a swipe of thumb across the throat. Sam had given the kid some food rations and a few dollars. Had a chat to calm his tears.

'Qadim,' the kid said.

'Sam.' A pat on the shoulder and off we go.

He seemed to think you weren't like the others. He hoped you'd do the right thing when the time comes. He said you'd promised him that you would.

—

Had Ros really been so far out of it these last several months that Niamh couldn't share anything with her? She hadn't thought so. She'd been trying to wean herself off the medication under supervision from the GP. She'd started going out more, on walks with Niamh or to the shops now and then. They'd caught the odd movie at the State Cinema, even had a drink in the adjacent wine bar afterwards. Ros had been holding it together, gradually rebuilding until … until.

Until the pandemic, the doom, the rupture in the social contract. The right and the wrong, what is real and what is false, what is truth and what is a lie. Men, a killer virus, unfettered power – a match made in hell. Night after night, every news story seemed to trigger something in her: women, even powerful competent women, reduced to chattels again and again by sneering apes and their enablers. Nothing specific to tip her over the line, but Ros would often find herself back in that office in St George's Terrace in Perth. Doubting her sanity, wondering where and when she went wrong. Blocked, tormented, isolated and abused at every turn. Unknown error. The pandemic seemed to act as a fast breeder reactor for bullies and abusers. Behind its cover, they hid. Under its auspices, they flourished. Every news story came with a warning and a helpline.

'Let's put some music on instead,' Niamh would say, but once those images of entitled cocky grey men and their vile abuse of power had worked their way under her skin, that was it. The music just seemed to fade and die like a disbelieved victim. After a while, Niamh too seemed to lose patience. 'Enough is enough. We need to start taking the fight back to those bastards.'

And that's what she must have done. Teaming up with young, fit Zeb Meyer. Ros had googled him. It seemed the young man was something of an eco-warrior, but media reports on Meyer's death were sparse. Tragic misadventure seemed to be the conclusion. No warning diving buoy, no buddy, injuries consistent with a collision with the propeller of a passing boat. He'd been found on a beach on the Labillardiere Peninsula on the western side of Bruny Island. The Selkies had mourned him, as they now mourned Niamh, and would name their annual Spring Fling swim in their joint honour.

Clicking into Niamh's social media accounts. As she follows the thread of their messages to each other on Facebook, it's clear that Zeb won Niamh over to his cause. They must have got talking one Saturday morning over post-swim coffees while Ros would have been moping under her doona More messages. Shared URL links to negative stories about the local salmon industry: the pollution, noise, marine environment, animal welfare, you name it. Petitions, meetings, demos. **Meet you at the boat ramp x. Don't forget your hot water bottle for after.** Followed by a smiley face. A few weeks later. **You OK? Been better.** Paranoia creeping in. Zeb spooked by bumps in the night and other encounters on lonely Tassie back roads. Phone calls in the night from unknown numbers. Vandalism. Then a whole series of empty bubbles. Zeb unsent a message. Niamh unsent a message. Again and again, rinse and repeat.

Did Niamh buy into Zeb's paranoid world of cloak-and-dagger and is that what led her to lodge this envelope full of nothing with her lawyer? The two crusaders had obviously developed a fixation on how shitty the salmon industry could be. Ros was once a corporate lawyer, and she knows how shitty most industries can be as it was often her job to help them dodge any consequences. It was never that hard, especially if the government and public servants have your back and the media is easily distracted. A quick scan of the other contents of Niamh's envelope and a glance at the folder contents on the USBs: digital versions of these same photos, the reams of official-looking documents sourced, hacked, stolen, or leaked from wherever and dumped onto one of the thumb drives.

She knows they count for very little in this age of explicit government corruption and pork-barrelling. All the President's Men are now expert spin doctors and number-crunchers; Woodward and Bernstein dismissed as fantasists. Conspiracy? Niamh got knocked off her bike by a distracted driver who drove off rather than cop a fine. Zeb went diving one morning and surfaced into the propeller of a passing boat that probably never noticed he was there. Ros is yet to open the second thumb drive but foresees a wasted evening ahead when she could be doing something useful like sleeping or crying.

4

Thursday. Jill doesn't like the look of Mark Limace one little bit. Except she does. She's beginning to fancy him for the hit-and-run. She's checked out his social media profile and noticed how many men's-rights pages he likes, the creepy misogynistic memes he finds funny, how free and easy he is with the words 'bitch' and 'slut', with or without asterisks filling in for vowels. Do the people who hire him to maintain or create their websites realise what a prick he is? She's sought and obtained permission to have his phone movements retrospectively tracked for the key dates in question. Pity he's got a white Mazda instead of a black one. Otherwise, she'd already have him in the cells in a spit hood and be bouncing telephone directories off his kidneys. Shame today's telephone directories are too slim to do the job properly.

'Good stuff. Want any help with that, Jill?' Ian is feisty this morning.

'Good for now, Sarge. How's the drive-by shaping up?' There'd already been a reprisal shooting. Tit, tat, tit and all of a sudden, you're in a war.

'Laugh a minute. Keep me posted if things ramp up. Don't want you feeling left out. Unsupported.'

Far from it. The gradual winding down towards retirement had begun to feel like a drudge. Volume crime. Stats bashing. No place for her in Cavanagh's young dynamic team of chosen ones working the juicy cases. So she's loving this new-found sense of purpose and independence and wants to hold on to it for as long as possible. 'It'll probably come to nothing,' she lies. 'But we need to tick those boxes.'

'That's the spirit.'

'Couldn't have done it without your tip-off, Cav.'

'How do you mean?'

'Ros Chen telling you about the ex. We weren't looking at the victim's life while it was still in the realms of failing to report an accident. On that, maybe I should have a chat with Ros myself to get more background on the ex.'

'I'll do that if you like. Call in on my way home this evening. Save you the trip.'

'Not a worry, Sarge. You've got plenty on your plate already.'

'It's fine,' he insists. 'She's in a fragile state, still. Only just got used to me. Better if we keep things simple.'

'Sure.' Something is off here, but he's in charge. Not worth dying in a ditch for, she thinks, then realises that might not be the best analogy. 'Oh, and we've had a request from a lawyer, Jo Burke, acting on behalf of Ros. Wondering when we're going to return Niamh's belongings.'

'Belongings?'

'Bike, riding gear, phone listed here.'

He shrugs. 'It's still an active investigation. They'll be returned in good time.'

'I'll let her know. Enjoy your day, boss. Keep your head down with those drive-bys.'

He laughs and is on his way.

Jill decides to head over to the stores and take a look at that phone of Niamh's.

—

Sam now knows that the 'T' in DTS stands for Trembath and the 'S' for Strategic. Dave's name signed with a flourish on the MoA. They're on the Bruny Island ferry, out of the company ute, getting some fresh air on deck. Today's island tour, explains Dave, will be all Sam gets by way of an induction into his new role.

'I'll be talking, you'll be listening, the sun will be shining and we can grab a beer at the hotel on the way back.'

'Can I ask questions at any point?'

'Within reason and I may or may not answer them.'

The ferry slows for the approaching berth. 'When do I get to meet Q?'

'You're a riot, mate. Hop in the car and pin your ears back.'

It's a beautiful, still, sunny day as they climb the hill away from the port and head towards Dennes Point at the northern tip of Bruny. Maybe he and Kaz should dump Blue Wren Estate and get a place over here with a bit of land around it.

'Nice,' Sam says, as if by accident.

'Nature boy, eh?'

'Grew up on a farm. Got used to the space, the quiet.'

'But in the end, you always knew what came first. The land had to produce, right? Sheep, cows, wheat, whatever. Without that end result it's just a hobby.'

'S'pose.'

'Lot of people coming to Tassie the last few years. First, they were drawn by the cheaper houses and cooler climate; now they're just fucked off with the fast lane. Cashed-up, retired or semi-retired, a lot of them. Time on their hands.' Dave flicks his hand at the surroundings. This is their slice of Eden, they think. Home at fucken last.'

Sam has an idea where this might be going.

'Shit me to tears, some of them. Nimby bastards.' Dave swerves to avoid a pothole.

'So, you want me to kill them? Horse's head in the bed?'

A grin. 'Not so fast. Plenty of other options first.'

'Where do you call home, Dave?'

'That's too many questions already. You were meant to listen and I was meant to talk, remember?'

Sam feels that familiar rush of blood, the harbinger of stupidity and regret. But he won't heed his own warnings, he never does. 'Thing is, Dave, if you want me to abide by your rules you need to convince me you're not an impostor. Don't mean to be rude but I'm guessing the reason you're offering me this good money is that you want me to skate close to the edge on your behalf. I'm prepared to do that if I believe I have the right backing.'

Dave opens a window to let some fresh country air blow through but they're on an unsealed dusty stretch of road so it's not the best idea. 'Contract signed this morning, mate. Bit late to be asking awkward questions.'

'Awkward? By the way, it isn't a contract, it's an MoA. Gives you more wriggle room if you feel the need to hang me out to dry. I need to know if you're the real deal or just some bloke who likes playing with soldiers until shit hits fan.'

A sharp intake of breath as Dave pulls over to the side of the road in a swirl of gravel. He turns to Sam. 'Fucken cocky, I'll give you that.' He scans the landscape, the bays, shining water, gently swaying eucalypts. 'You can have the first crack for free. Shows spirit. The next one will cost you.' A nose scratch to punctuate the carefully chosen words. 'I don't have to prove myself to anyone, least of all you. Live with it or walk away. Good luck finding a job ever again in this state.'

Sam sees how close he's come to blowing it. Kaz would never forgive him if he let this chance get away because of his stupid mouth. A wry smile. 'Consider my head well and truly pulled in.'

'Good,' says Dave. 'Sitting comfortably? Then I'll begin.'

—

Ros hadn't been able to face a trawl through the second USB last night. Instead, she'd opted for half a bottle of pinot noir, happy pills, and early to bed. Okay, she thinks now, I'll do this for you, Niamh. I'll check out everything you left for me in that envelope. Then I will get on with mourning the beautiful woman I loved. She checks the time, midmorning. Inserts the thumb drive.

Video files. Half a dozen or so, they seem to be in date order. The first in mid-February, just after Zeb's death. Ros clicks on the play arrow.

'Where do I start, Ros?' It's Niamh. She's been crying, 'Zeb is dead.' She shakes her head, wipes a smear of tears and snot from her face with her sleeve. 'What am I meant to do now? How do I go on without him?'

Ros feels a cold knot in her gut. Had all this time with Niamh been an illusion?

'They asked me to identify him. They said he had no-one else but me.' A sob. Eyes lifted heavenward. 'Jesus.' Niamh straightens, tries to bring herself under control. 'I barely recognised him. That beautiful face bruised, bashed, bloated.'

Ros fights the urge to slam the laptop shut and throw it in the bin.

'Ros, my love, they murdered him. You must believe me.'

Here we go. How could Niamh have signed up to this conspiracy-fuelled nonsense? How many other lovers, families, friends, had been swept apart, this last year or two, under the tsunami of tinfoil-hat irrationalism flooding the globe?

'They said it was an accident, a boat propeller.' Niamh shakes her head. 'No way. You know why? There wasn't enough damage. I've seen what damage a propeller can do on the Rottnest swim. Nasty gashes, mauled, ripped up. No sign of it on Zeb. Any real damage to him was internal, invisible.' More tears. 'My beautiful, brave Zeb.'

'Stuff this.' Ros starts to close the laptop.

Sniffling. 'He'd been warned. He knew this was coming.'

What had happened to Niamh? Strong, down-to-earth. Now this stupid, ranting, crazy— Who the hell was she, what other secrets had she held back?

—

They've pulled up at a farm gate. Sam recognises the property, the Tibetan prayer flags: it's Mad Cow's place. Down the hill, beyond the weatherboard farmhouse which needs a lick of paint, the salmon pens float on the blue water and there's the constant thrum of engines, pumps and generators. Out there he hadn't noticed – it was just a job he was doing – but from up here you can see how it would drill into you, like that muffled roar he wakes up to every day from the Brooker Highway, only harder to ignore. This place must have been paradise once, but who wants to wear ear plugs just to live your life?

'You grow up in Tassie, you learn to keep your mouth shut,' says Dave. 'Sure, there's been notable exceptions. Greenies like to bleat and don't know when to stop. And there's always the odd one here and there looking to make a name for themselves, sell some books, get a following on Twitter. But by and large we're a compliant, complicit lot.'

'You're Tassie?' Sam reappraises Dave. 'Wouldn't have guessed.'

'My cunning disguise.' He lifts his chin towards the farmhouse. 'She doesn't like the noise. Can't say I blame her, but there's the big picture to consider. She doesn't get it.'

'Noise complaints? Seriously?'

'What is that Paul Kelly song? The one about big things growing from little things.'

'Care to elaborate?'

'No.'

By 'big picture', Sam assumes that Dave is talking about profit and loss. The woman has come out onto her porch and is staring their way. Lifts her smartphone to take a pic but she won't be able to see them through the tinted windscreen. 'You've tried persuasion, I take it?'

'Of course. Not interested in money, or relocation. Offered to buy her place off her. Could use it for storage or something. Nah, she likes to fight for her cause.'

'Which is where I come in?' Sam's not convinced. 'If you want somebody to put a brick through her window or leave a gutted wallaby at her door, I'm sure you could get it done for less than you're paying me. Any bloke down the pub ...'

'Already done that. She made a video and put it on Facebook. Got a lot of likes and angry faces.' Dave starts the engine up again, gives Mad Cow a wave out of the window. 'She doesn't scare so easily.' Grins at Sam. 'And *that* is where *you* come in.'

Sure, thinks Sam, he has the skills. He's fully trained to terrify the crap out of people. 'I can't believe you're bringing me in for something this petty.' But it's clear that Trembath intends to follow through. 'How scared do you want her? Like physically hurt scared?'

'If that's what it takes. But sometimes what you plant in the mind can be enough. A graduated approach, if you like.' Reversing out onto the gravel road. 'There is a deadline of sorts. She needs to get the message quickly.'

'How quickly?'

'Within the next fortnight, we want her closed down. The D'Entrecasteaux board will be meeting to discuss a takeover offer and we don't want her bleating to the faint hearts.'

'Bleating about the noise? Surely that wouldn't affect a big money takeover. Or does she have more influence than you're letting on?'

'Did you ask this many questions when you were chasing the towelheads?' Dave thumbs towards the back seat. 'That envelope tells you all you need to know.'

'She took our photo back there. That bother you?'

'No. If you do your job properly, her only thought will be about seeing the next dawn. Grateful. Obedient.'

A glimpse into Dave's perfect world. A warning too, maybe.

—

Jill surveys the deceased's belongings through the plastic covering of the evidence bags.

'That's it?'

The civilian storekeeper glances up from her smartphone. Her lanyard says 'Charlotte'. 'Yeah, far as I know.'

'No phone.'

Charlotte puts hers away. 'Sorry.'

'I meant there's no phone among the belongings. But there's one listed in the database record.'

'Oh.'

'There's definitely nothing else tucked away in a bag or box of its own, on the wrong shelf, in the wrong drawer?'

'If it's not there, it's not there.'

'Who's been in to look at this stuff before me?'

Charlotte checks her computer. 'Nobody in the last week or so. Oh, wait. Ian Cavanagh, way back just after it was all logged in. First day after the incident.'

'Death.'

'Hmmm?'

'The incident was a death. She was killed in a hit-and-run.'

'Okay. Right. Nasty.'

'You keep a check of what comes and goes, right? If somebody wanted to take the phone away for any reason, they need to log it out?'

'Yes.' A beep on Charlotte's screen. She can't resist checking it.

Would it be that hard to sneak a piece of evidence away from a distracted civvy clerk? Of course not. But if Cav had done that, then why? Jill returns everything to its container and lets Charlotte know she's finished. 'Can you do me a favour and buzz me if that phone shows up?'

'Sure thing.'

Jill leaves Charlotte to her social networks and goes back upstairs to the office. It's nearly empty save for herself and a couple of civilian data inputters – clock-watchers. Everybody else is out chasing the drive-by wannabe gangsters. Nudging lunchtime, and the clockies will be heading out too. She'll have the place pretty much to herself then. To do what? Rummage through Cav's drawers? What does she think he's done? There could be any number of innocent reasons for him taking the phone from evidence storage. He had a hunch, checked it, didn't work out. Forgot to return it, distracted by gang shootings, et cetera. Maybe he didn't take it. Maybe the records were wrong – human error. Why doesn't she just ask him?

'Won't be long.' The clockies give her a wave and leave together. Jill thinks they might be an item. She nods their way and smiles. The door glides shut behind them.

What's stopping her?

Well, for a start, the three CCTV cameras dotted about the ceiling. She heads for Cav's desk. Makes a show of looking for something and finding it. Scrawls out a note on a yellow stick-it pad, some bullshit enquiry. Blocking the camera with her body, she tests the drawers. Top one opens, pens and such. Second one doesn't. She sticks the note on his computer screen and returns to her own desk.

—

Dave treated them both to a paddle of beers and a cheese platter at the Bruny eatery. Now they're back on the Tassie mainland parked over the road from a plain-looking suburban home in Margate, the northernmost of the string of Channel towns.

'Why the personal tour?' Sam had asked over his brie and cracker. 'You could just give me the instructions and set me running.'

'Professional pride. A way of letting you know we're all in this together.'

Sam had little option at this stage but to accept it at face value. The rest of the Bruny Island trip was a getting-to-know-you exercise, trading inconsequential snippets of personal information to try to build trust. Dave was testing him, and Sam knew that game from way back.

'Item number two,' says Dave, emitting a soft beery belch.

Sam cracks a window to release the fumes. It's the end of the school day. Parents trailing kids up the street. Dogs bark at the passing footsteps and childish chatter. Sam and Dave, two men huddled in a car like a couple of perverts and nobody pays them any mind.

'Nice place,' he says, lifting his chin at the brick veneer and the view of the mountain beyond.

'The occupier died in a tragic traffic accident.'

'When was this?'

'Very recently.'

'Our doing?'

'Like I said, accident. Best of my knowledge.'

Sam stifles an impatient sigh. 'So why are we here?'

'We believe something of value may have been left there.'

'Like what?'

'Video or sound files, documents, photographs. Probably all in electronic form.'

'So, we're looking for laptops, phones, thumb drives, stuff like that?'

A nod. 'Trouble is, she never seems to go out much.'

'She?'

'The widow.' Dave shows him a photo on his phone. A woman somewhere in her forties. A professional-looking woman, groomed and confident. 'She used to be a lawyer; that's from the archives. Not so flash these days.'

'Meaning?'

'A breakdown. Unfair dismissal case. Workplace bullying. Got a nice settlement out of it. S'pose that's her training coming into play, eh?'

'She's been giving you—' Sam corrects himself— 'us, grief?'

'No, that was her dearly departed. But the idea of a corporate lawyer having that ...' he searches for a word, '... material in her possession, well, you'd get nervous, wouldn't you?'

Sam sums up. 'So, it's a monster job on the Bruny woman and a burglary here. That it?'

'For starters.'

'Deadline?'

'Yesterday.'

—

Ros assumes the other videos are more of the same, and she's had enough. That tight tangle of jealousy inside her is overpowering. She's been trying to distract herself the last few hours. Some yoga, piano practice, a list of gardening jobs. Lunch. A list of meals for the coming week. Lists, lists, lists. What's the point? She glances out the window at the schoolkids skipping across her driveway, sees the ute parked over the road: two blokes, probably from the housing development down the hill, no doubt figuring how to cram more overpriced retirement villas into the decimated acreage. A walk and some fresh air might have been nice but she can't face dodging the kids on the footpath or shielding her jagged nerves from the barking dogs. Is it time for her next round of meds?

The ute starts up and, with a glance her way from the driver, off it goes. Why was he looking at her? Ros dismisses the question. That's the kind of thing Niamh would think. Ros pops her meds, puts on Classic FM, and starts chopping vegies for a curry; a favourite recipe of Niamh's which will no doubt be delicious but may, from now on, leave a sour aftertaste. After a while the meds kick in and she's nicely drowsy. She pushes the ingredients to one side, reaches into the fridge for the half bottle of pinot gris, and grabs the cheese and bickies.

The couch beckons.

It's so hard to wake up these days. Eyelids so heavy you feel the need to prise them apart with your fingers. Head mummified in choking old rags. A taste in her mouth that could be formaldehyde. Ros feels dead already and may as well be. Has she gone blind? She's sure she opened her eyes but it remains pitch black. How long has she been asleep?

Thump.

That's what woke her. There's somebody in her home.

A scrape. A drawer opening. Being opened. By somebody.

She should stay still, silent. Let them take what they want and go. I'm insured. Just go. Please.

Why is it so dark?

'Where is it?' A male voice, close to her ear.

If she wasn't on tranquillisers, she might well be crapping herself by now. Instead, just a cold paralysis. And perhaps a wish for the worst, so she can be reunited with Niamh.

'What? What do you want? Money? My wallet is in a basket on the kitchen counter. Take it.'

'PC. Laptop. iPad, phone. Where are they?'

If this was a desperate junkie, she'd expect more urgency and less control in their voice. Perhaps also an unwashed smell, bad breath, chemicals, something like that. But this voice was calm, unhurried. The smell? A hint of brine like a windy day at the beach. Where was her laptop? Good question. 'Can I turn the light on? I can't see.'

'No need.'

A surge of impatience. 'This is stupid. I can't see, you can't see. How am I supposed to find the things you want?'

'Just tell me where they are.'

'I don't fucking know!' Then she does. She'd slipped the laptop and phone under the couch before she dropped off to sleep. Feels down in that direction.

A staying hand on her shoulder. 'Oh, right. Got it.'

She hears them being lifted, put into a bag. He can see in the dark. How?

Oh my God. Night-vision goggles?

'This thumb drive in your laptop. Is it the only one or are there more?'

'That's it.' He's not a thief. He's not taking the wallet and gadgets for selling. He wants information. Niamh's information. The stuff that got her killed.

A gloved hand cups her chin. 'I hope that's the truth, Ros. You don't want me coming back.'

He knows her name. 'It's the truth,' she lies.

And then he's gone.

5

Friday. Sam wakes up in a strange room, bathed in sweat. A house in Middleton, overlooking the D'Entrecasteaux Channel, keys – along with ex-military hardware and other goodies – handed over by Dave Trembath as they parted yesterday.

'If this all goes well, you're going to be in clover.'

And if it doesn't? thought Sam.

He'd wound his way back down the Channel Highway from Margate around midnight, every headlight in his rear-view surely a cop. In his mind he saw the woman, Ros, rushing next door to the neighbours to call for help. When they arrived, they would find the mains switch in the power box turned off. They would find the smashed leadlight panel in the front door. What else?

Relax, they'll find nothing.

He flicks the kettle on and spoons coffee into the plunger. Nice place, he thinks. Lovely view. Peaceful. A house with all the mod cons and a big yard. Maybe he was aiming too low with Blue Wren Estate. The booty is in his backpack. He hasn't examined it; that's Dave's department. Using the burner phone Dave supplied, he'd left a message as he drove south to Middleton in the dark.

'Got it.'

There are a few notifications on the mobile when he turns it back on. Missed calls from Trembath. No audio messages or texts; nothing leaving a guilty trace. He pours himself a cup, then returns the call as he takes his coffee out onto the front porch.

'You rang.'

'Mission accomplished?'

'Got a phone and a laptop, if that's what you mean. Plus a USB.'

'I'll drop by this morning to pick them up.' Dave punctuates whatever he's thinking with a sniff. 'Any grief?'

'The meds and the half-bottle of plonk must have kept her calm.' Out on the water, it's flat calm and sunlight glints on the glassy surface. Further out, the dark circles of fish pens hover like a mirage. 'She'll call the police.'

'Who will have nothing of substance to work with. Unless you were careless?'

'I wasn't.'

'Great, see you in a while.'

Sam lays the phone on the table. Takes another gulp of coffee, topping up his mug from the plunger. Gets back to enjoying the view.

—

A couple of barely interested uniformed constables have wandered through Ros's home this morning. After a quick phone consultation, it had been deemed that her place doesn't need the full crime-scene treatment. She's been given a case number to quote for insurance purposes for the cracked leadlight and any missing valuables. Is that it?

No. There was an intruder in her house. He switched off the mains power. Wearing NV gogs. He's Buffalo Bill from *Silence of the Lambs*. He was after information, not money. The same information that got her life partner killed. Get bloody interested. The plods had conferred. Seriously doubted her goggles claim but would make enquiries about the coincidence of her partner dying recently in a road accident.

She's summoned a locksmith and had some security devices put on the doors and windows and installed a sensor alarm. Got a quote on the broken leadlight and learned it'll cost an arm and a leg to replace. Now she's calling Ian Cavanagh, who was ever so attentive last time they met.

'Ros, how you going?'

'Somebody broke into my place last night.'

'Anything taken? Are you okay?'

She tells him what happened and what's gone. In the background she can hear traffic and voices.

'Night-vision?' he says, unable to keep the scepticism from his voice. 'You told the attending officers?'

'Yes. They didn't believe me either.'

'I believe you, Ros. Of course, I do.' No, he doesn't. 'This stuff of Niamh's. What was it exactly?'

Documents, she tells him. Photographs. Videos.

'Videos?'

'Video diaries, I suppose. Messages for me, I was the intended audience.'

'You've watched them?'

'I started to.'

He offers a sympathetic *hmmm*. 'Must have been upsetting.'

'Yeah.' Only she's not here for sympathy. 'Are you going to look into this, like properly?'

'Absolutely.' The phone is muffled for a moment, then background murmurs. 'Look, Ros, I'll be able to get away from here around lunchtime. I'll drop by your place then, okay?'

'Okay.'

'Don't worry, Ros, I'm on to this.'

Great. So why does she feel like she's yelling into the void?

—

Sam has hitched a lift over to Bruny on one of the company boats which picked him up from the Middleton boat ramp and dropped him at a quiet bay away from everywhere else. It looks more legit this way: there's a bunch of salmon pens nearby and every reason for the boat to be pulling into the ramp to drop personnel off. Nobody wants the Bruny ferry operators or fellow passengers looking too closely his way. Remembering him. It's a hike to where he needs to be but an innocuous white any-ute is waiting at the Labillardiere Jetty car park, arms-length courtesy of Trembath. Sam slings his holdall in the back and reverses across the gravel. A couple of grey-nomad campervans, an SUV parked at the beginning of the walk track. The place is midweek out-of-season quiet. He settles in for the drive up north towards Dennes Point. Early afternoon and he's got several hours to kill. A diversionary swing down to Adventure Bay where he parks up over the road from the general store, gets himself a pie and a coffee, and sits looking out over the white sand and blue water.

What on earth did he think he was getting himself into?

In Afghanistan, in uniform and under orders, it was still possible to believe you were on the side of the good guys. Even after a day of slaughtering peasants in a field, a brutal and ugly but ultimately necessary sideshow in the global war on terror. The Great Crusade, as his highly decorated and now egregiously persecuted ex-brother-in-arms would say. Vietnam,

Northern Ireland, Iraq, Afghanistan: it was the loyal foot soldier's burden to carry the weight of dark deeds demanded for the supposed greater good. Always had been, always would be. It didn't compare to the petty bully-boy gangsterism Sam had just signed up to. And for what? To put a deposit down on an overpriced shitbox in outer suburban Hobart?

And yet.

If he doesn't take this dirty money, someone else surely will. And that leaves him and Kaz paying extortionate rent on someone else's shitbox in outer suburban Hobart. To hell with that. As Trembath might say, there was the bigger picture to consider, and Sam was obliged to take it into account.

Nobody would get hurt, nobody would die. A scare maybe, but it's a scary fucken world these days. All it needed was smoke and mirrors and a few chills like on the ghost train at the fairground. And all Mad Cow needed to do was buy some earplugs, look out a different window and shut the fuck up. Or sell up and piss off. Right?

Right.

Sam chucks his cup and pie bag in a nearby bin. Starts the motor and heads north again past the dazzling coastline and sweeping bays. He always felt better after he'd given himself a pep talk.

Even after a blood-soaked day in the fields of Uruzgan Province.

—

'Have you given up on Niamh?'

Ros didn't intend to sound so blunt. She knows that Ian is here to talk about the break-in. Fine. But it's been over a month since Niamh's death and Ros feels suspended like a wasp in amber. She needs to move forward but things keep holding her back. Things like paralysing grief, things like psychos invading your home and threatening you in the dark.

'Of course not, Ros. We're doing our best.' Ian heads for Ros's kettle. 'Do you mind?'

Yes, she does. 'Take a seat, I'll make it. What do you want?'

'Coffee'd be great.'

Kettle boiling, mugs, milk and such. Ros trying to gather her thoughts. 'If you believe it was a cowardly hit-and-run, just say so. Does that make life easier for you?'

'It's not about making things easier, Ros. Believe me.' A pause as Ros gives him his coffee. 'So, the break-in?'

She recounts what happened. 'It was no random burglary. He was after Niamh's files and information.'

'You said you read those files, watched the videos. What was in them?'

'Niamh was upset about a friend of hers who died. She believed it wasn't an accident.'

'Who was the friend?'

Ros tells him and he makes a note. 'I'll look into it. What about the files and stuff, read any of that?'

'The salmon industry. Niamh and her friend thought they were stuffing up the environment.'

Ian frowned. 'Hardly a secret. I can't see it being worth killing anyone for. Any particular company named?'

'D'Entrecasteaux featured a lot.'

'How did she come by all this material?'

'I don't know. Her activist circle I presume.'

A few taps on his iPad. 'And now all this information, videos, whatever, has been stolen, you say?'

'That's right.'

'Probably coincidental. It was on items that are popular anyway with thieves: phones, laptops and such. Easy to offload for quick money. We'll check the local Cash Converters.'

'He was wearing night-vision goggles.'

'You saw them?'

'No, but it was obvious he—'

'When you wake up suddenly, sometimes it takes a while for the eyes to adjust ...'

He doesn't believe her. Previously he was hinting at foul play and wanting to know if Niamh had enemies. Isn't this an answer? 'Are you going to look into the salmon company link?'

'Sure, I'll look into it.'

No, you won't, thinks Ros. 'Why did you come here?'

'You rang me.'

'Are you going to seriously, properly, investigate this burglary?'

'We seriously and properly investigate all crime, Ros.'

But she can see she has annoyed him. He doesn't respond well to criticism, implicit or explicit. He's the white knight and obviously Ros needs to get back to being a damsel in fucking distress.

'How exactly are your inquiries progressing?' she says.

Shoulders back, he straightens himself in the chair. No longer the slump of an underappreciated prime minister. 'What can you tell me about Mark Limace?'

'Mark? You think he …?'

'We think everything and nothing, Ros. We're just gathering information.'

'He's a prick.'

'Care to elaborate?'

'Controlling, manipulative, threatening.'

'Violent?'

'He never left any marks.'

'So, was he?'

Ros has to admit that Niamh never said in so many words. 'Coercive control, you've heard of that?'

Ian smiles grimly. 'Quite the buzzword, isn't it?'

Two actually. 'He controlled the finances, who Niamh could communicate with, when or whether she could leave the house, where she went.'

'But not actually violent.'

'The threats and control seemed to be enough. Until she got up the nerve to leave the bastard.'

'He didn't take it well, did he?'

'It needed a court order to get him to back off.'

'Your doing?'

'No. I specialise – specialised – in corporate law. But I knew people.'

'Do you think he's capable of murder?'

'Isn't anybody?' Ian looks at her expectantly. It's as if he's waiting for permission. 'Yes, I think he is. There are plenty of examples of men who've progressed from control to murder. And why the hell did he follow us to Tasmania anyway?'

Go fetch, thinks Ros. If you're not going to help me with the other things, I will look into them myself. Meanwhile feel free to give Mark some grief.

—

Sam has the woman cable-tied to her kitchen chair, a hood over her head. It's just gone 2.00 am and he's left all the lights off. He can see her in hazy-green through the NV. He'd woken her up, slapped gaffer tape over her mouth and led her at knifepoint into the kitchen.

He's shifted his voice to a higher register, slipped in the hint of a northern English accent, flattening vowels similar to an old army mate he knew when they shared patrols with a unit of Poms. 'Lonely out here. How do you stand it?'

A muffled noise from behind the tape.

'Rhetorical question. No need for a reply.' She's lost control of her bladder. A sob follows. 'You must be sick of all this, eh? And you know it'll never stop, that feeling of being alone, vulnerable. Never.'

Sam gets up, walks around the kitchen, sees the photos on the fridge. Kids. Grandkids. Friends. Happy times. He takes one of them down.

'When was the last time your family saw you happy? Can't be much fun for them these days.'

Standing behind her now. His head bowed to her ear. She flinches at his breath, his proximity.

'What use are you to them stuck out here? Alone, angry? Fighting a war that you'll never win? You should be with them, swapping recipes, playing games, celebrating life. Not poisoning yourself and everyone around you. You're toxic.'

Back to his chair directly in front of her, knees touching. 'It's alright for you, Stephanie. You get to be an artist. Live in this big, nice house all on your own while people are sleeping in tents and cars. But you want to take away the livelihoods of thousands of decent hard-working Tasmanians. Nimby. That's what you are.'

She shakes her head. Frustrated. Must have heard this argument countless times. No doubt has an answer for it.

'It has to stop, Stephanie. You have to stop. Otherwise, this goes on, and on, and on. And before you know it, you're dead from stress or cancer or summat, and it were all for nothing.'

Sam lifts the container up in front of her face, knows she can't see it.

'Know what this is?' He shakes it so she can hear the sloshing noise. Undoes the cap so she can smell. Petrol. A squeaky sob and a struggle against the cuffs. He wanders around the kitchen. Sloshing and splashing, sloshing and splashing. Some goes on her. 'The problem with living so far away from everything is how long it takes for help to arrive. You think you're living the dream and all of a sudden, it's a nightmare.'

Right beside her ear, he clicks the lighter.

'Now then, Stephanie. One last time. Do you promise to stop?'

A strangled sob but yes, unmistakably a nod. He tears the tape from her mouth.

'Let me hear it.'

'Yes.'

6

Saturday. Early. 'Mainly water?'

'That's what the fire investigator says.' Jill Wilkie has been up since about four and feels herself fraying, ready to snap. That birthday of hers, yesterday? A non-event, drowned by more pressing matters. No cheesecake, no nothing. Cavanagh's manner isn't helping. It's like she has to repeat everything three times or attribute it to an expert, preferably male, before he takes it in. 'Heavily diluted mixture, like ninety-nine percent, barely combustible but enough of the petrol smell to scare the bejesus out of anyone.'

'What else have we got?'

'She was hooded, and the lights left off. The intruder was male, had some kind of northern Pommie accent; reminded her of a cop show she'd watched recently. Spoke calmly the whole time but threatening.'

'Threatening what?' says Cavanagh.

'To not leave her alone until she stopped.'

'Stopped what?'

'Her campaign against the salmon farm,' says Jill, thumbing over her shoulder to the pens visible through the kitchen window. 'She's on our books. Wallabies left on the porch with their throats slit. Being followed in her car and nearly rammed off the road. Abusive and threatening phone calls at all hours. Bricks through the window.'

'Has all that been investigated?'

'Yes, but no action taken. No perps identified.' Jill could murder a coffee. 'Apart from the watery petrol, or petrolly water, the intruder left no other significant trace of himself. The techs can check for fibres and stuff and may get a cast of prints from outside for if we find someone of interest later.'

'Neighbours? Other traffic?'

'We're on it. Will keep you in the loop.' They shuffle out of the way of a masked technician. 'You must have a lot to juggle? I can keep things ticking along here.'

'You seem like you're suddenly enjoying the job, Jill. Second wind before retirement?'

'Justice never sleeps, Sarge.' He gives her a look but she can't decipher it. 'We do know our man can see in the dark. Either he eats lots of carrots or was wearing NV. Maybe we need to look at where he might have got them from? Check local suppliers?'

'NV? Interesting.' A pause. Cav staring at the scenery like he's deep in thought. 'Good idea, Jill, I'll leave it with you.'

'One more thing.'

'Yep?'

'We should encourage D'Entrecasteaux to assist us with our inquiries. Want me to follow that up too?'

'That might require a touch more finesse. Diplomacy and such. I'll kick it upstairs for advice.'

'Sure, Sarge. No worries.'

'Mark Limace. Any progress with him?'

'Not without authorisation to dig deeper into his affairs – business, technical, personal, whatever.'

'Consider yourself authorised. Fill out the forms and zap them to me for the tick.'

—

Ros digs out the second thumb drive from the bottom of the basket on the kitchen counter. She had found it inside a spectacle case. Why? Likely a med-haze accident rather than cunning design to thwart the invisible enemy. This one has all the files and documentation that Niamh seemed to think was important. The videos of her are on the drive stolen the other night. Ros feels a pang at not getting the chance to watch those remaining videos or a last glimpse of Niamh. But if it was the conspiracist version, is that really what she wants as her last memory of her soulmate? Yes, she supposes so.

She's just got home from a mad dash up to the city for a new laptop and smartphone along with various accessories. A pot of coffee and some choice expletives later, she's got the phone and computer set up and ready to go. She logs into her bank, credit card and super accounts and changes the passwords. Thankfully the accounts haven't been touched. Then likewise with email, social media and whatever else needs it. She had stopped using social media when she was depressed; her own last post was of her and Niamh in a happy land far, far away and long, long ago.

They'd been bouldering. Along the cliffs at Blackwall Reach on the Swan River. Another of Niamh's many physically demanding hobbies she was trying to share with Ros. Free-climbing, but not at a height where you could badly hurt yourself. Indeed, on that glorious Perth spring day, any fall from those Blackwall cliffs would have resulted in a refreshing dip in the river.

Use your legs to push and reach. Feel the strength in them.

Yeah, love, I'm trying.

So, Niamh's USB.

Reports. Shitloads. Internal D'Entrecasteaux Salmon reports, some marked classified or secret, some not. Environmental reports, financial reports, invoices, receipts, shipping and freight dockets, personnel reports, health and safety reports. Where to start? And where the hell did Niamh get all this from? Or rather, who the hell? External reports by independent consultants, government bodies, subcontractors. It was like a mass dump from WikiLeaks: what was meant to be significant, and what was not?

Back to basics: who owns D'Entrecasteaux, how is it organised, a brief history, summarise the current state of play, what's on the horizon. All or most of that, Ros could find out through other channels. Then, and only then, might this information dump begin to take shape.

A knock at the door.

Was it the burglar?

I hope that's the truth, Ros. You don't want me coming back.

If he knew what he was looking for, then he must know what was still missing.

Another knock. Maybe it was Ian Cavanagh with an update on the investigation. He could tidy the place up while he was here, run the vacuum over the rug.

Again. More insistent. 'Rosalyn? It's Mark.'

Jesus. Mark Limace.

But he wouldn't go away. She knew that of him. He would have seen her car, known she was home. Maybe had been watching and waiting all along. Maybe he was the one who killed Niamh and had come around to gloat. It would be just like him.

Knock, knock. 'Rosalyn?'

She sets the camera on her new laptop to record and goes to answer the door. 'Mark. Hi.'

Mark has a sad look on his face and a bunch of flowers in his fist. 'I just heard about Niamh. I'm so sorry.' He looks like he's about to offer her a consoling hug. Instead, he hands her the flowers.

'Thanks. You needn't have.'

'I was wondering how you were going.'

Let's get you sat down and record anything you have to say. 'I was about to pour myself a tea. Want one?'

'Sure. This isn't an awkward time?'

'No, no, it's fine.'

Mark has put on a few kilos since she last saw him, his hair has grown and he sports light stubble and the demeanour of a Tassie artisan. He plants himself at her kitchen table in the chair she hoped he'd take. 'What a shock.' He shakes his head. 'Horrible.'

'How did you hear?'

'Some mutual friends contacted me. 'They asked me how I was going.'

That would have been at least a month ago. 'Have the police spoken to you?'

'Yes. A few days ago.'

'It makes sense, I suppose.' She hands him his tea.

He blows on the cup to cool the liquid. Glances at her over the rim. 'Yes, I suppose.'

'Were you able to help them in any way?'

'No. They don't seem to know where to look. Probably some tanked-up bogan reading his phone while he's driving.'

'Who knows.'

'Is there anything I can do at all?'

Like what? Let police examine the tracking software you used to control her in the good old days? 'What did you have in mind?'

'Nobody should be alone at a time like this. If you need someone to talk to …'

'Was it you?'

'What?'

'Did you kill Niamh?'

'Are you serious?'

'Deadly.'

He puts his cup down. Shakes his head slowly. 'I can see you're in a dark place, Rosalyn. And you might not believe it, but I really am sorry for your loss.'

'Why are you here, Mark? Come to gloat?'

He stands to go. 'We never really got on, you and I. It's a shame. Times like this, we all need a friend. Is there anybody who can be with you?'

'You didn't answer my original question, Mark. Did you kill her?'

'You're in my thoughts, Ros.'

He can't keep the twinkle out of his eyes when he says it. She won't grant him the dignity of a reply.

—

Once again in the Middleton weatherboard, out on the front porch looking at that gleaming water and the overlapping verdant contours of the hills falling to the sea. A mug of tea at hand, a plate of toast and Vegemite, and a craving for the smokes he gave up years ago. Sam had woken late. With what was left of the morning, he'd luxuriated in a long hot shower to try to flush away his demons. He'd left the borrowed ute on Bruny at the Jetty Beach campground where he found it and was picked up by an early morning boat which took him directly to Middleton. He'd climbed into bed as the sun flashed across the calm surface of the Channel. Sleep had been fitful.

We gunna pop this fucker?

Whether it's a Star of Gallantry or a downpayment on a shitbox in suburban Hobart, in the end, what's the difference between one mercenary thug and another? Qadim, the kid in the cornfield, had no reason to believe Sam would do the right thing, ever. We don't even do the right thing by our friends and allies, he thinks, never mind our enemies. How do you clamber back out of that hole you've dug for yourself? The sides are muddy and slippery, there's nothing to hold on to. He'd recognised that sour stench of Stephanie's terror-induced piss from countless episodes in the line of duty. Her loss of control had shamed him.

The farmer in the field had pissed himself in terror before he died. You can see the damp patch in the photo trophy taken of the war hero. The grin, the devil-horns hand signal, the corpse. Photos leaking out now to the media. A steady drip-feed. Somebody wants to bring the war hero down. Sam turns his phones on: messages and missed calls from Kaz and from Dave Trembath, two each. It's late morning but he can't for the life of him recall what day it is. Saturday, that's right. He should be at home, mowing the lawn, playing with bub, messing around with Kaz. He responds to Trembath first.

'Job done?'

'Yep, I believe so.'

'You believe so?'

'She promised, crossed her heart, but I didn't actually get a signed MoA off her.'

A pause to absorb the insubordination. 'Best keep your head down for a few days. It's on the news. Go home, see your family.'

Sure thing. Next, a call to Kaz, who's happy he'll be home for a few days even if she hadn't been expecting him back so early. 'Is the new job going okay?'

'Great, babe, I'll tell you all about it when I see you.'

Except he won't.

Was all this inevitable? Seeded, perhaps from the day he claimed the coveted SAS beret, or the night he'd agreed to put a bullet in the head of a kneeling, captured, defenceless man. Or maybe from that day eighteen months ago in a nondescript office in Melbourne. Two suits – one of each gender – across the desk from him. Army investigators, tasked to investigate – and, if possible, bury – allegations of war crimes.

'You were there that day, Sam. We know you were. You saw everything.'

'This guy's a war hero. Powerful friends. Always on the telly giving his two cents' worth. Are you seriously going after him? You really want me to betray a fellow soldier?' asked Sam.

'We want you to tell the truth.'

What they did in Uruzgan is already known, all the way up the chain of command. Somebody is being lined up as a sacrifice. 'I didn't see anything.'

The woman slides a series of photos across the desk. Flashlit red eyes. Sam popping one in the skull of the prisoner. 'Maybe you'd like to talk to us about this instead?'

'You want him badly, don't you?'

'We want the truth, Sam. About him or about you. Your choice.'

No, he won't tell Kaz all about this new job when he sees her. Won't tell her she's married to a monster.

—

Jill Wilkie finds Stephanie Howden sitting up in bed in a side room on the third floor at Hobart Private. The security options here are better than the public wards in the neighbouring building. There's a uniform outside her door, alert and respectful, the way Jill likes it. No visible signs of injury on Stephanie, but she has the unmistakable look of someone who has been somewhere she never expected to come back from.

Jill introduces herself, shows some ID. 'How are you going?' Stupid question, but she can't think of another opener.

'I don't need to be here. I'm not hurt.' An embarrassed smile that crumples immediately.

'You've had a huge shock. Traumatic. The doctors need to keep you under observation.' You're safer here than at home, goes unsaid. 'Are you okay to chat, Stephanie?'

'Steph.' A lost look. Tearful. 'I didn't see anything, him. I was hooded.'

Steph again describes the voice, northern British accent, high-pitched. There's something in the background, a flicker, that Jill can see. She leaves it to percolate in Steph's memory.

'Yorkshire? Liverpool? Geordie? Scots?' Jill spent a few years over that way after she finished uni. Learned to tell the difference.

'I don't know.'

Jill makes a note to organise expert advice on the matter, get some recordings of accents. They move on to the things that were said. Menacing allusions to how dangerous it was for Steph to live alone and isolated. How this menace would never go away until she stopped.

'Stopped what?' Jill already knows the answer but wants to hear it from Steph.

'Campaigning against the salmon farm.'

'He said that?'

'No. But that's what it was about. There's nothing else I'm doing that needs to stop.' A snuffle. 'It occupies every waking hour.'

'This isn't the first time you've been threatened though, is it?'

They go through the sorry history: mutilated wallabies on the porch, midnight phone calls, a smashed window, a ute doing doughnuts at her gate in the middle of the night. Then there's the daily harassment from on water: shouts, boat revs, sirens and klaxons, seal bombs, gunshots at all hours. If it was Jill, she would have buggered off years ago, but that's not what Steph needs to hear. If this was happening in suburban Hobart, they'd be rounding up the ringleaders. As far as Steph is concerned, it's obvious who is behind it: a multinational corporation with close ties to government. But this is next-level brazen thuggery.

'It seems to be escalating. Any idea why? I mean, normally they might ignore campaigners like yourself, drown your message in PR spin, get the lawyers onto you, offer to buy you out. This seems pretty desperate.'

'They've already done all of the above.'

'So why single you out? There's a campaign group, a few in fact. What makes you so special?' Jill checks herself. 'Don't mean to be rude.'

Steph manages a chuckle and her face lights up. 'You remind me of my little sis. Foot-in-mouth disease.' She shrugs. 'I don't know what makes me so special. Maybe I don't realise what I know, or there's a personal grudge.' A hesitation. Something realised? 'There's a takeover on the horizon and someone stands to make a shitload of money.'

Or lose it, thinks Jill. But that's not what you're holding back. And the question remains, what makes you so special? 'Whatever the reason, I think we need to start talking to the company. Anybody there you've had dealings with?'

'There was somebody up at my gate just a few days ago. A vehicle.' Another flicker. 'I took a photo with my phone.'

But Steph's phone was the only item missing from the break-in. 'Do you back your photos up on the cloud?'

'Cloud? What cloud?'

—

After a morning of googling and trawling through other sources such as company registers, social media, news articles, Ros pretty much has the picture. D'Entrecasteaux Salmon has been haemorrhaging financially the last few years and is ripe for a cut-price takeover. Even at cut-price, the figure is still in the billions and would net a tidy sum for the company founder and principal shareholder Edward 'Teddy' Milsom, proud son of Hobart, LNP stalwart and major donor, descended from convict blood, residing in Sandy Bay on prime waterfront. Early sixties, he's eyeing retirement and establishing a golden bulwark for his twilight years. Two companies are circling the prey. One, a Norway-based conglomerate with extensive salmon-farming interests around the globe, seeking world domination of that particular niche. The other, a Queensland-based coal billionaire looking to diversify his portfolio as fossil fuels fall out of global favour, greenwashing his image by pursuing the increasingly lucrative avenue of 'protein' production – fish farming seemingly less evil than coal-mining, relatively speaking.

Ros's tummy is rumbling. Checking the time, she sees it's early afternoon. She takes a break from the computer screen and puts together a sandwich and pours a glass of apple juice; keeps the snack simple and anodyne in memory of the nauseating fish farm images she's already seen. Outside, the sun shines, and birds flit between the trees and bushes – blackbirds, wattle birds, wrens. The vegie garden looks neglected, knee-high weeds and creeping triffidry. It had always been Niamh's territory; Ros wouldn't know where to start. Get a chap in, she thinks. Take control. Another item for the to-do list. Clouds float around the mountain, and next door the lawnmower hums. Ordinary folk are doing ordinary things while she peers down this infernal rabbit hole. Yet it doesn't depress her. She feels an awakening of parts that have been dormant for so long now. The vegie patch might have been Niamh's territory, but this labyrinth of commerce and contracts is hers; Ros knows this stuff, can read the fine print, decipher the clues.

She ignores the mountain view out the window and returns to the screen. Knowing the basic backstory and key players of the company, she can now try to construct a new narrative from the myriad documents on Niamh's USB.

The timeline.

Niamh's videos and photographs date back to early February. Is that just because that's when she was first won over to Zeb's cause or is there a more significant reason? The documents range back over the last few years, some of them nearly three years old. The takeover speculation has been swirling for at least nine months but solidified early in the new year.

So. What?

Late last year, around October, a member of the committee charged with environmental oversight of D'Entrecasteaux resigned. A well-regarded marine biologist. There's no indication of her name appearing in subsequent news reports. If she's the leaker or whistleblower, she's keeping quiet about it. Odds-on, she's under a gag order. But she would certainly know how to make sense of the science and stats embedded in this info dump. Ros notes her name for follow-up later: Jennifer Nguyen. All the documents here are official records and presumably obtainable under FOI to anyone interested, such as a takeover bidder. Ros knows that company law requires full disclosure and access to the books in the event of a serious bid. Anything hidden or undisclosed could be the basis of subsequent damages/compensation litigation. But there are ways, there always are. What if these documents are not the main game, that it is the video and photos that got Zeb and Niamh killed? Or that they back up, complement, or reinforce in some way the dry numbers and stats in the background?

Something that could derail or devalue a multibillion-dollar corporate takeover. Something definitely worth killing for.

—

It's a beautiful day in Claremont and Sam is mowing the front lawn. Honeyeaters flit between the bushes, and the nearby traffic on the Brooker Highway is reduced to the hum of an inquisitive bumblebee. Kaz is happy to have him home early, but he knows from the look on her face that she doesn't buy his story.

'It seems funny that you're working such irregular hours with this consultancy thing. Away for a few days, back for a few. On that money, I imagined something more defined, longer hours, structured. It's good they're being so flexible.'

'Sure is.' He switches off the motor, lifts his sunnies to his head and gives her a smooch to stifle the anxiety behind her probing. 'Gives me a chance to get some overdue chores done.'

'And spend quality time with me and Ollie.'

'Goes without saying.'

'It needn't.' She leans into his embrace. Sniffs. 'You need to change this shirt. Smells of petrol.'

'Will do. I was topping up the lawnmower and some splashed on me.'

'Chuck it in the basket. I'll put a load in the machine later. You nearly finished here?'

'Nearly. Then I'll do the edges with the whipper.'

'Pity there's not a rental inspection due. Would have been all shipshape for them.'

Sam brings his sunnies back down, mock businesslike. 'No more rental inspections when we move into Blue Wren, huh?'

'Do they still pay you for this ... downtime?'

'Of course.'

'So, what's a day in the life of super high-flying consultant Sam Willard?' She'd highlighted the word 'consultant' with finger quotes. 'Lay it out for me, hotshot.'

The wail of a waking bub saves him. 'I'll go and get him.'

'No, I'll do it.' She puts her hand against his chest. 'No secrets. Promise?'

'Promise.'

'Cross your heart.'

He does. 'Hope to die.'

—

Police are investigating a terrifying home invasion overnight on the otherwise sleepy holiday retreat of Bruny Island. The incident occurred in the early hours at a property near Dennes Point in the island's north. According to sources, the owner of the property, fifty-five-year-old Stephanie Howden – a vociferous critic of the salmon industry – was woken by an intruder, tied up and doused with petrol. She was also threatened.

Neither Tasmania Police nor Ms Howden have been able to confirm the nature of the threats and Ms Howden has declined to issue a statement. Police confirmed that they are following a number of leads.

In other news, a peak Tasmanian tourism body has called for further relaxation of Covid restrictions and the reopening of state borders even as cases continue to climb on the mainland ...

7

'According to sources? Which fucking "sources"?'

Jill Wilkie hasn't ever seen Cav this angry. Saturday evening's news story was followed on Sunday by a deluge of speculation – mainly on social media and fuelled by the salmon-farm opponents. That, in turn, had led to annoyed phone calls to Cavanagh from his bosses who, as a consequence, were fielding 'please explains' from Big Salmon, various politicians and the police minister. Cav's weekend had been a write-off. Monday morning. Somebody must pay.

'Well?' says Cavanagh. 'Any takers?'

'Whoever they are, they're well informed.'

Cavanagh turns his gaze to her. 'Thanks, Jill, you're right. It's as if they're at the centre of the investigation. Any ideas?'

'Sorry, boss, haven't a clue.'

'Whoever you are,' he casts a menacing scan across the faces, 'when I find you, you're finished here.'

I'm theoretically finished in a few months anyway, thinks Jill. Big deal. 'How do you want to proceed with the inquiry, boss?' She's not normally the 'boss' kind of gal, but she's enjoying the tickle of it.

His answer is to move her aside, back to the hit-and-run, and assign the Bruny job to two of his favourite boys. Not unexpected. That's why she'd leaked pre-emptively; it would make it harder to sweep it under the carpet. She and Steph Howden were women of a certain rage. They'd sort this their way.

Jobs are handed out. Cavanagh will stay in the office today dealing with the internal politics. The gangsters can wait, shoot each other out of existence if they want. This lonely, scared but determined woman at Dennes Point is the immediate priority he didn't need.

'I was thinking of having another look at Mark Limace, boss. Okay with you?'

'Who?'

'The hit-and-run victim's ex.'

'Sure, Jill. Knock yourself out.' He gives her a smile but doesn't look like he means it.

—

Ros saw the news over the weekend, alerted by the multiple red dot summonses on Niamh's still active Facebook page. She'd linked her phone and new laptop in, to keep channels of communication open with Niamh's old networks. Fellow campaigners against Big Salmon: tune in, check it out. Ros had spent most of Sunday neck deep in social media speculation and conspiracy theories. She had to admit, toxic as it was, it was quite compelling.

Interesting timing too.

Ros had then sent a message via Niamh's Facebook account to Stephanie Howden and to the marine biologist Jennifer Nguyen, who had resigned from the government oversight committee. Both were FB friends with Niamh. Ros had explained who she was, why she was contacting them through her dead partner's account, and hoped each would be available for a coffee and a chat sometime. Soon. Gave her own mobile as a reply contact.

Out on the deck, a brisk breeze flaps the sun canopy, and the chooks burble in the space below the boards. The mountain is in sharp focus today, the striations of the Organ Pipes clearly defined. Beautiful, she thinks, and some dickhead wants to have a cable car going right through all that. Is there nowhere these pricks won't ruin for a dollar? Her phone dances on the rain-warped pine table beside her coffee. A reply from Stephanie Howden. **No. Sorry**

Shame. Maybe in time. Ros is aware she's edging into cold-lawyer mode and it feels good to be heading back there. Is this Niamh's farewell gift to her, a renewed sense of purpose? A renaissance? Ros resolves to enjoy it while it lasts. She knows only too well how fragile it might turn out to be. A distant siren kicks off and the neighbouring dogs start howling. A few mad minutes then it's all quiet again. Ros didn't need the anti-barking zapper, didn't need a gobful of calming medication. Peace of mind? It feels good. No more coffee, she decides. Instead, a walk down to the

Margate waterfront at Dru Point; stand on the jetty, enjoy the tranquility of North West Bay. Fresh air, vitamin D, a change of scenery. The stats and leaked reports can wait.

The phone throbs in her hand. Steph Howden. **OK then**

Ros decides not to reply immediately. Give the woman every chance to change her mind again.

—

Sam is back on that winding road down through the Channel towns. In some ways relieved to be away from home. The rest of the weekend had been fraught, not with tension exactly but a sense of dancing around each other. The old 'let's not go there'. Things unsaid. He'd left at dawn without offering a rationale for the early departure and knowing that one wouldn't be well received right now anyway. It will blow over, he knows; all she needs is a distraction or a project – like, signing on the dotted line for Blue Wren Estate, for instance. To kill time and settle his nerves, he'd taken a breakfast break at Banjo's in Kingston. On the burner mobile, three missed calls and messages from Dave Trembath. On his own phone, two from the ABC journalist. How did she get his number? He's not interested in either of them right now. The sun bounces off the Channel as he rolls down the hill through Kettering, watching the Bruny Island ferry nosing its way through the slight chop out deep. Nudging the hour, he switches on the radio news. The headlines are all about the Covid numbers. Then:

> *To Melbourne now, and a growing party-room rebellion over the Prime Minister's Captain's Pick of high-profile author, political commentator and decorated Afghanistan war veteran Michael Turnell, for preselection for the blue-ribbon seat of Foyle in next year's federal election. Allegations have recently resurfaced of Turnell's possible involvement in war crimes in Afghanistan, with key party figures now questioning his suitability as a candidate. The ABC news website today posted video testimony of an Afghan citizen, known only as Qadim, who witnessed the killing of his father in what Defence Department records describe as a firefight with enemy insurgents but local villagers describe as cold-blooded murder ...*

Somebody had tracked Qadim down. He'd be what, twenty by now? Was this what that journalist wanted to speak to Sam about after all this time? The original documentary aired nearly three years ago. The allegations were already out there. All that remained was the question of whether Turnell was provably culpable. True, the bastard's war-hero reputation was already shaky in the eyes of some but maybe that wasn't the point here. The atrocities were known about and condoned all the way up the chain of command. Turnell has major financial and political backing and the Captain's Pick message was *Don't fuck with the big guys*. So, the ongoing probing by this ABC journo was a middle finger to those big guys.

Sam pulls off the road, turns the engine off, and listens to the first message from the journo. 'Hi Sam, Larissa Barclay here from the ABC. A mutual acquaintance gave me your number. Just wanted to let you know that your name has come up in our investigations. Qadim has been telling us his story and citing you as a witness to corroborate his version of events. Wondering if you'd like to comment? My number ...'

He seemed to think you weren't like the others. He hoped you'd do the right thing when the time comes. He said you'd promised him that you would.

You've got me all wrong, mate, the world has changed. Don't go looking for heroes and good guys anymore. Just because I'm called, doesn't mean I'll answer. Second message. 'Hi Sam, Larissa again from the ABC. Just had a call from somebody in Defence who recommended I talk to you. Very intriguing. Apparently, you've already given evidence to an internal inquiry which would support the resurfacing of certain war crimes allegations. Is that correct? Please call me on ...'

Some fucker in an office in Canberra is trying to put a target on Sam's back. Some mutual fucking acquaintance.

He checks Trembath's messages on the burner. 'You need to keep your phone on, buddy. I don't want to have to chase you. Meet us in the Middleton house. Nine, sharp.'

Us?

Sam eyes the dashboard clock. He should only be about ten minutes late.

—

Jill has Mark Limace's telcom records and movements for the last two months, specifically for the day or two either side of the hit-and-run, and they don't help at all. Ideally, he would ping somewhere on Sandfly Road at around the time and place that Niamh Cassidy was thrown into a ditch and left for dead. But he doesn't. The phone is at his home in Cygnet during that timeframe. That doesn't mean *he* was, but it could have been more useful in nailing the bastard. There's no evidence of any calls or messages between him and the deceased in recent times, or of emails or social media contact. Jill revisits the cesspit of Limace's men's-rights groups likes. How many of these names would crosscheck with VROs and violence offences around the country? Might any of them have done Mark a favour? Far-fetched, she decides. But not inconceivable.

Jill catches Ian Cavanagh staring at her across the partitions and gives him an enquiring look. He ignores it and takes a call on his mobile. How long before she is outed as the leaker, the 'source'? She's not sure she can rely on the loyalty or discretion of the journalist she called. Knows the kind of pressure they'd be under. Maybe she could set the ball rolling on her retirement after all. Get the pension and other entitlements locked in now and work out her time to a set date. Or would that be the sign of a guilty conscience? It's a strange feeling, both scary and weightless. Jill's enjoying giving free rein to this new spirit of independence, assertion and devil-may-care, yet the old anxieties nag. Along with those invoice reminders from the care home.

'A word, Jill?'

Where did he come from? Cavanagh is standing by her desk.

'Sure. What can I do for you?'

'The meeting room's probably best.' He leads the way and Jill follows, kissing goodbye to her pension. Single now and with the mortgage not paid off, maybe she'll join the growing number of middle-aged women forced to couch-surf or sleep in their cars when their world turns to dust after divorce and retrenchment. Maybe now Dad will become eligible for a public-supported care home, moved up the waiting list once his daughter is cast into the wilderness. What was she thinking, pulling a stunt like that?

—

Ros loves it down here. The end of the jetty at Dru Point, looking out across North West Bay to the soft green hills descending to the shore. Sailboats stir on their moorings. Ducks, black swans, plovers, seagulls, pelicans. Here, in the shelter of the bay, the water is flat and clear enough to make out the energy-drink can lolling in the sand two metres below. If the water was not so icy it would be nice to swim here on a morning such as this. But she knows, even if she wanted to, it would be a bad idea. There are signs around advising against swimming, fishing, any of that. Effluent disposal pipes, since sealed but, you know. But oh, the view and the peace. Out around the point, left towards Tinderbox, the salmon pens float on the near horizon. Over to the right, more of them between Electrona and Snug. And she sees now the oily, rust-coloured sheen on the water, like the burley her dad used to cast to attract the fish. Overflow from the farms. No, you wouldn't want to swim in that. The only sign of life in the water, the odd flurry of tiny sprats. An old bloke casts a line from the neighbouring jetty a few metres away on the opposite side of the boat ramp. He gives her a wave and a smile.

'Any bites?' she asks.

'Not this century. Live in hope, eh?'

'I don't have the patience.'

He shakes his head. 'It's my meditation, these days. Last time I caught a worthwhile feed here was before those arseholes moved in.' A nod out onto the water.

'The salmon farms?'

'Yeah. Stuffed everything up.' He rubs his thumb across his index finger. 'Money talks.' Looks worried. 'You don't work for them, do you?'

'No.'

He reels in and recasts. 'Nice view though, eh?'

'Beautiful,' she agrees.

He turns back to his meditation with a farewell nod.

Ros's phone buzzes. Steph Howden again through the Messenger app.

Tomorrow best 4 me. Am in Hobart, can meet here? No car

From refusal, to grudging acceptance, to pushy. Ros messages back **OK** and they arrange a place and time. In the distance, the big blue-and-white salmon farm wellboat edges away from its moorings and out into the Channel. From this far away there's no noise, just the lapping of water and the competing cries of bird life. Ros turns for home, leaving the old guy casting his rod into the cold, dead water.

—

Dave and Kristin are waiting for him on the front porch at the Middleton house. A pot of coffee and some Danish pastries on offer.

'Nice,' says Sam. 'Lovely day for it.' Admires that view again. 'Great spot.'

'Got it cheap when the owner was persuaded to sell up,' says Dave.

'Milk and one, right?' Kristin hands him a mug.

She's her usual serene self, but Dave seems agitated.

'You're a hard man to pin down in an emergency. Maybe we should have included a clause in your contract about leaving your phone on.'

MoA, not contract. 'Emergency?' Sam accepts a plate of flaky delicacies.

'We've got police and media all over us,' says Dave. 'Asking difficult questions, upsetting those at the top, the board, the shareholders.'

'I thought you had police and media under control?'

'It only takes one or two to break ranks and make life difficult.' Kristin lays a hand on Dave's arm as if to calm him. 'But it'll quieten down soon enough.'

'You told me you got everything from the Margate house, and that the Howden woman would pull her head in.' Dave, on a short fuse.

'I did.' Sam wipes some crumbs from his lap. 'I can only tell you what she said. If she didn't mean it, then she's clearly more resilient than we planned for. If you want certainty, you could always have her killed.'

Kristin frowns. 'Let's dial it down, guys. Dick-waving won't get us anywhere.'

Sam wonders if the Blue Wren lifestyle is floating away from him. A bit of pushback from cops and journos and all hell breaks loose. From dream home to house of cards in a few days? 'What do you want me to do about this?'

'The police have already backed off and will bring their people into line. Meanwhile we've done a data crosscheck and we believe there might still be items missing from your haul at the Margate house.' Kristin checks the plunger, sees it's empty. 'A number of files that we know to have been leaked from our system remain out there somewhere. We need you to pay a return visit.'

Kristin's all over this, Sam realises. She's running the show and Dave is just the narky errand boy.

'And we'd like you to keep tabs on Stephanie Howden over the coming days. See who she talks to.'

'Tabs?'

'Follow her,' says Dave. 'Don't let her out of your sight.'

'So, Sam.' Kristin gets up to make a fresh pot of coffee. 'Tell us about your weekend. Nice?'

—

Jill can see that Cavanagh isn't sure what to do next. She's seated on one side of the oval meeting table. Him on the other. The room smells of yesterday's takeaway and old coffee; under-used, it's become an unofficial lunch spot for those hermits who are jack of shop talk and looking for some peace and quiet. People like her.

'So,' she says. 'You wanted a word?'

'What's your game, Jill?'

'Game?'

'I know it was you who leaked.'

'You've got the wrong person, mate. But if you want to make accusations then I'll be having a union rep in.'

He smiles. 'C'mon, Jill. No need for that.'

She makes to stand. 'We've all got stuff to be getting on with.'

'Sit.'

She doesn't. 'I'm not a fucking Jack Russell.'

'You've got what, six months left before retirement?'

Here it comes. 'I've got as long as I choose. If you're thinking of threatening my pension, you know I can tie us up in a tribunal for those six months, and more.'

He gives her an appraising look. 'You've been underestimated all these years, Jill.'

'By some, yeah.'

'It needn't be this way.'

Jill makes a show of checking the time on her mobile. 'I really have got work to do.'

'We all have, Jill. I think I know why you did it. You don't want stuff swept under the carpet. Fair enough, very noble, but it stops now. Got it?'

'Finished?'

'There's a bigger picture. We're a team here, Jill. All of us—'

'In this together?'

'There's a lot at stake, more than you realise.' He dismisses her with a curt nod. 'Nobody is immune.'

She stops on the way out. 'Is that meant to be a threat of some kind?'

'An observation.'

—

Sam heads back up the Channel Highway to Hobart where, he's been told, Stephanie Howden is due to be discharged from hospital later this morning.

'Shouldn't I just wait for her at her place on Bruny?' he'd asked.

'The forensics cops haven't finished with it yet.' Dave had handed over a slip of paper. 'She'll be staying here until further notice.'

How do you know?

Kristin seemed to read him. 'Hobart. Everybody knows somebody.'

A tame cop, then, maybe several.

No arrangements for any city accommodation for Sam. 'You can't be watching her if you're sitting in an Airbnb stuffing your face with Uber Eats,' Dave had said with more savagery than necessary. 'Stock up on your way there, sleep in the car, piss in a bottle. Pretend you're back out on Ops.'

Which had been triggering for Sam. As intended.

His first tour. Uruzgan. North of the provincial capital, Tarin Kowt, a hamlet in a strip of fertile green farming land where the river runs through. Three in the fucking morning.

It had been a long wait but worth it. Their objective: a high-value target, a bomb maker whose IED had killed their colleague a month before. The patrol commander has just called him over, eyes shining possum bright in Sam's NVGs.

'Your turn, big boy.'

'What?'

The patrol commander nods down at the kneeling, blindfolded prisoner. 'Pop him.'

It's a joke, to test him. A packet of sky hooks, SAS-style. The prisoner can provide intel, they need him alive, surely? Sam chuckles. 'Yeah, mate, I'm good thanks.'

'Pop him.'

The rest of the patrol seem to shuffle in a step closer. The bloke's serious. Sam's seen what happens if you don't play the game. The freezing out, the white-anting, the career-ending sabotage. And he's already seen the atrocities. The killing of innocents, the throwdowns, the cover-ups. He'd thought if he could just close his eyes to it, keep his mouth shut, that would be enough to get him through. It isn't. They want him implicated, as guilty as them, sharing their dark secrets.

'Pop the cunt, Sammy. I won't say it again.'

A chill wind blows along the valley. It'll be winter soon. The prisoner hunches in, perhaps from the cold, perhaps from his impending fate.

Sam levels his M4, pops the guy and the skull splits open like an overripe melon.

'Good boy.' The PC pats his shoulder. 'Welcome to the club.'

Sam's blooding. Only obeying orders as they say. The kill captured on someone's mobile. Collective insurance.

They fit the corpse with a battle bra, two ammunition clips, a mobile and a handgun – an old Russian one they've used over and over in these set-ups. Take the happy snap. Bye.

Sam had surprised himself. Not by what he realised he was capable of, but by how little he had hesitated.

—

Ros needs to get out more. The walk down to Dru Point has done her the power of good. There's a message waiting for her from the marine biologist who'd resigned. Happy to meet, any time and place suits. How about my house, today? Ros replies. No problem. Ros offers lunch, any dietary requirements?

No salmon, is the reply.

Jennifer Nguyen arrives ten minutes earlier than expected. Tall with the same outdoors air that Niamh always had. Ros gauges her as a similar age too. 'Clear run through,' she explains. 'Used my Jedi powers on the traffic lights and the bridge was quiet.' She's come from the eastern shore, the Sunshine Coast as some call it because it avoids the mountain shadow in the afternoon.

Salad, some posh cheeses, avocado, crusty sourdough. They adjourn to Ros's deck and settle in, jumpers on against the nippy breeze. The mountain is sharp today, the dark verticals in the Organ Pipes clearly defined. A flock of white cockatoos drifts on the updrafts in the intervening valley.

'Thanks for seeing me at such short notice.'

Nguyen smiles ruefully. 'Nothing else on. The contracts and consultancies have dried up. Plenty of time on my hands.' She spreads some avocado on her bread and takes a bite. 'It was terrible what happened to Niamh. I'm sorry for not reaching out earlier.'

How would she know where and who to reach out to? 'How well did you know Niamh?'

'We met a few times. Campaign meetings, once or twice at Zeb's place.' Suck it up, Ros. You can do this. 'How did they, she, seem?'

'Seem?'

Ros is looking for clues in Jennifer's demeanour but there's nothing forthcoming. No guile, no games. 'Both Niamh and Zeb have died, as you know. Did they seem troubled, worried, afraid at all for their safety?'

'Zeb, no. I guess he thought he was invincible. But after he died, I only saw Niamh once and she was … anxious. Wary.'

Ros wants to know when that was, the circumstances of the meeting. Why had she never picked up on that anxiety and wariness herself?

'At his funeral. She was a mess.' Jennifer gives Ros this look as if to say, 'What, you didn't notice?' No, I'll have been somewhere under the doona.

The breeze picks up and the roller shade flaps and judders in protest. 'Do you think their deaths are linked? Deliberate?'

'I've been getting death threats for over a year now. So yes, I can believe it. Look at what happened to Stephanie Howden over the weekend. If this is all pure coincidence, that would make me very happy. As it is, I'm selling up and getting the hell out.'

Ros wants to know the nature of the threats Jennifer has received. Text messages, phone calls, social media trolling, graffiti at her home. What about the police, asks Ros, didn't they investigate? But the answer is already apparent. If they had, Jennifer maybe wouldn't be leaving.

'But it's not just the trolls and the threats. I can't make a living here. Not in my chosen field, anyway. Big Salmon has warned them, and nobody will touch me with the proverbial barge pole. I've got school-age kids and a partner to think about.' Tears prick her eyes. 'I'm really sorry about Niamh. She was so lovely. You must miss her terribly.'

Lunch is mainly untouched. 'Coffee, tea, whisky?' They smile through their tears and hug. Before Jennifer leaves, Ros has one more question. 'Did the information Niamh had, all the files and reports, come from you?'

'No, I'd be the obvious suspect, I know, but …' Palms upwards. 'No, it wasn't me.'

'Any ideas who?'

'If I did, I wouldn't be telling, sorry. Suffice to say, I wasn't alone in despising what was going on. But people have mortgages, not everybody can afford to display a conscience.'

On her way out the door, Jennifer turns. 'What will you do now?'

'I don't know. What would you do?'

'I've already told you, I'm getting out.'

'Maybe I should too.' Ros is curious about where Jennifer is moving to.

'Queensland. They're hiring marine biologists to chart the death of the Great Barrier Reef.'

A job's a job, Ros agrees.

—

Jill sits outside Mark Limace's home in Cygnet. Wind slapping the side of her car, churning up the Huon. Salmon company dark deeds may or may not play a part in the assault on Stephanie Howden but the death of Niamh Cassidy remains open to question. There's nothing solid on Limace yet but the murder stats point to people often known to the victim, and ex-partners figure heavily in those numbers. She knocks on his door.

No reply. His Mazda is in the driveway, he should be home.

Another knock.

Nothing. No wait, a yelp?

Jill tries the door handle. Unlocked. She opens it and steps tentatively over the threshold. 'Hello? Mark?'

Murmuring from the back of the house, a room way down at the end of the long hallway. A meeting? The radio or TV?

'Hello?' she says again, louder.

No reply.

Something isn't right. Jill pulls the Glock out of the holster on her hip. What's missing? That's right, the yappy dog, Maxie. No sign of it. She edges down the hallway, nudging doors open with her foot. Master bedroom, empty and scrupulously in order with bed made and no sign of clutter. A spare room, some boxes stacked, furniture too. Empty. A shadow flits at the window. A bird in a bush.

As she nears, the murmurs become more distinct. It doesn't sound like radio or TV. More disjointed, and one-sided. It does seem to be Limace's voice, though. Maybe he's on the phone, or a Skype or Zoom call.

A hoot. 'Bitch didn't see that coming.'

Chuckling.

'Oooh, yeah dude. Give her some.'

Livestream? Porn? Something worse? She pushes open the door.

Limace is seated at a large computer monitor, his back to her, headphones on. Over his shoulder Jill sees what looks like a shooting game paused, several split screens of other players with nicknames and some with locations around the world. In a smaller screen bottom right, Judd from London, Ontario, seems to be beating a woman live on camera.

Jill taps Limace on the shoulder and he jumps, turns. Face flushed. The little brown dog wanders through the door. Roused from a nap. Sniffs Jill's ankle, uninterested.

'Busy, Mark?' asks Jill. 'Need a word. Sorry to interrupt.'

—

Sam has trailed Stephanie Howden from the hospital to a single-storey terrace house in Macquarie Street, South Hobart, just over the road from the Cascade Hotel. She's been taken there in an unmarked police car. Two women detectives, or maybe one of them is Victim Support. They've settled her in, and a marked patrol car has passed every half hour or so. That must be very comforting, he thinks. He could be in and out of there in a few minutes to take her out of this life and nobody would know until and unless they went inside to check. I'd ask for a refund if I were you.

He sits down the road a little, seat slightly reclined, playing with his phone and giving all the appearance of a bored bloke waiting for his partner to come out of the nearby hairdresser. He'll change position every now and then, move up the street and park on the other side. Then in the hotel car park. Then. Then. Then. What the fuck were they expecting out of this dumb routine other than Trembath putting Sam in his place?

Sam's stocked up with a couple of ham-and-salad rolls, some lollies, a banana and an apple. Water and energy drinks, one in a bottle big enough to piss in. But it won't come to that. Surely. He cracks a window to stop feeling drowsy. What's the objective here? It probably doesn't matter what it is. Since when did missions have a clear objective? Twenty years of war and an untold number of deaths in Afghanistan are counting down to an inevitable Taliban victory. Sam pops a can of Red Bull, takes a slug. Stop thinking and do your job. Stay awake. He suspects the real objective here is to keep Howden and her fellow troublemakers from stirring up shit until the D'Entrecasteaux takeover is finalised. Two months, they reckon, tops.

Suddenly both his rear doors open and two uninvited passengers climb into the back seat. They bring the smell of cigarettes and hard liquor with them. They must have been watching him from the window of the pub.

'Sammy J,' says one. 'They told us we'd find you somewhere along here.'

Two blokes from his old patrol in Uruzgan. Still big and fit-looking but a touch thicker around the jowls and belly these days. Sam shakes his head, not in an unfriendly way. 'Who's they?'

'Nice to see you too, comrade. How's it hangin'?'

The talker is Brett Somebody but Sam can't recall the surname. He was always Moose anyway. The other? Footrot. Never a way with words but always good for covering fire. Both of them joined at the hip. Inseparable.

'Good, mate. Down below the knee as usual. Who's they?' he says again.

Brett leans forward. 'Reckon we could take a drive, maybe somewhere discreet?'

'I'm workin' right now, Moose. Maybe later?'

'Now's best,' says Footrot, letting Sam catch a glimpse of the pistol under his armpit.

Sam eyes him in the rear-view. 'You're threatening a brother-in-arms?'

Brett sighs. 'Fucked-up world, eh Sammy?'

They drive.

—

Jill came here to shake the tree but it seems like the tree has done fine, shaking all by itself. She reholsters the Glock.

'Habit of yours?' She nods towards the screen behind Limace where the young chap has finished hitting the woman and is now swearing at her. The woman, apparently, is his 'mom'. 'Watching livestream violent misogyny?'

A shrug. 'We're gamers. I'm not his keeper.'

'You seemed happy to cheer him on.'

'Commentary, that's all. Is there a law against that?'

'I'll check and get back to you.'

'I'd like you to leave my home now. Please.'

'Please. Love your manners. Why?'

Limace first mutes then kills the screen behind him, no doubt realising that the disembodied voice of a young man screaming and threatening violence to 'Mom' might not best serve his interests right now. 'You entered my house uninvited, snuck in, trespassed. Unless you intend to arrest me, you need to leave, now.'

'What could I arrest you for?'

A snort. 'I get it. This is your last hurrah before they send you on your way. Your "MeToo" moment to round off an unblemished and unexceptional career.'

'Do go on.'

And he does. Revved up perhaps by the display of male dominance he's just witnessed online. Wants his share of the action. 'All the younger, smarter, faster, prettier ones getting promoted ahead of you. Eating your lunch alone from a Tupperware box. The weekend barbie invites that never come. The husband that left you for someone spicier in bed. Or did you never actually get married in the first place?' He sees from her face the truth of it. Abandoned, ten years since. Sneers. 'That's about right.'

'And how am I supposed to turn all that onto you?'

'You'll think of something.'

'Stand up and face the wall, put your hands behind your back.'

'You're kidding.'

'Do it.'

He stands, as ordered, then pushes her hard in the chest with the flat of his hand. 'Look, just fuck off, fatty.'

Triggered, as they say. Her retractable baton does most of the work. Multiple strikes about the knees to bring him down, a few in the area of the kidneys. Defence wounds on arms and hands see one broken finger and a dislocated thumb. Somewhere along the way the baton must have found his face too. He's whimpering and blood-caked by the end of it as she leans over and cuffs him.

'You're under arrest. And yes, I have thought of something.'

'Me too,' he chuckles through bloody lips. 'My computer camera was on the whole time, bitch.'

—

The usually spectacular view down from kunanyi/Mt Wellington over Hobart is partly obscured by wads of cloud floating below.

'Never spent that much time in Slowbart.' Brett offers Sam a ciggie but he declines. 'Given up, huh? Best, if you've got a new baby. Don't want them breathing your filth and picking up bad habits.'

Okay, they've checked up on him recently. With the sun falling behind them, much of the city is in shadow. Here on the pinnacle of kunanyi the tourists and sightseers are thinning out and going home. The end-of-day breeze has sharpened.

'What's this all about, Moose?'

Sam had tried the same question as they wound their way up Pinnacle Road but there had been no reply. Moose had simply fiddled with the radio until he found Triple M and cranked up the volume. Barnesy. 'Khe Sanh'.

'Remember that exercise up in the south-west mountains, midwinter?' Brett draws long and hard on his ciggie and lets loose a cloud of acrid blue. 'Forty Ks a day with a fifty pack, no food, no warm gear, knee-deep in snow with the ninjas tracking us. Preparing us for what? War with fucking Norway?'

'Character building, Moose. Answer the question'

'But we made it through, didn't we? Footrot with his frostbite. Me with my dodgy knee. T-Rex and you, you got us through. Flying colours. The Awesome Foursome.'

Sam knows now what this is about. T-Rex – Michael Turnell, war hero under a cloud of suspicion. 'Seen Mikey lately? Enjoying the spotlight, is he?'

'Sends his regards. Look, Sammy, we both know much of his trouble is self-inflicted. He believes his own publicity. But some things are bigger than ego. Even his.'

The Code. 'Surprised and a bit disappointed that you feel the need to remind me, Moose.'

'The kid from the village named you. The enemy's getting all excited, thinking you might be their key.'

Which enemy? 'They'll be wrong then, won't they?'

A nod and smile, still staring out over that view of the city, the Derwent, the Channel. 'Good boy.'

Turnell used to say that. Good boy, this. Good boy, that. Pop the cunt. Good boy.

'How'd you get into Tassie with the border closures and such?'

'Essential workers, Sammy. Exempt.'

DTS. The old army contacts, wheels within wheels. Tassie in a nutshell.

'Tell T-Rex not to worry about me. He needs to focus on his exit strategy from these holes he digs for himself.'

'Cool, mate. We'd hate for things to get messy.'

'Mikey's a micromanager,' says Sam. 'Always was.'

'A worrywart,' Moose agrees. 'Time on his hands and a shitload of money behind him to feed his fears. Brutal cocktail.'

'Yeah, brutal.' Sam receives the nod to restart the engine. Below, Hobart hunkers down for the evening.

8

Limace was still in hospital, having been examined, X-rayed and sutured, but hadn't wasted any time bringing his assault complaint, with supporting footage uploaded to any platform that would take it. Jill was stood down, pending an internal investigation, and is now enjoying her fifteen minutes of viral notoriety. She's everywhere this morning and trending even ahead of #ScoMothefukwit.

Maybe if she'd been more computer savvy, she might have wiped the evidence but Limace's gamer mates have already seen and stored it. So now she sits at her kitchen table drinking tea and staring at her breakfast. Toast. That'd be right.

But God, it felt good.

And bad at the same time. He'd known which buttons to press. The loneliness she sometimes felt. The abandonment. Sure, it had been a childless and loveless marriage for years, but those last few months of Geoff flaunting his infidelity, the cracks about her weight gain. Yeah, 'fuck off, fatty' would be triggering. Geoff Wilkie. A carbon copy of Dad, really. Charming on the surface and spiteful just below. She'd already endured years of emotional abuse at her father's hands, the belittling, the self-hatred. No wonder Mum died early of cancer. The only upside? The old bastard is in a nursing home, and with his dementia he's forgotten to be a bastard. He's actually a nicer, gentler person now he's lost himself.

Tuesday. Not yet nine o'clock. She should really get on to the union and organise some representation. Maybe even her own lawyer. Nobody from the office has rushed to her support. No texts with heart emojis. She knows that even from footage this bad, officers have stayed out of jail and in the job. Seen it countless times across the country and over the years. But you need to be a brother to belong to the Brotherhood.

She makes the call to the union. We've been expecting you, says the smirker at the other end. They can fit her in later this morning or sometime this arvo. They agree on a time. Jill asks whether she should engage her own lawyer. Maybe, Smirko says, and an agent too? Hilarious. Jill spends a while googling industrial lawyers. They all look the same.

Jill's still about ten years from paying off the mortgage on this three-bedroom brick veneer with a tippy-toe view of the Montrose foreshore and the constant thrum of the Brooker Highway. The Hobart property boom hasn't quite touched this area yet so if she opted to sell up and downsize it would be to somewhere scummier. Any lawyer she gets would have to either be pro bono or a guaranteed rainmaker. She might be better off saving her money for the next mortgage payment. Superannuation? Jill's sixty next birthday. No government pension for the best part of eight years and it might not even exist by then. A ration card, probably. Food stamps. If only she had franking credits. Either way the super, what of it she might be able to access, isn't going to get her very far. As for Dad's nursing home bills? Maybe a pillow over the face will do the trick.

Her phone rings. Probably another journalist; her mobile number seems to have been leaked from the cop shop and is in wide circulation. Jill ignores it. Moments later, the ping of a message. She checks it. Stephanie Howden.

'Fancy a coffee?' Steph enquires when Jill returns the call. 'Can't wait to hear your news.'

—

Ros is elated. Somebody has finally done to Mark Limace what she could only have fantasised doing. She had slept soundly and unmedicated last night for the first time in months. Years even. The radio news had alerted her to the attack on Mark. TV news and internet then supplied the pictures in technicolour. Texts and social media messages from old friends: have you heard? Yes, indeed.

This wouldn't bring Niamh back, nor would it undo what that other bastard had done to Ros in Perth all that time ago. But hey, chalk this one up as a win for the girls. You take your rainbows wherever you might find them. Today she would meet with Stephanie Howden, a Facebook buddy of Niamh's and a tireless campaigner against the salmon farms for which, it would seem, she had been targeted in a vicious and terrifying attack. Ros was keen to compare notes. Was the person who had attacked

Howden the same one who had invaded Ros's home recently? And the same person who had possibly killed Niamh and Zeb Meyer? A long bow, maybe, but one worth drawing.

For now, it's a blessing to be able to focus on this possible external threat rather than dwell on the one from inside that has consumed her for so long. Somebody knows something. This is Tasmania: the six degrees of separation are halved here. People can't get away with murder, threats, home invasion, theft. Right? Then again, wasn't Van Diemen's Land founded on exactly that?

Phone buzz. Stephanie with a suggested time and place. And a heads-up. Would it be okay if disgraced and suspended detective Jill Wilkie joined them? The woman who just beat the crap out of Mark Limace? Why, sure. The more the merrier.

—

Sam hadn't returned to his posting outside Stephanie Howden's safe house last night. To hell with Dave Trembath and his power games. Instead, he'd checked himself in to The Pickled Frog backpackers on Liverpool Street and taken a room to himself. Sparse, verging on spartan, but it suited his mood. He hadn't wanted to inflict this on Kaz and the bub. He'd sunk a sixpack of Boag's and followed it up with a quart of the cheapest whisky he could find in the bottle shop. He could afford better these days but this was about self-abasement, not reward.

The alcohol seeps from his pores, and the sun is too bright as he checks his phone messages outside Ginger Brown, the café just up the road from Stephanie Howden's lodgings. Nothing from Kaz, thank God. She's not expecting to see him for a few days yet and he suspects she might have the shits with him. Join the queue. On the burner a couple of pings from Trembath wanting to know where he is, wanting an update. Sam ignores them. If this was a legit surveillance, properly funded and resourced, they'd have supplied him with gizmos to monitor Howden's phone and internet use. Listening gear. Tracking devices. This is half-arsed 1970s gumshoe bullshit. A waste of time and no clear objective; just like his last days in Afghanistan. Look how that turned out.

A marked car has been and gone, checking on Howden's welfare and cruising by every half hour since. And here she is now – obviously at liberty to come and go as she pleases. Headed his way, checking her phone screen. Hadn't he taken hers and dropped it in the Channel on his way back that morning? Maybe she had a spare, an old one. He hadn't bothered searching, keen to get out of there as fast as he could. On the surface, she looks none the worse for wear from the ordeal he inflicted on her. As she passes the car, he dips his head as if she could recognise him even though she was hooded and the lights were off the whole time. Ghost shapes through the NV goggles, terrified and all too familiar. How many times had he done that to some wretched being? She goes into Ginger Brown.

Sam opens the car window to release some of the stale alcohol fug. Takes a swig from his water bottle. A coffee would be good. Strong, black, sweet. Moose and Footrot had left him with a matey menacing pat on the shoulder.

'Good to see you again, Sammy. Let's not be strangers, eh?'

'You guys in town for long?'

'Long as it takes, Sammy.'

Emissaries from Turnell to ensure he held the line. Trouble is, Sammy isn't the only problem Turnell has. Enemies inside and outside the fold. And now some new ones: blue-blood LNP politicians with their own excellent contacts looking to settle a score or two over the pre-selection shambles. By all accounts, people are lining up to accuse him of exactly what the media has previously reported. These people were there, on the ground, at the time: interpreters, comms technicians, intelligence analysts, medics. Colleagues. Former brothers- and sisters-in-arms. Then there are the surviving witnesses from the villages: brothers, sons, fathers, friends, cousins, mothers, daughters, sisters. Why does it matter whether Sammy stays mute?

Qadim must be the key. The kid from the village, eyewitness to his father's murder, along with Sam, the soldier from the opposing side who he believes will tell the truth. From the blizzard of circumstantial evidence, conflicting accounts and misinformation emerges the clarity of one specific instance with an eyewitness and corroboration. The fog of war lifts for a moment. Bang. Game over. And that's where Samuel Jason Willard comes in.

—

Three months earlier in a dingy first-floor office at Anglesea Barracks on Davey Street. Homeward-bound rush hour traffic banked up as far as the eye could see. Sun still high, a pleasing late summer's day in Hobart.

Outside on the verge, next to the painted cannon, an electronic sign exhorts you to consider an army career. Drivers wanted, apply now. No, thinks Sam, don't listen to them. Stick with the Uber gig, run a mile.

'Are you with us, Sam?' A bloke in jeans and polo. Soft, likeable face. Uni educated. Calls himself Liam.

Am I with you? In what sense? 'It's not what we do. We don't snitch. I already told you lot, last time.'

'He wouldn't think twice, believe me. Loyalty's a one-way street with Turnell.'

'That's him, he's not me.'

'There's a greater good at stake. A much greater good.'

Liam doesn't give a fuck about war crimes, he says. It's what we pay you guys for. Win at all costs. Except now there's a higher, more pressing, imperative. The Taliban expect to be back in power by year's end, if not sooner. The Americans, the British, us, we all accept that as inevitable, no matter what bullshit we pump out about the capability of the Western-backed Afghan army to hold the line. After twenty years, there will be scores to settle. All our interpreters, Afghan support personnel and their families are marked for death. Just watch. But Liam and some spook friends have opened up a channel of communication with the resurgent insurgents. We'll do a deal. Put the war criminal Turnell on trial, say the Talibs, and we'll spare some of your little infidel traitors. Let them catch the last plane out.

'How many?'

'Couple hundred.'

'Out of how many thousands?'

Liam shrugs. 'Along with their families, it adds up. Better than the alternative scenario.'

'Surprised you want to buy into it. Isn't the Digger legend worth the sacrifice of all those brown people?'

A wry smile. 'Usually, but that fucking idiot Turnell has already trashed the brand. He should have kept his head down after that doco three years ago but no, he's on breakfast TV teaming up with the fruitloops and cookers. Drawing attention to himself as a prize dick. He's tainted goods. The top brass have had enough.'

'Isn't the bad press he's getting enough for the Talibs?'

'Nah, they want blood. A bit of sharia. Proper criminal show trial.'

'Then prosecute him.'

'The burden of proof is high, as it probably should be. It's not easy to carry out a proper criminal investigation after all this time, and under the current chaotic circumstances in-country. Besides, war crimes cases are hard to prove and take decades to happen. Look at the Nazis, the Balkans. Shit up a hill.'

'So?'

'We go through the motions. For that, we need to entrap him, try to get him to convict himself. The bloke's got a big mouth, shouldn't be that hard. But we need to get a move on.'

'And if I still say no?'

Liam flicks a copy of the red-eye photo across the desk. Sam about to split open a defenceless man's skull. 'We'll give them you instead. Not worth as many saved lives of our gallant Afghan interpreters and brothers-in-arms, maybe half the number or less, but we'll take whatever we can get.'

'You trust them to keep to the deal?'

'Have to, not much choice.'

'You're serious.'

'Deadly. Look, the PR and intelligence value of the saved interpreters is worth far more than that tosser has left to offer. It's a no-brainer for us.' Another photo. Helmet-cam screen capture of a young boy with raised hands and terror on his face. 'How about a sweetener? We put your little mate Qadim top of our list for those to be spared. Of course, he's not so little these days. Him, his lovely family, his dear widowed mum. Your shot at redemption, what more could you ask for?'

Hobson's choice. Sam gives the matter all of a moment's thought. 'How does it work?'

There's a job coming up, they told him. We've laid the groundwork. Take it, bide your time, do their bidding. It will lead you to Turnell.

Hey presto, three months on and Moose and Footrot had made contact. Now here we are today. More comings and goings from the café. A middle-aged matronly type squinting at her mobile before scanning the QR check-in code. Another just behind her, younger. Something familiar about the hair and shape. The second one turns as a dog barks nearby. Sam recognises her. The woman he stole the computer and phone from in Margate a few days ago.

—

Jill doesn't know why she's here and suspects she might come to regret it. The café is too busy, too loud, too exposed. She feels too seen. Her image was blurred by most of the news outlets reporting on the Limace assault, but maybe some didn't bother blurring and somebody here saw it. Saw her. If people knew the whole story about him then, fair chance, she'd be getting fan mail and accolades. But for now, she feels vulnerable and guilty. Jill spots Steph at a corner table at the back, signals she's going to put in her order then join her. Notices another woman head straight for Steph's table to be greeted with a smile and a long hug. What is this, thinks Jill, brunch with the girls? It takes an effort of will not to just can it and scarper.

'Large flat white, please. Extra hot,' she says to the beautiful young thing behind the counter. When offered a table number she points to where Steph is sitting. 'Just bring it there. Thanks.' Then braces herself and turns to the table, plastering on her best effort at a smile.

'Here she is. Woman of the moment.' Steph Howden's got a ten-paddock voice. Probably what comes of living on your own at the tip of an island off an island off the bottom of Australia. 'Ros, this is Jill, who I was telling you about.'

Ros? Jill pauses. A photo on the office board. The partner of the hit-and-run victim. Ian Cavanagh's little secret that he won't let anybody else in the team talk to.

'My heroine,' says Ros, offering a hand to shake.

The orders arrive. Two flat whites and a chai latte for Steph. Ros must have phoned her order ahead because Jill is sure she came in after her.

'So, here we all are.' Steph Howden glances at Jill over the rim of her cup. 'You've been busy. That thing with Slugface, business or pleasure?'

'Slugface?'

Ros explains, *limace* in French means slug.

Ah oui, gotcha. 'Sorry, not allowed to talk about it.'

'Is he a suspect for what happened to Niamh?' Ros wants to know.

'Like I just said.'

Gradually they wheedle it out of her and it feels good to share, however guardedly. Hey, she's already halfway out the door and past caring about protocol.

'In the end, we still don't know if it was him. Just that he's the misogynist

97

wanker we always thought he was.' Ros shakes her head. 'What the hell did Niamh see in him in the first place?'

'Love-bombing, dear. She wouldn't have been the first to succumb.' Steph mops chai latte froth from her lips. 'Young, naïve, optimistic. We've all been there.'

'So, if it's not him, then who else might it be?' Jill wants this to be more than a gossip session.

'Big Salmon,' says Steph unequivocally. 'The common denominator.'

'We need proof. Evidence.' Jill notices an affirming nod from Ros.

They begin comparing notes, especially on the attacks against Steph and Ros within twenty-four hours of each other. Jill seeks, and is granted, permission to record this on her phone. She also takes notes as they speak.

At one point, she presses the stop button on her phone. 'You're both absolutely sure of that?'

Yes, they are.

In both cases the intruder was able to see in the dark. He had to have been wearing NVG. Is Ian Cavanagh aware of this remarkable coincidence? Hasn't he been in contact with Ros after this burglary which nobody saw fit to tell Jill about?

More. In both cases the burglar/assailant spoke in a calm northern English accent but Steph recognised it as not wholly authentic.

'In what way?'

'Put on, cartoonish, like "Eeh by gum, lad" and all that. Monty Python's Four Yorkshiremen–type thing.'

The case records should show reference to both observations, but Jill has no sense of any crosschecking or follow-up occurring.

Out the corner of her eye she notices something. A bloke at a nearby table taking too much interest in them. Mid-thirties? Needing a shave and a shower. Powerfully built under that hillbilly flannel shirt. Playing with his phone as if engrossed in the screen but it's been pointed their way a couple of times. Was he taking pictures? Maybe he's one of those who has come across an unblurred photo of her on the Limace news stories. A men's rights–type looking to put her on his Facebook page as Public Enemy No. 1. Jill decides the best course is to ignore the sad seedy fucker. For now.

'Where to from here?' Ros seems fired up. A crusade in the offing.

'There's not much I can do to advance this while I'm suspended.' Jill sees the disappointment. What were they expecting? She picks up her phone. 'Give us a smile then, you two. We're a team, right?'

They do as asked, albeit reluctantly. Never mind, it's enough to catch the seedy fucker in the background as he's looking away.

'When are you heading back to Bruny, Steph?'

'I've been given the all clear from tomorrow.'

'Feeling okay about that?'

She has to. Not much choice.

'I'll try and follow up a couple of things as best I can,' says Jill. 'How about we reconvene at your place in a couple of days, Steph?' Absolutely. Steph and Ros are both up for it. 'New phone, Steph?' enquires Jill nodding at the one on the table.

'Old spare,' she says. 'Still had the old SIM. Just needed to charge it up.'

They all swap contacts then say their goodbyes.

'You work with Detective Cavanagh?' asks Ros before leaving.

'Yes.'

'He must have a lot on his plate, eh?'

'Goes with the job. Why?'

'Ian was very attentive in the first days after Niamh's … death. Weirdly so, in fact. But not so much lately.'

'Weird how?' Jill asks.

Tagines, housework, overfamiliarity. Yep, Jill has to agree, weird.

'What do you make of it?'

Jill, frankly, doesn't know. But she'll store it away for a rainy day.

Ros looks up, eyes bright. Brimming. 'I hope this stuff of yours blows over, Jill, and we can get back to finding out who killed Niamh. And why.'

'That'd be good.'

A hug. Awkward and fleeting. 'And thank you for beating the shit out of Slugface.'

—

What to make of all that?

Sam zaps the pic through to Dave Trembath, see if he can identify the third woman. Trembath comes back quickly.

'Looks like the cop from the assault case that's in the news.'

'What assault case?'

'Where've you been the last twenty-four hours?'

Wasting my time on this shit job for you. 'On surveillance.'

'Why haven't you answered any of my calls or messages?'

'Been busy.'

A release of breath at the other end of the line. 'Tell me about this meeting.'

Apart from place, time and duration, there's little he can say. 'They seem thick. Friendly. The cop and the Margate woman swapped contacts at the end. Gave each other a hug.'

'Sweet. Did they clock you?'

'Don't think so, but the cop was on her guard.'

'She's meant to be suspended, according to the reports. Whatever she was doing today wasn't official.'

'Going rogue?'

'I'll look into her. We need to know what she's up to.' A pause. 'The boys find you?'

Moose and Footrot. 'Yeah, they did. Friends of yours?'

'Old boys' network.'

'Didn't know you were out there.'

'You never asked.'

'They said they're going to be around for a while. Do I need to watch my back?'

'Always, mate. You know that.'

A young bloke whizzes by on a bright orange electric scooter, nearly bowls over a pensioner crossing the road. 'What do you want to do about these three?'

'Clearly the Howden woman is tougher than we thought. Doesn't respond well to your subtle methods of persuasion.'

'So?' But Sam already knows what's coming.

'We need to raise the stakes. Pay them both a return visit. Be more convincing.'

'The cop?'

'Leave her to me.'

—

Jill had sat in her car waiting for that dodgy bloke to exit Ginger Brown. Enough is enough with these men's-rights nut jobs. If he wanted to make her a target for his inadequacies, then he was going to feel some consequences. She'd watched him climb into his ute and taken a pic of his rego plate. He sat talking on his phone for a while. Who to? *Guess what?*

I saw that bitch from the news. Yeah, that one. No way! Eventually the ute started up and pulled away.

Out the lounge room window, wind whipping the grey water at the Montrose foreshore on the far side of the Brooker. Afternoon stretching before her. Life without a job. Endless weekends. She hates weekends. Get busy, she thinks. Don't dwell. How long since she visited Dad? Too long or not long enough? Maybe spend a bit more time now the old bugger has turned nice. Trouble is, he might not remember what he used to be like, but she does and finds it hard to let go. Lose the grudge, she tells herself. But she's not mentally ready for the filial-obedience gig; that's not going to fill this yawning gap.

Could an investigation really be stymied by higher powers for whatever reason? Of course it could, there were any number of examples across the country and across the years at both federal and state level. In this case, you have a government seemingly in the pockets of Big Salmon; pressure could come down from the police minister through the hierarchy. If there were specific cops in the pay of Big Salmon then you'd have a very effective pincer choking off the truth.

Ros's observation: Ian was very attentive in the first days after Niamh's death … but not so much lately.

Was Ian Cavanagh such a cop? It would be easy to believe so right now. Jill hates his guts, no other way of putting it. Had he pointed her towards Mark Limace, knowing that would push her buttons, in order to distract her? He'd kept Ros to himself, then filtered out the titbit from Ros about Limace. Let Jill run with it, he must have thought. Sit back and bring out the popcorn.

And what's with that weird tagine shit? Had he fixated on the widow Chen? Like, what? Where to start?

Or is she just overthinking all this?

It's not as if she has anything better to do with her time. Without access to the system to verify what has and hasn't been done on the Niamh, Ros and Steph cases, the only thing Jill can do is to make some inquiries of her own until she's back in the fold. If ever.

There's only so much one person can do, especially if they're suspended. She can't go door to door up and down Ros's street asking if anyone saw anything. At some point someone is either going to ask who she is or, if they've been following events on the internet, recognise her anyway.

Besides, as a minimum, door-to-doors should already have been done. The hit-and-run on Sandfly Road has similar limitations. But Steph's attack on Bruny? That has potential.

The assailant needed transport to get to, and move around on, the island. Had the ferry operator and CCTV been canvassed? If the ferry wasn't used then that meant either a private boat drop-off/pick-up, or a light plane at the aerodrome, plus a vehicle parked for him to borrow. If that was the case, that suggested logistical back-up. Which, in turn, supported the Big Salmon conspiracy theory. And wasn't it the speculation around the salmon companies and the news reports on the attack on Stephanie that triggered the internal police furore?

Her phone has been buzzing while she's been musing. One message from the internals inviting her to an interview tomorrow morning at nine sharp. Bring a rep if you like. The second from Cavanagh wanting a word. She phones and organises for a union rep to be with her in the morning and texts Cav back to say she'll drop in after she's had her interview. He replies with a thumbs-up.

—

Sam is back outside that Margate house. Just down the road a little, parked in with the tradie utes from the retirement village they're building on a cleared hillside rumbling with earthmovers. The day has turned out nice, for a while anyway. School's out and families are trailing back up the street. It's busy and he'd be better off grabbing a feed and returning later.

He had warned her.

I hope that's the truth, Ros. You don't want me coming back.

He's changed into a fluoro top, wraparound sunnies and a baseball cap. On the passenger seat next to him is a tradie's toolbox. There's a gap in the foot traffic; the nearest cluster of pedestrians a few hundred metres away down towards the school. He makes his move. Across the road, cap pulled low, purposeful stride, toolbox in hand. He knows from the previous visit that once you cross the driveway the last few metres to the front door are hidden from the street by bushes, bricks, shadow and helpful angles. He raises his fist to knock.

'Hi, can I help you?' Sam turns. Ros is behind him on the driveway. Garden shears in her hand and a wide-brimmed sunhat shading her face. Probably no real need, the UV factor isn't high this time of year, but each to their own. A family approaching and two tradies across the road packing up their ute and having a chat.

Tactical retreat. 'Missus Gerrard? Electrical fault?'

She smiles. 'Not me, you've got the wrong house.'

He takes out his phone and makes as if to read the screen. Grins and shakes his head. 'Sorry, I'm losing the plot, been a long day. Didn't see the extra four in there.'

'That'll be a long way out.' She nods her head westward. 'Woop Woop.'

Sam starts to leave.

'Know anything about garage roller doors?' she says.

'I can take a look if you like.'

She puts down the shears and rolls the door up as far as she can. It sticks halfway. 'Not electrical, I know, but you look the practical type.' She dips her head under the gap and invites him inside to the garage gloom.

Two kayaks, a bike, folded camp chairs, a chest freezer, paint tins, garden tools. A dusty and neglected place. The pedestrian family has passed but he hears more approaching. One of the tradies has driven off, the other is taking his time, having a smoke and checking his phone. Ros removes her hat and blows air up from her lower lip to cool herself. She reminds Sam of a teacher he once had a crush on. The dark hair and eyes and an air of sadness only just held at bay. Like that woman in the town south of Tarin Kowt, begging on the street after they'd shot her husband a month earlier.

Sam sees the problem immediately. 'That bracket up there has come loose. It's forcing the door out of its track.' He opens the toolbox. An array of screwdrivers, hammers, spanners, a power drill. All capable of doing whatever is necessary. 'Two-minute job.'

'I didn't mean—'

'Not a problem. Really.' He fixes it. Rolls the door open. Rolls it down shut. Checks the locking mechanism works. It does. Just the two of them now, behind closed and locked doors. 'Sorted.'

'My hero,' she says. 'Can I get you a cuppa or a cool drink?'

Would those tradies remember him? Would they figure which ute in the line had been his? Dave Trembath wants the stakes lifted, to be more persuasive. Why not just kill her now and be done? The other one would get the message. Two birds, one hammer.

'No, of course not. You've still got that job to go to up the road, haven't you?' She bends down and draws the roller door open again. Daylight floods in. 'Like new. Really appreciate it.'

Across the road the tradie looks up from his phone. Gives them both a wink.

'I'm Ros,' she says, offering a hand to Sam.

'Jake,' he conjures, on the spot.

'You're a good man, Jake.'

9

Wednesday. Jill finds herself across the table from two suits pretty much dead on nine. Beside her is Greg from the union. He seems intimidated by the suits and Jill lacks faith in his ability to look after her interests. It's a cool morning and there were a few spots of rain in the blustery wind that accompanied her from the multistorey car park on Argyle Street. They're all socially distanced, all squirted sanitiser on their hands, and the machine is recording.

The older of the two speaks. The lanyard says Brown and his thinning hair matches his name. 'You understand why we're here, Jill? The process we need to go through?'

'Yes.'

'Perhaps you can tell us, in your own words, what happened when you visited Mark Limace on the day in question.'

She does.

The younger one leans forward after a while. The lanyard says Owen. He has tobacco on his breath. 'Would it be fair to say that as you entered that room, pistol drawn, you were in a heightened and nervous state?'

'Yes.'

'You could hear sounds of violence.'

'Yes.'

'Mr Limace has previously had violence restraining orders taken out against him. Is that correct?'

They've worked out an escape route and are leading her down it. 'Yes.'

'Go on,' says Brown. 'What happened next?'

Owen leans in again. Pours them all some water from the jug. 'Take your time, Jill. It must have been very traumatic, confusing, a blur even.'

'Exactly,' she says. And proceeds to describe it thus. She pinches some flesh on her wrist so hard it draws tears. That goes down well.

Finally, Brown asks, 'Do you regret your actions?'

'Of course. Every day is a high-pressure environment. We don't always get it right.' She sees immediately she's gone too far. Mouthing platitudes and half apologies like a busted politician. They're after something more sincere. 'Yes, I do regret what happened to Mr Limace. I do, really, regret it.' Really, really.

'Did you interfere at all with Mr Limace's computer equipment?'

'No.'

'You made no attempt to cover up your actions?'

'That's correct.'

'Were you aware that Mr Limace had abusive material stored on his computer?'

Yeah? Perfect. 'Not at all. Of what nature?'

'Seriously prosecutable, but we are unable to go into detail at this stage.'

'Shocking,' says Jill. 'I never knew.'

'That might be a good place to stop.' Owen switches off the recording equipment. Slides a form across the desk for Jill to sign.

'What's this?'

'A month's notice of your intention to retire. You're owed at least a month in various leave entitlements. So, you can clear your desk and say your goodbyes today if you like.'

'That's it?'

'An apology, mitigating circumstances, and out the door with full entitlements. Mr Limace is happy to call it quits given other developments. Better than a long, drawn-out court case and dismissal, don't you think?'

Jill turns to Greg the union rep. 'Feel free to jump in and support me here.'

Greg shrugs. 'He's got a point.'

It's probably a good thing she doesn't have her retractable baton immediately to hand.

—

Sam wonders to what extent he's blown it with the Margate job. She's seen him now, talked to him. Those tradies clocked him too. He can't simply threaten Ros anymore. The Defence spooks, DTS and D'Entrecasteaux, how far will they make him go? Is nailing Turnell really that important?

What's worth more – the lives of a couple of Australian innocents like Ros and Stephanie, or those of a few hundred Afghan innocents?

You're a good man, Jake.

Maybe, but Sam isn't. All these people believing in him: Ros, Qadim, Kaz. They don't know him at all. Back on Bruny now. As per Trembath's instructions, he's parked his own car over at Kettering, joined the ferry as a foot passenger and picked up the ute left for him at the terminal on the other side. Up the hill a bit, away from any cameras, unlocked with keys in the glovebox as usual – you can do that kind of thing on Bruny. Why not the same level of precaution as earlier – the boat drop-off at Labillardiere? Too much scrutiny of DTS and D'Entrecasteaux at the moment, according to Trembath. Need to be arms-length plus some. Relax, he'd counselled. Strangers come and go all the time on Bruny. Sam not fully convinced. On the ferry it was cap pulled low and shoulders hunched against the breeze in a corner of the boat away from other folks and any CCTV.

Up that gravel road on North Bruny to Stephanie Howden's isolated farmhouse just south of Dennes Point. There is still an opportunity to push it further with her without having to take it to the extreme. Dust cloud in the rear-view. A vehicle following him. Well, not necessarily following. A vehicle travelling the same road behind him. And why shouldn't there be? Dennes Point is a significant settlement with holiday shacks and permanent residents. People have a right to drive there if they want. Too far behind to discern the make or check out the driver. Just another car, that's all.

He decides to drive past the farmhouse all the same and head on to Dennes Point. Just as well. The vehicle behind turns into the Howden driveway. She's got visitors. After a couple of Ks he pulls to the side of the road, chucks a U-ey, heads back that way. A conservation fire trail offers an opportunity to park off-road and out of sight in a clump of stringybarks. The borrowed ute is thoughtfully equipped with a water bottle and a set of binocs. DTS going all out. Sam grabs them and sets out through bush and paddock the kilometre or so back to Stephanie Howden's property. Normally he would tool up with some kind of weapon for a thing like this but decides it's not needed. He's just going to take a squiz.

It's windy but not enough to modify the intensity of the sun on this unseasonably warm day. You can burn at twenty degrees down here if you don't take heed and he's glad of the pockets of shade the gum trees provide. The conservation bushland rises, allowing Sam a view down over Stephanie Howden's farmhouse. He finds a spot where he can see everything but nobody can see him, and settles in. There are two vehicles parked outside her home. Hers is the old green Volvo station wagon. The other is a white Toyota SUV. The Tibetan prayer flags flutter in the breeze. Some chickens free range in the backyard, a mixture of browns and blacks and whites. A rooster among them yodelling now and then. Raised and netted vegie beds. Out on the water, the salmon pens: twelve of them, each about ten metres in diameter. The runabouts, the hydraulic pumps, engines, sirens, clanking, whooshing, the constant heavy thrum of industry. One day you're living in paradise, the next a twenty-four-hour factory opens right next door. No wonder the woman is pissed off.

Who is her visitor? A friend, a neighbour, a relative? Back out on the water, through the binoculars Sam spots his old work buddy lobbing seal crackers at a spot just beyond the last pen. It seems a lifetime since he was in that job. Jake. The first name he'd grabbed when Ros had introduced herself and held out her smooth, cool hand for him to shake. *Thrump.* The water fizzes and bubbles where the seal cracker lands. The pens erupt into life, salmon leaping to avoid the shock waves. Jake revving the runabout, doing doughnuts. *Thrump.* Another one. Sam scans the water with the binocs. No bubbles or froth. The seal cracker didn't come from Jake's boat and there don't seem to be other boats in the immediate vicinity. Suddenly there's movement outside the Howden farmhouse. Two men exiting. Not running exactly, but purposefully walking. Sam recognises them.

Moose and Footrot.

—

The white SUV has disappeared south in a cloud of dust by the time Sam makes it down to the farmhouse. He fears the worst and expects to find it. Knocks on the door. Nothing. Does it again.

'Missus Howden?' He tries the handle and it gives.

Across the threshold.

This side of the house is gloomy; he hadn't noticed when he was here last time in the dead of night. For all the landscape, sky and surrounding sea, it's a poky little hole.

'Missus Howden?' Sam's hedging his bets. Maybe she's knitting with her headphones on and will want to know who this trespassing stranger is once she's recovered from the shock. A tradie, missus. Sent by the police to fix something they broke when they were swabbing the place. Nothing broke? No problem, some mistake in the bureaucracy. Bye, then.

'Missus Howden?' Nudging doors open with his foot as he passes down the hall. A spare bedroom. A toilet. A linen cupboard. Main bedroom. Musty. Curtains drawn. A dreamcatcher above the bed. Cobwebs.

The next door, he knows, leads into the open-plan kitchen, dining and living area. This is more like it. Bright, spacious, the kind of light an artist would need. That anyone would need. But she's long since given up on painting. The easel is folded away, leaning against a wall. Canvases stacked on the floor. Paints and brushes gathering dust on a shelf. One of her paintings is on the wall. A landscape before the salmon pens arrived. Light dappling the water, rolling green hills. Her initials bottom right.

'Missus Howden?' Louder this time, as if by being more insistent she might answer him and make everything fine. Why the disquiet? He's a trained killer. Who cares what Moose and Footrot might have done here? The smart thing for Sam to do would be to get the fuck out, leave no trace, cover his arse. Yet he pushes on.

'Anyone home?'

The room off the kitchen is the bathroom. The last place inside before heading outside. There she lies, facedown on the tiles, blood trickling down the drain outlet for the shower. The back of her head blown away and a spray of crimson on the ceramic wall. The noise he thought he'd heard out on the water, the second thrump, hadn't been a seal cracker. It would have been the muffler on the gun they used. Not a silencer exactly, just enough to dim and distort the sound. Hardly necessary anyway in a place this remote with the accompanying noise of the adjacent salmon farm.

Already he can hear sirens in the distance. Yes, Moose and Footrot had been following him and knew he would be nearby. Would the police have seen them on their getaway south or would the lads just pull off into a sidetrack until the coast was clear? They aim to pin this on him. Good boy, Sammy. Take one for the team.

Fuck that.

He makes himself scarce.

—

'I need you to do something for me, babe.'

'What's happened?'

At this stage he still doesn't fully know but there's no time to ponder the possibilities and permutations. 'Some old army stuff. Can't explain right now, but it could be heavy, and I need you and Ollie to be safe.'

'Fuck, Sam.'

'You need to leave. Today. Now. Find someone to stay with.' But not your folks. That would be too easy. 'That friend of yours over in Dodges Ferry. Can you go there for a while?'

'I'm sick of all this, Sam. Really.'

'Please, babe. This is serious.'

'Where will you be?'

Who knows? 'I'll call you when things settle. Love you.' He closes the call, takes the SIM and battery out of his phone and stamps them to smithereens. He can't return to the car and already the ferry and ports either side will be a trap.

Remember that exercise up in the south-west mountains, midwinter? Forty Ks a day with a fifty pack, no food, no warm gear, knee-deep in snow with the ninjas tracking us. Preparing us for what?

For times like this, Moose. But you knew that, didn't you?

Binoculars, a half-empty water bottle and his training; that's all Sam has at his disposal. Along with a sharp knife he took from Stephanie Howden's kitchen as he left. It wasn't sirens he could hear in the distance, just a single siren. The main police post is down at Alonnah on South Bruny – forty or so Ks away. Unless they were out and about on patrol nearby, they've arrived much too quickly. Or maybe they were pre-alerted. Timing is everything.

Sam is way back, further under the cover of bush, but still has a view of the farmhouse as a single paddy wagon skids into the drive and two officers exit the vehicle drawing their weapons. Even from this distance, it's clear they're scared. The plum Bruny posting was never meant to be like this. Sam leaves them to it. He needs to be away before reinforcements arrive along with dogs, search choppers and drones. Or should he simply hand himself in and explain? Explain what? Maybe he was sloppy, left traces each time he visited the Howden property. Maybe they can be linked to more at Margate Ros's place. His phone call to Kaz will have pinged the nearest tower within minutes of Stephanie Howden's murder. He's cactus. He could say 'I was only obeying orders'. Bring Trembath and D'Entrecasteaux down with him. Or at least pressure them to fight his corner.

Or was Sammy the Scapegoat the plan all along?

And what if key cops are in on it? What if their orders are to shoot first and deflect questions later?

T's crossed, i's dotted. Sam Willard – deniable and expendable as per the MoA. To what end? The big picture isn't important at the moment. Sam just needs to get through this next phase on his own terms and take it from there.

Bruny Island. A place of escape, peace and solitude for many. Historically, no doubt, of incarceration too. And, like the whole of Tasmania had once been, a bloody hunting ground.

–

Ros hears the sirens rushing down the Channel Highway. They set the neighbours' dogs howling again, only it is prolonged by the number of passing klaxons. The hounds will get laryngitis at this rate. Something big, she assumes. A multi-car pile-up, or a fire. A random, shivery thought. Please, not another Port Arthur. She was in her teens when news broke of the shooting massacre of dozens by a lone gunman on the Tasman Peninsula. Twenty-five years later she still recalls the shockwave it sent through the whole of Australia. Catastrophising. A symptom of a wider societal existential dread, or just her own?

She raises the garage roller door to bring the green bin out, full of prunings. Grateful again to the handy tradie Jake for fixing it and only slightly guilty for batting her eyelashes at him to get the job done. Shameless but fun, and a reminder that there are good people left in this world.

If she, Jill and Steph are to collaborate on this great mystery, like some superannuated Nancy Drews, then she needs to do her part – the paper sifting. She's looking forward to catching up with them again tomorrow on Bruny. Looking forward to checking out Steph's place. To once again being part of something meaningful, a joining of purpose.

Back to her desk with a fresh mug of coffee. As Deep Throat might say, follow the money. D'Entrecasteaux Salmon company founder and principal shareholder Edward 'Teddy' Milsom. Two companies vying for takeover: the Norway-based conglomerate seeking salmon farming world domination, and the Queensland coal billionaire wanting to diversify and greenwash his ill-gotten gains with 'protein' production. Both entities, it seems to Ros, would have little to gain from being involved in dark deeds in deepest Tassie. Unless, of course, those deeds broke into a scandal that diminished the share price and made it a cheaper buy. But D'Entrecasteaux is already something of a bargain, particularly for two such cashed-up and image-conscious suitors. The taint of corruption and murder wouldn't play well.

No, thinks Ros. There's a lack of subtlety and finesse that she would expect from bigger players. That sense of arrogant untouchability. This has Tassie small-town vibes scrawled all over it. Teddy Milsom, let's take a closer look at you. Who are your mates, your family connections, your business connections, who did you go to school with? A helicopter flies low overhead, then another. Something really is going on down south. Maybe she'll tune into the radio news on the hour. For now, though, resist the temptation to hang out on the news websites waiting for reports on something bad. Teddy Milsom has a Wikipedia page.

Born in April 1959, Edward Arthur 'Teddy' Milsom AO is the eldest son of former Liberal parliamentarian James Arthur Milsom. Educated at Clements School then at University of Tasmania, where he graduated with a Bachelor of Arts and a Bachelor of Laws in 1984. Twice married, he has a son from his first marriage, Peter, and a daughter, Harriet, from his second. He is founder, Chief Executive Officer and Managing Director of D'Entrecasteaux Salmon, and patron of several charitable foundations, including Hearts and Minds, a veterans mental health initiative, and the Peter Milsom Leaders of Tomorrow Foundation. Born into an established Tasmanian family with farming and aquaculture interests, he has over thirty years' experience in fish farming operations, is responsible for the leadership and strategic direction of the company, and is committed to delivering high-quality salmon, raised responsibly and sustainably.

Blue-blood squattocracy, thinks Ros. The consummate silver spooner. The kind of face she has seen in law chambers and courtrooms across the land. The kind not used to hearing the word 'No'.

—

Late morning. Jill had been on the point of departing with a cardboard box of personal effects from her cleared desk when Cavanagh called her into his office.

'Forget that, you're with me.'

'I'm retired, as of now, and you're eating into my leave entitlement.'

'All leave cancelled. There's been a murder and the hunt's still warm. All hands on deck. Especially yours.' He'd strapped on his kevlar vest and handed her a spare. 'Stephanie Howden. Remember her?'

Like a cold hard punch in the guts. 'Steph? How?'

He told her as they collected a pool car and headed for the ferry port at Kettering. Shot. Execution style. The local plods had found her.

'What, they just happened to be passing?'

'Anonymous tip-off.'

Helpful, thinks Jill.

'Ferry points sealed off, aerodrome closed. Choppers and police boat looking for random vessels leaving the island. He's trapped, we've got him. Just a matter of time.'

'Bruny's not that small, Cav.'

'Where's he gunna go?' They were in a convoy racing down the Channel Highway. Lights and sirens all the way, clean run through.

'Do we know anything about him?'

'Not yet.'

The Bruny ferry has been commandeered, police and authorised personnel only. Two vans of black-and-camo ninjas checking their equipment. A third batch being choppered in. Overwarm in her kevlar, Jill feels surplus to requirements and says so.

'You're involved,' Cavanagh says. 'Simple as that.'

She suspects it's not as simple as that and, as always with Cav, there's an agenda. Still, it feels like a reprieve. A breeze flutters the surface of the Channel as the ferry noses into Roberts Point, the Bruny side. Seagulls wail. Poor Steph, she thinks, it's come to this. There's a long line of vehicles waiting for a ferry they can't have for hours yet. At the front of the queue, two blokes lean against their white SUV, munching on pies.

Bored. Restless. How long before their entitlement bursts its banks?

Out on the water to the left, as they drive up the hill, a dozen salmon pens. Spreading around the coastline like ringworm. They weren't there just a few months ago when she had that long weekend on the island with a visiting rellie. The car stuffy, the ninja van up their arse. Jill cracks a window for some relief. 'What's my role in this?'

'We'll assess the scene and take it from there.'

'Forensics?'

'On their way.'

A step up from threats, she muses, from watered-down petrol to an execution-style killing. All within what, a week? Steph hadn't taken the hint, hadn't listened. They mean business, that much is evident.

The ninja van overtakes, one of the masked men gives a jaunty wave in passing. 'They'll be loving this,' says Cavanagh.

'Meat and veg to them, I suppose.'

'Ever killed anyone, Jill? No, course not. It'd be on your employment record, wouldn't it?'

'Possibly.'

'When we find our man, we can assume he's very dangerous.' Cavanagh gives her a look. 'No prisoners, no heroics. Whatever it takes, Jill. We need to take care of each other.'

Shoot to kill. 'Sure.'

—

The logical thing to do is to swim his way off the island. The northern tip near Dennes Point over to Tinderbox is no more than two kilometres; one and a half, even less maybe. Sam can swim that distance. He just needs to make sure he isn't found before nightfall – six or seven hours away – then off he goes. He can hear the choppers approaching. They will have cameras, perhaps with thermal imaging capacity, and he's a sitting duck unless he does something about it. The adjacent property, beyond this no-man's-land of conservation bush, has a paddock populated by cows. That might be an option for later, mingle and moo a little, but in broad daylight in a cleared, no-shade paddock, it's not the best idea. Back down to the ute at a trot to salvage whatever may be useful. The foldable windscreen sunshade might help distort whatever the chopper thermal camera thinks it can see. A tourist map of the island. Break some branches and disguise the vehicle to buy time. Then it's outta there.

But which direction? If he heads north-east, the island narrows to its tip and they can bottleneck him, closing off his options. Consulting the map, he sees that the main roads in this area tend to skirt or parallel the coastline. Inland is best for now, south and east, keeping to the trees where possible. The helicopters have faded away a little, probably focusing on the roads and on the coastline.

Moose and Footrot.

They're armed and probably still on the island. Will they get caught up in the dragnet or has somebody arranged for them to be waved through? Can that level of conspiracy be sustained among so many players? Sure it can. Sam was part of an SAS Death Squad once and, over a decade later, it remains consequence-free.

Or does it?

There's a dip in the terrain. A clump of shoulder-high bushes, soggy damp earth towards what remains of a farmer's dam – long since abandoned. No road nearby, not even unsealed, but a rough, rutted track perhaps a hundred metres away. Stamp your feet to clear out any snakes in the vicinity and climb into the cool shade on offer. It's as good a place as any to wait things out.

The water bottle is less than half full. He needs to ration his intake. He's hungry too, but that can wait. Sirens, cars, helicopters. Those seeking a peaceful island retreat will be disappointed today.

How long can he keep this up and to what end?

The immediate aim is survival. He knows too much and cannot be allowed to talk. The same forces that have recruited him and set him up for Stephanie Howden's murder, the same forces who have brought Moose and Footrot into play, can easily arrange that he is not captured alive.

Evasion and insurance: his immediate and longer-term goals.

Early afternoon: a solid five hours more before it will be dark enough to move again and attempt his swim over to Tinderbox. Over the coming hours this area will be swarming with cops, vehicles, dogs, whatever. To be honest, he doesn't fancy his chances.

10

Jill is nauseated by what they encounter at the Howden property. Steph is facedown on the bathroom floor, shoulders and head over the sill of the shower cubicle. A lot of blood must have run down the drainage hole but there remains a crimson spray dripping down the tiles along with brain and other cranial matter in the shower well. Half of the top of her head has been taken off.

'Jesus,' says Cavanagh.

The forensics team has arrived and it's best to leave them to it. Officers have been despatched north and south to block off the road passing the farmhouse, and to check and redirect any traffic in the vicinity. Others are canvassing neighbouring farms.

'What do you want me to do?' asks Jill. They've both masked and suited up. What with that and the kevlar and the unseasonably warm day, Jill is suffering with her own fluctuating thermostat. She needs to get out and about. 'Happy to take a look around the immediate vicinity, see if anything gels?'

'Yeah, yeah.' Cavanagh is fielding messages on his phone as they retreat to the kitchen. 'Take a look around. The K9 is due any moment. I'll let you know when they arrive.' His phone rings. 'I'll just take this.'

Outside, Teletubby suit off. Relief at last. There are deep gouges in the gravel from a vehicle different from Steph Howden's own. Was that the murder car? Jill directs a uniform to have them taped off and marked, receives a glare from an approaching forensics tech for encroaching on his turf.

Where to start looking? The property, farmhouse aside, is large and sprawling. Sloping down to the water's edge, visible through the gum trees, along with the salmon pens out on the Channel. Tibetan prayer flags flutter on lines strung between the main house and a smaller outhouse, also constructed from weatherboard. Jill wanders over and looks through the window. A self-contained granny flat or perhaps an Airbnb offering. It also has a storage area for some of Steph's artworks. From the fence line marking the northern boundary, the land rises thick with trees and bush. Unspoiled, uncleared. Council or state land maybe, preserved as a conservation corridor.

The first responding officers found no other vehicles in the driveway when they arrived and encountered none heading south on their drive north. The killer or killers, if driving, must have turned left out of the driveway to head north around the tip of the island to take the alternative route south. Jill starts walking that way.

'Wait.' Cavanagh, waving his phone at her. 'The chopper has spotted what might be a vehicle parked under trees just up the road. Let's take a look, eh?'

Jill's not sure what to make of this new Starsky-and-Hutch approach of his. Sure, pardner. Whatever. The chopper is landing in an open paddock on the adjacent property and they'll be joined by a handful of ninjas. The two vanloads that accompanied them on the ferry have already fanned out south and east. With the paramilitaries taking the lead, Jill and Cavanagh work their way up the dusty road to the conservation track turn-off.

The vehicle is visible now, tucked in under the trees and strewn with extra branches to try to disguise it further. A bog-standard white Toyota ute. While the ninjas check it is unoccupied and safe, Cavanagh has phoned through the rego details.

'A hire car. One Samuel Jason Willard. Address in Claremont.' He shows her the driver's licence photo sent through to his phone. 'Him.'

Jill has seen him before. He was in Ginger Brown café a couple of days ago taking a great deal of interest in her, Ros and poor Stephanie.

—

Jeez, that water's cold, but. Sam is knee-deep. It's dark now. He's found a secluded cove around the tip from Dennes Point. Nobody came near him over the course of the afternoon. With the sunshade deployed whenever a helicopter flew over, he even managed a reckless, restless snooze. Ant and other insect bites plagued him but he's experienced worse. The choppers have departed for the night but he still hears cars racing around the area and there are boats out on the Channel ahead of him. Across the water lies the Tinderbox peninsula and he can see the lights of houses dotted along the hilly coastline. There are salmon pens out there too, over to the east, floodlit for twenty-four-hour operations. He needs to avoid being swept over to them by the outgoing tide which, even at this shallow depth, tugs fiercely at his ankles.

Boats. Lights. Sharks maybe? The Channel can be deep here and the salmon farm, already an attraction for hungry predators, will also be leaching the high-protein feed. Burley, for want of a better word. Is he crazy doing this? Hand yourself in – put your fate in the lap of the gods, for goodness' sake. Only goodness doesn't feature in what's at play here. Thigh-deep now, feet edging along the stony bottom. His Blundstone boots, along with the windscreen shade and his Craghoppers fleece, are in a clump of bushes he passed en route to this point. If found, they'll provide a feast of forensic traces that will possibly link him to various crime scenes. Such is life. Too heavy to swim in, too awkward to carry. He knows he'll regret ditching them when, if, he reaches the other side. But that is then, this is now.

Intake of breath as the water eddies around his waist. He needs to get on with this, start swimming. Apart from the boats servicing the salmon pens, there seems to be just the one runabout in the area. A rigid hull inflatable powerboat with a spotlight about two, maybe three, hundred metres away to his left. A determined grid-style search back and forth. No police markings from what he can see – which isn't much – but they might have commandeered it. Surely, they would keep the chopper and its spotlight out for such a search? No matter. He's procrastinating. Get the hell on with it. Swim.

Freestyle would be faster but noisier. He opts for breaststroke – that way he is also better able to see if the RHIB or anything else is heading his way. Under he goes, gasping at the cold, face and ears burning with the freeze. Steady strong strokes pushing through the water. Already Sam feels the current tugging him towards the salmon pens. He tries to keep a visual lock on one of the houses brightly lit on the far side. Aim for that, don't drift. Hardly much more than a kilometre to go now, you can do this. No worries.

Looking back, it feels like he's barely covered any distance at all, and the lights of Tinderbox seem as far away as ever. Push on. Steady the breathing, stay calm. A cloudy moonless night and that, at least, is in his favour. No strong wind to battle but that tidal current tears at him. The house he was focused on, where is it? There? Really? He's drifted further and sees now that the lights of the salmon pens are brighter, details clearer, noises sharper. How long has he been in the water? Ten minutes, twenty? Five? The cold disorientates him. He really needs to concentrate, stay alert. The RHIB, where did that go?

Bump.

What was that? His left leg had hit something as it kicked out. A change in the energy of the water around him. A sense of new currents, a rush of movement.

Bump.

Again. His right hip this time. Jesus. Shark? He dips his head below the surface but it's black. Nothing. He's cold inside and out. Frozen to the bone.

Over to his right about a metre away. A ripple and soft splash as something surfaces then slips under again.

A bark, more like a cough, nearby, and another rush of water around him.

A seal, he realises. A fucking seal. The relief warms him a little. He'd laugh if he could. He pushes on. Where's that house light? More drifting, it's way off to his left now and he's ever closer to those salmon pens. The RHIB is over that way now too. Pulled up alongside a runabout from the fish farm. Murmurs in the gloom, good-natured. The odd laugh.

Is that—? It's Jake, his former colleague. Must be pulling some overtime.

'Nah, mate. Seen nuthin. You cops?'

'Kind of.'

'Cunt killed that old sheila in the house? Shit. Never liked her but she didn't deserve that. S'pose.'

Both boats drift under the floodlights. Yes. Sam sees now, it is Jake. The men in the RHIB are known to Sam too.

Moose and Footrot.

'What's that?' says Jake, pointing Sam's way. 'Something in the water.'

Sam goes under, pulling hard against the current and aiming out further into the gloom. Down into the ice-cold depths. Spotlights turned on the shimmering, shifting surface above him. He can't stay down much longer, lungs bursting. Sam heads away from the spotlights. Surfaces as softly as possible.

'Fucking seal,' says Jake. 'Hey, watch this.' A chuckle as he lights and lobs a seal bomb in Sam's direction.

–

'Ex-SAS?'

The follow-up on Samuel Jason Willard has taken all afternoon and into early evening. Two secretive organisations – the salmon company and the military – moving at glacial pace to answer their queries. Or rather, avoid doing so. Willard, it emerges, was recently sacked from his farmhand job at D'Entrecasteaux Salmon on account of his unreliability and inability to fit into the team environment.

'He was on probation,' the HR person had informed them. 'Just didn't work out.' Sure, she'd said, she could send through his employment record, brief as it was. That's where Jill had seen the reference to a military background.

'Military?' Cav had said. 'Really? Interesting.'

The Department of Defence had promised to get back to her but didn't. After an exchange of phone calls from higher up the food chain citing urgent murder inquiry and political disquiet at an executive level, they had this: ex-SAS, trained killer, expert survivalist. A real tough nut and possibly deranged with PTSD or whatever. Unexploded bomb.

Except he'd now exploded.

'Shit,' says Cavanagh. 'He could be anywhere.'

'So, our theory is what? Rogue ex-soldier goes off the rails? Fixates on salmon farm opponent as cause of all his problems?'

'Hangs together,' says Cavanagh. 'First job he's had in yonks and here she is stirring up trouble, wanting the place closed down. Him back on the dole.'

They're ensconced in a commandeered Airbnb at Dennes Point, tidy place with an excellent view, and waiting for the ninjas to come back with some good news – Willard's head on a pole maybe. A coffee plunger on the go, some bickies filched from the owner's stash, and half a dozen colleagues on the phones or dozing. It's just gone 8.30 pm and looks like being a long night.

Because Defence took so long to get back to them, they've missed the deadline for the evening news bulletins. It's been decided to hold off until morning but a doorknock has been organised for all the properties on North Bruny – figuring the guy won't be able to get very far on foot and will be caught by the roadblock on the narrow isthmus leading to the south if he ventures that far. A text alert has been sent to the properties further south and across the water at Tinderbox and Kettering – do not approach. Police social media helping to spread the word.

'Fingers crossed the mad bastard won't take any hostages in the next few hours.'

Cavanagh is philosophical. 'Might be a blessing in disguise. At least we'd know where he is.'

A dull crump in the distance.

'What's that?'

'Seal bombs,' says Cavanagh. 'To protect the valuable stock. Bit like stun grenades.'

'They do that often?'

'As needed.'

'Day and night?'

'Prob'ly.'

With neighbours like these, thinks Jill, who needs enemies. Poor Stephanie, tormented day and night while alive, then brutalised for speaking up. Was Willard behind the earlier petrol attack on her too? One presumes so. And was he behind the burglary and intimidation of Ros around the same time? Again, presumably yes. A pair of boots and a fleece found by a search team. Sent off to the labs. Maybe they'll link him to the other crimes.

Yet the original incidents seem measured and calm, not like this explosion of violence. Deranged rogue male? Maybe. Maybe he was on calming medication previously and it ran out. Note to self: check his medical record too. Jill hasn't mentioned yet to Cavanagh that she saw Willard in the café a few days before. Not sure why she's holding back.

To raise it begs the question of what she was doing meeting with those women anyway. Jill, despite herself, is enjoying being back in the thick of things and doesn't want to jeopardise that just yet. But she does feel beholden to Ros to alert her about developments. She takes out her phone.

—

Ros wakes to her phone buzzing on the armrest beside her. She'd fallen asleep during some SBS documentary about Great British train journeys. Not sure why SBS were showing such Pommie rubbish or why the hell she was watching it. A half-eaten bowl of pasta on the coffee table in front of her, an open laptop with a dark sleeping screen, and her notebook with dot points about Teddy Milsom. The phone. A message from the cop, Jill Wilkie.

Steph has been killed

The sirens. The helicopters.

Ros returns the call. 'What happened?'

Voices in the background, phones ringing. 'Hi, Ros. Not so easy to talk right now. Maybe check out the news or internet, you'll get the idea.'

There was an unspoken 'but' hanging there. Ros articulates it as she scrolls the news on her laptop, sees the murder headlines. The photo of Steph Howden.

'Is there anywhere you can go for a few days, Ros? Lie low?'

'I'll think of something. You reckon I could be next?'

'Just a precaution.'

'Do you know who did it?'

'We think we do, yes.'

'And?'

'Watch the news, Ros. And find somewhere to stay for a few days.'

'If this person shows up on my doorstep, wherever I am, I want to know what I'm dealing with. You know it, Jill, that's why you messaged me.'

Movement. Shuffling. Jill's voice even lower, an urgent whisper. 'I shouldn't be doing this. I'll send something through. Wipe it from your phone as soon as you've seen it.' Hand muffling the phone. 'Yeah, Cav, be right with you.' Jill again. 'Stay safe, Ros. This bloke is dangerous.'

The call closed. A few seconds later the bing of an incoming message.

Ros opens the attachment. A pic of a driver's licence. She enlarges it with her fingers. Looks closer to be sure. Yes, it is him. The nice guy who helped her recently with her stuck garage roller door.

—

He's made it to shore but doesn't know which one. Or is he already dead and in hell? Maybe if Sam hadn't dived under again just as Jake lobbed the seal cracker, he wouldn't be deaf now, maybe his right ear wouldn't be leaking blood. His head wouldn't feel like it had just been crushed in a carpenter's vice. He might still have his balance, be able to kneel then stand without the world tossing. He vomits again: raw, sour. Shivers. Whole body spasming. He's in shock and probably has hypothermia. What now?

He lies still, unable to do anything else. Sand scrapes his cheek. The cold takes hold, burrows bone-deep. If he could just close his eyes and sleep for a while. A siren. A siren? He hears something, he's not completely deaf. Muffled, sure, but it's there. No, it wasn't a siren. A boat horn, out on the water. A huge wellboat, edging near the pens. Getting ready to suck all those fish up, rinse them and spit them out again. But something has changed. The salmon nets are to the left, not the right as they were before. Has he drifted even further east out beyond the pens? It would be hard to do that and not get spotted under all those floodlights. No. He's made it. He is on the other side, near Tinderbox. But the world needs to stop spinning.

He needs to be dry, to be warm. Needs to keep moving. Lying here, he's no use to himself at all. Remember the training. Push through, reach deep. Prevail. It takes an age but gradually he pulls himself into a kneeling position and, once the universe settles, climbs to his feet. Surveys his surroundings. A small, mainly rocky cove with hills sloping steeply down to the beach. Bush and gum trees in what he can see and smell of those looming silhouettes either side of him. He slowly picks his way across the sharp, stony beach, cursing silently as his bare feet take the brunt. Out on the water the wellboat roars into its vacuuming and sluicing action. No sign of Moose and Footrot in their RHIB.

Clothes. Warm, dry clothes.

Stubs his toe on a rock.

And fucking shoes.

The nausea and dizziness ebb and flow. He picks his way up a narrow, muddy track leading uphill out of the cove. Wonders about snakes and decides that, after tonight, why worry. The path widens and the floodlights from the salmon farm and the wellboat light the way. Sam is aware he needs to avoid presenting as a moving silhouette on the skyline. Crouches where necessary. A warm trickle down his neck from the leaking ear. He must look a sight.

Lights ahead. A house. Over to the left, through the trees. Sam tries to listen, favouring the ear that still nearly works. No sound except for the wind and the rumble of activity around the salmon pens. The exertion of walking uphill temporarily helped him forget the cold. He shouldn't have stopped to listen. Once again, shivering uncontrollably, as if his very bones are rattling. He edges towards the light, pushing off the path and through the undergrowth. More stubbed toes. Then a fence, waist-high, three strands of wire, star pickets leading off to left and right. He's confident it's not electric. Crouches through between middle and top strand, catching his shirt and jeans on the barbs. Keeps going, tearing cloth as he does.

What time is it? Mid to late evening he assumes. The Channel, either side, is dotted with the lights of homes still awake. It can't be easy trying to sleep with the thunder of that wellboat, the throb of the engines, the hiss of the hydraulics and spray. What the fuck has he been working for these past few weeks? Sam feels that familiar self-disgust he'd felt in Uruzgan Province, if less intensely, when it became clear that what he was doing served no-one and nothing good. Take the money and keep schtum. Survive another day. Live on, even if your soul dies.

But even that wasn't enough. Neither the army nor the salmon company were content to leave it there. Rewarding his silence and loyalty with this frame-up and manhunt. They want him dead.

The useful idiot.

To hell with that.

—

Ros still hasn't worked out where to go, but the Subaru is packed and ready. She's even thrown in her walking boots, tent, sleeping bag and camping gear as an option. Who knows? The fact is, she has no family and nobody she could honestly call a friend to stay with. Every year it's on her New Year's resolution list – make some pals – but she never seems to get around to achieving it. Sociability had been Niamh's thing. Ros has left the chicken coop door open, topped up the feeder bin and the water bowls and hopes for the best. A note in the neighbour's mailbox – help yourself to eggs, back in a few days. Or longer. Monica can come and go through the cat flap. There's a bowl of nibbles to start her off, but otherwise she'll have to fend for herself. Kill a few birds, catch some mice.

Nearly midnight. Ros has organised to stay the night at a waterfront motel in Lutana just north of the city. A nice view out over the murky, heavy-metals-tainted river. From there she'll take it one step at a time. Front door locked, zap the car. Toss the last bag into the boot. A scrape behind and suddenly she's smothered: an arm around her neck, a hand over her mouth, hot breath in her ear.

'Take it easy, Ros. Keep quiet, nobody gets hurt.'

Him.

A tiny prick of pain in her side. He has a knife, or something just as sharp. 'You've seen the news. You know what I'm capable of. Nod if you understand.'

She nods.

'We'll get in the car through the passenger side, and you slide over behind the wheel.' An increase in pressure with the knife to remind her.

And in no time at all they're off north up Channel Highway with Ros's eyes firmly on the road ahead and that sharp thing pricking her side. So far, the news sites haven't named the wanted man, just offering a general description and age range. But Ros knows, she's seen his driver's licence. 'Jake, is that right?'

'Yep.'

What if she veers off the road suddenly? Or flashes an oncoming car or sounds her horn? Same result, she expects. He has nothing to lose. It's not that long ago since Ros felt she too had nothing to lose, she'd already lost it. Now she's not so sure. She wants to fight, survive, win. Like Niamh would.

'Are you going to kill me?'

'Shhhh. Focus on the road.'

'Are you?'

'If I was, I'd have done it already.'

'Today, tomorrow. Next week. They're going to get you, Sam.'

'Who's Sam?'

Ros shakes her head. 'If killing us was your job, you're not finished yet. Will they still pay you when you're in prison?'

'I didn't kill her.'

'So, what's this all about? Kidnapping me at knifepoint?'

'What?' It's like he hasn't realised what he's been doing this last fifteen minutes. The sharp pressure on her side recedes. 'I'm sorry. I won't hurt you.'

She risks a sideways glance. Sees for the first time his weird outfit. Scuffed trainers with the smell of a teenager about them. No socks. Jeans too short on his legs and too tight everywhere else. A t-shirt bearing the image of a blinged-up gangsta rapper. Sees the blood dribbling from his right ear. The grey pallor.

'You're a mess.'

'Thanks.'

'You need to be in a hospital.'

'No.'

'What? We just keep driving all night?'

'Any chance of stopping the car? I need to spew.'

She does, and he does. After a moment he wipes himself down and they press on.

'What's to stop me just driving to a cop shop now?'

'The people who killed Steph Howden, who want to kill me, they also want to kill you.'

'And?'

'The cops won't be able to protect you. Us.'

'But you will?' A nod. 'Why should I believe you?'

He shrugs, hands her the knife. 'A huge leap of faith, for you and for me.' Reclines his seat. 'Mind if I nap for a while? Don't feel too good.'

—

Jill has decided to turn in. Well past midnight and, so far, nada. No sign of Willard although a ute registered in his name has been found parked on the Kettering side of the ferry crossing. Why leave a vehicle registered in his name on one side and take another, hired again in his name, on the other side? The vehicle has been impounded for further scrutiny. As for the man himself, well, we should just leave it to the bloodhounds. It's a waste of time and money having all these Ds hang out in some Airbnb on

Bruny when they could be getting a proper night's sleep, ready to take on the new day. Cav's loving it though: working the phone, issuing orders, conferring with the ninjas, poring over the map and pointing like he's in charge. She can hear them in the next room. Low murmurs and the occasional laugh. A pop and hiss. They're even cracking open the tinnies like it's Schoolies Week.

Sam Willard.

He must be feeling the pressure now. Does he know his employers at the salmon farm have thrown him under a bus? Does he know his former military masters have distanced themselves from him? Is he really the embittered rogue male he's painted as? He certainly looked feral that day in the café. According to his online Medicare health records, he's not on any prescribed drugs but that doesn't rule out the over-the-counter or prohibited variety. The Claremont home abandoned, wife and child missing. Has he done something to them? He seems capable of anything and certainly has the training to carry it out.

And yet.

Why the abandoned vehicles? And the trail of ownership so easy to follow. If you're a trained assassin you want to get the hell away as fast as possible and have your tracks covered so you can live to fight another day, and maybe earn yourself another murderous dollar. And having avoided the ferry on previous jobs, this time he takes it, bold as brass. There's CCTV of somebody who could be him huddling in a corner of the boat. From *Day of the Jackal* to *Day of the Jackass* in one fell swoop? Sure, that can happen when the meds run out. An increasingly erratic and stressed Willard might be easier to track and capture but that unpredictability could also take a tragic turn. Innocents in the crossfire. Has Ros managed to get away and lie low? Jill bloody hopes so.

11

Sam wakes with a cricked neck and nostrils twitching to the smell of wet dog. The wet dog is him. He badly needs a shower and some clean clothes that fit. Ros is staring at him, face blank. She looks tired and he wonders if she slept at all.

'An hour or two,' she says, reading his mind. 'You were snoring.'

'Sorry.'

They're angle-parked in the centre of New Norfolk, a town about thirty-five Ks north-west of Hobart. Like other towns within that fifty-kilometre radius of the capital, there's been a serious effort to rebrand as a cool, chic, foodie mecca but without necessarily informing some longstanding locals. They haven't come far but Sam isn't about to complain.

'Now you've had a good sleep I'm hoping you've woken refreshed and full of great ideas about what to do next.'

'Breakfast?' he suggests. 'And maybe a change of clothes.' Cash only, no cards.

Ros agrees to organise that.

By now his name and face will be on TV, the internet and in the papers. There's a Maccas down the street, anything from there will do. The Vinnies on the main drag won't open for at least another hour but they should be able to meet all his sartorial needs. Ros asks him about his size requirements. He gives them.

'We should probably find a new car too.'

'Why?' says Ros. 'I'm not declared missing yet. The police should have no interest in this vehicle.'

'It's not just the police on our tail,' he reminds her. But they agree that, on balance, obtaining a new car right now could draw as much attention to them as proceeding as they are. Sam studies Ros as she heads off to Maccas. She's decided to trust him for now, that's clear. Why and for how long remains to be seen. Okay, great ideas for what to do next. What's the desired outcome? They're both alive, the truth prevails, as does justice, and everyone lives happily ever after. Timeline? He thinks about Kaz and the bub. They can't live for too long with this hanging over them. A week should do it, then. Maybe two. A cop car rolls by, occupants not paying him any mind as he dips his head and feigns interest in Ros's extinguished phone. This is useless. He should turn himself in and end this bullshit.

'Double Sausage McMuffin meal and a flat white. Times two. You owe me.' Ros slides into the car, passing the package over. 'Twenty years or more since I was in one of those places. They don't seem to have changed that much.'

'You're taking all this remarkably calmly,' he says through a mouthful of mince. 'Like you were born to it.'

'Probably a build-up of anti-anxiety medication in my system. I've developed natural immunity.'

'I'm thinking of handing myself in.'

'One option,' she concedes.

'But?'

'But nothing. I can take my chances with the state apparatus. You're the one in the biggest trouble.' She offers him her hash brown with a look of disgust, and he gladly accepts. 'Do you think surrendering will solve everything?'

'They might leave you alone if I do.'

'Only might?'

'Hard to say. There's some big money behind this.'

'Teddy Milsom?'

'Who?'

'Your ultimate boss.' She starts the car and they reverse out onto the road. 'See, you need me more than you realise. Now let's go and find you some better clothes. Those tight jeans are putting me off my food.'

—

Jill is halfway through her second coffee and third slice of toast, enjoying the solitude before the others wake up. They'd gone into the early hours with their tinny popping, murmurs and cruel jokes. Some, she could overhear, were at her expense. Tee-fucking-hee.

'Any water in the kettle?' Cav has emerged from his room. Shabby. Yawning. Needs to set a better leadership example.

'Just boiled, not long ago.'

'Sleep well?'

'Eventually.'

'Yeah, that was naughty. Sorry.' But it's clear he isn't really. He drops two slices of wholegrain into the toaster. 'Figuring if you want to head back over the water, we can try to survive without you.'

'Back on track with my early retirement plans, huh?'

He smiles. 'If you like.'

'There's no word on Willard, is there? We've lost him.'

'I think our friend plays the long game, but we'll get him.' Cavanagh's phone goes. A few grunts, yeahs and an expletive later he closes the call. 'The spare chopper's been called away to an activated emergency beacon on the South Coast Track and there's some weather coming in, making the boat crews nervous.'

'Otherwise, no sign of him?'

'He's still on the island, we just need to tighten the net.'

'A matter of time and patience,' she says encouragingly. 'Happy to play my part, Cav. You know that.'

'Cheers, Jill. Tell you what. You get back over to the office and chase down the missing wife. Maybe we can get her to convince him to give himself up. TV appeal. Tears, baby, all that.'

'Good idea, boss.' Women's work. Leave the boys to the chase. Some smoke and a background click. She gestures behind him. 'Your toast is ready.'

They've agreed she can take his car and he'll hitch a lift with whoever. Jill wastes no time packing her bag and hitting the road. Happy to be out of that house, which is already beginning to feel and smell like the boys change rooms at the local footy club. Reversing out on the gravel drive she sees Cavanagh standing at the window. He turns to say something to one of the other guys in the room. Has a laugh at the reply and gives her a wave as she's leaving. On down that dusty road back to the ferry port. She can't get away from there fast enough.

—

Ros hasn't yet told him what she saw on the news on the wall-mounted TV in Macca's. Would he want to know? They're on the road beyond New Norfolk, heading north and west. Aimless, for the moment. To the left, the Derwent flows black and strong to the coast. Ahead, gentle rolling hills with the shadow of mountains in the distance. Dark clouds loom from the north-west and already there are spots of rain on the windscreen. Sam has nipped into a public toilet in the park, changed out of the overtight rent-boy outfit he'd been wearing into the clothes she'd found for him in the New Norfolk Vinnies. Dark brown cords, a flannel shirt with plain white tee underneath. Uni lecturer, casual, part-time. The brown slip-ons are a tad *outré* but, in general, an improvement. Besides, they were the only shoes in his size. All paid in cash. While he was changing, she called the Lutana motel, apologising for the no-show. No problem, they'd said, but they had to deduct from the credit card anyway because of the late notice. Ros ambivalent about leaving traces of her recent movements. Thinking maybe she needs a little insurance.

'Is it true, what they're saying about you?'

He stiffens slightly, as if he'd forgotten he was on the run. She needs to repeat herself sometimes and she finds herself talking louder. If that burst eardrum of his gets an infection that will complicate matters. How do you get antibiotics without a prescription?

'What do they say?'

'On the news in Maccas. Do not approach. You're ex-SAS. Trained killer. Probably suffering PTSD. Unstable, they sacked you from your salmon farm job.'

'Four out of five ain't bad.'

'What's the fifth?'

'Didn't know I'd been sacked for being unstable.'

'It was you who broke in, took my laptop, threatened me.'

'Yes.'

'Did that terrible thing with the petrol, to Stephanie.'

'Yes.'

'When you turned up and fixed the garage door, you planned to do something more?'

'Yes.'

'You're a monster.'

'S'pose.'

'That's all you have to say? No excuses, no apologies, no denials?'

'I'm not a killer.'

'That's not true either. The news linked you to some war crimes allegations along with that famous author bloke. Said you were implicated too.'

'I meant—'

'Are you going to kill me?'

'No.'

'Did you kill Niamh?'

'Who?'

Maybe he doesn't know the name of the person he killed. Maybe he hasn't a clue who she's talking about. Maybe he's messing with her mind. This whole situation is madness. The rain is heavier now. The wipers go on. 'Maybe you should hand yourself in after all.'

'Or you could drop me somewhere and I can push on alone.'

The town sign says Hamilton. Old convict-built stone buildings. Everything proudly closed for business, like they want to encourage people to keep on shooting through and leave them alone. 'Explain to me, fully, what is going on. Persuade me as to why I shouldn't just pull into this cop shop up ahead and hand you over.'

As they draw near, it's clear why not.

'It's closed,' says Sam. 'But yeah, I'll try and put it together for you.'

'I'm listening.'

—

Jill has the police radio tuned in as she motors north from the ferry port at Kettering. Any developments of substance on the Willard manhunt will be on radio silence anyway, but the odd coded message might emerge which could offer a clue to anyone in the know. Passing through Margate, she decides to drop in on Ros and check she took the warning seriously, made herself scarce. Pulling into the driveway, Jill notices a bike abandoned on the verge a short way down the street. It's that kind of area; you can leave your bike out, reasonably safe in the knowledge that nobody will nick it overnight.

The driveway is empty and the security screen door locked. A good sign. Ros has taken the hint. The neighbour pops her head out of her front door.

'Gone away for a few days, I believe. Left me a note to check the chooks. Want me to tell her you called?'

'No, it's fine,' says Jill. 'I'll message her. Thanks.'

'Is everything alright? There were a couple of blokes here earlier looking for her, too.'

'Really?' Jill wheedles a description of said gents and vehicle, hoping she doesn't seem too inquisitive and copperish. Tough-looking types in a white Toyota SUV. Tradies maybe. Didn't offer any conversation. Time?

'An hour ago, something like that.' The sound of dogs howling in the background. A twist of the head. 'Shut it, mongrels.'

Jill thanks her and drives away, scanning for properties and businesses that may have CCTV she could access if needs be. On the police radio, chatter about a burglary over in Tinderbox. Any units able to respond? It seems not, all are fully stretched with the Bruny incident. It's a short detour so Jill offers her services.

'You sure?' says the operator. 'Bit beneath you, isn't it? Usually a uniform job in the first instance.'

'Team player, mate. Give me the name and address.'

A big timber place clinging to a steep, tree-shrouded block sloping down to the water. The bush needs thinning out and the house needs some space between it and the trees. This area isn't called Tinderbox for nothing, and every summer is a bushfire lottery. A woman emerges from the house as Jill's car comes to rest on the gravel driveway. She's gym-fit and dressed to continue the regime.

'Police?' she asks, scanning Jill from head to toe and noting that neither she nor the car seem to be in uniform.

Jill presents her ID. 'What's happened?'

'Some scumbag stole some clothes and a bike. Pathetic, these people, I tell you.'

Jill is led to an outhouse that serves both as a laundry and a storage shed for tools, leisure equipment, gardening stuff.

'Bloody kids.'

'What makes you think that?'

'The gear they took. The clothes belong to my son. Fifteen. It's his bike too.'

Jill gets a description, a few more details and gives the woman a job number for any insurance claim. 'And this happened when, last night?'

'We found the stuff gone this morning. Sometime between about eight last night, when I set the dryer running, to about seven this morning.

Xavier's gutted about the skate shoes. He'd just about worn them in to their smelly best. Me? Less sad. But the bike wasn't cheap.'

Jill wraps things up. Gestures out across the view, the water, the salmon pens, the rolling hills. 'Nice place you've got here.'

A snort. 'Wanna buy it? Like living next door to an iron foundry, only they'd have rules to abide by. We've had this place on the market three times in the last two years and had to withdraw it.'

'No takers?'

'Our only hope is out-of-staters or overseas buyers who don't do their homework on the salmon farms. Bloody activists, wish they'd pipe down at least until we've sold the place.'

Jill once again looks out at that view across to North Bruny. Wonders how the search for Sam Willard is going.

—

'That doesn't make sense. Or, at the least, it's far-fetched.'

Sam's inclined to agree. It sounds dodgy to him too. Salmon, war crimes. War crimes, salmon. WTF? 'I'm not saying the two threads have always been linked. I'm saying someone has spotted an opportunity to kill two birds, or more, with one stone. And I get to play the part of the stone.'

'I thought you were claiming to be one of the birds?'

'Good point. Maybe I'm both.' Sam is giving Ros a break from the driving. She looked exhausted and his dizziness has receded enough to make it not too unsafe.

She shakes her head. 'One man's reputation, another man's fortune. They're really prepared to kill for that?'

Sam knows it goes further than a matter of Turnell's reputation. Sam could help convict him in a criminal trial, if it ever got that far. Has Turnell got wind of that? Sam can't give Ros the whole story yet. As for killing an activist who is causing trouble for a big business? This wouldn't be the first time that's happened. Sam knows how cheap life can be. 'It seems so.'

'Even if it could be made to hold together, be proven, why would anyone believe it? The world is full of conspiracy theories. The simpler narrative is of you: lone wolf, disturbed war vet. I don't see you coming out the other end of this without some consequences and, to be frank, you deserve it.'

Yes, he acknowledges, he probably does. 'Whereas you can emerge from this and move on, if you want to.'

'I suppose.'

It's hard to tell on roads like this. Just the one major route, snaking its way north and west. Once you're on it, you're on it for the duration and it wouldn't be unusual to spot familiar company along the way. Except that ute behind has been maintaining a regular pace and distance long past the time when it could have overtaken safely and zoomed on its way. Could they really be on the tail this quickly? He speeds up. The ute does too, keeping that two-hundred-metre distance behind. He slows a little, and it does too. The gap remains the same.

'So?' says Ros.

'So, what?'

She gestures out the windscreen. 'Where are we going? Wouldn't a big city like Hobart or Launceston be an easier place to hide in?'

'Know any vacant properties we could shelter in?'

'No.' Helpless shrug. 'What are we going to do about this?'

'The options are that you drop me at a cop shop and go home. Que sera, sera. They may or may not come after you. Maybe you could leave the state or the country for a while.'

'Or?'

Or what? Drive this car as far as they can, abandon it out west? Then get the bus back to Hobart. 'I don't know,' Sam says.

'Why do you keep doing that? Speeding up, slowing down, staring at the rear-view?'

'There's a ute ... Don't turn around. I don't like the look of it.'

'Why?'

Why? Because it's given up on the two-hundred-metre gap and is racing up on them, headlights flashing.

—

Jill goes back to Margate, to Ros's house. Only she stops halfway up the street where that bike lies abandoned on the verge. It's the stolen one, right down to the Vans skate shoes sticker on the crossbar as described by Xavier's mum. Sam Willard isn't on Bruny any longer. He swam across to Tinderbox. Stole some dry clothes and a bike. And the first person he chose to visit was Ros. She's near and she has a car. She is his insurance. Now Sam Willard has a hostage and a vehicle and could be any-damn-where. She takes out her phone.

'Cav? Jill here.'

'Yeah?'

'I don't think Willard is still on Bruny.' She explains why but can tell by his impatient punctuating 'ums' and 'yeahs' that Cavanagh doesn't buy it.

'Not a bad theory, Jill, although I think it's unlikely. Why is he going to steal kid's clothing? How about you track down the wife and we take it from there?'

'If he has taken Ros Chen as a hostage, we probably need to start putting some resources into that situation, boss. The longer we leave it...'

'Tipping Ros Chen off about Willard was probably a good idea of yours, Jill. Getting her to lie low for a while. Would have liked to have been privy to your thinking but top marks for initiative.' Background noises. Male. Low energy. 'See if you can contact her. Put your mind at ease. Meanwhile, the wife. We'll talk later, yeah?'

'Cav—'

But he's ended the call.

Is the man wantonly stupid? Stubborn? Negligent?

The first and only useful thing she can do is put out an alert on Ros's car. If it's spotted, she wants to know. Likewise, credit card and ATM use. Maybe she should be running this action past Cavanagh too but fuck him. Now back to the office to start tracking down Willard's wife. On the way, she calls the Tinderbox lady and lets her know where she can find her son's stolen bike.

'Great. No sign of the smelly skate shoes, I suppose?'

'No, sorry.'

'Don't be. I'm not.'

Back in the office. Empty. The *Mary Celeste* of cop shops, not counting the civilian staffers. She gets one of them onto chasing up the wife's social media accounts and her phone. See where it's pinging. That's if she's still alive. Bank accounts, ATM withdrawals, credit card usage. Whatever. There's an early result. The phone's on and pinging over in Dodges Ferry. Jill calls the number.

'Katherine Willard?'

'Yeah?'

Jill introduces herself, explains her business. 'Can I come and see you?'

'S'pose. Is Sam in danger?'

'Possibly. But you can help him, Katherine. Help get the best result possible.'

'Sam told me to trust nobody, including the police.'

'And look where that got him.' An insistent child's cry in the background. 'The address, Katherine?'

'He's not what you say he is. All that stuff on the news. Bullshit, all of it.'

'And you can help make sure he comes in safe and sound to tell his side of things. Mmm?'

Jill notes down the address and promises to be straight out there. Closes the call. And releases the breath she hadn't realised she'd been holding. Katherine and the kid are unharmed and that's a good start.

—

It's clear when the ute driver draws level with them that he hadn't expected to see Sam behind the wheel. It was Ros he thought he was closing in on. He abandons his attempt to overtake them, drops back. Right back. Sam can see in the rear-view that the man is now on his phone.

'Shit.'

Sam slows, then reverses at full speed back towards the ute.

'What are you doing?' Ros grabs the cissy handle above her door, bracing her feet against the footwell.

A spin of the wheel, some fancy work with the brakes, and he's now facing the ute, driving full at him, head-on.

'You're mad,' she says between gritted teeth.

A hundred metres, seventy, fifty. Has Sam miscalculated? Thirty.

The driver of the ute blinks first and veers off the road into a ditch. Sam slams on his brakes and is out of the car, crossing the distance in a few strides, hauling the ute driver out of his cabin. The man is facedown, Sam's knee on his neck and an arm twisted up his back to breaking point. The spare scrabbling uselessly in thin air.

'Who are you?' says Sam.

'Nobody. What the fuck. Get off me!'

'Your arm will be out of the shoulder socket in five seconds. Answer the question.'

'Fuck off.'

Snap, crackle and pop followed by a howl.

'I warned you.' Sam takes hold of the other arm.

'Sam, stop.'

'Stay back, stay out of this.' Sam applies pressure to the remaining arm. The man is hissing, trying to control his breathing against the pain.

'Sam.'

'Listen to your girlfriend, Sammy. She's a humanitarian.'

To Ros. 'Check the ute, glovebox, whatever, for ID or weapons. Anything else you can find.'

'But—'

'If you don't do it, I'll have to put him out of action and do it myself.' That'll keep her busy. While Ros is otherwise engaged, Sam leans down, all the while maintaining the pressure on the man's arm and neck. 'You know we don't take prisoners, mate. You were there.' Prods the bicep. 'Got the tatt to prove it. Who are you and who sent you?'

'Not telling.' As Ros returns with a pistol and a wallet, the man raises his voice. 'I. Can't. Breathe.'

'Sam, please. There's no need for this.'

A car approaching in the distance. The help he called or just another traveller? Either way, this needs to stop. 'Stay where you are,' he says to the prone man. He takes the gun and ID and, with his knife, punctures all four tyres on the ute. 'Sit up, smile, play nice.' He's banking on everyone having their own good reason to not give the game away.

The car slows, a window wound down. 'Need any help?'

Sam has kept his face low, feigning concentration on the ditched ute, trying not to be recognised. 'All good, mate. We've called a tow truck.'

'You alright, cuz?'

'Arm's a bit sore, but I'll be good,' says the prisoner.

'Missus?'

'All good. Thanks for checking,' says Ros, smiling. 'Lovely of you.'

The car moves on and they all try to act natural for the rear-view mirror.

Sam would like to kill the guy but realises he probably shouldn't. Checks the ID. Robert Beckett, address in country Victoria. Another one of Trembath's essential workers allowed access to the state in these pandemic times? How did he catch on to them so quickly?

'Robert, Rob, Bob? What is it?'

'Wouldn't you like to know.'

Sam turns to Ros. 'Know how to use a gun?'

'No. Why would I?'

He shows her. 'I need to check something.' Back to her car, lowering himself to the ground for a look. There it is. A tracking device magnet-clamped under the driver's side. He disconnects it. Stamps on it.

Then he hears the yelp and the shot.

12

Katherine Willard is waiting for Jill on the porch of a charming Dodges Ferry weatherboard. Inside, the sounds of a chuckling infant and an attentive female adult. It's a community of holiday shacks, boats in the driveway, wetsuits on the washing line. Be nice to live out here, thinks Jill. Short walk to the beach. No traffic noise, no commuting. Just string shells together and grow your own vegetables. Maybe start a book club and have a dog. Root the local handyman who's probably called Bill and still surfs. Jill and Bill, nice. She adjusts her gun holster for sitting with ease on the porch furniture.

'Thanks for seeing me, Katherine.'

'Call me Kaz, everyone else does, except my mum.'

Jill accepts a cup of tea from the pot. Helps herself to an Anzac. 'How are you going?'

'Worried. Scared.'

'For Sam?'

'Sure, and us too.'

'Sam told you to lie low?'

'Yeah.'

'What were his words exactly?'

The woman is compact and streetwise. Cop-wise even. Jill wonders if this is perhaps not the first time they've had to go into hiding. He hadn't given any details, Kaz says, just told her to get herself and the kid out of there and he'd be in touch.

'You know he needs to give himself up. If he really believes that he, and you, are in danger, then we're your best bet.'

'Unless you're part of that danger.'

'He said that?'

'No.' Kaz seems to be weighing things up in her mind. 'Ever since he took on that new job he's been acting strange. Like the old days when I first knew him.'

'Strange? In what way?'

'Secretive. Distant. All that money that was going to come in, gone now. Good job we didn't sign the contract on the house.'

'By new job you mean the one he had at the salmon farm, right?'

'No, they offered him a better one after about a month. A promotion. A consultancy they called it.'

'What kind of consultancy?'

Kaz shrugs. 'Dunno. Security stuff maybe, given he was in the army and that.'

'This was with the salmon company?'

'Not direct. A subcontractor. Can't remember the name. He signed something but I don't know where that document is.' A single tear bursts from those big eyes. 'Did he really do those things they say he did?'

'It's what we need to find out, Kaz. And we can't do it without talking to Sam. That's where you come in. We need you to persuade him to give himself up.'

A nod. 'Okay.'

—

Robert Beckett is dead, chest bleeding.

'What happened?'

Ros is white with shock. Trembling. 'While you were under the car. He pulled a knife from down near his ankle. Must have thought I wouldn't shoot.'

They need to get out of there fast. 'Give me the gun.' She does. 'Go and sit in the car. Drink some water. Try to stay calm. I'll take care of things.'

The most recent sighting, by the passing motorist, is of a rolled ute and a possibly injured driver who was being helped by another passing car. All seemed relatively well and normal. Sam needs to separate the body of Robert Beckett from the location of the abandoned ute. That means driving the corpse some distance away and dumping it.

He clears space in the boot of the Subaru. Shifting camping gear and other bags onto the back seat. In the absence of a tarp, he extracts the flysheet from around the rolled-up tent and wraps Beckett in it. Hefts him into the back of the car.

A groan from Ros up front. 'Is that what I think it is?'

'No choice. We'll get rid of him further down the track. Drink water. Stay calm.' He scoops up the shattered pieces of the tracking device along with Beckett's phone, which had been used to monitor it. Both will be discarded along the way. There are some of the dead man's belongings that could prove useful. Sam grabs them, chucks them in the boot with the body. All that is left is a ute rolled into a ditch on a country road in the lengthening shadows of the day. Praise be, no more passing traffic during that time. Soon they will also need to get rid of Ros's car and find a new one.

'How are you going?' he asks.

'I'm a murderer.'

It happens to the best and worst of us. 'Self-defence. He had a knife. He meant you harm.'

She lets out a shaky breath. 'Get me out of here.'

—

Mid-afternoon by the time Jill organises, through police media, okayed by Cavanagh and the top brass, to get Katherine Willard in front of the news pack in time for the evening bulletins. Kaz has the kid in her arms and stares straight down the barrel of the camera like a pro, eyes brimming with tears.

'Wherever you are, Sam, we need you to come home and sort this out. I need you.' She kisses the child's head. 'Ollie needs you. Come home, tell the truth. Tell your side. Whatever happens, we'll be with you all the way.'

The police media guru shields Kaz from any questions from the pack. She is shepherded out of the room and a car will take her back to Dodges Ferry. Police will keep watch on the property, for Kaz's safety, to deter gawpers and the press, and in case Willard shows up there.

Jill's phone goes. Cav again. 'Good work finding the wife.'

'Wasn't that hard, but thanks.'

'Still a dead end over here. Tell me more about that theory of yours, Jill.' She does so.

He *hmmms* and *yeps* a bit. 'Maybe we can put an alert out on her car.'

'Good idea, boss.'

'Stop taking the piss. I know you already did. Any reports?'

'Nothing so far on the car, but Ros's credit card was used at a motel in Lutana. She was a no-show. Then her mobile pinged this side of New Norfolk.'

'She's with him, isn't she?'

'Possibility.'

'Where do you think they're headed, Jill?'

'Up north? Try to reach the mainland. Lose himself there.'

'We can block that. Other ideas?'

Jill has the feeling of being played in some way. Like he already knows the answer to these questions. 'Out west maybe. Use his survival skills to disappear into the big wilderness over there. Could take weeks if he's as adept as they claim he is.'

'That was my thinking too. Same page, Jill. Initiative suits you.'

Patronising git. 'Got a plan, boss?'

A sniff. 'If he heads out bush with his skills, it'll need a specialist team to track him. Maybe even military. I'll talk to some people. Meanwhile, I'll get them to cover the northern ports too. Back in the office in an hour or so, will call a meeting then.'

'What could he hope to gain heading into the wild for a few days, weeks, whatever?'

'Buy time? Negotiate? Especially if he's got a hostage. Plenty of currency for dragging this out.'

Who's playing catch-up, her or Cavanagh? And this hot and cold business. One minute she's invisible – to be patronised or ignored – the next, a peer and confidante, a trusty lieutenant. What's that all about? Jill checks the time; nudging 4.00 pm. Realises she hasn't had lunch yet. Heads to the kitchen to make a cuppa and rummage through other people's food stashes.

—

The rain has cleared and sun pokes through the clouds. Low in the western sky, blinding through the windscreen. Ros has remained silent since they started driving again. Deep in her own thoughts, eyes focused on an inner distance. Sam took a side road that allows them to tack generally in that same direction north and west. The advantage is that they're off the slightly busier highway. The downside is that they're even more conspicuous on these minor roads. No vehicles have passed so far, but a tractor driver working one of the paddocks may remember them if prompted by, say, the nightly news. Is it Sam's imagination or is Robert Beckett's body already showing signs of ripening? A literal dead weight in the back of the car, it may as well be sitting up front with them it so occupies their thoughts. The body needs to go. The car needs to go. Ros too needs to go; blame the killing on him. He's already in enough trouble and one more won't matter.

The high hills in the west loom closer. Jagged dolerite bluffs, towering snow-capped ranges. Sam longs to hide among them. But is it sustainable to have Ros along for the ride?

As if reading his thoughts. 'We're headed for those hills?'

'That was my thinking, yeah.'

'How long for? Are you Bear Grylls or something?'

'I don't have a plan as such. Making it up as we go along.'

Maybe there'll be a cop shop at the next town, Ouse. He could drop her there; it may even be a town big enough to provide him with new wheels. Maybe.

'When and where are we going to get rid of the body?'

He ignores the question and outlines his idea for dropping her at Ouse and him taking the blame for Beckett's death.

'Why would I want to do that?'

'To keep out of trouble, get on with your life.'

'But it's not the truth. You didn't kill him, I did. So back to the original question. When and where do we get rid of the body?'

She's clearly in shock. Not thinking straight.

'Ros, I'm already in the shit. I can deal with it. It's what I'm trained for.'

'Big guy.'

'Ros—'

'You said yourself. He didn't expect you to be in the car. He was coming after me with a gun and a knife. I was fair game. There's nothing for me to return to until this is finished.'

'The police can protect you.'

'No. Maybe. For a while, but not forever.' A pause. 'The body?'

'Why are you doing this, Ros? This isn't your fight.'

She turns on him. Fierce. Eyes brimming. 'They killed the love of my life. If it was Niamh in my place, it would be her fucking fight. But it's me, so it's mine.'

A sidetrack heading down towards what looks like a river or stream. No buildings for miles. 'This looks a good spot.'

—

The big meeting room at HQ. Cavanagh seems able to float between one reality and the next, like a politician in election mode. Now he's committed to the theory that Willard has left Bruny and is headed for the hills with Ros as his hostage, like it was his idea all along.

'By this time, he could already be there,' says Cavanagh, between mouthfuls of pizza. 'If so, we don't have the manpower to hunt him down. Choppers and drones are only so much use, but it's a big area to cover and where to start?'

Jill is enjoying her pizza. Several boxes have been ordered in from Room for a Pony in North Hobart. Classy stuff beyond your standard melted mozzarella and chorizo. She's happy to sit back and let Cav go on a bit.

'All the stations on the roads accessing the national park are now on alert for the target vehicle but are under orders not to intercept. We're weighing up a media alert but don't want that to undo the wife's plea for him to come in.' A nod towards Jill Wilkie. 'Good work on organising that, Jill.'

Heads turn her way. Some nods of encouragement.

'As to whether Willard will see or hear that appeal, we can only hope.'

Jill's been doing her homework ahead of the meeting. 'Not a sighting of the target vehicle as such, but there is a report of an abandoned ute in a ditch on the Lyell Highway between Hamilton and Ouse.' She checks her notes. 'Four flat tyres. Vic plates. Registered to a business name, TSS Pty Ltd.'

'Add it to the database, might come in handy for crosschecking later.'

'Four flat tyres. Unusual. Maybe it warrants a little further digging, now?'

Cavanagh frowns. 'If you like, Jill. Go for your life.'

They briefly adjourn to catch the six o'clock bulletin on the wall-mounted screen and check out Kaz's performance. Everyone reckons she did well. Back to business.

Cavanagh pauses, almost theatrically. He has some big news. 'We've had consultations with the military about precisely what kind of threat Willard presents.' Grave, statesmanlike. 'He's a piece of work. Suspected of committing atrocities in Afghanistan. Been under investigation for some time. But for all that, regarded as one of their best soldiers. Very, very capable. In turn, Defence has cautioned that only our most capable should engage him.'

Fair enough, thinks Jill, bring out the ninjas. That's what they're paid for.

'And they've offered us some specialised contract personnel to consult and advise as required.'

Not the police Special Operations Group, or Soggies as they're known. Instead, some ex-military advisors who come highly recommended by their former masters.

'Long as they don't steal our glory,' says one voice.

'Or our beer,' says Hughesy.

'Our Soggies will still be on hand as back-up,' says Cavanagh reassuringly. 'But we'll let these other blokes have first crack as they're paying for their own petrol.'

It's agreed then, at a high level. We've got more commandos and ninjas than you can point a stick at. Jill joins the exodus from the meeting room, taking a couple of slices of pizza with her in a napkin.

Cavanagh says, 'See you tomorrow.'

'I'll just run a check on that ditched ute before I go home.'

'It'll wait, Jill. Save your energy for the new day.'

She demurs, but he seems insistent. It's as if he'd prefer Sam Willard to get as far away as possible before releasing the hounds.

—

Dark by the time Robert Beckett is laid to rest. They'd been hampered by hard-packed stony ground and lack of digging tools – all they had was a hand trowel intended for toileting purposes in the great outdoors. The grave is shallow as a result, and the body is covered with branches and earth. The tent flysheet has been retrieved from around the body and rinsed in the rivulet. They will have greater need of it. Sam also has greater need of Beckett's boots – even if they are a size too small – and the bloke's fleece will come in handy too. As will his phone. At this stage in the game, they've given up on the idea of getting a new vehicle. Instead, they'll hightail it to the nearest national park access point and take it from there. Then a late-night hike into darkness and who knows what.

How does this end?

Ros foresees a few days of cold, hunger and fatigue before they give themselves up, having wasted their – and everybody else's – time. Or a chopper or drone spots them and the police corner them on some windy ridge. Maybe, like the Maccabees at Masada, they throw themselves to their doom rather than be captured. Or perhaps they are simply cuffed and dragged away to their fate. Or maybe they wander for days growing thinner and weaker, finally succumbing after eating the wrong wild mushroom. Skeletons discovered by wayward hikers some months hence. It all sounded equally fanciful, unreal, dire. How many days or weeks have passed since she was a simple suburban depressive content to self-medicate and repose under her doona? Now she's a murderer and fugitive. Still, she can't deny it: she feels more alive now.

'Good to go?'

No, thinks Ros, I'm not. 'I need some kind of insurance that I'm not wasting my time. I don't want all those suspicions, conspiracies, whatever just to dissolve into nothing while we bust our arses tramping around the wilderness for the next however long. Somebody needs to be set the task of joining the dots and seeing where, if anywhere, they lead.'

'Who do you have in mind?'

Who indeed?

In fact, they each have someone in mind. Sam is thinking of the pushy and persistent ABC podcast producer Larissa, and Ros has decided to place her faith in the detective, Jill Wilkie, who seems to be stubbornly interested in the truth when many of those around her are not. Ros has Jill's card in her wallet, Sam doesn't have Larissa's number but he remembers that her work email is on the ABC investigative tip-offs page on the website. He'd looked her up when she took an interest in him.

But how to get them on board and at such short notice?

They'll send each the same message from Beckett's phone and suggest each contacts the other. Once done, they will destroy the phone, keeping Ros's as back-up. No impassioned rant in the message; instead, dot points and names or references to follow up in the first instance. The journalist and detective are investigators – let them do the rest of the work if they're interested. It's a risk. The sending of the messages will tip the authorities off as to their whereabouts. Beyond Derwent Bridge, at the foot of Lake St Clair, the phone signal is an unknown quality. That's their last opportunity. Timing will be everything.

Fully dark now as they bump along that river track they took earlier. Headlights off and the car lighter by about ninety kilos, even if the metallic tang of blood remains.

—

Heading home, north on the Brooker, traffic solid all the way, Jill Wilkie's phone lights up in its dashboard cradle. A text from unknown sender. She pulls off into a side street and parks. Opens up the message.

Look into David Trembath DTS, Edward Milsom, D'Entrecasteaux takeover, connections to Turnell & war crimes, Sam Willard innocent

Jill imagines Ros texting, a madman in her ear, a gun or knife at her head. A dictated conspiracy theory bathed in spittle and bad breath.

Are you OK Ros? she texts back.

Some moments later. **Yes**

Not reassured at all, Jill tries phoning the number but gets the disconnected or out-of-range signal. A call through to the techs, gives them the number, can they trace this?

Yep, she's told, a few minutes later. Number registered to one Robert Beckett. Call made from Derwent Bridge. Ops centre notified; Cav not available, but all units within cooee of Derwent Bridge scrambled. So, Sam and Ros are indeed headed for the hills. Jill caught the weather forecast on the radio: cold winds, rain sweeping in from the west. Snow down to five hundred metres. That's going to test Willard's survival skills. Can Jill really go home with all this happening?

Who is Robert Beckett and why send this text to her?

It could have gone to police HQ, any one of the media or Crime Stoppers numbers on the website. Or to the news media. Why had they chosen Jill? Maybe Ros was buying into Willard's claim of innocence. Surely not. Grieving and vulnerable she may be, but there was a level head there too. She's the hostage of a disturbed killer. She's doing what she's told. Isn't she? Even if not, if they've got something useful to say, then they can walk into the nearest cop shop and spill the beans.

Her phone lights up again. Cavanagh. 'What's going on?'

'Ros Chen made contact. From Derwent Bridge.'

'Saying what?'

'Willard is innocent and we should look into this other stuff.' She lays out what the other stuff is.

'Bullshit diversion. She in on it, you think?'

'Hard to tell based on a text. Could be under coercion.'

'Course she is.' Chewing noises. He's back in the office, snaffling what's left of the pizza. 'You weren't thinking of following up on any of that crap, were you?'

'No, boss.'

'Good.'

Some spots on the windscreen, trees bending in a sudden gust. That weather forecast kicking in. 'You'll be heading up there then, Cav? Be in the thick of it.'

'Yeah, leaving soon.'

'Take your winter woollies and thermals.' Jill won't ask if she's invited. He'd have said so by now. 'Here's to a nice clean happy ending.'

'One way or another, yeah.'

Meantime it wouldn't hurt for Jill to inquire further, would it?

13

Friday. Snow. Knee-deep in frigging snow. It isn't even dawn and they're on their way. Ros is cursing all the things she neglected to bring. Like gloves. Thermals. The list grows. Having no doubt given away their location with the messages sent from Derwent Bridge, they had then destroyed Beckett's phone. They had stolen a car parked at the Lake St Clair Visitor Centre, perhaps a guest of the Lodge, although probably not, as the car had to be old enough to hot-wire – a bit low-rent for someone who can afford the Lodge. Abandoned Ros's vehicle there, along with stuff they didn't intend to carry – laptop, Ros's Kindle, things like that. Then they'd kicked on with a few more hours of driving in a meandering fashion north to Mole Creek then back south along Mersey Forest Road to the bottom of Lake Rowallan, allowing access to Cradle Mountain National Park or Walls of Jerusalem with options taking them down into The Labyrinth. They parked the stolen car out of sight and covered it in whatever branches and foliage were available. A delaying tactic to try to throw their trackers off the scent: it could take a few hours or a few days for the car swap to be noticed and the stolen car located. Those on their trail not sure which direction to follow given all the options. A limited delaying tactic, though, and sooner or later helicopters, spotter planes, drones and possibly dogs to contend with. They'd slept a few hours in the stolen car before setting out, Ros feeling guilty as she snuggled into the relative warmth of her sleeping bag, Sam insisting he would be fine.

'You okay?' He's a few metres ahead, electing to carry the main backpack and setting a cracking pace.

'Yep,' she says. Hopefully they'll be captured by the end of the day and it'll be all over. A nice warm prison cell and a life sentence for murder.

They're keeping off the main walking tracks. Even at this time of year and this hour of the day, there are hiking zealots out there – usually Tasmanians – and it's not a good idea to risk an encounter, especially while Sam is still kitted out in Vinnies smart-casual and limping along in borrowed ill-fitting boots.

'Yell out if you need a rest.'

Yeah, yeah. 'I'm good, cheers.'

The hike had kicked off almost immediately with a steep climb, six hundred metres in elevation. They're keeping parallel, about a hundred metres distant, with the lesser used, they hope, Lake Myrtle Track taking them across Blizzard Plain. It feels like it too. The wind is bitter, slicing through any chinks in her Gore-Tex, numbing her exposed face and hands. Taking the heavy pack and yomping at double speed is probably Sam's way of keeping warm, she realises. But surely this isn't sustainable. The sky slowly turns from black to grey over to her left. Sam has the head torch, the light dancing out front. It's important to keep up so she can reap any residual benefit. How long since she did something like this? Like what? Take a hike in the wilds? Kill a man and go on the run? Either way it's been a while. She used to do this often, had been working her way through sections of the Bibbulmun Track before … before everything. It was how she'd met Niamh. The Bibbulmun and the Munda Biddi Trail intersecting, not far out of Donnelly River in south-west WA. Ros with her backpack, a rest break and some scroggin. Niamh on her mountain bike, slowing down and smiling. At her. At Ros. Stopping to chat. The rest, history.

It should be you here, she thinks. You're the kick-ass one.

'Say something?' Sam halts for a moment, turns to her.

'No,' she says. 'All good. What's the rationale here? The aim?'

'Buy enough time for them to investigate. Stay alive. Survive. Think of something.'

—

Jill is woken by next door's ute starting up. He's a tradie and, according to the stickers, supports the Bulldogs and the cable car and doesn't believe in vaccinations or the virus. It's still dark. Feels like she hardly slept at all. She'd taken ages to get to sleep, then woke up again not long after midnight. Tossing and turning for the next couple of hours.

Coffee.

Once again, Jill feels in limbo. Just a matter of days ago she signed up to early retirement to escape disciplinary action for beating Mark Limace up. How is he doing, the poor lamb? Internals had reassured her that she had nothing to fear from rogue copies of the beating video, Limace had said he would sort it. They must have put the fear of God into him. Moving right along. A murder and a manhunt and, momentarily, back in the thick of things. Now, yet again, on the outer it seems. What to make of it all? She flicks on the kettle and spoons coffee into the plunger. Hears the throb of traffic on the nearby Brooker Highway. As the sky lightens, it's possible to discern the dense white of the Bridgewater Jerry hanging over the Derwent. What's the weather like where you are, Ros? Are you even still alive? That text from her, famous last words?

Look into David Trembath DTS, Edward Milsom, D'Entrecasteaux takeover, connections to Turnell & war crimes, Sam Willard innocent

What if Ros means and believes what she says? However misguided. The coffee tastes good, warms Jill through and is strong enough to give her a jolt. How much effort would it take for Jill just to have a quick nose around? Cavanagh has made it clear he doesn't want her wasting any time on this. Still, what else is she meant to be doing? If she is early retired, she can look into whatever the hell she likes. If she's still on the team, then why hasn't she been tasked accordingly?

A couple of slices of wholemeal in the toaster and a top-up for her mug. Blackbirds twittering in the backyard. Jill switches on the morning TV, ABC News 24, and settles down with her toast and that second coffee. More federal versus state wrangling over pandemic border closures but Tasmania remains immune; the Forgotten State and long may it remain so. Then, above the strip banner, TASSIE MANHUNT CONTINUES:

Tasmanian police have descended upon the tiny tourist town of Derwent Bridge, adjacent to Cradle Mountain National Park, as the hunt continues for Samuel Jason Willard who is alleged to have murdered environmental activist Stephanie Howden on Bruny Island two days ago. He is believed to be in the company of Rosalyn Chen but police at this stage are not able to say if she is a hostage. Willard, an SAS veteran of the war in Afghanistan, is believed to be armed and people are warned not to approach him, but to report any sightings. As a precautionary measure, walkers are being evacuated from the Overland Track and the park is closed until further notice. Local residents are advised to keep their houses and vehicles locked and report anything suspicious.

To Melbourne now where the fallout continues and pressure builds on the Prime Minister in the pre-selection battle over high-profile war veteran and author Michael Turnell ...

Jill turns off the TV. Cav looks like he's enjoying himself in his kevlar and windcheater out in the wilds. Some familiar faces surrounding him, some ninjas and a few guys in camo she's never seen before. Maybe Cav's secret weapon, on loan from Defence, the outdoor survival experts. Trackers, for want of a better term. The kind of faces that give nothing away, forgettable in an instant. Yet somehow familiar.

—

Sam's feet are numb with the cold and wet, but numb is good, it dulls the pain from the blisters. Light enough now to extinguish the head torch. A steady freezing drizzle sets in, occasionally whipped by a wind gust. They descend gradually, the track slippery and treacherous underfoot – but at least there's no more snow at this elevation.

He should have insisted she be dropped off.

He should not have even gone to her house.

He should. Should. Should.

Have told DTS where to stick their special consultancy offer. Should have told the war crimes task force what to do with their toxic entrapment deal. Lock me up and make the world go away.

Helicopters. Or maybe tinnitus. He knows at least one eardrum is perforated from the underwater blast, any sound coming from the end of a long corridor through a thick oak door down in the dungeon. Accompanied by an itch that presages an infection. The other ear hears better but rings and pops like an exotic bird seeking a mate.

'Is that a helicopter?' Ros has heard it too.

They crouch under thick tree cover, shielding the bright blue backpack with the grey of the tent flysheet. One chopper. Coming in low from the south-east, Derwent Bridge direction. Not police or rescue. Dark. No markings. Not military, something private. Three-hundred-and-sixty-degree cameras mounted front and back. Thermal? Infrared?

'Don't look up, don't move. Let it pass.'

As the whomp of the blades draws closer, Sam feels that familiar tightening in his chest. The leap into the void for a hot landing, bracing for a sniper's bullet, the yawing in the pit of the stomach.

We gunna pop this fucker?

If only he'd said no. Just once.

The helicopter banks left, heading west out over the Overland Track and Sam breathes again.

'Will they be back?' Ros asks.

Of course they will. With bells on. 'I expect so.'

'This isn't going to end well, is it?'

'Chin up.' Sam finds a smile. 'Might never happen.'

—

Jill has just edged into a parking spot on level four of the Argyle Street multistorey when her phone buzzes. Unknown number. She leaves it in the cradle and presses loudspeaker.

'Yeah?'

'Jill Wilkie?'

'That's right.'

'My name's Larissa Barclay. ABC. Sam Willard told me to call you.'

'Yes?'

'Is it possible to meet somewhere? It's a sensitive matter.'

'Can you explain a bit more, please.'

'He sent me a message, an email rather. Last night.'

'Saying what exactly?'

'I should look into certain matters. Claiming his innocence.'

'Why did he choose you? Do you know him?'

The journalist explains her interest. Her ongoing investigation into the war crimes allegations against Michael Turnell. Sam Willard's connection to that matter.

'Right. How can I help you, Larissa?'

'You received pretty much the same message, didn't you?'

'Sorry, I'm not at liberty to comment.'

An impatient expulsion of breath. 'The links he talks about exist, I already checked.'

'Links?'

'Company links between D'Entrecasteaux and DTS and between specific personnel and elements of the Defence Force.'

'Tassie's a small place. It gets like that.'

'There's more, but I'm getting the impression you're not interested.'

Jill relents. If this journo has already done the initial digging, it'll save her time doing the same. 'Okay, you up for a coffee?'

'No, but I'm a sucker for a good chai latte.'

'Perfect,' says Jill and they agree a time and place.

—

Despite everything, Ros is struck by the beauty of the landscape they're trekking through. Rugged dolerite ridges rising out of swirling mists. Cool, whispering forest. Rushing rivulets and waterfalls. More shades of green than she imagined possible. Lichen-laced boulder fields tracing the path of a long-gone glacier. It really does feel like the land that time forgot. Birdsong, hollow and haunting. The fall of light among the trees. A thousand types of fungi, some like delicate new coral on an endangered reef, some could be an illustration from *Alice in Wonderland*.

Sam is head down, ploughing on. It's clear he's struggling. Limping. Those tight boots, Robert Beckett's posthumous revenge. Sure, the Vinnies slip-ons and nylon socks would have been useless in this environment, but this seems like torture. The thin jacket, Beckett's fleece, shirt, pants, all soaked through. Limping and shivering like a condemned man. He's not fully recovered from whatever happened to him to make his ears bleed. He seems dizzy and not there. But every so often he'll halt and turn, catch her concern and draw upon some inner reserve.

'Can we stop?'

'Sure,' he says. 'No problem.'

They break out crackers and cheese, dried fruit. Take a few glugs of water. Ros studies him, sees the exhaustion he's holding at bay. 'We need to get you some serious outdoors gear if this is to work.'

'I'm fine.'

'No, you're not.'

'Short of ambushing a fellow hiker, hopefully my size or bigger, that's not going to happen.'

'Spare clothes of mine in the backpack, you know that.'

'Might be a bit tight.'

'Socks, jumpers. Something, whatever. Use them.' She feels herself getting impatient. 'There's a first-aid pack in there too. Let me see your feet.'

He's reluctant, but she's insistent. It's hard not to shudder at the sight. Flaps of skin, red raw flesh, blood, blisters. Some Betadine, Blistex and elastoplasts later, it's not such a dreadful scene. Ros digs around in the backpack and finds dry socks that should fit. Hands them over, along with her biggest t-shirt that he can wear as an extra layer.

'No argument.'

'Thanks,' he says.

'Your ear is bleeding again.'

He dabs it with his sleeve. 'Do you want us to hand ourselves in?'

'I don't know. What do you think?'

'I think the odds are against us.'

'So how does it end?'

'God knows.' He shakes his head. 'I'm sorry for dragging you into this.'

—

A café on Elizabeth Street, North Hobart. Jill happy to be away from the city centre where any colleagues might see her. She'd rather Cavanagh doesn't get to hear about this just yet. It had taken a while to pin Larissa down on her preferred coffee shop, too many choices it seemed. Never a good thing for young people.

'How's your chai latte?'

'Had worse. The coffee?'

'Tepid.'

Some dancing-around-the-subject pleasantries. They'd both found a parking spot easily enough. Yep, the weather was a bit brisk, and Jill admired Larissa's new Tassie Tux puffer. Larissa gave her a business card and explained what a content producer was. Jill didn't have any business cards with her today but explained her role in the investigation. So much chat, they'd ordered a second round of beverages. Jill asking for hers to be extra hot this time.

'So how does a content producer making a podcast about war crimes in Afghanistan find herself in a café with a detective investigating a homicide in Tasmania?'

'Summed up nicely,' says Larissa, tucking a dark lock of hair behind her ear.

She's pretty, thinks Jill. Obviously smart too. 'I've come across all sorts in my time. Idiots who believe they're master criminals. Recidivist losers with remarkable street smarts. Thugs, psychopaths. Sad people who really don't belong in handcuffs. They're often needy in some way, manipulative. Sometimes all they've got left is their ability to spin a yarn. That's where people like them and people like us intersect.'

Larissa sips her drink. 'You've got me down as young and gullible, right?'

'Not necessarily. I just need convincing. Is there any substance to those messages or is it just a diversion?'

Larissa brings out her iPad. 'Key names. Edward Milsom, Mr D'Entrecasteaux himself.' Associated picture. Swipe left. 'Kristin Baker. D'Entrecasteaux Sustainable Business Team.'

'What's that?'

'Hard to pin down, seems like a catch-all fixer and troubleshooter role. High-flying.' Swipe left. 'David Trembath, DTS. Consultants. Current clients include D'Entrecasteaux.' Swipe. 'Finally, Michael Turnell. War hero. SG recipient, celebrity author and pundit, and now political candidate.' Another swipe. In fact, a series of them. A photo of Edward Milsom next to a young man in full dress uniform. 'Milsom's son, Peter, died in Afghanistan, 2007. Next, Peter Milsom, David Trembath and a younger Michael Turnell among others in combat gear in a theatre of war. Another. More drinking and revelry with the usual suspects. Recognise the woman in the background?'

'No prizes for guessing, huh?' Kristin Baker. Other faces in the drinking crowd seem familiar but Jill can't think why.

'Finally. A few years later. Twenty twelve.' A pic of four soldiers beside an armoured personnel carrier. Camo. Sunnies. Beards. Guns. Devil-horn gestures. 'Centre is Turnell, now patrol commander. Over right there is your fresh-faced recruit, Sam Willard.'

'Where did you get these?'

'Various sources helping us with the podcast.' Whistleblowers.

'Do we have names for these other two?'

'I asked, but my sources couldn't name them.'

'Couldn't or wouldn't?'

'Whatever. Same result until and unless they change their minds.'

'Interesting.' Very interesting. Suddenly, Jill remembers where those familiar faces are from – two men munching pies at the head of the queue at Bruny ferry port while emergency services rush past them towards a murder scene – and they're there in that final happy snap, flanking Michael Turnell with young Sam Willard outside and a little apart. Unable to believe his luck to be in such fine company.

—

Sam is shaken awake. 'Hear that?'

Course he didn't fucken hear it. He was catching some shut-eye, his turn. Where is he anyway? Oh yeah, the compound. They'd secured it this afternoon. Three dead insurgents. On the white hat side, a Wakunish commando with a bullet in his leg and an Aussie radio operator with a sore head; he hadn't ducked enough going through the small doorway.

'*Raouza!*' Pashto for 'come out, show yourself' but spoken with a Queensland drawl.

Sam was sure they'd already cleared and secured the compound. He gets up, dusts himself off, edges towards the doorway. Sunrise. Choppers approaching, two for the squad and one for the exfiltration of the HVT they captured. Sam wasn't convinced this target was particularly high value but that was T-Rex's call. The bloke looked to Sam like any other dirt-poor fucken peasant.

'*Raouza!*'

The HVT emerges from the room they'd locked him in. Hands cable-tied behind his back, a hood over his head. Waiting to greet him: T-Rex, Moose and Footrot. The choppers maybe two or three minutes away, discernible now as silhouettes against an orange sky.

'Squirter!' yells someone. Moose? Footrot? A burst of gunfire and the HVT lies in the dust.

A hoot of approval. T-Rex slaps Moose on the shoulder. 'Diamond, mate. My shout when we get back to Club Foot.'

I know what I saw, thinks Sam. He was no squirter. Where was he going to run to? The threesome turns to look at him. Raise their guns in his direction and squint down the sights.

'*Raouza!*'

Sam jerks awake, shivering.

A staying hand on his chest. Ros. 'It's okay.'

He checks his watch. Late morning. A bitter wind blowing across the high plain. 'I slept?'

'Not for long, but you obviously needed it.'

They'd stopped after another steep ascent. Pack down. Breather. Gulp of water. Head back and close his eyes.

Sam's exhausted. His feet are agony. He knows he doesn't have much left in him. Ahead, another mountain. They're at alpine level and that big dark bank of cloud out west is likely to dump more snow. This is madness. He's a Judas goat, leading Ros to slaughter.

It needs to be said. 'Out here, we're invisible. They can do anything they like and concoct any story they like.'

'Yep,' says Ros.

'We should go back the way we came. Hand ourselves in to the police. We need to have as much control as possible over our surrender.'

'Wish you'd said that before.' Ros stands and shoulders her daypack.

Back out onto Blizzard Plain.

—

It's agreed, then. Jill will focus on putting names to faces while Larissa will do a deep dive on D'Entrecasteaux Salmon and Edward Milsom. Larissa has zapped through all the photos, plus any supporting info, to Jill, who has promised to return the favour.

'Are you in or out of the fold?' Larissa wondered aloud.

'Both, I suppose. You're no doubt aware of the assault charge against me. It was in the news for a while.'

A rueful smile. 'Yes.'

'That's receded, but theoretically I'm still headed for voluntary early retirement.'

'But?'

'But here I still am. Not dead yet.'

'Good to hear.'

Back to the office, practically empty save for the civilian staff. Anybody authorised to tote a badge and gun is out on the manhunt where many of them will be hanging out by the coffee van and freezing their arses off. Today would be a good day to go on a violent rampage in downtown Hobart. Tumbleweeds. Crickets.

Jill logs on to the system, wanting to know who's on duty, who the supporting personnel are. Those specialist trackers on loan from Defence.

Nothing. Fair enough, you get that with Defence spook types. But if they're on the scene, they have to be authorised by somebody in order to pass through various cordons and enter inner sanctums. She tries another tack. Keys in a phone number.

'Jill?'

'Hughesy, how's it going up there?'

'Cold as fuck. Brass monkeys. Hoping to retire in front of the log fire at the Derwent Bridge Hotel. Try the Sri Lankan curry, play Tetris on my phone.'

'Not in the thick of things then, eh?'

'Nope. What can I do for you? Need to speak to the boss?'

'Nah, like a morgue here. Just wanting some gossip.'

'Not sure Cav would approve. He's gone all double-oh-seven. Windcheater, sunnies. You name it.'

Jill laughs. 'Shaken not stirred. What do the real spooks think of him?'

'Haven't seen 'em. They're off in the chopper sweeping up and down. Needle in the proverbial if you ask me.'

'Our ninjas with them, I suppose?'

'Nah, they're kicking their heels by the coffee van. Not used to being on the outer.'

Really? 'Love to be a fly on the wall.'

'Too fucken cold for that. I'm off for a curry. Get back to work, you. File some stats or something.'

Call closed. Hughesy's gone before she can weasel any more out of him. Our ninjas on the outer, the Defence trackers ruling the roost. Cavanagh letting them. Interesting scenario but no real answers. Jill still needs to put names to faces.

Horse's mouth it is.

—

The wind is up, the snow almost horizontal and Blizzard Plain is again living up to its name. To their left, Nescient Peak is no longer visible, and remains as unknowable as ever. Only the sign at the track junction tells you of its presence. They're back on the marked trail, banking on nobody being out in these conditions, hardy Taswegian or otherwise. They've been making better time as a result. Until now.

Ros can see Sam is struggling. He's changed out of Beckett's tight boots to give his feet some respite but the Vinnies slip-ons offer no grip and he's already taken a few tumbles. Cursing, standing, pushing on. Pace slower, back bent. Whole body racked by uncontrollable shivering. She's offered to swap her daypack for his heavier one but he refuses.

'Enough.'

He stops, turns.

'Give me the pack, you're slowing us down.'

'No. I'm fine.'

'No, you're not. And your damn pride is going to get us killed. I refuse to freeze to death out here. We need to move quicker.'

Breath fogging in front, he lifts his face and the snow whips at him. It doesn't disguise his tears of frustration and defeat. Reluctantly he unbuckles the backpack and lowers it to the ground.

'Thank you,' she says.

Swap done, on they trudge. Ros taking the lead now and setting the pace. The silver lining with all this, she supposes, is that the weather will ground the choppers. One less thing to worry about. A dull thud. Ros looks behind her, Sam has taken another tumble. Another thing she notices is the pink tinge in his snowy footprints. Another blister must have burst, blood leaking through his socks and out of his shoes. They need to get back to the car before all this turns into some Scott of the Antarctic tragedy.

They start the steep descent through the stunted eucalypts still recovering from a bushfire many years earlier. Moving as carefully and as slowly as it takes. The last thing they need right now is a twisted ankle or a busted leg. Behind her, Sam's breathing is laboured, interspersed with hisses of pain.

'Not far now,' she says. 'Just a few Ks.'

'Yep.'

The lower they descend, the clearer the weather becomes. Still windy, but no more blizzard. If anything, it's even more slippery here, as snow melt turns the stony track into a muddy rivulet. Finally, tortuously, they find themselves back on the gravel road. The car is just a few hundred metres up the hill and off to the side. Mid-afternoon. Given the conditions, barely an hour or two of daylight left. Ros is ready for the break, pack heavy on tight, sore shoulders. Frozen and wet to the bone, even with her regulation outdoors gear. As for Sam, she turns to look back.

And sees him kneeling, hands behind his head, a man pointing a gun at him.

14

The view is stunning, even with rain sheeting down onto the water and the hills shrouded in low cloud. A big airy office with panoramic windows overlooking the Channel. Kristin Baker has led Jill away from the desk to a couple of comfy armchairs and a low coffee table. Jill tries, in vain in the over-soft chair, to emulate Kristin Baker's perfect, almost Scandinavian, posture. Even in shapeless fluoros, the woman looks elegant.

'Excuse the work gear, just back from a site visit out on the water.'

'No worries,' says Jill. 'You must be very busy.'

They agree tea would be nice and they chat about the shitty turn in the weather until the mugs arrive. Company merch.

'So how can I help you?'

'As you might know, I'm on the team investigating the murder of Stephanie Howden.'

'Dreadful business. I understand you're closing in on Willard?'

Do you? Who from? 'Hopefully, yes. I'm just trying to get more background on him in the meantime.'

'We sent through what we had in the personnel file.'

'Yes, very helpful and much appreciated.'

'So …?'

'What were your impressions of him?'

A pensive sip from the mug. 'I didn't have much to do with him. He seemed quiet and keen. I don't think he fitted in well with his workmates.'

'What makes you say that?'

'There was a certain awkwardness. I think he was a bit of a loner.'

Not a bad observation of someone you didn't have much to do with. 'But obviously his work was satisfactory because he was offered a job with one of your subcontractors.' Jill checks the notes on her phone. 'DTS.'

'That's probably a matter you should take up with them.'

'Of course. But in the days immediately following the murder of Ms Howden you made some effort to distance your company from Willard, saying he was sacked for unreliability, poor behaviour.'

'In the days immediately leading up to the … tragedy … Sam was behaving erratically and we advised him his probation period would not be extended.'

'In writing?'

'Verbally. He was counselled.'

'And he was taken on by DTS instead?'

'Yes. As I already said, that's their decision.'

'What kind of services does DTS provide for D'Entrecasteaux?'

'That's commercial-in-confidence I'm afraid.'

'This is a murder inquiry.'

'Yes, sorry. But I'm not completely au fait with them.'

'Really? But you know the proprietor David Trembath, don't you?'

A frown. 'Not really, I—'

'Sure you do.' Jill finds the pic on her phone. 'That's you and him enjoying a drink or two back in the day. Old army buddies, right?'

'Where did you get that photograph?'

'Commercial-in-confidence, I'm afraid.'

'Your boss, Ian Cavanagh. Is he aware of your inquiries? I'm surprised you're not out there with the main team looking for Willard.' Sip from the mug. 'Oh, wait. Now I remember where I've heard of you before. That vicious assault on a poor defenceless man.' She picks her phone up from the coffee table. One press, Jill notes. A saved favourite number.

'Ian? Kristin here.'

—

In some ways, Sam is relieved it's finally all over. Shame about Ros, though, she doesn't deserve any of this. She hasn't met his eyes since that last moment on the gravel road when they were bundled into the ute and brought here. Wherever here is. Her fate is his fault. Look at him, trussed hand and foot with cable ties, a pig ready for the spit. No such indignity for Ros. She stares at the dirt floor. Is that disgust or disappointment on her face? Both maybe.

What happened up on the mountain? There he was, blubbering like a baby and losing it. Okay, so his feet hurt, and he was cold, wet, a bit tired. Seriously? Once were warriors, for fuck's sake. The Chosen. His kind are meant to be able to tramp naked in the Antarctic for days on end with no food rations and still be able to take out an enemy machine-gun nest single-handed. Mind over matter, they were always told. Yeah, you need to be fit and strong, but in the end it's all about what's up here in the skull. Triumph of the Will. The crucial difference between cannon fodder and commandos. Sam knows now that he doesn't have what it takes, probably never had. Another bout of violent shivering sweeps in.

'What were you thinking, Sammy?' Moose is crouched before him. 'Letting the little lady carry the big bag, while you' – he flicks his fingers at Sam's sodden op-shop attire – 'ponce along like a dero on the grog.' He slaps Sam dismissively across the cheek. 'Fucken disgrace.'

Sam wonders why they weren't just killed on the road. Do they really mean to bring them in and hand them to police? Surely not, awkward conflicting stories – particularly if Ros gets to tell her tale. No way. Moose, Footrot, T-Rex, himself; they were all well-versed in murder, in rigging evidence, creating fictions. Clearly a roadside execution didn't fit the narrative. They are waiting for instructions. Who from?

It's a hut, not one of the many walker's huts dotting the landscape. This is more a maintenance worker's storage shed. Perhaps connected to the power station at the northern end of Lake Rowallan. Iron shelves with assorted small tools, oil, degreasers and the like. Lower down, plastic tubs of chemicals and cleaning agents. Windows. It's dark outside. While Moose pays insolent attention to Sam, Footrot is looking at Ros intently. Sam has seen that look before. Knows what Footrot is capable of, given the opportunity.

'What are you waiting for?'

'What? What's that Sammy? Speak up, mate.' Moose theatrically cups a hand to his ear. Turns to Footrot. 'Did you catch what he said?'

A wry smile, shake of the head. Footrot was never one for party games. Quiet achiever. Own agenda. Sam suspects he would have been the one who put the bullets into Steph Howden. Job done, get the hell out. Meanwhile, Moose plays to the crowd.

'What are you waiting for?'

'That, Sammy. Hear it?'

He can now. A chopper. Arriving in the dark to take them away. Maybe they are just going to hand them over to the authorities. Footrot finally takes his eyes off Ros. Whatever he was thinking, it'll have to wait.

—

Jill is grabbing a tasty pho at Cyclo in North Hobart when Cavanagh gets back to her.

'What's going on?' he wants to know.

'I was wondering the same.' Attack, the best form of defence.

'What?'

'Why's Kristin Baker got you on speed dial?'

'Ask her. No wait. Don't. What the hell are you doing barging in on her? You're meant to be twiddling your thumbs in the office, maybe keeping tabs on Willard's family, generally being helpful. Pissing off D'Entrecasteaux is not helpful.'

'She and Trembath were in the army together. With Edward Milsom's son who died in Afghanistan. Trembath employed Willard, another Afghan veteran. Join the dots.'

'Join the dots? What you get then is a fucking Jackson Pollock. People know each other. Welcome to Tassie. Get a grip, Jill.'

That's the blurry thing about Tasmania, admits Jill. Some people see nepotistic conspiracies, others just see inbreeding. Maybe she really does need to get a grip. Her pho is getting cold – a film of fat on the surface, chicken skin yellow and sickly in the spare bowl.

'Have you located Willard yet?'

'No. The Defence scouts went out but their chopper was grounded by the weather. Stop changing the subject.'

'The owner of D'Entrecasteaux is tied in with all these dodgy ex-soldiers. Isn't it an amazing coincidence that one of them is now on the run for killing one of the salmon farm's key opponents during a multibillion-dollar takeover bid?'

'You watch too much TV, Jill. You should get out more.'

Her career is over and she's out in the cold. But she signed the paperwork the other day that secures her entitlements, so fuck him. 'Something is off about all this, Cav. You know it. What I still don't get is whether you're an idiot, wilfully blind, or part of the problem.'

'Strong words, Jill.'

'Honestly, mate, I'm past caring.'

'Consider yourself suspended. I'll submit the paperwork this evening.'

—

The cable ties have been snipped. Finding a body in the Tasmanian wilderness in winter is one thing. Finding it cable tied is a different matter. They're flying low over the snow-covered ranges heading south and west. Sam, Ros, Moose, Footrot and the pilot. The doors are slid back and it's bitterly cold. Sam and Ros are facedown on the floor of the chopper deck. A boot on the back, a pistol at the neck. Sam now knows what the story will be; two bodies in the snow far from anywhere. Perhaps a fall from a ridge in shocking conditions and poor visibility. One of them woefully unprepared for the conditions but desperate, nonetheless. The other, his hostage, an innocent victim. What a tragedy. So where would the dump site be? It has to be a credible walking distance from where they allegedly started out. A radius from Lake St Clair of not much more than thirty kilometres, especially in those conditions. Time left to live? Minutes surely. The gun is removed from his neck, the boot from his back. Here it comes. Sam is being dragged by his feet towards the open door. He hears Ros yell out. She knows what's happening to him, but with Footrot kneeling on her she is helpless to prevent it. Sam tries to grab at whatever he can, a seat stanchion, dangling safety belts, anything. His grip swatted by the stronger and fitter Moose.

'Sorry, Sammy mate. Nothing personal.' Sam is surprised he can hear the words above the roar of the rotor blades and the howling wind and him with his bad ear and all. Did something pop internally and clear the tubes out? Or does he just wish he'd heard it? Head and shoulders out over the edge now. A snowy, rocky world racing below him. Sam lashes out, kicking his legs desperately. Moose stamps him down, crouching to land a few punches. 'Behave. It'll be over soon.'

Moose shouldn't have crouched and brought himself so close. Sam headbutts him, pushes him back forcefully, both of them a mess of flailing limbs wrestling in the open doorway. Sam positions his legs to upset

Moose's balance. Teetering, a foot shove, and Moose disappears through the gap. Flying into the blizzard.

Footrot has decided that Ros isn't so important anymore. Now he's crouching over Sam, pistol pressed into Sam's cheek. The trigger needing only the lightest of touches.

Sam goes for the wind-up. A bloody grin through busted lips. 'Hey, Moosey can fly! Who knew?'

Footrot mashes the butt of his pistol into Sam's cheek. The splinter of bone.

'Stop! Drop it!' shouts Ros.

Back on that gravel road they'd taken the knife from Sam but neglected to search the backpack Ros had been carrying. Robert Beckett's Glock was in there. The backpack was to have been thrown out of the chopper after them as part of the fiction.

'Drop it. Throw it out the door.'

Footrot is calculating. It's clear neither Ros nor Sam has anything left to lose. Dead this way or that, who cares anymore? Sam remembers Footrot on patrol. Strong survival instinct. Always live to fight another day. He throws the gun onto the chopper deck. Sam brings him down, a few punches – uncalled for since the man has yielded, but God they felt good. They use spare cable ties to connect Footrot to some steel brackets out of harm's way.

The pilot is aware of all that's happened. Radioing in the commentary, but focused primarily on flying in the shit weather. Sam takes the Glock from Ros and shows it to him.

'Reckon you can land us somewhere nice and safe around here?'

15

Saturday. Liberated. Jill had expected a sleepless night but, in fact, has woken rested. Pincer movement, she'd decided, over tea and toast. Larissa does the background, Jill knocks on doors. Maybe today she'll choose a big, solid, posh one. Nice and early too.

It might be waterfront Sandy Bay but it still seems surprisingly modest. Lovely little blue wren hopping around in the front garden. Jill is old-school in her approach to home visits, she doesn't phone or email ahead to forewarn them, however rich and powerful they might be. Knock, knock.

Eventually the door is opened by a young woman, perhaps late teens or early twenties. 'Hi?' Looks like she's just woken up: sleep-gummed eyes, rumpled Save the Organ Pipes t-shirt, trackie dacks.

Jill shows her ID. 'Is Mr Milsom available?'

'Dad? Not sure, I'll check.' She turns and walks away, door still open. Over her shoulder. 'Come in if you like.'

Huon pine flooring. Expensive rugs. Art on the walls. The place is bright, airy and looks out onto the Derwent with picture windows. Jill hovers in the entrance, foyer she supposes you'd call it, awaiting the young woman's return.

'Golf,' is the explanation offered through a yawn.

The rain has stopped but it's still windy and cold as hell. Jill mimes a shiver. 'Keen, eh? Early start too.' A look over the young woman's shoulder. 'Mum around?'

'She doesn't live here anymore. What's this about anyway?'

'Police business,' says Jill. 'Where does he play?'

'The Royal. Seven Mile Beach.'

'Great, thanks.' Jill turns to leave.

'Is this about that activist woman on Bruny?'

'What makes you think that?'

A shrug. 'Dad's been acting funny since it happened.'

Is this kid totally guileless? The kind that comes with the privilege of never having faced anything worthy of guile in her life? 'Funny?'

'I'm Harriet by the way. Hattie, if you like.' Hand held out for shaking, mock formal.

'Jill,' says Jill. 'Funny in what way?'

'Nervous, secretive. He used to take his business phone calls over the dinner table like we weren't there. Use his big boss-man voice. Not anymore.'

'Why do you link this change to her death?'

'She knocked on our door one night about a month before she died.' A smile. 'I answered that time too.'

'Any idea what her visit was about?'

'No, but he was in a foul mood when she left.'

Jill wonders if this kid is a natural oversharer or whether she's just lonely. 'So, it's just you and Dad here, mmm?'

A nod. 'Dad says everyone leaves him. His first wife did. Mum did. Peter did.'

'Peter?'

'My brother from his first wife. Much older than me. Peter died in a war, he's Dad's favourite. Talks about him all the time. You should see Peter's bedroom, like a shrine. Saint Peter.' Audience coming to an end, Hattie shepherds Jill towards the open door. 'Poor Dad, I suppose I'll leave him soon too. Only it's hard without money, isn't it?'

'I suppose so.' Jill smiles her farewell. Not sure if she feels sorry for the kid or not.

'Tell Dad I said hi. We're practically strangers these days.'

Jill promises she will and excuses herself to check an incoming text.

—

All bets are off. Ros, like Sam, is no longer convinced of the merits of handing themselves in. They need to survive and find insurance of some sort to stay alive. They let the chopper go. What else were they meant to do? The body count is already too high, they're not equipped to take prisoners, and Ros doesn't want any more blood on her hands.

They've confiscated phones, weapons, anything vaguely useful, binoculars, outdoor clothing – including boots for Sam – taken from Footrot.

'Footrot? And you're wearing his boots?'

'Beggars can't be choosers. Same size as me and I believe he's had treatment since.'

Among the haul, police-issue handcuffs. They'd used one set on Footrot, in addition to the temporary cable ties, connecting him to a safety handle by the sliding door. Gagged and hooded and well out of reach of his colleague. The second pair of cuffs on the pilot, securing him to the controls. Hopefully they won't crash in a lake on the way back.

'There's no need to do this,' the pilot had said.

Sam clicking the handcuffs home. 'Isn't there?'

'I'm not like them, I'm just doing a job.'

'Heard it all before, mate.'

'I suppose we could hijack him,' mused Ros. 'Take us to Hobart. Land at the ABC. Cameras blazing.'

'Not enough fuel,' said the pilot. 'Look.'

He was right, the gauge was low. They had to make a decision and live with it. Buy time and work out what to do. So, they were back out there in the wilds, like it or not.

To try to even out the game they'd sent a second round of messages to Jill Wilkie and Larissa Barclay using Ros's phone while the signal was still strong enough.

Police shoot to kill? We will surrender but not to mercenaries! Publicise this! Need help not hunting

Chances of it working? Slim. Ros had to tamp down her petty anxiety about the exclamation marks. She wasn't a fan of hyperbole. On the upside, a return to her pedantry of old was surely a good sign.

'Great Outdoors, take two,' says Sam, grimly.

The chopper had taken off in the dark, buffeted by the wind, charting a course north-east according to Sam's newly acquired compass. Daylight now and they've been walking for best part of two hours. The weather has cleared but it remains freezing cold and blustery. They are surrounded by mountains, snowy ridges, black crags. Climbing into the sparse cover of a eucalypt tree line, they see small lakes scattered to their north-west. Ahead and below, heading south-east, the clear outline of a walk track threading between those big hills.

'The pilot would have known where he dropped us. Taken GPS coordinates. Chosen certain landmarks as back-up. Make us easier to come back to.' Sam checks the compass again. 'They expect or hope that we'll take that walk track.'

'Let's not, then.' Ros shoulders the daypack, having once again relinquished the large one to Sam. 'I'm guessing that means more climbing?'

—

Jill sits in her car on Sandy Bay Road studying the text from Ros's number.

Police shoot to kill? We will surrender but not to mercenaries! Publicise this! Need help not hunting

Call incoming. Larissa. Yep, she got it too. Email again.

'Okay, what do we do?'

Hard to say. Larissa probably has more options than Jill. At least she isn't suspended, exiled and in disgrace. She has half a chance of being listened to. 'Whatever you think necessary, and I'll do likewise,' Jill tells her. 'Any other developments from your end?'

'As I suspected, Milsom's backing Turnell financially for some reason. A sugar daddy helping him with his investment and property portfolio. Pulling some political strings too. You?'

Jill tells her about her encounters with Kristin Baker and Hattie Milsom. Maybe Edward Milsom is supporting Turnell out of some kind of homage to his beloved son, Peter? Or maybe he just has cash to burn? 'It'd be good to know why Stephanie Howden paid him that house call back then.'

'Sure would.'

'I'm off to see Milsom at the golf club. I'll ask him.'

'Don't mess about, do you?'

'Life's too short. Stay in touch.' They close the call. Jill immediately makes another. 'Hughesy?'

'You again.' He sounds like he's having breakfast.

'How's the manhunt going?'

'It isn't. Don't you have a life?'

'No sign? Defence cowboys haven't come good? Our ninjas still kicking their heels?'

Hughesy's not stupid. Lazy yes, stupid no. 'If you've got something to say, say it.'

'I'm going to forward a text to you. Received this morning from our runaways. Maybe you can show it to the ninja squad leader. What's his name again?'

'Her name is Josie. What's your game, Jill? Why would they be contacting you?'

'Charisma, mate. Here it comes.'

'Hold on, what about the boss? Cav should see this too, surely?'

'Of course. After Josie though, eh? And tell him the ABC also has it.'

'Crikey, Jill, you came in from left of field, didn't you?'

'In with a whimper, out with a bang, Hughesy.'

—

From up here Sam has his bearings and finally recognises the terrain.

'I think I know where we are.'

'Really?' says Ros. 'Where?'

He points east to that track they saw earlier, winding between the hills. 'Lake Elysia Track. The hills to the left are Mount Geryon and The Acropolis. Then The Parthenon. Right is Mount Gould. Those little lakes there, The Labyrinth.'

'How do you know all this?'

Sam explains. He walked these hills often when he was younger. Getting himself army-fit. Eyes on that prized SAS beret.

'Good memory all the same.'

'Etched into me.' He drags the binoculars from the side pocket of the backpack. Takes a sweep of the landscape, coming to rest on the north slope of The Parthenon. 'Ah, there he is.' Hands the binocs to Ros. 'Moose.'

'Where? Oh, right.'

It's hard to mistake the red stain in the snow. 'He'll act as a helpful marker for the chopper when they come back.'

'Did he have a proper name?'

'Brett.'

'And the other one?'

'Footrot? Shane, I think. Yeah, Shane.'

'Brett and Shane. Okay.'

'Don't go getting close to them,' says Sam. 'Acting like they're human.' They've been lucky with the weather so far today, but another dark cloudbank threatens from the south-west. 'Need to keep moving.'

'Okay. One condition.' Ros slips off her daypack. 'Bag swap.'

'No need, I'm good now.'

'Me too. Hand it over.'

He could argue and insist. Try to salvage whatever fragments of male pride remain after yesterday's debacle. But what's the point? Besides, he can see this sense of purpose and camaraderie is fuelling Ros. They both need motivation and inspiration in whatever form it comes. 'Okay.'

By Sam's reckoning they're near the top of Walled Mountain. A drop down the far side between here and the adjacent Macs Mountain might offer them the kind of protection they need both from the weather and from patrolling aircraft. Whatever the options, there's quite a hike ahead. A final scan with the binocs, one last look at poor Moose – a dollop of strawberry jam on the pristine white tablecloth.

'Fuck.'

'What?'

'Moose just moved. He's still alive.'

—

Jill finds Edward Milsom at the nineteenth hole. There are three well-heeled old duffers with him and they've all started early on the pinot noir. She flashes her ID and they make themselves scarce. All except Teddy.

'I assume this is important?' he says, after a sip.

'I wouldn't be giving up my Saturday morning otherwise.'

'Do I need my lawyer?' He nods towards a table by the window. 'He's just over there.'

'Your call, but you're not under arrest at this stage.'

He's picked up on her combative tone. No longer slouching in his chair. A wink towards the lawyer now taking an interest in them. 'How can I help?'

'I called at your place this morning. Met Hattie. Nice kid. She said Stephanie Howden paid you a visit about a month or so before she died. What was that about?'

'Stephanie ...?'

'Howden. Anti-salmon-farm activist. Your farms, in particular. Lived on Bruny. Shot dead a few days ago.'

'Yes, yes, of course. Dreadful. Visited me you say?'

'Hattie says.'

'Harriet is mistaken.'

'She seemed pretty certain.'

'It's been a difficult few years for Harriet. Ups and downs. I think the pandemic brought things to the surface for so many young people.' Another gobful of pinot. 'And the antidepressants make her a bit unfocused, confused.'

'Stephanie Howden didn't pay you a visit?'

'Not that I recall, no.'

'What's your relationship with David Trembath?'

'Client and service provider.' No hesitation.

'What kind of service?'

'Commercial. In-confidence.' The old bastard looking smug.

'Trembath was there when your son died in Afghanistan. So was Kristin Baker. That bit of connection; important, isn't it?'

'I'm not sure of your point.'

'Your favourite child. Tragically taken.'

Makes a point of checking his watch. A raised eyebrow towards his alert lawyer pal.

Let's run this up the flagpole and see who salutes. 'How precisely did your son die?'

'None of your business.' Another swig of wine.

Switch tack. 'Why are you backing Michael Turnell in his various business endeavours? Must be costing you millions yet it looks worse every day to be connected with this bloke. Hanging with an alleged war criminal? Money down the drain, I reckon.'

'Reputation is important. Courage and sacrifice should be supported, rewarded. Too many people these days are ready to tear down our heroes, attack our values.' He drains his glass. 'We finished now?'

'For the moment, yes.' Jill slides her business card his way.

He dismisses her with a curt nod, already reaching for his phone and summoning the lawyer with a flick of the fingers.

—

'A word, Ian?'

He turns. It's Josie, the tactical squad commander, all kitted out in a mix of bush and white/grey alpine camo as a change from all black. She's as tall as Cavanagh, a few years younger. He recalls her entering the academy as he was in the process of leaving. Expects her to overtake him on the ladder soon. 'Sure.'

'What do you make of this?' She shows him her phone.

Police shoot to kill? We will surrender but not to mercenaries! Publicise this! Need help not hunting

'Where did this come from?'

'Our targets, at a guess.'

'You know what I mean. They wouldn't have had your mobile. Who forwarded it to you?'

'All in good time. Me and my squad, we're hanging around here stamping our feet in the cold while your Defence buddies lock us out and yeehaw their way around the mountains. Who are they and what's going on?'

'Above my pay grade.'

'Over your head, more like. They've obviously had contact with the targets and not reported it back to us. To you. Who's in charge here, us or them?'

Cavanagh is still processing the text. How did they send it? Who to? And why has it taken until now for him to know about it? 'Leave it with me.'

'No. You know what happens if those cowboys find and kill the targets? They melt back into the shadows and leave us to take the flak.'

'Or the glory. Is that necessarily a problem?'

'Maybe not in regard to the soldier. But the civilian, as far as we know, is a hostage. We want to at least bring her home.' A pause. 'Don't we?'

'Like I said, leave it with me.'

'No. Ground their choppers. Put ours up. Any killings or rescues, it's ours to do.'

'At this stage, I outrank you.'

'Better show some leadership then, Detective Sergeant.' A nod beyond the cordon down the road. 'A hungry media pack there waiting for some news. You could be the one that gives it to them. Or do you want me doing it?'

He nods. 'Okay, I'll sort it.' Waits until she's out of earshot then rings Dave Trembath. 'Call your boys off.'

'Explain.'

Cavanagh does.

'Love to help you but it might be too late. They're already airborne and we've lost radio contact.'

'I don't believe you.'

'That's your problem.'

—

'You're serious.' Ros is vaguely ashamed of the way that sounds.

'I never expected to have to convince you.'

'He's a killer.'

'He's alive.'

'Only we know that. And nobody else knows that we know that.'

Sam shrugs. 'We had a code in the army. No-one left behind.'

'He tried to kill you. He would have. He's your enemy.'

'Now, yeah. But he saved me once. I owe him.'

'That's some twisted code you've got there, Sam. Didn't you say something earlier about not getting too close to them, acting like they're human?'

'I thought he was dead, then.' He shrugs. 'Like I said, I owe him. Settling this debt is about my peace of mind, not his. You can stay here, or head on and find a camp spot down that hill. Somewhere out of sight of any choppers.'

'No way.' She lifts the pack. 'We're in this together. Better or worse.'

'As it's my stupid idea, I'll carry the big bag.'

'You know what? I'll let you.' They swap again and head back down the hill towards the distant red stain in the snow. 'You're sure he moved? It wasn't just a delayed nerve spasm like when you chop a chook's head off?'

'He moved.'

'The wind?'

'He's alive.'

The wind is even stronger, buffeting them as they clamber down across snow-covered boulders, treacherous underfoot. At this rate, it'll be a solid three hours at least before they reach him. 'He could be dead anyway by the time we get there.'

'Maybe.'

'He'll need more than a first-aid kit.'

'Probably.'

They're both tiring again. Of the effort, of the landscape, of each other. But they push on regardless. Wind. Sleet. Snow. Stumbles and curses along the way. By mid-afternoon they've crossed The Labyrinth, skirted the small lakes, rejoined the Lake Elysia Track briefly and now begin to ascend the northern slopes of The Parthenon. Despite the atrocious conditions and the fatigue, Ros can't help but be struck by the magnificence of it all.

'There he is.'

Sam points to a spot about three hundred metres away to the right.

Drawing nearer, the snow is fresh, knee then thigh-deep. It would no doubt have cushioned Moose's landing and the chopper was flying relatively low at the time. Still, a miracle is a miracle – if he's still alive. The red smudge of blood visible from up on the mountain has paled to pink and slowly disappears under new layers of snow.

A groan.

'Coming, Moose mate. Hang in there.' Sam's voice is gentle as he crouches over the man who, just hours ago, would have killed him.

A sharp intake of breath as they survey the damage. One leg splayed at an unnatural angle. Moose is on his back, blood all down his chest and under his torso. There must be massive internal damage. Left shoulder not quite where it should be. Where to start?

'We can't move you, mate. Let's just get you warm as possible, eh?' Sam takes a sleeping bag out of the backpack, unrolls it and spreads it over the destroyed body.

'Mad, Sammy J. You're fucken mad.' Moose is reduced to a feeble hiss. 'You're a dead man.'

'Better shape than you right now, Moosey.' Sam looks up at the sky and shakes his head. 'Nine lives, buddy.'

'Should've let those Talibs take you that time.'

'But you didn't, mate, and I'm grateful.'

Ros sits on one end of the sleeping bag to stop it from flapping in the wind and blowing away. She feels an outsider in this bizarre exchange between murderous old comrades. Tries to tune out, bowing her head against the gale and the blizzard.

'The Code, eh Sammy?'

'Yeah.'

'All bullshit.' A wheezy chuckle that brings fresh blood frothing over his lips. 'T-Rex never gave a fuck about any of us.'

'So why fight for his cause?'

'Money. What else?' Eyes closed against a spasm of pain. 'Start out thinking you're doing good. Up against hard-core armed Talibs, all's fair, eh? Then the poison seeps in. Killers, mate, all they ever wanted us to be. Ain't rocket science.'

Behind the howling gale another noise. Unmistakable. A helicopter approaching.

16

Sam hears it too. Retrieves the Glock from the lid pocket of the backpack. He knows there's nearly a full clip, he checked. A dozen bullets. He'll have to make each of them count.

'Time's up, Sammy J. Thanks for the soldier bro-love.' Moose closes his eyes.

'What now?' says Ros.

'I don't know.'

The chopper lands nearby but unseen. The driving snow has reduced visibility, but Sam also guesses prudence on the part of the pilot: flatter, more open ground lower down the slope and around to the north. He wouldn't have been able to see them or the crimson smudge of Moose with the naked eye. Perhaps a thermal-imaging camera coupled with GPS coordinates recorded at the moment of Moose's exit from the chopper. The blades are still turning; the pilot not taking any chances. He won't want to hang around in this weather.

Out. Do the job. Back in. Get the hell away. Three Fs: Find, Fix, Finish.

How many times has Sam himself been in that situation?

There was that time of the mad dash after the squirter near the river. Sam first to take the jump from the hovering Black Hawk, leading the chase, blitzed on adrenaline. And then he found himself cut off from the others with two insurgents emerging front and behind. Where did they come from? He's done for. That's how easy it can be. Then Moose emptying his M4 into them and giving him a move on. 'Fuck's sake, Sammy, keep your eyes open.' Yeah, he'd owed Moose for that if nothing else.

There's a clump of boulders over to their left. Sam points Ros towards them. 'Quickly, stay there. Stay low.'

Sam slides along on his belly downhill to another rock cluster, creating some distance between himself and Ros, offering her half a chance to get away. What with the wind and the helicopter rotors, it's hard to hear much else but gradually, closer and closer, the crunch of boots through snow. How many sets? Two, maybe three, he thinks. And surely one of those will be Footrot.

Out of the blizzard they emerge. In a line, about two metres apart. Swaddled in their alpine gear, it's hard to tell who might be who. All armed with short-barrelled lightweight automatics. The one on the right needs a hand free to hold up his thermal-imaging device.

'Over here.'

Sam presses himself further down into the snow as they head his way.

'Yep, Moose alright.' Footrot's voice. Gently. 'Ah, mate. What'd they do to you?'

Sam risks a look. Sees the three surrounding Moose. Footrot kneeling.

'Gone?'

'Yep.'

'But they wrapped him up cosy, eh?'

'That'd be Sammy, he's got a good heart.' Standing. 'That right, Sammy?'

Sam has Footrot lined up in the sights of his Glock. Are they wearing kevlar under all that Gore-Tex? It makes sense if they don't intend hanging around. Better safe than sorry. A head shot then.

'Tell you what, mate, this is all getting a bit messy. Hear me, Sammy? Course you do.' Footrot has to shout to be heard against the competing rotor and wind noise. Thermal camera guy does a slow scan as Footrot speaks. Pausing momentarily on the clump of boulders shielding Ros. Her body heat will be giving him a reading as it rises above the rock cover. Continuing the sweep round towards Sam. 'None of us needs this shit.' Sam needs to act. Take the shot. Footrot raises his hands slightly as if in surrender. 'You've got a gun, probably pointed at me, yeah?' The thermal camera has now picked out Sammy's location. 'I just want to take Moose home. Give him a Christian burial. You okay with that, Sam? He saved your life back then, after all.'

Sam now has two machine-guns pointing his way. Thermal camera guy has packed away his gizmo and once again has both hands free. Sam crushes himself down behind the rocks just before the firing begins. He missed his moment. That's what it said in his performance reports: 'Lacks decisive thinking when it matters.' T-Rex's own words. The firing stops,

Sam knows why. He heard the yelp as Ros was hauled out from her hiding place. Sam looks up again. Footrot has her in a headlock.

'*Raouza*, Sam. Throw your weapon out.'

What are his options? Footrot is a known predator. He can't be trusted with Ros as his captive. Will the comrades curb his instincts or give him free rein? Join in, even? If Sam throws away his weapon and surrenders, he's probably a dead man. Maybe a bloody blaze of glory is best all round.

'Sam?'

He stands. Throws down the gun.

And Footrot pulls the trigger on his.

—

Jill's run out of people to piss off for today. Back home, she's made herself a sandwich and a cuppa and settled down in front of the heat pump and a sudoku. Cavanagh wants to talk but he can't have it both ways. If she's already suspended and halfway out the door, she's not going to let him haul her back in for a ticking off. Edward Milsom is no doubt on the warpath too, phoning anyone of influence who'll listen. Kristin Baker? Sticking pins into Jill's effigy maybe, summoning the dark forces of spin and reputation management. It would be nice to know what Stephanie Howden's home visit to Milsom was about. Jill didn't believe Milsom's denial that it ever happened. Not for a second.

Of more immediate concern: has Cav called off the mercenary attack dogs? Another call to Hughesy. 'What's new?'

'I've just been bawled out by Cavanagh. How's your day going?'

'You passed the message on then? Thanks, Hughesy.'

'No worries. Our ninjas have just kitted up and taken off into the wild blue yonder. Josie gave Cav a blast. He's storming around with the phone glued to his ear, fielding calls from brass, media, pollies and other bigwigs.'

'Cats and pigeons, Hughesy, my new speciality. The cowboys been grounded, then?'

'Not sure. I think they might still be in play. Poor timing rather than ill-intent.'

'Who's in charge of them, if not Cav?'

'A mob called DTS, according to the briefing.'

David Trembath. 'They based on site?'

'Not to my knowledge.'

'Where, then? What's the point of having an emergency or incident management centre?'

'Good point, Jill. Maybe ask Cav when you see him next?' A sigh. 'Look, much as I appreciate these calls from you, and the faith you place in me, I'm feeling a bit fucking used at the moment. If you've got an agenda, come up here and run it yourself. Last time I looked we were of equal rank and I was nobody's lapdog.'

'Sorry, Hughesy. Fair point.'

'Yeah.'

The doorbell rings. 'Love your work, champ. Take care, right?'

She signs off and goes to see who's there. Hears a car start up and take off at some speed. Opens the door to find a gutted pademelon on her welcome mat. Still warm, blood pulsing out of the wounds.

—

Sam is dead. Ros is sure of it. She lies facedown on the chopper deck, their boots on her back pinning her. The landscape rushes past the open door. Do they mean to push her out at some stage? Deliver her to safety? Unlikely. What story will they concoct? An armed confrontation. Sam killed in an exchange of gunfire. Hostage Ros killed in crossfire? Then why not kill her there and then? She can't be allowed to tell her version. Their problem, she thinks. They'll work something out.

Sam is dead.

She watched him drop after Footrot fired. Footrot, Moose. Shane, Brett – they're human beings. Almost. They're real, they're culpable.

After Sam dropped, there was a crackle on Shane's radio. The pilot summoning them. Time to leave, weather shit. Ros dragged away, more gunshots behind her. What was that about? Finishing Sam off, maybe. The wind inside the chopper is fierce enough to kill all by itself. What the hell is she doing here? A matter of weeks ago she was a semi-comatose, medicated wreck facing early widowhood and the gradual but inevitable descent into … into what? Something so dark and hopeless it was impossible for her to imagine. And yet here is Ros, today, playing Princess Xena in the Tasmanian wilderness. That's one way to stave off crippling depression and, in its own way, was fun while it lasted. Survival can be exhilarating, revitalising. Up to a point.

But Sam is dead.

Footrot talking into his helmet headset. 'Yeah?' Pause. 'It's done. No worries. But Moose didn't make it.' Pause. 'Your fucken problem, mate. You lot never understand that.' Pause. Increased pressure from his boot. 'Yeah, we got her.' The boot edges down to her backside in a stroking movement. 'What do you suggest?'

Ros wonders whether she should just jump of her own accord. Is that even an option? Her fate lies with them. With him.

'Pity,' says Footrot. Pause. 'Yeah, but we could blame that on Willard. She was his hostage after all.' Pause. 'Davey, mate. You might do the hiring and firing and drive the flash Audi these days but you know fuck-all about real war. You never did.'

A break-in crackle.

'While we're on ops, the pilot answers to me. Go fuck yourself.' Footrot tears off the headset and chucks it to one side. Looks down at her, shaking his head. 'What's to be done with you, Rosalyn?'

—

Jill has binned the poor creature and hosed the blood off her front doorstep along with the bloody footprints and trail down her path. Doorknocked some of the neighbours, but nobody saw nuthin. They tend not to around here. She took a photo with her phone of the pademelon in situ before cleaning up. Should she report it? Obviously a threat of some kind. She's keeping an open mind but top of her list are associates of Milsom and/or Kristin Baker. A bit beneath them, for sure, but they keep such distasteful stuff at arms-length. It could be Mark Limace or one of his incel mates but if it is, she's happy to go and smack him again. Gutted wallaby? In some parts that's a standard Tassie greeting. Join the queue, she thinks, after thirty years in the job you pick up a few enemies. But still, she leans towards Milsom or Baker. Plain umbrage at Jill's uppityness or had she, in fact, struck a nerve?

The alleged Steph Howden visit to Milsom's home. The old army relationships and interconnections. Now Trembath's DTS guns for hire leading the charge on the Willard manhunt. Take your pick, any or all. Her phone lights up with a text message.

Pull your head in bitch

Umbrage still a factor then, but with a degree of ambiguity. Was it a serious threat to her safety or just the Taswegian version of the spilt-drink death stare? Jill hasn't handed back her police-issue gun yet and that feels like a good thing. A call to Larissa the journalist to give her a heads-up that she might be in the line of fire too.

'Thanks for the warning. You okay?'

'Yeah, yeah, but let's keep in touch, eh?'

'Anybody there with you?'

'No,' says Jill. 'There's not.' She's been tough the last several days, but saying that brings an unexpected tightness to her chest.

'Is it worth staying somewhere else for a while?'

'I'll be fine, don't worry.' Out on the street a car revs loudly. A common enough occurrence in Montrose but Jill feels nerves jangling. Where did all this jumpiness come from?

'Have you reported the threat?'

'Not yet.'

'Don't take it lightly, Jill. We already know how far some people will go.'

'Yeah. No worries.'

—

What would Niamh do? Probably not find herself in such a position in the first place. They've landed. Ros hasn't a clue where she is but at least she hasn't been chucked out of the chopper from a great height. That's a start. The pilot took straight off again for who knows where. A parting glance her way. Hard to interpret. Driving now along a gravel road, one side deep bush, the other more trees and rocky outcrop. Daylight receding. Well down below the snow line now. It's raining, not so windy. Dare she say it's even marginally warmer? Ros is in the back of the car with Footrot while the other two are in the front. They don't mind her seeing where they're going as she's not meant to survive.

'Where are we going?'

'Shhhh.' A pat on the knee.

Sam is dead and Ros is beginning to wish she was too. The driver looks into the rear-view. Gives Ros and Footrot a wink.

Ros shifts in her seat. 'I need to go to the toilet.'

'Go ahead, sweetie.'

'Big time.'

A sigh. 'Pull over, Aaron.'

A frown in the rear-view. Aaron didn't want his name used.

'Don't worry about it, mate,' says Footrot. The implication chilling Ros deeper. The car stops, engine still running. Footrot gets out and goes round to Ros's side, opening her door. 'No toilet paper, you'll have to find a big leaf maybe.' A smile. 'Sorry, I'll have to watch.'

Ros steps up off the road into the undergrowth. Thick eucalyptus and myrtle from here on in until the crag rises out of the gloom. Footrot is fit, as are the other two. If she runs, they'll catch her in an instant. Ferns. Moss. That magical green-out that she would appreciate under any other circumstances. Further on into the bush, the rich damp humus smell.

'Please, Shane. A bit of privacy, for pity's sake.'

The look in his eyes says no. Says worse. A few steps on, a clearing. Already they're out of sight of the car, engine grumbling. Ros looks around as if for the perfect shitting spot. Sees what she wants and edges towards it.

'Oh, while I think of it.' She reaches down into the leg pocket of her hiking pants. They never bothered searching her. 'The pilot. I still have his phone from earlier. He'll be wanting it back.' She holds the phone out to Footrot's outstretched hand. And drops it. 'Oh, sorry.'

As he bends to retrieve it, Ros sweeps up the fallen branch, swinging it against his head. Softened by damp, it disintegrates on impact. Still, he's stunned, collapsing to the earth, wincing. She follows up with a kick to his face. A stamp. He's still not out and grabs her leg, pulling towards him. Losing her balance, she falls. Clawing and kicking, Ros tries to free herself. Her hand comes up against something hard. She relaxes her struggle and Footrot climbs to his knees to reclaim his prize. Close enough now, Ros smacks him full force in the temple with a rock, and there's a sickening, bone-splintering sound. He's out cold. Dead, she hopes.

The car engine still throbs. 'Hurry up, you two lovebirds,' Aaron shouts.

Ros collects the dropped phone, strides through the undergrowth, arriving at the base of the rocky outcrop.

And starts climbing.

—

Late Saturday afternoon. Jill has locked all the doors and felt the need to close a few curtains. Illogical, she knows, but if you can't see the beast and it can't see you, then maybe it doesn't really exist. The reckless swagger she had the last few days seems to have dissolved. This is the same woman who takes a truncheon to slimy misogynists, who speaks truth to entitled power. What happened? Yeah, well. Sometimes a door clicks behind you and a small voice whispers in your ear, reminding you just how alone you are. Depending on the timing, and your true emotional state as opposed to the front you put on, that tiny voice can bring you to your knees.

Thanks Dad, you old bastard. This is your doing.

Netflix murmurs away on her TV, some American nonsense but it fills a gap. On the coffee table in front of her: phone, Glock, taser and a mug of cold tea. What should she have for dinner? God knows. Eggs? An omelette maybe. Nothing too complicated. Or maybe something complicated and distracting is exactly what she needs? No, fuck that. Eggs. Boiled. With soldiers.

Samuel Willard. Are you what they say you are? Are you even still alive? And Ros, poor Ros. Jill mutes the TV; no Hughesy this time. Straight to the top.

'Yeah?' He takes her call, that's a good start.

'I know I'm suspended, Cav, but I thought you should know, as my superior, that I have received threats to my personal safety.'

'Yeah?'

Don't get overexcited, chum. She gives him the details. Gutted pademelon. Menacing text. 'I believe it to be connected to my recent inquiries into the Willard case.'

'What makes you think that?'

You wanting to close me down. You possibly in cahoots with a bunch of mercenary killers. 'The timing, Cav.'

'Reported it?'

'That's what I'm doing now. Boss.'

'Right. Sorry to hear that. Maybe report it to the local station too, yeah? Tell them I sent you.'

'Cheers, Cav. I will.'

'I haven't submitted that suspension paperwork yet. Been busy.'

'Any developments at your end? Just inquisitive, nothing more.'

'Might have an announcement soon. Our SOG chopper has spotted something. They're checking it out.'

Josie's Special Ops Group finally got a guernsey then. 'Let's hope it's good news, boss.'

'Fingers crossed.'

—

Breaking news in Tasmania now where police have been searching for army veteran Samuel Willard, wanted in connection with the murder of environmental activist Stephanie Howden on Bruny Island this week. The search efforts have been hampered by deteriorating weather conditions with high winds and snow down to three hundred metres in places, affecting visibility for spotter aircraft. Late this afternoon police announced a breakthrough.

'Two people have been recovered from an area in the southern section of the Cradle Mountain – Lake St Clair National Park. Tragically one is deceased and the other, in a critical condition, has been flown direct to Royal Hobart Hospital.'

'Why not Launceston? That's closer, surely?'

'The person in question has life-threatening injuries and Royal Hobart is best equipped …'

'… Who are the two people? Is it Willard and his hostage?'

'I'm unable to comment further at this stage. Thank you.'

Police spokesperson Ian Cavanagh there, rounding off that dramatic development in the Tasmanian highlands …

17

Ros is tiring. Her hands are numb with cold but she needs the gloves off so her fingers can grip whatever is available. It's blustery again, the higher she climbs. The rock face is wet, slippery, treacherous. Ros feels spacey, how long since she ate anything? Yesterday?

Her jacket is reversible. The olive-green lining now faces out. Black beanie pulled as low as possible to protect her ears from the cold. Is it enough to merge in against the background? She can only hope so. The wind and rain will discourage anybody from looking up. Instinct and presumption will tell them she's made a dash for it through the bush. What idiot would commence a free climb without ropes on a sheer cliff face in these conditions?

Is Footrot dead? Ros is not sure she cares. Hell, she must be getting a taste for it. All she can try to do now is to survive to tell her story. A month ago she didn't care if she lived or died. Not now. Here, fifty metres up a dolerite crag, Ros has rediscovered her life force. If this really is Niamh's last gift to her then it's as twisted as Ros had come to expect. The woman had a very dark edge to her humour and some of the revenges they cooked up for Mark Limace over a bottle of wine left her giggling in delighted horror. What might Niamh have dreamed up for this misadventure? Pushing Moose out of a helicopter and crowning Footrot with a rock would probably have met with her hearty approval.

Shouting below. Ros is surprised it's taken them so long. There'd been a 'Fuck's sake, mate. How long does it take?' call from Aaron a few minutes ago. This obviously wasn't the first time they'd been out and about with Footrot, allowing for his proclivities. If the bastard is dead, then good riddance.

'He's here. Shit, mate. What happened?' Groaning. 'Where is she?'

Crashing through the bush noises, more cursing. 'Fuck it, let the bitch die out here. We need to get going.' Damn, Footrot still lives.

A few minutes later she hears the car roar away.

Alone at last. For how long?

Mist creeps in, cloaking her. A good thing but bringing with it a further drop in temperature. Light fading, she's destined to spend the night here. She won't take the chance of climbing down in case they return. She just needs to find somewhere to wedge herself, defying gravity and the big freeze. If she survives the next few hours it will be a miracle.

—

Keep busy, keep those demons at bay. Jill has cleaned up her plate of scrambled eggs; so many eggy choices in the end, dizzying. It hardly touched the sides going down. Cracked open a bottle of Devil's Corner pinot noir and settled in front of her computer. Steph Howden. Where did she fit into all this? Her Facebook, Insta and Twitter pages are still up. Immortality granted under the terms and conditions. Plenty of tributes following her death. A few trollings. Nobody around to delete or hide the unwelcome postings. Steph lived and breathed her anti-salmon-farm campaign. Posting photos of debris, videos of late-night noise and harassment, sound recordings of threatening phone calls, screenshots of vile texts, sharing of news reports from around the world, petitions. If you were to base your perception of Stephanie Howden purely on her social media presence, then you would guess at a sharp, bitter, angry woman. Passionate for the cause but little joy to behold.

And yet. The Steph Howden that Jill met following the first attack and subsequently in Ginger Brown's coffee shop had a positive energy about her. The twinkle was still in her eyes, despite everything.

According to Hattie Milsom, Steph had paid her father a visit about a month before she died. Sometime possibly in late April, drifting into May. The postings from around then on all platforms show nothing out of the bizarre usual that was Steph's daily existence. Jill takes some screen captures anyway for insurance.

Her friends and followers. A lot of campaigners and activists, it seems. Jill recognises the names of some journalists among her followers. A few who insist on having their academic and scientific qualifications before and after their names. Jill takes a few more screenshots in case any of this stuff suddenly disappears. The techs would have gone through all this already, accessed Steph's messages, her emails, her search history, everything. If there was anything of note, it would have been passed their way. Wouldn't it?

Perhaps not. They would have been searching for specific threats, probably. Not friendly invitations to coffee a month before her death, or emails with 'interesting, read this' attachments from followers and contacts way back when. The police had a suspect in the frame within hours of the killing. Sam Willard. Why dig deeper? Cavanagh wasn't interested and his team weren't encouraged to be either. A studious lack of curiosity all round. A deliberate whitewash of the truth or just lazy police work? To be fair to Cav, all signs do point towards Willard. He was, and remains, warm for it. So why is Jill pursuing the matter based on a couple of texts from Willard saying 'it wasn't me' along with some possibly justified snarkiness from Edward Milsom and Kristin Baker?

Because somebody had messaged her to back off, shanked a wallaby and left it on her doorstep, that's why. And in Jill's experience, people tend to have serious reasons for doing things like that.

—

'Use your legs. Remember they're much stronger than your arms.'

'Says who?'

'Take your time, pumpkin. Don't forget to breathe.'

It's great to have Niamh back. That boundless self-assurance, comforting and infuriating in equal measure. 'Remind me. Why did I agree to do this?'

'Because you love me.'

'I could be home under the doona, eating chocolate, reading a book.'

Niamh reaches out her hand, smiling, encouraging. 'Nearly there. Come to me.'

Ros is bursting with happiness and relief. 'It's amazing having you back. I never thought ...'

'Back? I haven't been anywhere.' That hand again, stretching out. 'Nearly there. Come on, you can do it.'

It's windy and Ros shivers violently. Notices the grip Niamh has on the wall. Less than a centimetre wide for her toes and for her fingers. Tiny notches of nothing. Hairline cracks in the rock. How does she do it? 'Niamh?'

'Hmmm?'

'You won't leave me again, will you?'

'Never.' That hand. 'Just one more step and we'll be together again, forever.'

'I'm scared.'

'Don't be. C'mon. Do it.'

Ros steps out. And starts falling. The wind howls, Niamh screams. It's so, so cold.

But at least it's over now.

'Rosalyn?'

She opens her eyes. Bright lights shine on her. A wintry blast of daylight. The noise is deafening.

'Rosalyn?'

That's what Footrot calls her. They've found her.

'Rosalyn. Look up.'

She does. A helicopter hovers high above. Spotlight beaming down. Rain and sleet slanting through it. A man dangling just above her.

'Nearly there,' he says, reaching out his hand and smiling.

18

It's the first time in days that Ros doesn't feel chilled to the bone. Hobart Private, her own room. The last few hours a blur: flashing lights, movement, strangers, reassurances, various medical checks then, blissfully, sleep. In a real bed. She awakes to the feel of crisp, clean sheets, a view of snow-capped kunanyi, and Ian Cavanagh sipping on a takeaway coffee.

'Hi,' he says, sliding a second cup her way. 'Sleep well?'

'Yes. Thanks.'

'It's good to have you back safe and sound.'

'Yeah. How did you find me? I mean it's a huge area.'

'Anonymous tip-off. We were able to narrow the field and the thermal camera on the chopper picked you out. How good is that?'

Miraculous, thinks Ros. A tip-off from who? A guilty and remorseful henchman pilot maybe? 'Sam?'

'You're safe from him now. He can't hurt you.'

No. I suppose not.

Ian stands. 'I was on my way to work. Thought I'd call in and see how you're going.' A nurse appears and, just behind her, an orderly with a trolley of food. 'Breakfast,' says Ian, as if he made it himself. 'I'll leave you to it. We'll talk later.'

And away he goes.

Talk later. Yep, plenty to talk about. Murder, et cetera. Meantime, food glorious food.

'What day is it?' she asks the young woman removing her breakfast tray.

'Monday.'

'How long have I been here?'

'Two days, according to your chart.'

Has Ros missed a day? She's lost track. Okay, it's Monday. Monday and she's safely back in Hobart. And Ian wants to talk to her later. Fine.

—

'You survived the weekend, then?'

Cavanagh is cheery and Jill's not sure what to make of it.

'So far, so good,' she says. 'You wanted a chat?' He'd phoned her on Sunday. More dramatic developments than you could point a stick at. In essence, the manhunt was over, and Jill could play her part in tidying up loose ends. Starting Monday, 9.00 am sharp. What the hell?

'Yep, grab yourself a cuppa, I'm gathering the team in the meeting room. We'll debrief and distribute tasks from there.'

Jill retreats to the kitchen and sets the kettle boiling. Teabag in the mug, slosh of milk. Hughesy crosses her line of vision but ignores her enquiring gaze. Meeting room is standing room only. Cavanagh calls everyone to order.

'A communal pat on the back for us all for this weekend's work. Mission accomplished.'

Really? thinks Jill.

'Rosalyn Chen is safe and sound and recovering well in hospital. Expected to be discharged later today and, either today or tomorrow, we'll do a follow-up interview with her.'

'How was she located?' asks Jill.

'Anonymous tip-off.'

'Some passer-by just nipped into the phone box and suggested we look on that particular mountain?'

No reply.

'Which brings us to the next phase. Rounding off various lines of inquiry, clearing up the—'

'Loose ends?' Jill doesn't look up from her notepad. Why does she insist on winding him up? He's brought her back into the fold, for goodness' sake. Enjoy the moment.

'So,' says Cavanagh, staying calm. 'Summing up. We need a debrief interview, or plural, with Ros Chen to clarify exactly what happened out there.'

'And before, right?'

Finally, he looks her way, exasperation written all over him. 'What's your point, Jill?'

'Why Willard chose her. The events leading up to that. The texts that she, they, sent to myself and the ABC journalist before setting out, and the text during the weekend.' Jill looks to her colleagues for affirmation. 'The whole picture.'

'Sure,' says Cavanagh. 'But as for Willard, we won't know why he fixated on Ros until and unless he comes out of the coma.'

'Not looking good,' affirms Hughesy. 'One of the bullets lodged near his heart. A couple of mils to the left and he'd be a goner. Probably still is.'

'Would make life easier for us,' admits Cavanagh. 'In that regard, Jill, I'd like you to talk to the wife again. Find out what she knows or doesn't even realise she knows.' A smile. 'The whole picture, eh?'

—

Ros is cleared to leave by lunchtime. They just need a final sign-off by a doctor and to work out who's taking her home.

'I can manage myself,' she says. 'No worries.'

'It'd be better if there was somebody to pick you up.' The nurse checks something on his clipboard. 'A relative? A friend?'

'Is there a phone I can use? I lost mine ... out there.'

'Sure, I'll bring one for you.' Two minutes later he hands her a cordless, freshly wiped of any Covid germs, and shows her how to get an outside line. He leaves her in peace while she makes the call. Ros's capacity for remembering people's mobile numbers is shot to hell, so she tries good old-fashioned directory assistance and is eventually put through.

'Jill Wilkie.'

'Hi, Jill. It's Ros Chen here. I didn't know who else to call so ...' Ros realises tears are streaming down her face. A weekend of playing Warrior Princess in the wilderness; a few hours back in Hobart and she's blubbing for Australia.

They work out an arrangement and Ros advises the nurse. An hour later she's in the reception foyer with her ticket of leave and a prescription for another box of anxiety medication if she fancies it. Jill Wilkie comes through the sliding doors, Covid mask on, smiling with her eyes. 'Let's get you home, eh.'

Ros has no words while they dodge through the city streets. No tears exactly, either. Some deep breaths as she tries to regain equilibrium. Replaying the last few days – the terror, the privation, the exhilaration – the state she's in now feels like mourning. A return to the old Ros.

'Sam ...'

'Is still in ICU, not sure how he'll go.'

'What?'

'ICU, he—'

'He's alive?'

'Yes. Only just.'

Ros feels unmoored. 'Can I see him?'

'No. No way.'

They drive in silence for a while, up and over Tolmans Hill. Fluffy clouds in a crisp blue sky. Nothing real anymore.

'I killed a man.'

'I didn't hear that, Ros. Get yourself a lawyer. One of my colleagues will be speaking to you later today, or tomorrow.' She turns her face to Ros. 'Get a lawyer.'

'I am one.'

'Not good enough. Things are going to get complicated. You'll need help to steer your way through it.'

'Is Sam going to make it?'

'We don't know yet.'

—

'You know what you are, Sam?'

T-Rex holding forth; hear him roar. They've all had a few too many in Club Foot, the bar back at base where only the few are chosen and who dares wins.

'What?'

Turnell has the look in his eye. Sly, spiteful. Moose on one side, Footrot on the other. Egging him on. Between them all, enough alcohol fumes to cook a dinner.

'Fucken coward.'

'Tell me more.' Sam knows it's his turn today. Best just to take one for the team then move on. T-Rex has had a shit day and he's a kick-down kinda guy.

'You're not one of us.'

'How's that then?'

'Fucken dog.'

Here we go.

T-Rex softly flicks Sam's cheek. Leaning over to blow Bundy and Coke vapour in his face. 'Soft. Soft on the enemy. Soft cock, I reckon. Am I right?'

'Nah, mate. Another Bundy?' Sam stands to head to the bar.

'Sit the fuck down. I'm talkin' to ya.'

Sam grins, mirthless. 'Go for it, T-bone. Fill your boots.' He knows Turnell doesn't like being called T-bone. It's got to be T-Rex or nothing.

'That time on exercises in Tassie. You didn't have a fucken clue. Passenger, mate. That's what you are.'

'Hard to believe you had that fancy education, T-bone.'

The eyes narrow. 'Yeah, mate? Something to say?'

Sam doesn't need a fight. Especially one he knows he's not allowed to win. 'Nothing, no worries.'

'Say it, you fucken fraud.'

Sam shakes his head. T-Rex isn't going away. The fight isn't going away. 'Fraud? Try looking in the mirror, you entitled private schoolboy cunt.'

A few stitches and a lost tooth, but it was worth it.

Sam opens his eyes to a glare of white. Closes them again. Hears beeping. Footsteps. 'He's awake. Fetch the doctor.'

—

Jill took the message from Cavanagh on her way to dropping Ros off.

Willard awake. Meet the wife at hospital

Ros had decided not to stay at her own house. No explanation, but Jill could guess. The bad guys were still out there. The powers that be, Cavanagh et al, believe the only threat to Ros comes from Sam Willard, who is in custody. Why then would Ros need protection? Head meets brick wall, yet again. It's easier to lie low. Cat fed and stroked. Chickens fed, watered and re-released to free range. Eggs collected and donated to Jill. Nice, cheers. Overnight bag packed.

'How are my colleagues meant to find you?'

'Tell them I'm only prepared to speak to you. You know where I am.'

'Cavanagh will want to know.'

'Leave him wanting.' It was nearly lunchtime when Jill deposited Ros at her new temporary digs, a winery resort near Kettering, ten or so kilometres further south. It was the first and most absurd choice on the Booking.com search, Jill securing the booking with her card.

'Can you do me a favour?' asked Ros. 'I'll need a new phone.'

'I'll drop one off later today.' A smile. 'Try to relax, rest.'

And now back up the Channel Highway and Southern Outlet to Royal Hobart Hospital. Jill finds Kaz Willard sitting in the waiting room, nursing a cup of tea.

'Hi,' says Jill. 'Remember me?'

'Yes.' The woman is hollow, dark-eyed.

'Your baby?'

'With my friend. Back at Dodges.' A sigh. 'Why can't I see Sam if he's awake?'

'I expect they're doing tests and such.'

'You here to charge him, now he's woken up?'

'No.'

'Why then?'

Why indeed? This woman knows nothing more that will help them. Has Cavanagh given Jill this job to keep her out of the way? Why give her a job at all? She was already out of the way. 'This isn't a good time, and the most important thing is for you to get to talk to Sam. To focus on him.'

'And then?' She's no fool.

'Maybe I can make an appointment to have a longer chat with you.'

'What about?'

'Everything that's led up to this day.'

'Why?'

'To build a complete picture.'

'Of my husband? The man you intend to lock up for the rest of his life? The man you lot just tried to kill?' A snort. 'Get fucked.'

—

No car, no phone. Neither of those were much use out in the mountains of the national park. Here, now, they seem indispensable. Ros is floating between parallel worlds. One icy and unforgiving; time measured in blisters, distance, daylight, almost cartoonish in its extreme otherness. This alternate world, mundane and dependent, easy to navigate if you're suitably equipped. Seemingly impossible if not. No ID either. The vineyard accommodation outside Kettering wants ID and doesn't like the idea of being paid in cash. Ros had collected some cash from her home, but her wallet and ID are in a car parked up near the Walls of Jerusalem. Is it still there? Let me explain, I've just spent the weekend trekking through a snow-white rugged wilderness fleeing ruthless assassins. Not sure where my wallet is.

'I forgot it,' she says to the sceptical receptionist. 'That nice lady who dropped me off? She's my friend, a police officer. I'll get her to bring it later this afternoon. Okay?'

Reluctantly, yes, okay.

The room is pleasant enough. A glimpse of the Channel, and the decor is reasonably tasteful.

A nice long hot shower and perhaps a nap.

Drying before the full-length mirror, Ros examines herself. Sees a woman drawn and pale who seems to have visibly aged over the last few weeks. But she sees something else too. A sureness in the stance, a memory of the younger Ros. The spark in the eyes. That life force.

It would make sense to not stay here either. To keep moving, trust no-one. But where does all this end? It isn't sustainable. Almost immediately Ros has learned how troublesome daily life can be without your wallet and ID, a phone, a car. When Jill returns later today, she can vouch for Ros and give her a phone. Maybe she can organise to retrieve the car and her belongings from up north. That's a start.

The question remains though. Where does all this end?

It ends when Ros is sure nobody means her any more harm.

It ends when whoever killed Niamh faces justice.

—

'You're lucky to be alive.'

Sam realises that already. Wonders how long it will last. 'I was shot?'

The doctor nods, checks a beep on her phone and pockets it. 'Three wounds: left hip, high stomach, right shoulder, pectoral. Diagonal sweep, bottom left to top right.' She gestures to each spot on her own torso. 'The first and third, we've removed the bullets and cleaned up what we could. The middle one is still in there, bit too close to your heart. Too risky.'

'So?'

'Got a specialist flying in from Adelaide today. He spent some time in the US. Has more experience in dealing with gunshot trauma.'

'What are my chances?'

She smiles. 'Better than zero.' A nod in the direction of the door. 'Police guards. Australia's Most Wanted. Do I and my colleagues have reason to fear you?'

'No.'

'I can see I'm just going to have to take your word for that.'

'How did they find me?'

'Two bodies. Snow. Lot of blood. Not too hard to pick out from the chopper. Thermal imaging helped, at least one of you was still warm.'

'There was a woman with me. Did she …?'

'She's okay. I'm probably not allowed to tell you any more than that. Some police officers would like to talk to you. Okay with that?'

'Do I have a choice?'

'I doubt it. But don't let them drag you off to prison just yet. Might dislodge that rogue bullet.'

'Don't feel well, doc.'

She shrugs. 'I don't imagine they'll take long. Anyway, I won't let them.'

In they come, a man and a woman. Both masked as per the pandemic regulations. He's the younger of the two, looks like he aims to take charge. Sam recognises the other. She was among those women meeting for coffee at Ginger Brown that day. They introduce themselves: he's Ian, she's Jill.

'Won't take up too much of your time, mate. Know you're not well. Jill here is going to read the charges to you, explain your rights at this time, ask you a couple of basic questions for formality. Confirm you're who we say you are, stuff like that. Got it?'

'Got it.'

'Happy with me recording this on the phone?'

'Sure.'

Jill reads it out. Two counts of murder, some assault, trespass, theft. Any questions?

'Ros Chen?'

'Is no longer any of your business,' says Ian.

—

Jill has a PAYG mobile for Ros on the passenger seat next to her as she exits the city on the Southern Outlet. Late afternoon now, sun already behind the mountain and casting a creamy glow behind the black bulbous silhouette. Traffic building for the home commute. Cavanagh had been happy for her to do the honours on the formal charging of Sam Willard. His preferred offsider was running late, Cav was impatient to get it over with, and Jill was already at the hospital, after her terse encounter with the wife. Kaz Willard had been advised to return later as there were a number of medical and legal matters taking priority. That hadn't helped Kaz's mood either.

'How'd it go with the wife?' he asked after the encounter with Sam.

'Not good,' Jill explained.

'Win some, lose some.'

Jill, exasperated. 'So, am I suspended or what?'

'Don't mind me, Jill. We've all been under enormous pressure lately. Sometimes we need to let off steam. Pressure's eased. All hands on deck to nail this one, eh?'

'See you tomorrow, then.' Jill now knows why she never cracked that glass ceiling into management. She could never be so fucking erratic.

A tailback of traffic at the Kingston roundabout. School pick-up time exacerbated by a minor prang at the Blackmans Bay exit – somebody misjudging their dash for freedom. Some Classic FM to soothe the frayed nerves, except it's a martial piece with clashing cymbals and blaring horns. Station hop: ABC Radio Hobart taking talkback on the need for a Tassie AFL team, nah. Radio National discussing the resurgence of the Taliban in the face of the withdrawal of coalition troops. Up ahead, the pranged cars are being pushed to one side. Traffic begins to move again. Four o'clock, news time.

> *The body of a man has been discovered in bush in the Lake Binney Forest Reserve east of Derwent Bridge. Police are at the scene and unable to comment on whether the body is that of Victorian tourist Robert Beckett, missing since last Thursday. The area has also recently been the scene of the police manhunt for former SAS soldier and Afghanistan war veteran Samuel Willard, wanted for the murder of environmental activist Stephanie Howden. Willard is now in a critical condition at Royal Hobart Hospital being treated for bullet wounds. Police are yet to rule out a connection between Willard and the missing Robert Beckett ...*

Of course they won't rule it out. Jill had received a text from Willard and Ros using the dead man's phone. Jill has a bunch of questions for Ros as she heads down the highway towards Kettering. A couple of messages come through on her phone, both from Cavanagh. One wanting to know if Jill has any idea of the whereabouts of Ros Chen. A colleague has been trying to contact the woman for follow-up interviews but to no avail.

Sorry haven't a clue. Keep me in loop

The other asking if she heard the news about the body.

Yeah interesting

Jill needs to stop texting and focus on the road. She's setting a bad example, car veering towards the centre line. One day she'll master the art of bluetoothing. Back in control and dropping down the final hill to the turn-off for the Kettering vineyard accommodation. The car behind, slowing as she turns. The guy in the passenger seat giving her the middle-finger salute as they accelerate away.

—

'Babe?'

'What have they done to you?' Kaz tears up, gently strokes Sam's cheek.

'It's good to see you.' He wishes he could detach all the wires and tubes and hold her close. 'Ollie?'

'He's good. Misses you. I'll bring him in soon.' A pause. 'What's going on, Sam? This is all so fucked up.'

'Can't argue with that.' He feebly pats her hand. 'It's not over yet. Who knows where you are?'

'Best of my knowledge, the police, that's all.'

'Not sure we can trust them.'

'We have to, Sam.' She shakes her head. 'What did you do?'

'Nothing, Kaz. I never killed that woman on Bruny. I wouldn't.'

'Wouldn't you? It's what you were trained for.'

'Not cold-blooded murder.' Oh, hang on.

'The ABC journalist who came to the door that day? She keeps trying to call me on my mobile. Leaving messages. Where did she get my number from?'

'I don't know.'

'She wants me to pass her number on to you. Insisted. Don't know who she thinks she is.' Nevertheless, a slip of paper now on his bedside table. 'Is this linked to what she wants to talk to you about? The war crimes stuff on the news. Were you part of all that?'

'I was there, I know those involved.'

'Were you involved?'

'It was impossible not to be.'

Kaz looks like she wants answers and yet doesn't. 'Me and Ollie. We're still in danger, aren't we?'

Sam nods. Helpless, hopeless. 'You need to get away, Kaz. Before they find you.'

'I think it's too late. There's been someone watching the house for a few days.'

'Kaz ...'

'What, Sam? Run away somewhere? You've brought this on us because you've done wrong sometime or other. Some terrible thing. Stop ducking and weaving, making excuses. Man up and do the right thing, whatever that is.' She stands to leave, her face a hard mess of tears and determination. Flicks her fingers at the beeping machinery. 'If you're going to die, at least make me proud of you at the going down of the fucking sun.'

—

Ros has had a nap and feels refreshed. Met Jill in reception and got her to vouch for her on the matter of ID. Jill handed over the phone and now they're back in Ros's room. It's nearly dark outside. Jill will have to keep an eye out for wallabies on the way home.

'Up for a chat then, Ros?'

'Sure.'

'Let's take it minute by minute from when Sam Willard turned up outside your house as you were preparing to leave.'

'Minute by minute? This might take a while.'

'Figuratively speaking. As much as you can remember.'

Ros does exactly that. The guy in the tight teenager clothes, smelling musty and damp. Dazed. Blood oozing from his ear. Wielding a kitchen knife. 'He swam from Bruny to Tinderbox. Somebody threw a seal bomb near him in the water.'

Jill winces, looks sympathetic. Curious woman, emanating tough love.

'He convinced me that I was in danger. That he was the best person to protect me. Then he fell asleep.'

'You didn't drive straight to a police station. You believed him. Why?'

'It rang true.'

'You recognised who he was?'

'Yes.'

'But still you went along.'

'Yes. Did I mention the knife?'

Jill shifts in her seat, a hint of impatience. 'Do you realise how this looks?'

'I suppose so.'

A Macca's breakfast in New Norfolk followed by a new outfit from Vinnies. Then back on the road. Westward ho. 'We eventually got to Derwent Bridge. Sent those messages to you and to a journalist called Larissa something from the ABC.'

'Larissa Barclay.'

'Right.' A pause. Ros looks straight in Jill's eyes while she omits the earlier encounter, the shooting, the bush burial. 'Stole a car at Lake St Clair, left mine there. Then we drove for a further few hours around to the southern end of Lake Rowallan, parked up and started walking.'

'Why?'

'Desperate delaying tactic.'

'You never encountered anyone between New Norfolk and your final stop?'

'No.'

'You said you killed a man. Tell me about that.'

'That was later, when I escaped. I hit him with a rock. I'm sure I must have killed him.' Lie upon lie.

A frown. 'There was a report of a ute in a ditch on that very stretch of road at about the time you would have been going through.'

'I remember that, yeah. But there was nobody around, so we didn't stop.'

'Didn't see anything strange around then?'

'Like what?'

Jill sighs. 'Radio news today. The owner of that ute was found buried in a bush grave this afternoon.' She waggles her phone at Ros. 'Just updated on the website. His name was Robert Beckett and he'd been shot. You and Sam sent me a message using the bloke's phone. Stop messing about, Ros. Did Sam Willard kill him?'

Long pause. Panic mounting.

'No,' says Ros, finally. 'I did.'

19

Yes, she really did say that. Jill studies Ros. The woman seems remarkably calm for someone who just confessed to murder. 'I'm listening.'

An encounter on a lonely road winding north and west between Hobart and the Central Highlands. An exhibition from Sam Willard in the art of defensive-offensive driving. Four flat tyres. Jill had since learned that was deliberately inflicted with something sharp. Willard's doing.

'What made Sam think the guy was a threat?'

Ros shrugs. 'His actions. Plus he had a gun in his glovebox and a knife strapped to his ankle. He also had a tattoo that Sam recognised. A military one.'

Jill can easily check the latter when she gets the pathology report. 'Go on.'

A moment of panic, a killing.

'We wrapped him in my tent groundsheet, put him in the car and pushed on until we found that place down a back road.'

Lake Binney Reserve. 'What was going through your mind? You were digging yourself into further trouble.' Maybe digging wasn't the best way to phrase it.

A teary smile from Ros. 'I can't undo it.'

They buried him, retrieved the tent groundsheet and pushed on.

'You said there was a second killing, later?'

A pause, pregnant with calculation. 'I think I might have, I don't know.'

'Out with it.'

'No. The second one wasn't dead.' She starts to explain.

'Okay, I'm going to stop you there.' Jill doesn't like the way Ros seems to be dancing around this story. She's obliged to arrest the woman and charge her. Take her into custody and let the law take its course. But once Ros disappears into the system, Jill could lose access to her version of the truth, however erratic. There's an external semi-official narrative forming and if Ros finds herself in strife, it won't be difficult to persuade her to conform to that narrative. Jill is already well aware of the business and political pressure that has been brought to bear on this investigation and suspects there's plenty more where that came from. To what extent is Ian Cavanagh part of that nefarious network?

It's fully dark outside now. 'Fancy a drink? I could do with a stiff one.' Jill gathers her stuff. 'Just the one, mind you. Let's check out the bistro.'

'Bit public, maybe?'

'We'll find a quiet corner, keep our voices down.'

'Then what?'

'Then I can decide whether or not to arrest you.'

'So, it's not a sure thing, then?'

'Not yet.'

—

Sam is just drifting off to sleep when he senses a presence in his room. Probably the nurse with another vital signs check. He opens his eyes.

'Kristin?'

'Thought I'd drop by to see how you're going.'

'All these visitors today. Exhausting.'

Kristin is out of the usual D'Entrecasteaux uniform of company fleece or fluoros and is dressed for business. She notices that he's noticed. 'Conference. Sustainable Aquaculture – The Global Challenges Facing Protein Production.'

'Catchy.'

'Can't stay long, there's a conference dinner. Some movers and shakers in town.'

And purchasers too, thinks Sam. The takeover for D'Entrecasteaux Salmon. Ros had shared her research with him on the drive from Hobart to Derwent Bridge. 'I'm here,' says Sam. 'Still.'

'Yes,' she says, almost regretfully. 'You are.'

'I'm surprised they let you past the police guard.'

'Are you?'

S'pose not. 'So, what happens now? Pillow over my face? Lethal injection?'

She smiles. 'That's more than my job's worth. I'm hired to solve problems, not create more.'

'I'm all ears.'

'What a mess, eh?' A loose thread or hair on her lapel. Swept away. 'To be honest, Sam, what's gone on so far. Not the way I like to do things.'

'What *has* gone on so far?'

She tilts her head. Maybe wonders if he's wearing a wire. 'Let's call them errors of judgement.'

Sure. 'How would you have handled it?'

'With more finesse. Too late, it is what it is.' She glances at her watch. 'We're on a deadline, Sam. Time to draw a line under this.'

'I'm still not clear what *this* is.'

'Take responsibility, Sam. Do the right thing. Everybody knows you killed Stephanie Howden. You have history. It wouldn't be your first taste of cold-blooded murder.' Leans forward. 'Instead of tearing down heroes and blaming others, it's time you paid your dues – this one, that one, it all balances out in the end.'

The nub: keep quiet and take the rap. 'Then what happens?'

'Life goes on and the things we hold dear remain safe and sound.'

A threat to his family. Eloquently delivered but one all the same. Isn't it all too late? The genie is out of the bottle, surely? 'Where does Ros Chen fit into your clean-up plan?'

'Who?'

Sam observes Kristin rise from the bedside chair, brush herself down and straighten out the creases. 'Anywhere else in the world you, your mate Trembath, those dogs you set on us, whoever is paying you and pulling your strings, you'd all be busted by now. Facing a few decades in the slammer.'

'You think so?' She gives him a parting wave.

–

The bistro is doing relatively well even with the state borders still closed and mainland tourists down to a heavily regulated trickle. There's talk of open slather by the end of the year. People are impatient to get back on with their lives, for scientific reality to remould itself around their personal preferences. For the virus to just bugger off. Jill and Ros have found a booth in a quiet corner. Should do nicely. Jill has a gin and tonic, just the one as she'll be driving. Ros a lemon, lime and bitters.

'This is the picture based on what the police and emergency services have observed and experienced this weekend,' says Jill. 'Sam Willard and a man called Brett Armstrong were located by one of our police rescue helicopters. Willard in a critical condition from bullet wounds caused by a weapon in Armstrong's possession. Armstrong, in turn, dead from bullet wounds from a weapon in the possession of Willard. The inevitable conclusion: the men encountered each other and there was a shootout.'

'That's not what happened. That's not how Moose died.'

'Moose?'

'Brett. What's your understanding of what Brett was doing there?'

'He was a member of a specially trained remote and extreme terrain operations group—'

'Hired killer. He and Sam were in the SAS together in Afghanistan. They had history, something nasty that happened back then. Moose and Footrot.'

'Where do they get these nicknames from?'

'Boys. Go figure.'

'Okay, let's hear your version.'

A gruelling trek through snow, tempest and grim terrain. Sam woefully ill-equipped and suffering. The decision to turn back and hand themselves in. Moose and Footrot waiting for them near where they parked the stolen car. The helicopter ride and the intention to throw them out; as if they'd tumbled from a high crag in the poor weather. The struggle. Moose losing. 'Surely some forensic person could tell that Moose died from the fall, not from being shot?'

Jill nods. 'In a perfect world, yes. But I suppose these are ex-military types. Sometimes the usual rules don't apply.'

They got the chopper to set them down safely. Relieved the pilot and Footrot of guns, phones, walking equipment and gear to make life better for Sam and his blistered feet. Sent that second message to Jill and the journalist; blessed with good fortune in an area with very patchy mobile reception. Pushed on, with no immediate plan except survival. From a distance, through binoculars, spotted the fallen Moose. Still moving, still alive. Sam's decision not to abandon the guy.

'What?'

'A brothers-in-arms thing,' explains Ros. 'We made him as comfortable as possible, wrapped him in my sleeping bag. Then the others returned.'

Ros's capture. Sam throwing down his weapon and surrendering. Footrot shooting him. Ros recalls hearing two further shots as she was being dragged away. Assuming they were to finish Sam off. 'But he's alive.' Silent tears.

Yet another helicopter ride to somewhere, maybe the north end of Lake Rowallan? A guess only. Footrot in conversation with a bloke called Davey.

'Trembath?' asks Jill.

'Not specified. They were arguing. This Davey wanted him to bring me in. Footrot had other ideas. A sleaze. He would have killed me, eventually. After.'

Names flying around. Davey, Aaron. No longer careful. They did not intend her to live to tell the tale. A car ride, a bush stop. The struggle with Footrot. The climb up the cliff face.

'And here I am.'

Jill studies her, gobsmacked. 'You've been through a lot.'

'Yep.'

'You've told me everything?'

'Yes.'

'And it's the truth?'

A nod. 'Am I under arrest?'

'You should be.'

'But?'

'Until Footrot, Davey, Aaron and all the other mates are neutralised, I'm not sure I can guarantee your safety in custody.'

And that means confronting Cavanagh.

—

Sam doesn't believe Kristin will keep her side of the bargain. He also knows that he and Ros are key to the success or failure of Kristin's clean-up strategy. He and Ros are the only eyewitnesses contradicting the official version. If they are taken out of the game, then all that is left is research and conjecture by a cop and a journalist – easy enough to bury. Even if Ros somehow does make it, there can be no chances with Sam, he's also the only eyewitness to those events back in Afghanistan. He and Qadim. Qadim can be silenced any number of ways: threats to him and his family, he too could be killed. And where does all this leave Sam?

In prison for life or, more conclusively, dead. He needs a phone. Needs to warn Kaz, make her listen, stay safe. Warn Ros. Warn Qadim. Do the right thing, everybody keeps telling him. Kaz really does mean the right thing. Kristin means the smart thing.

The smart thing won't guarantee Kaz and Ollie's safety and it won't keep Sam alive. The people behind this are relentless, worrying who might have told who, who might have left something incriminating. Look at Ros, she had nothing to do with any of this and her activist partner was already dead. But that wasn't enough for them.

Sam tries to sit up. Body screaming at him to stop. It is as if he can feel that rogue bullet shifting inside, ready to nudge his heart. Game over. But he has to move. If not, then Kristin may as well have finished him there and then with a pillow over the face. He swings his legs over the side of the bed and almost passes out. This isn't going to work. Less than two days after being raked by a machine-gun, you don't get up and stroll out of hospital.

One thing at a time.

'Doc? Nurse?' No reply. Try the buzzer. Nothing. 'Hello?'

He lies back down. Exhausted. Dizzy. Hurting.

The buzzer again. Finally, a head around the door. But not a familiar one.

'I need a doctor, or a nurse.'

'I'm neither, friend. I push trolleys.'

'I need help.'

'I'm not sure I can, on my own. O, H and S, you know?'

'The guard, where's he?'

'Guard?'

'There's a police guard, outside the door.'

A quizzical look and a head bob to check. 'Nobody here. You sure?'

'Is there a wheelchair around?'

'Yes, down the corridor. You mentioned police guards. Are you a criminal? I don't want them to accuse me of helping any escapes.'

'Where are you from?'

'Moonah.'

'Not with that accent.'

'Ghazni, it's in—'

'Afghanistan. I was there. You're Hazara, right?'

A tentative smile. 'You know Ghazni? You were a soldier, maybe?'

'Long time ago. What's your name? Mine's Sam.'

'Iqbal.' They shake hands.

'Iqbal, I need your help, mate.'

'Yes?' A frown, replaced by a look of concern. 'Oh, you're bleeding.'

Sam looks down and yes, there's a spreading red stain at his hip. 'The guard has disappeared because people are coming here to harm me.'

'Like Don Vito in *The Godfather*?'

'Yes.' If you like.

'That is bulldust, my friend. What do you take me for?'

'Okay, one small thing. I don't want to get you into trouble, and I understand your concern. Perhaps you could help me to the chair by the door. Then bring the wheelchair and park it just outside. I'll do the rest and you walk away. How does that sound?'

'I don't know.' A pause. 'Did you kill Taliban when you were in my country?'

'Yes.' And more.

'Then just this once, I will repay the favour. Good luck, and don't dob me in, my friend, or I will find you and slit your throat.' A chuckle. 'Just joking.'

—

Jill has promised to phone in the morning if anything develops. Handed over her business card. For now, her advice is to rest up, try to relax.

Easier said than done.

While she's in the bistro, Ros orders from the room-service menu before heading back to her crib. Sliding the key card from her back pocket she sees her door is already open and slightly ajar. A housekeeping trolley just down the hallway. Restocking soaps and shampoos maybe. Plastic thimbles of UHT milk. But they did that this morning. Turning down the bedsheets, perhaps? She places her hand on the doorknob to push open. Sees the housekeeping woman emerge from a room a few doors down, take the trolley and go. Notices for the first time the scuff of soil on her threshold.

Withdraws and retreats down the corridor. This is crazy, she thinks. Paranoid. I need to be able to get back to my room. Relax. Eat. Sleep. Work out what to do next.

Back to the bar, find a seat in the corner where you can see everything, everyone. Have a drink to settle the nerves. It's the first time in days, weeks possibly, that she has felt the need for her old 'medication'. What happened to Ms Invincible? How fragile did that turn out to be? The pinot arrives; take a gulp. Breathe deeply.

Ros retrieves the phone from her backpack. Puts it together – SIM, battery, et cetera. Plugs it into the socket in the wall near her feet to charge up further. Puts the packaging back into her bag. Continues drinking and messing with the phone. Inserts Jill's number into the contacts. A covered tray at the kitchen outlet. Ros's room service order? Hard to see from here, but it looks like the club sandwich and fries she ordered. She leaves her wine and follows the room service order down the corridor. The young guy knocks on her door and announces himself. Ros dips back around the corner out of sight. Listens intently.

Her door is opened and Footrot's voice says, 'Yeah?'

'Room service? Club and fries?'

'Oh right, sweet, yeah. She just popped out, back in a sec.'

Back to the crowded bar, regain the seat, drink, think. He'll be out in a moment, wondering where she is. How did Footrot slip past her and Jill and access the room? Ros had been sitting with her back to the reception area. Jill perhaps too focused on Ros. Access the room? He's Footrot, special forces, ways and means. And now he waits for her in there. She looks around the bar. Is someone here watching her and communicating with him? Several people on their mobiles: texting, talking, scrolling. The guy in the corner, not even pretending not to check her out. Or is he just one of those blokes who likes to ogle? Why speculate? Time is running out.

Where to?

Stay here in plain sight, lots of witnesses. Summon the police at the same time. Which police? Summon Jill. Ros does so, Jill's phone is busy, so she sends a text instead. Looks up to see Footrot standing by her table.

'Mind if I join you?'

20

Jill has just finished talking with the journalist Larissa Barclay, updating and comparing notes, when she sees she missed a call from Ros. Brooker Highway northbound, the evening rush hour traffic thinning out. A message comes through.

footrot here help urgent

Fuck.

Returns the call, but no reply. For Kettering, the nearest police stations are at Woodbridge or Kingston. Woodbridge may or may not be manned right now. Jill takes her chance to do a U-turn and head back south, trying both stations as she goes. Is this, in fact, a job for the Soggies? Footrot and Co are ex-military and odds-on will be armed. That bistro was crowded with civilians. If the ninjas go in, it's fifty-fifty whether it degenerates into a hostage situation or is swiftly nipped in the bud. Besides, she'll need Cavanagh's say-so. Woodbridge rings out but Kingston picks up. Jill introduces herself and asks a favour. Tries Ros again. It rings out. Texts:

Police on way. Me too

The ninjas could be there quicker than her. She makes the call to Cavanagh. Explains the situation.

'Are you serious?'

'Yes.'

He whinges about her lack of protocol, shielding Ros from his interviewing team. Colluding with her, even.

'Add it to your list of grievances, mate. Are you going to do something or not?'

A studied pause. 'I'll sort it.'

'Make it quick.' Jill kills the phone and goes faster than the speed limit.

Along Domain Highway. Up Davey. Over the big hill. Minutes slipping away and Ros quite possibly already dead. Jill tries ringing again. And again. No reply.

These people are relentless. What, in this age of soul-numbing scandals, could be so worth killing for? War crimes? People stopped caring about that somewhere between Srebrenica and Aleppo. Environmental disaster? Financial impropriety? Corruption? Mate, we're just coming out of a pandemic that's killed millions. All we want is our freedom back and to get rid of those pesky face masks. Or is that the key to the relentlessness? A loss of perspective. It's been something of a theme these last few years, especially among entitled white men. Murder, corruption, war crimes? Yes, Your Honour, but this person was rude about me on Twitter, and I want you to throw the book at her.

A message from the Kingston patrol: they're in position. Jill lets them know she's about ten minutes away. Tries Ros again. Nothing. Tries Cav. Yes, the ninjas are on their way. He'll meet her there.

—

Footrot's wearing a beanie, puffer, jeans, blundies: Tassie winter formal. The edge of a gauze dressing peeping out the left side. A bruise where she stomped him. Head obviously harder than Ros had hoped.

'Yes, I do mind actually. Somebody will be joining me soon.'

'I'll just take the weight off until they arrive, eh?'

She raises her hand to summon one of the staff.

'Don't panic, Ros. Just want a word, that's all. No dramas.' He pours himself a glass of water from the jug on the table, loosens off his jacket and leans forward. Lets her see the gun in there, snug in its holster. 'We're not desperadoes.' Waves at the surroundings. 'Places like this, people like us, we've sworn to protect and uphold all this shit. We don't do indiscriminate. Unless we have to.'

She checks her phone and sees the message from Jill. How come she missed the preceding call? 'Have your word, then. The police will be here soon.'

'Reckon you could turn that thing off for me?'

'No.'

In a swift movement he takes the phone out of her hand and drops it in his pocket.

People are noticing. Sideways glances. A stiffening of postures in the immediate vicinity. He checks an incoming message on his own phone.

Glances around the room and frowns. Types a quick reply. Someone applying external pressure?

'Better make it quick, Shane. Say your piece and piss off.'

'Language.' Footrot doesn't like her attitude but he has a job to do. 'We're happy to let all this drop, as long as you do too. Forget everything and get on with your life. The world is full of conspiracy theorists, they drive everybody and themselves mad. Nobody listens and you'll never win. But if you persist, we will find you, even if we wait ten years or more. We'll always be out there. Got it?'

'Yes.'

He hands back her phone, having removed the battery. 'Be good.'

—

Jill joins the Kingston patrol blocking the unsealed road leading to the winery accommodation. Waves her ID at them through the windscreen, learns their names too. Exiting the car, she's aware of a buzzing noise. Looks around for the source. Finally looks up and sees a drone hovering high above. Bloody news crews.

'Either of you guys a crack shot?' She gestures subtly to avoid tipping off whoever's watching.

'Happy to have a go.' The younger of the two pulls out her gun, grips two-handed, aims and shoots.

Bullseye. The drone drops into the adjacent paddock.

'Nice one, Bev,' says her colleague.

'No comings or goings since you arrived?' asks Jill.

'Nothing.'

'How long's that drone been around?'

'Dunno,' says Bev, shamefaced. 'We stayed in the car to keep warm.'

'Fair enough.' Out north along the Channel Highway, blue and red flashing lights winding down the hill into Kettering. The ninjas that she'd expected would already be here. Jill lifts her chin at Bev's colleague. 'Matt, was it?' A nod. 'Mind retrieving what's left of that drone, Matt? I'd like a closer look.'

'Sure.' And off he goes.

'Are you aware of any other roads leading into the winery?'

'Nothing on the maps,' says Bev. 'Matt checked while I drove down here.

There are walk tracks, maybe wide enough for an ATV or quad bike.'

Too late to block those off, Jill realises. The price for her initial decision to go low-key. Her phone lights up. Ros.

He's gone. Where R U?

Jill rings. 'We're at the end of the lane. If he comes down this way, we'll have him.'

'I looked outside when he left. It was on a quad bike in another direction.'

Damn. 'I'll be up there soon. You okay?'

'Bit shaken but otherwise, yeah.'

Jill leaves instructions with Bev and Matt for the ninjas to search and seal any other entry and exit points, then heads up the track. A couple of wallabies and a bandicoot later she pulls up in the gravel car park outside reception. Notices the tyre marks from a quad bike which clearly took off at a skid. Ros is waiting for her in the reception area.

Blowing out a breath. 'He was waiting in my room but I didn't go in. He found me in the bar. I tried calling you but ...'

'Tell me what happened.'

'He told me to forget everything, keep quiet, get on with my life. If I did, they would leave me alone. If not, he'd come after me.'

'That's it?'

'He confiscated my new phone, kept the battery.' She smiles. 'I used the spare you supplied.'

Jill's thinking. Thinking about cars taking a great interest in her as she signals right and turns up a country lane. An abusive middle-finger to disguise true intent. Cars staying with her all the way from the city to Kettering and back again. About Footrot making a hasty exit. Tipped off about the imminent arrival of the ninjas? A colleague monitoring the drone. 'We must have been followed right back from when I first dropped you off at this place. Maybe even from leaving the hospital.'

'I can't stay here.'

Jill's not so sure. 'He's made the threat and left.' Examines Ros. 'It must be tempting to do as he says?'

'It doesn't get me any nearer to knowing who killed Niamh.'

A sigh. 'We might never know, Ros. Or never be able to prove it, anyway.'

'I can't drop this. It's the only thing that keeps me fucking going.'

'Woman after my own heart,' says Jill. 'I'll make some arrangements to get you shifted.'

—

Sam has parked himself in a room at the far end of the block on the same floor. It serves as storage for miscellaneous stuff: cleaning gear, stationery, and the like. It wasn't easy to manoeuvre the wheelchair through the door into the narrow space but he managed eventually. Now he sits there, light out, waiting.

It doesn't take long. Purposeful footsteps in the hallway. Two sets, he thinks. Urgent murmurs. A third set of footsteps, intervening. Iqbal's voice.

'Sorry, friend, I haven't seen anyone.'

'You sure?'

'I would like to think so, yes.'

'Check those wards down that side.'

Sam's pretty sure that's Dave Trembath speaking. He'd been wondering where the bloke had got to.

'Excuse me, gentlemen. May I ask what you are doing here?'

'No. This is a police matter. Now be a good boy and get lost.'

'It's just the Covid restrictions, sir. We're not meant to have members of the public walking around as they please. Especially without a mask.'

'Did you hear me, son? Off you go.'

Don't argue, Iqbal. Just do what they say.

'As you wish.'

'You wouldn't be messing with us, would you … Iqbal, that your name?'

'That's what it says on my badge, sir. No, I am not messing with you. I'll leave you to your business and get on with mine.'

'Cheers, mate.'

Steps approaching, doors being opened and shut. Sam has snicked the lock on this one and hopes it is enough to deter enquiry. Nearer and nearer. Just a few metres away now. Bump, twist of the handle.

'Oi, Iqbal, before you get in that lift. What's in here?'

'Storeroom, sir.'

'Got a key?'

'Not on me. I can try to find one if you like?'

A pause. 'Nah, fuck it. Don't worry.'

The steps move on. The lift doors close with a ding.

Trembath. 'Somebody tipped him off. Let's get out of here.'

'Isn't the bloke meant to be fucken half-dead already?'

'That's what I was told. Fucken Cavanagh couldn't organise a piss-up in the proverbial.'

'Cunt.'

'Yeah.'

—

The ninjas found nothing and have been sent home. Cavanagh wants a strong word with Jill. She's happy to oblige.

'What the hell's going on, Jill?'

'I was thinking the same thing.'

They're taking a stroll down the lane, out of earshot of whoever. Ros is busy packing her bag for another move. God knows where. It's getting colder, wind picking up. Scratchings and scurryings in the undergrowth. Dark out here, away from the glow of the hotel.

A sigh. 'What's your game, Jill?'

'Ditto, Cav. Previously I've been prepared to view your erratic, blowhard behaviour as just basic male incompetence. There's a lot of it about. But now I'm beginning to think there's more to it.'

He stops. Turns to face her. 'Meaning?'

'I believe that, at best, you're obstructing and undermining the investigations into Niamh Cassidy and Stephanie Howden. At worst, you're conspiring with others to murder certain individuals and to pervert the course of justice. Why? I don't know. Maybe they're paying you well, maybe they've got something on you. Maybe both.'

A bitter laugh. 'Don't hold back, Jill. Spit it out.'

'I'm guessing number two or three. What is it they're holding over you, Cav?'

'You're way out of order.'

She shakes her head. 'No, I'm not. How did it all start? Bit of mortgage help in this crippling housing market? Help with the career, some introductions. Before you know it, that helping hand is squeezing your nuts. It's turned into leverage. Blackmail even. That it?' Sees the truth of it in his eyes.

'Thin ice, Jill.'

She pulls her jacket tighter against the freeze. Feels the reassurance of the Glock clipped to her hip. 'All this blowing hot and cold. One minute I'm out, the next back in. Like a fucking yo-yo. That's your paymasters telling you what to do, changing their minds, back and forth. Wanting to know what I know, what I'm doing. If I'm in touch with anybody they're after, can lead them that way. If I'm onto them or not. Micromanaging you. Must be driving you crazy.'

'It's meant to be me giving you the talking to.'

'Sure, but your heart's not in it. You're sick of all this. Looking for a way out. Am I right?'

Jill sees calculation creeping into his eyes. 'And, hypothetically, what do you think my options are?'

'Hypothetically asking for my advice?'

'If you like.'

They continue the stroll. Off the gravel road and in among the vines. 'You could have me killed so none of this comes out, but where does it stop, Cav? You could leave the dark side and rejoin the Jedis. I could arrest you. You confess all and throw yourself on the mercy of the Commissioner, who might let you quietly slip away with your redundancy money, maybe piss off to the mainland or somewhere. All sorts of possibilities, mate.'

'Number one sounds best so far. Hypothetically.'

Jill is too slow to duck as something smacks into the side of her head. She's flat on her back, dazed, dizzy, sore. Cavanagh is straddling her, hand on her throat, the other curled into a fist.

'Why couldn't you just—'

Jill claws at him as the blows rain down. Feels her nose buckle, her lips burst. On and on, he won't stop. She can't shield herself anymore. Submits. Slides into the blackness.

—

They've gone. Sam unlocks the storeroom door and edges his way out, scraping his knuckles on the door jamb as the wheelchair squeezes through. The police guard should return soon: friend or foe? Maybe he was only obeying orders and is not necessarily part of the plot. Nursing staff, will they too magically re-materialise? Are they part of it or were they too sold a story? There's no point speculating. Sam needs to get out of here and go somewhere safe. Impossible, he realises, in his precarious medical condition.

The only way to remove the threat is to remove the point of the threat.

They want him to shut up and go away, preferably forever. If so, then his only viable option for now is to stay alive long enough to make a noise.

He needs a phone.

Over to the lift, press the down button and, ding, here it comes.

The doors open and he presses for the ground floor. Where might his new mate Iqbal be? At the very least there may be a public phone booth somewhere. Will he get that far? It's now mid-evening. Lift doors start to close but an arm comes through to stop them.

'I'm not sure you should be moving around, my friend. You look terrible and you are still bleeding.'

Sam checks. Indeed, he is.

Iqbal steps in and closes the doors behind them. 'Your friends are not nice guys.'

'You noticed.'

'I don't believe they are police, either.'

'Not wrong.'

'What a pickle.'

'Can I borrow your phone?'

'No.'

'Can you phone someone on my behalf? An ABC journalist.'

'ABC?' Iqbal beams. 'Of course. They are the best. Who?'

Sam gives him the slip of paper Kaz brought in. Larissa's deets.

'Never heard of her. Does she do the Breakfast show?' He hands the phone to Sam.

—

Ros is ready to hit the road. All she needs is for Jill to come back from the bollocking from her boss and away they go. Ros would like to call in at her Margate house. Pick up a few useful basics to make life and her ongoing researches easier. She wonders about Sam. Will he pull through? What fate awaits him? If he doesn't die, it seems certain that the powers that be will at least see him buried in prison for the foreseeable. She checks the time on her mobile. How long does it take to tell someone off? Maybe the boot is on the other foot and Jill is doing the telling. She certainly seemed in no mood for any nonsense when Ian showed up huffing and puffing. He was far removed from the calm, caring, nice guy he presented when Ros first met him. It seems clear now that his strange intrusive behaviour was aimed at finding out how much she knew about whatever it is that worries them. Whoever they are. Inconclusive in her case, she would have thought, but obviously they don't allow for that kind of uncertainty. Maybe her decision to join that meeting at Ginger Brown was the trigger for them.

Does Jill have a point? Maybe Ros should let this slide. Niamh was a fighter, but she would also want Ros to move on, heal, be happy. But this new drive, this impulse, feels like it is part of the healing process. Ros is loath to discard it so soon. Where the hell is Jill?

Outside in the car park she sees Ian Cavanagh walking purposefully towards his car, key fob in hand. The lights flash and in he gets. Ros tries to catch his eye but he looks right through her. Reverses in a crunch of gravel and drives away at speed. That must have been some row they had. Ros looks forward to Jill's take.

Two minutes pass. Three. Four.

Time to take a walk.

A hundred or so metres down, well outside the pool of light from the reception area, she finds Jill lying at the side of the gravel road. Deathly still. There's blood, a lot. Drag marks. She was placed there. Checks the pulse: weak but present. Checks breathing. Yes.

'Jill?' she says softly.

No response.

Ros summons an ambulance. Then phones up to hotel reception for somebody to bring first aid. Is there, by any chance, a doctor or nurse in the house?

There is. His name is Tony, retired now but happy to take immediate charge.

'Is she going to be okay?'

'Can't say yet. We don't know what's going on internally. The external injuries could look worse than they are. We'll see.'

The ambulance arrives and Tony wants to know if Ros is going to accompany the patient.

'I, um ...' She really doesn't know any more. They are everywhere. They're not going to stop. She feels once again that surge of panic and despair.

Jill opens an eye, says something, barely a whisper. Tony leans in to listen. 'She says you're to take the car.' More whispering. Tony gently feels in Jill's pockets. Retrieves a key fob. 'Here.'

The ambos do their bit and Jill is lifted onto the gurney. Ros gets as near as she is allowed. 'Was it Ian?' Jill winks in reply, or is that a wince? 'Whatever it takes, Jill. Hang in there. We'll win this.' Who is she to promise something so futile?

The paramedics take contact details from Tony, the retired doctor, and from Ros and away they go.

'She's a police officer?' asks Tony. He waves sadly at the ambulance. 'Line of duty, eh.'

'Yes.'

'And you're her colleague?' He's holding out a pistol, must be Jill's. 'You'll be wanting this, I expect.'

'Yes,' Ros says. Cold resolve settling in. 'Thanks.'

21

Tuesday. Sam wakes up to new surroundings. He's in a private hospital in South Hobart with an excellent view of the mountain, which is in fine fettle this early June morning. Larissa Barclay showed up late last night with, as requested, officers from the joint AFP–OSI war crimes investigation team. Sam was offering a full confession and full disclosure of all he knows. He's in their custody now. Two big guys, well-armed, outside the door. Murder charge or not, Tas Police can't have him until the Feds have finished with him; they've pulled rank and it's not gone down too well locally. Still, he knows, all this does is buy time. Postpone the inevitable.

Either way, for now, Sam's safe from any corrupt Tasmanian police and Trembath's DTS goon squad; and he continues to get the medical care he needs. He's scheduled for an operation later this morning to stabilise things in his chest. A period of recuperation to follow before some intense questioning. No breakfast this morning since he's pre-op, which is a shame because it smells inviting. Meanwhile, if he's up to answering some preliminary questions, that would be appreciated.

'You're entitled to legal representation,' says Grace from the Australian Federal Police.

'No, you're all good.'

'Great,' says her colleague Grant from the Office of the Special Investigator. Sam recognises the bearing of an ex-military man, a senior one at that.

Larissa has been granted permission to film the proceedings for her podcast on certain conditions of embargo and veto rights of the authorities. The war crimes team set their own recording equipment whirring.

Everybody's ready to go.

Grace wants Sam to identify himself, the SAS unit he belonged to, his tours of duty. He rattles it off. Any dirt he has on other people is for further down the track. For now, the priority is to nail him down on his own culpability. No backing out later or changing your mind. No wriggle room. Confession time.

Pop the cunt, Sammy. I won't say it again.

He recounts his first tour in Uruzgan. North of the provincial capital, Tarin Kowt, a hamlet in a strip of fertile green farming land. Three in the morning. Grant and Grace interrupting here and there to check dates, locations, who he was with.

It had been a long wait but worth it. Their objective, a high-value target: a bomb maker whose IED had killed their colleague a month before. Name and date check please, says Grant. The killed colleague, the date, name of the bomb maker. The latter escapes Sam's memory for now. No problem, says Grant. They'll come back to it later.

Chopper touchdown. Some running around. Shouting. The odd angry shot. Then the patrol commander called him over, eyes shining possum-bright in Sam's NVGs. Name of the PC please, says Grant.

Turnell. Michael Turnell.

'Your turn, big boy.'

'What?'

Turnell nodding down at the kneeling, blindfolded prisoner. 'Pop him.'

It's a joke, to test him, thought Sam. A packet of sky hooks, SAS-style. The prisoner can provide intel, they need him alive, surely? Sam had chuckled. 'Yeah, mate. I'm good, thanks.'

'Pop the cunt, Sammy. I won't say it again.'

Grace wants him to confirm that those were the exact words used. Yep, they were. Pop. The. Cunt.

Turnell was serious, he really did want Sam to kill the guy.

A chill wind blowing along the valley. The prisoner hunched in, shaking. Sam levelling his M4, popping the guy as ordered.

'Good boy.' The sergeant had patted his shoulder. 'Welcome to the club.'

Sam's blooding. The kill captured on someone's mobile. The collective insurance.

Grace and Grant making a note to follow that up. Some people in Defence have it, Sam says. They showed it to him. Who? Grace wants to know. Grant says, don't worry, I'll follow it up.

They'd fitted the corpse with a battle bra, two ammunition clips, a mobile and a pistol. Took the happy snap and away they went.

'That photo should be on the record somewhere too,' says Sam, looking directly into Grant's eyes. 'Bloke called Liam. Try him.'

No problem, Grant is on the case.

'You never hesitated, never believed what you were doing was wrong?' asks Grace.

'No,' says Sam. 'I was under orders.' He's suddenly aware that his face is wet with tears.

Larissa looks happy. She later tells Sam she'll call this episode 'The Blooding'.

—

After driving aimlessly for several hours in Jill's car, Ros had decided to rest up at Jill's place. The address was on an envelope in the glovebox and the sat nav took her straight there. Sure, the bad guys could be watching, they could be anywhere, but Ros needed sleep. It seemed mercenary to be using Jill's car and home like this when the woman was smashed up in hospital but she reckoned Jill would see the sense in it.

The place felt both neglected and lonely yet possessed its own homely individuality. The food cupboards and fridge spoke of a woman who didn't have the time or inclination to prepare healthy, fussy, labour-intensive meals for herself. No Ottolenghi nonsense here. No pictures of family or friends on the fridge door. No books, CDs, evidence of any external interests or hobbies. The centrepiece of the lounge room was an armchair with a recliner lever and a side table marked by coffee-cup rings. The TV remote lay on the seat. The TV itself a monster, the screen occupying most of the facing wall.

Ros had made herself a cup of tea then gone to bed in the spare room. It was cold and the sheets smelled musty. Did Jill ever have visitors occupying it? Ros had been unable to sleep at first, and when she finally dropped off it was fitful and populated by Jill's bloody face and Footrot's menacing presence.

And now here she is again driving around the suburbs on this cool, clean, sunny day. Her bag is in the boot and Jill's police-issue pistol is in the glovebox. She's also borrowed Jill's home laptop. Not password protected, very lax given her job, but there doesn't appear to be anything controversial on it.

Why would Ian Cavanagh do such a thing? Where is he now? Ros should report him, but who to, and who would listen? Maybe Jill is already awake and has given a statement. All Ros can do then is back up Jill's version with whatever she observed. Yes, he was there. He must have been the last person to see her before the attack. He made himself scarce. Ros wishes she still had her wallet and her original phone. His number was in one, his card in the other. Maybe she could phone him. To what effect? Hi Ian, was that you who half-killed Jill last night and scarpered? Aimless driving, aimless thinking.

Her wallet and laptop are still in the car parked up beyond Derwent Bridge. Maybe she could drive up there now and retrieve them? Or has the car already been impounded? Or are the bad guys waiting and watching?

No. Back to Margate. Pick up some essentials and hit the road. Ros joins the morning rush hour on the Brooker and heads south through the city and beyond. Davey Street southbound is snarled, an accident or breakdown somewhere ahead. She ducks down past the Conservatorium of Music onto Sandy Bay Road, then drives past UTAS campus with the Derwent on her left, glinting in the morning sun. Magnificent.

Sam had put all this madness down to war crimes in Afghanistan, but Stephanie and Niamh knew nothing of that. All they knew was that Big Salmon is destructive and dangerous. Sam will have to fight his own battles on the issue of war crimes. Ros, if she is to get to the bottom of this, needs to focus on fishy business. On through Taroona now, winding on to Bonnet Hill, the Channel and Storm Bay opening up before her. Salmon farms in the distance, floating on the surface of those calm, beautiful waters.

Ros has an idea where she can hide out.

—

Jill feels like she's been hit by a bus. Cavanagh beat the crap out of her and tried to choke her to death, but no permanent damage. Nose may need to be reset. Panda eyes. She'll feel sorry for herself for a while, the doctor had said.

'Business as usual, then,' Jill had joked, a raspy whisper.

Cavanagh had stopped, held back. He'd been unable to go through with it. She remembered the sensation of being dragged. He wanted to make sure she was found, didn't freeze out there.

From her hospital bed, Jill had made her report to the coppers in Hobart local. She hoped they would keep it out of HQ but they weren't stupid. They wouldn't want a bar of it, handballing it upstairs. Nobody knows where Cavanagh is. It's all a bit embarrassing and shameful. Everybody seems to wish it had just never happened. Jill couldn't agree more.

Was it a good idea to loan Ros her car? It seemed so at the time. Even more concerning, where the fuck is her gun? The mobile, thankfully, is still in her possession. She had pre-entered Ros's new PAYG number before handing the phone over. Ring, ring.

'Don't forget to refill the tank before you return it.'

'Jill! Thank God. How are you?'

'Been better, but the doc says it's nothing terminal. Where are you?'

'Just coming into Margate.'

'Your house?'

'A quick visit, pick up a few things.'

'Okay. Then where?'

A pause. 'Not sure yet. Are you still in hospital?'

'Should be released later this morning.'

'I can pick you up?'

'No. I don't think it's safe. Find somewhere, then let me know when you feel you're ready. Keep your head down.'

'Ian? Has he ...?'

'No word yet. Don't know what's happening.' Murmurs in the corridor. Footsteps approaching. 'Ros, have you got my gun?'

'Gun?'

'It's missing. Not recovered from the scene.'

'No, I haven't.'

The hospital room door opens. By the looks on the faces, it's not good. Jill will have to let Ros slide for now. 'Speak later.' She puts the phone down, notices Hughesy for the first time.

'We found Cav,' he says.

—

Sam has been provided with a mobile from the war crimes task force. They'll be monitoring it but hopefully it will be secure from the likes of DTS. He's tried to call Kaz but there's no answer. She must be wondering where he is, why he's no longer at the public hospital. Worried, maybe.

Man up and do the right thing, whatever that is.

Done, love. What now?

Several years in the slammer, if he lives that long. He wonders about the state of play with the Tassie cops and with DTS. Wonders if Michael Turnell has got wind of this early morning confession.

Sam has had all his vital signs checked for pre-op and will be wheeled down to the theatre soon. If anybody is to finish him off, then that's the place to do it. Out for the count, helpless, something unforeseen in the chest cavity, or a fatal mix from the anaesthetist. They don't even need to kill him, just render him a vegetable. These and other cheery pre-op thoughts assail him. What about Ros? How is she going, where is she? A knock on the door and Larissa Barclay pokes her head round.

'Can I come in?'

'Sure.'

'That was very courageous, what you did earlier.'

'My options were limited but yeah, thanks.'

Larissa bites her lip, perhaps not sure whether she should say this. 'Lot of buzz around, things happening.'

'Yeah?'

'A police officer, Jill Wilkie.'

'Yes, I know who she is.'

'Attacked last night. Badly beaten. She's in hospital.'

'Really? She going to be okay?'

'As far as I know.' A pause. 'Something else.'

'Yeah?'

'Her boss, Ian Cavanagh. He's been found dead.'

'How did he die?'

'Car crash, hit a tree on Woodbridge Hill Road.'

Channel country. 'Are his death and her attack linked?'

'Not known, yet.' A frown. 'What's going on, Sam?'

He shrugs. 'Wish I knew.' The porter arrives to take Sam to his immediate destiny.

'Good luck, Sam. See you when you wake up.'

Yeah, he thinks. That'd be good.

—

Ros pulls into the driveway of her Margate home and immediately knows something isn't right. The chooks are scratching and pecking in the front garden. They shouldn't be able to get around here unless one or both of the side barriers has been left open or blown down. The latter is possible, there have been some big winds through of late. But there's another thing. A gap at the bottom of her garage roller door and a buckle in one of the sides. The buckle probably stopped it from being closed properly again. Must have been jemmied open.

If somebody has been through her place, hopefully they're long gone. Still, she is comforted by the weight of Jill's service pistol as she turns the key in the lock of the front door. Slow leaden steps down the short hallway. A chill in the air. Push open the door that's already ajar.

The place has been trashed. No effort to disguise their visit. Main bedroom first: mattress half-pulled off the bed and sliced through, bedclothes and clothes from the wardrobe strewn across the floor, bedside table drawers open and contents scattered. En suite bathroom a mess. A similar picture in the lounge room: furniture slashed, bookshelves pulled over, TV shattered on the floor. Kitchen: drawers and cupboards open, foodstuffs strewn across the tiles, crockery smashed. She doesn't need to go into the other rooms to guess.

Except the office.

The desk drawers opened and tipped out, bookshelf upended, the usual. Luckily the new laptop she bought to replace the stolen one is, she assumes and hopes, still in that car parked up north.

These weren't burglars. They could have taken the TV, some kitchen gadgets, whatever. Someone was looking for something. And Ros knows exactly where to find it.

Out to the shed, rummaging deep into the chicken food bin and there, elbow deep among the layer pellets, is the USB. There are a few eggs in the nest boxes so she collects them. Thanks the chooks who've all hurried around from the front garden now they know she's here. Tops up their water bowls and food treadle bin. Reseals the side gates. She'll close up the house and leave the mess for another day. Wonders if the week's worth of food and water will be enough for the chickens.

Wonders if all this will be over by then.

From the corner of her eye, over by the saltbush, flies buzzing. The tree stump they use for chopping firewood for the rare occasions when they'd set up the fire pit in the backyard.

'Oh no.'

Monica the cat, held in place on the block by a tomahawk in the neck.

—

'Why would he do such a thing, Jill?' Hughesy seems genuinely perplexed.

'What? Attack me or kill himself?' Preliminary indications from Traffic are that Cavanagh's car drove deliberately into a tree. No marks suggesting loss of control. Early days though.

'Both, I guess.'

They're sitting in the hospital reception area waiting for Jill's clearance paperwork to come through. People are staring at her facial injuries, like she brought them on herself. She's got her obligatory face mask on but the damage still shows. Hughesy has agreed to drive her home. Hasn't asked where her car is or enquired about her gun.

'He was bent, Hughesy. I challenged him about it.'

'Serious?'

She points to her face and neck. 'You think he did this for nothing?'

Hughesy shakes his head. 'What'd he think that would achieve?'

Curb your empathy, mate. 'I guess we can't ask him now.'

The paperwork arrives and Jill agrees to wait for Hughesy to bring the car through to the entrance. Walks slowly to the doorway as he pulls up; it's not full-on pain she feels, more a sense of brittleness. Stoops into the car, wincing.

'You sure you're okay for discharge?'

'Yep.'

Out through the traffic onto Liverpool, sharp right up Argyle. 'Your car'll be back in Kettering, yeah?'

'S'pose so.'

'I'll check what's happening with it. Get someone to pick it up. You got the keys?'

'No. It was all a bit chaotic. No rush.'

'What was that all about anyway, the Kettering thing?'

'That Ros woman who was rescued at the weekend. She was feeling threatened.'

'Enough for the ninjas?'

'Yeah.'

'But instead, you ended up in a fight with Cav.'

'It wasn't a fight, Hughesy. He attacked me.'

'After you called him bent.'

'That's right.'

Right down Burnett and join the Brooker left heading north. Traffic steady but flowing. Sun shining and still a glimpse of snow on the mountain. Everything sharp and bright, too much so. 'You and Cav never really hit it off, did you?'

'No,' she admits. 'Not really.'

'And now he's dead.'

'Wasn't me, Hughesy. I've got a rock-solid alibi.'

'Poor bastard. Must have been in a bad way, mentally, to do that to you.'

'Yeah. Must've.'

—

Ros has never been to this part of the world even though she's been living in Tasmania for nearly four years now. No good reason, just never got around to it. Not quite sure where she's going but remembers the general area from news reports and feels sure she'll recognise it when she sees it.

Besides, it'll probably have crime scene tape still in place.

Steph Howden's Bruny Island house is pretty much where Ros thought it would be and is easily identifiable by the fluttering Tibetan prayer flags she remembered from the news. The cordon tape has been largely removed apart from across the front door. There's nobody around. Ros parks the car at the rear, out of view from the road, and approaches the back door, also covered by tape. She snaps it and tries the handle. Locked. Feels under the nearby geranium pot for the key. Bingo.

Inside, it's been cleaned up, the strong smell of industrial-grade cleaning agents hanging in the air. Other chemical smells, perhaps associated with whatever forensic activities were carried out. Even with sunlight streaming through the north-facing windows, the place feels chilled. Through the windows, that blighted view. A poisoned paradise of green hills, blue sky, silver shimmering water and ink-black salmon pens.

Ros checks the fridge, thankfully cleared. She'd picked up some provisions at the Oyster Cove store on her way through, plus she has her freshly harvested eggs. Foodstuffs packed away, she finds a room to sleep in. She's not Goldilocks, she'll leave the most comfortable-looking bed, Steph's, alone. There's a guest room, it'll do fine. Outside she hears the steady thrum of the salmon farm runabouts, the clanking of the hydraulics, occasional shouts, sees a large factory boat approaching from further out in the Channel. Steph Howden lived with this day in and day out. It must have gnawed at her, right up until the day she died.

Where exactly did Steph die? That detail wasn't reported. Ros can't see any sign, but that's probably the wonder of trauma cleaners. What will become of this place? Ros assumes adult offspring will sell it. Or a sibling maybe. She knows so little about this woman yet, in that brief encounter in the café in South Hobart, she'd perceived a fighting spirit still to be completely wrung dry of her residual joy and humour. She wishes they'd known each other longer, better. Ros suspects she could have learned much from the woman. It's afternoon now. Shadows stretching. Ros should probably get to work. Maybe she should also let Jill know where she is.

Maybe not.

Ros thinks about her trashed home. What was once meant to be a love nest for her and Niamh. The casual and cruel carnage inflicted on their pet cat. Some people are born into perpetual war zones, their lives always in turmoil, danger and uncertainty every day. How do they manage to live like that? Simple. They have no choice.

A dull whump out on the water followed by a splash and a triumphant hoot. Ros takes in the scene. A runabout circles what looks like a dead seal bobbing in the waves, revving and swerving, tearing up the Channel.

—

Hughesy has dropped Jill off at her Montrose home and told her to call him if she feels at all wobbly. She promised him she would. The hint of something different about the place. She wanders from room to room, then realises what it is. It's slightly tidier than she would normally leave it. The spare room gives it away. Ros, she thinks. Fair enough, not a bad idea to hole up here for a while. But something's missing. A few moments later she realises – her laptop. Ros is becoming increasingly wily and resourceful. A tad sly too, perhaps? She slept here, has Jill's car and laptop and possibly her gun, and is out there somewhere determined to push this as far as it will go. The woman might have made a good cop.

Jill flicks on the kettle and, a few minutes later, settles into her recliner with a cuppa. Pulls the lever and pushes back to get comfy. Zaps the TV with the remote. News 24. Taliban retaking Afghanistan following the pullout by Western forces and in the face of mass desertions by Afghan military. Women back behind closed doors. Old scores being settled. Collaborators fleeing for their lives. So, what was the last twenty years about then? Jeeps, utes, trucks all carrying heavily armed young men. A glint in their eyes, resolved to prevail no matter how long they need to wait, no matter what they might endure, no matter the overall cost.

A theme. Here too, young heavily armed men under cover of war fulfilling and claiming what they believed to be their destiny. A reckoning. Only these were our heavily armed young men. Was that really what was behind all this recent madness in faraway Tasmania? The case for the affirmative is building. Willard no longer in the custody of Tas Police and now in the hands of a federal war crimes task force. Lots of local noses out of joint. Who will lead the investigations now that Cavanagh is no more? And who will look into Cav for that matter? A whole bunch of 'shoulds' forming in her head but she's in no fit state to pursue them.

Maybe a nap. Some Panadol for her sore body.

The chaotic scenes on TV. The crime scenes in Tasmania. Both the inevitable outcome of something that's been brewing for years. Jill had tried being in a local book club once. Part of a New Year's resolution to make a few friends. It didn't work out, the meetings kept clashing with a robbery or a rape or a murder. Besides, she'd found it difficult to set aside the time and concentration needed to do the actual reading. But one book title had stood out for her. Maybe they'd chosen it knowing she was a cop, thought it might appeal.

Chronicle of a Death Foretold by some South American author.

She hadn't forgotten the title even if she still never got around to reading the damn book. It resonated now. All this grief over there and back here, foreseeable if you knew where to look. All foretold if anyone was listening. All of it a long time in the making.

22

I'm dead. This time for real.

Pinned down by enemy fire with nowhere to run. Two Afghan Wakas dead and the new guy, the Queenslander, wondering where the rest of his left leg is. Walking past the southern wall of the compound when the world exploded and everything went pear-shaped.

Dead. For sure. Minutes away at best.

Impossible to be rescued without coming under murderous fire. Call in an air strike? The building where the shooters are is less than twenty metres away. The air strike won't discriminate over a radius of at least a hundred metres. So, everybody dies. Another scorching, dust-filled day, sun casting its punishing glare. He's bathed in sweat; the stench of fear all around.

The other patrol, Turnell's, would be round the north end of the compound. They would have heard the shooting by now. But what could they do? Sam has never seen such a perfect ambush set up. The lay of the land, the lines of attack and defence. Sam can't even raise his gun for a blind rake, they'll take his arm off. Grenades? He would have used them by now if he could.

'Do something, useless cunt.' The Queenslander. Inferior to Sam in rank but part of Turnell's clique, so feels able to talk to him like this. Besides, he has just lost half his leg, so fair enough. 'Fucking do something.'

Dead. May as well be.

This paralysis. It goes against Sam's training, against what he stands for, against the Code. He's meant to be a fucking warrior.

'Do something.' Weaker now as the blood and life drain away. 'Maggot.'

Maybe Sam could at least put the Queenslander out of his misery. Shut the bastard up. The last few months have been like this since

Turnell started his campaign of isolate and demoralise. Firstly, demoted to another patrol. Undermined, excluded, ridiculed, despised. After a while you begin to believe they might just be right. Maybe he is a useless maggot after all.

Dead. One way or another.

May as well be in a hail of enemy fire.

'Fuck it,' says Sam. Yeah, he'll do something. Jumping up, bracing for the bullets that don't arrive. Full charge at the building. Unclip his therms – the thermobaric grenades that suck all the surrounding oxygen to create a high-temperature megablast. He's John Wayne, he's Rambo, he's the fucking *Die Hard* guy. Thumps on the kevlar, splinters of concrete chipping at his cheek, a sharp jab down his right hip. Bang, whoosh. Therm the bastards, kick the door in and spray them.

Yippy-ki-yay and all that.

Dead. Just don't know it yet.

'How are you feeling, Sam?'

He opens his eyes. Surgeon. Nurse. Behind them, a window, dust motes floating in the sunshine, and kunanyi beautiful as ever. 'Yeah, good.'

–

Ros didn't sleep well. Several times during the night she was woken by loud clangs from out on the water, or the sudden acceleration of a powerboat, or floodlights turning her bedroom from night to day, alarm klaxons. If you wanted to break down a terrorism suspect with sleep deprivation, just bring him from Guantanamo to North Bruny. Outside on the landward side of the house, away from the stunning but infernal coastal view, she cradles a mug of tea and nibbles at a slice of toast. Above her, the Tibetan prayer flags flap lazily in the gentle breeze: blue for the sky, white for the wind, red for fire, green for water and yellow for earth. Health and harmony achieved through the balance of the five elements. Ros knows this stuff, she lived in Fremantle for a while. Another clang and throaty engine roar out on the water. Tibetan prayer flags? Poor Steph must have been sorely deluded or else the eternal optimist to keep on flying the buggers. Better to put up the Jolly Roger and sharpen the cutlass.

Ros is feeling combative after getting out of bed on the wrong side this Wednesday morning, but combative is good. That's what she's here for. So much can happen in the space of a few days or weeks. Worlds turned upside down. And yet so little can happen too. Ros checks and finds that the NBN is connected and the modem is winking away in the pantry. Nobody has yet got around to disconnecting poor murdered Stephanie Howden from modern life. Maybe once they notice she's late on paying her bills. The wi-fi password is stuck on the fridge and she's cleared for take-off with the laptop she pilfered from Jill. Back to the USB and the electronic paper trail that Niamh thought meant something and that D'Entrecasteaux wants back.

Teddy Milsom. Founding father. The two multinationals circling for takeover were interchangeable opportunists. Whether you're a Norwegian salmon giant looking to master the universe or a fossil-fuel magnate diversifying your dusty lucre, where better to focus your energies than on this little slice of heaven devoid of environmental regulation and oversight? For salmon barons, loggers and gambling magnates, the state capture of Tasmania offers the benefits of third-world plunder in a stable first-world setting. Ka-ching, thinks Ros. Who wouldn't? But Milsom has known that all along, it's been his path to great riches and it's his marketing schtick now. So, what is out there that could threaten this?

Corrupt dealings and payments involving politicians? Pffft. Pass the smelling salts.

Evidence of environmental catastrophe? How many reports do you need? Just ask the climate scientists.

Accounting irregularities? A misrepresentation of the worth of the company, undisclosed massive legal liabilities? The takeover bidders would do their own due diligence and leave no stone unturned. Neither came down in the last shower.

What then? Murder? Atrocity? We're talking billions of dollars here, and in an era when life has never seemed so cheap.

All of the above? Yeah, maybe cumulatively it begins to seem a bit on the nose. Might sustain an hour of investigative current affairs coverage. Some social media outrage for a short while until another scandal comes along. But there's a big picture here, a long-term view, or a short- to medium-term profit motive.

What scares Teddy Milsom? If that's who is behind this.

Ros surfs the waves of documentation, frustrated by her inability to catch a solid break. Maybe there's nothing to see. Wade through the sludge. Break for another cuppa as the morning floats by.

Change of tack. The thing about Cluedo is that it's not too interested in motive. Colonel Mustard, in the library, with the dagger. If it's not possible to pin down whodunnit yet on the basis of motive, it is at least possible to know where and how and against whom. Niamh: on a quiet country road with a car. Steph Howden: in the isolated cottage with a gun. Zeb Meyer: out in the Channel with a boat propeller? Sam: on the snowy mountainside with a gun – but he survived. If the why and who still aren't evident, then maybe the chosen means might bear fruit. What's the relationship between D'Entrecasteaux and those thugs from DTS who were sent to kill them? They didn't just happen upon them in the Yellow Pages.

DTS. David Trembath. Footrot on the phone as the helicopter scudded away from the bloody hillside where Sam lay lifeless.

Davey, mate. You might do the hiring and firing and drive the flash Audi these days, but you know fuck-all about real war.

Sure, he's the key, rather than Teddy Milsom. But shady ex-defence operatives aren't as easy for Ros to track as high-profile Tassie billionaires. That is Larissa or Jill's department. Hopefully one or both of them is onto it.

Meantime, once more unto the paper trail.

—

The bullet has been successfully removed and Sam is reliably informed that all it comes down to now is a period of rest and recuperation. Things are on the up and up. A couple more days and he might even be ready for some more gentle questioning from the AFP–OSI team, Grace and Grant. Hell, in no time at all, he'll be back in the hands of Tas Police and getting the feel of his new surroundings in the remand wing at Risdon.

Man up and do the right thing, whatever that is.

So far so good, Kaz.

Lacks decisive thinking when it matters.

You'll be proud of me now, T-Rex.

Do something. Maggot.

Yeah, mate. Careful what you wish for.

The Queenslander had signed a statement about how Patrol Commander Michael Turnell had shown outstanding courage and selflessness in the single-handed rescue of his comrades pinned down by enemy fire and blah-blah and blah. Shipped home to Townsville, the

Queenslander would die of blood poisoning within weeks. Sam had woken up in the base hospital at Tarin Kowt with T-Rex and Moose grinning down at him. No serious injuries, the kamikaze dash hadn't fulfilled his expectations.

'Congratulations, Maggot. You're still alive.' Moose handing him paper and pen. 'Sign this.'

'What is it?'

'A citation. T-Rex here is destined for a fucken SG.'

Sam had read it. Star of Gallantry? 'Bullshit.'

'Six witnesses say otherwise. You're number seven.'

'That was me did that. Not you. You weren't there.'

T-Rex had tapped Moose on the shoulder. 'I'll leave this to you.' And excused himself.

'The helmet-cam,' says Sam. 'Mine confirms my story, Turnell's would destroy his.'

'Malfunctions,' says Moose sadly.

Play the game, Sam was told. Life gets so much easier if you do, and so much harder if you don't. 'Besides,' said Moose. 'Who's gunna believe a useless cunt like you could do something like that? It's T-Rex territory, mate. Not Sammy Maggot.'

Lacks decisive thinking when it matters.

Yeah, it was out of character with his performance reviews, for sure.

Sam had signed the paper and life did get easier. He'd survived that final tour of duty and chucked the game in. Went home. Got treated like a hero. Got pissed. Got into fights. Sobered up. Got a job. Met Kaz. Got married. Lost the job. And the next one. Then another. The war crimes investigators had paid him a visit at some point. Hoping to bury some ugly rumours. He'd helped them.

Anything for a quiet life. Sam hears the murmuring of the beefy armed guards at his door.

Lacks decisive thinking when it matters.

Keep thinking that, T-Rex. Sure path to extinction.

—

Jill thinks she knows where Ros is holed up and looks forward to paying a surprise visit. Based on the info Ros gave her, she's also arranged for the Deloraine cops to take a drive down past Lake Rowallan to see if the abandoned stolen car is there and, if so, bring it down to Hobart. They've already got Ros's Subaru that had been left in the Lake St Clair car park, back in custody at the Hobart police garage. Had it for a few days in fact, Cavanagh knew apparently but hadn't passed the news on to Jill. It's been forensic'd and, yes, traces of Robert Beckett in there, along with Willard and Chen. The thinking is, more ammunition to nail Willard with. If only they knew. Anyway, it's cleared to go. Not long after, there's a text telling her that the other car is there at Lake Rowallan and they'll have it down to Hobo-town later today. Great. She'll jag an Uber into the city and be waiting for them at the office.

The office is subdued, still in shock over the death of Cavanagh, and a few colleagues look at her like she's responsible. Or are they just ogling her bruises and boxer's nose? Hughesy sidles up. 'You sure you're meant to be here?'

'I'm fine.' They retreat to the kitchen and boil a kettle. 'What's happening?'

'Inquiry continuing into the circumstances of Cav's death. Apparently, the Traffic investigators have since found some anomalies at the crash scene.'

'Anomalies?'

'Things that don't match the lone crash scenario. Accident, suicide, foul play. Who knows? Watch this space.'

'Anything else?'

'Special task force being set up to oversee the gangster drive-bys and to be run out of Launceston, as this is their spillover anyway. Some tweaking still needed on the local angle.'

Jiggling of teabags. 'Meanwhile?'

'Meanwhile, I'm in charge. Acting.'

She looks at Hughesy. He seems as surprised as her. 'Congratulations.'

'Once more with feeling.'

'No, really. So, where are things at with the whole Willard–Howden circus?'

'Fancy postponing your retirement for a few weeks?'

'Happy to, but aren't the wheels of bureaucracy in motion?'

'Easy enough to put a spoke in them.' Almost apologetically he leads Jill into the office that used to be Cavanagh's. Sits down tentatively in Cav's old chair and nods for her to shut the door behind them. 'Half wishing the Lonnie gangs squad would take this fiasco over too.'

'Leadership becomes you, Hughesy. Born for it.'

'You're probably more across this whole schemozzle than any of us. What's your assessment?'

'The Feds have snaffled Willard for the foreseeable?'

'Bastards, yeah.'

'But we know that when they do give him back, which won't be that long surely, he's good for Howden and the DTS guy on the mountain?'

'Brett Armstrong.'

'Right. Brett Armstrong.' Jill can only think of him as Moose now. 'And probably this Robert Beckett character?'

He nods. 'Yeah, him too. Can we pin the last Tassie thylacine on Willard while we're on?'

'So, we just need to sit tight, maybe do the back-up and supporting paperwork while we're waiting, and that's three big outstandings cleared up.'

'The woman on the bike?'

'Be good if we could pin that on him too, eh?'

'Seriously?'

No. But Hughesy is looking to her for advice and guidance and she needs to dangle some goodies his way in order to get what she wants. 'One step at a time, I suppose. Yes, I'll stay on. But two, no make that three, conditions.'

'Conditions? Don't like the sound of that.'

She counts off on her fingers. 'One. I make the running, even if it looks like it's you that's doing it. Two. You back me up, administratively and in whatever way else necessary.' She thumbs beyond the door. 'I don't want any of Cav's little disciples giving me grief.'

He nods. 'Three?'

'No stone unturned. There're some lines of inquiry, some serious investigations of powerful people, that need to happen. The top brass will be in your ear telling you to back off.'

'That will be beyond my control.'

'Just be like Hodor in *Game of Thrones* for as long as it takes.'

He nods. 'Shared cultural references. This could be the making of a great team, Jill.'

A text. The Deloraine crew with the stolen Lake Rowallan car is waiting downstairs. 'First things first, I think we need to bring in David Trembath and Kristin Baker for questioning.'

'Who?'

Jill brings him up to speed. 'Cav held everything a bit too close. Could be why he's dead now. Don't want that happening to you, Hughesy, eh?'

'Yup. Hate to have any anomalies if I crash into a tree. What's our aim with these two?'

'Formal and official cage-rattling.'

'And this is to be presented as my brilliant idea?'

'It's what we pay you the big bucks for, boss.'

—

Nothing much on his military history but there is a financial trail courtesy of the USB downloads. The more Ros reads about David Trembath and DTS, the more she believes this is who killed Niamh. And, perhaps, Niamh's swim buddy, Zeb Meyer. Rewind seven years to when DTS first appears on the books of D'Entrecasteaux Salmon. Consultancy services to the value of $62,800 inclusive of GST. No further details provided. But a Google trawl for the same period throws up something interesting. A mysterious fire at a salmon pen over on the Tasman Peninsula causes a few hundred thousand dollars of damage and allows the escape of thousands of mature salmon into the surrounding waters. Bonanza for local fishers, financial embarrassment for the company concerned. It's an independent operator, a local landowner, commercial rival. Facing bankruptcy, he sells up to D'Entrecasteaux and gets the hell out. It emerges that the bargain sale also included a non-disclosure agreement of some kind. Some months later the said landowner puts his waterfront home on the market, again bought cheaply by a property investment subsidiary of D'Entrecasteaux. The owner, however, remains furious and vents his feelings to the local weekly newspaper, breaking the terms of his NDA and lashing out at the bullying, underhanded tactics of D'Entrecasteaux. One week later, he tragically dies in a diving accident off the Tasman Peninsula. A passing boat failed to see the diver warning flags and the poor bloke is decapitated. Six months from salmon-pen fire to beheading. The $62,800 DTS consultancy fee more than covered by the waterfront property profit. Some nine months later, a new batch of D'Entrecasteaux salmon pens become part of its western panorama.

Or this.

Three years ago. A Derwent Valley dairy farmer who drew her water from a rivulet adjoining the property that had been in her family for generations, filed a complaint about deteriorating water quality following the establishment of a salmon hatchery immediately upstream six months earlier. Previously clean and clear, the water had turned cloudy and was infested with algae and chemicals. The environmental watchdog doesn't act, the water company doesn't act, the local member isn't really interested and the media don't pursue the story. The dairy farmer pens a thought piece for an environmental blog and is threatened with a defamation suit. Unabashed, she posts the threatening legal letter on her next blogpost along with accusations of midnight phone calls, vandalism, the poisoning of her livestock.

Then nothing.

Except, a month later, the weekly newspaper reports that the historic homestead has been bought and the long-standing local dairy farming family will be leaving the area and relocating interstate. The property compulsorily acquired by the state government. Then peppercorn leased to D'Entrecasteaux so they can expand their hatchery. A neat way of bailing out D'Entrecasteaux from its environmental responsibilities at taxpayer expense. And look. DTS slung another fifty grand from D'Entrecasteaux during the same period.

Countless other happy coincidences, but Ros's question now is how did D'Entrecasteaux and DTS find each other to form this beautiful, productive partnership?

Ros takes a break. Sees a text from Jill asking if they can meet. She'll respond later. Sandwich and juice out on the back deck. The wind has picked up and carries most of the salmon farm noise away from her for a nice change. Leans back in the seat and enjoys the peace and those vitamin D rays on the face. Suddenly she's aware of something. Rare silence. The company runabout that was pottering between the salmon pens has cut its engine. The boat occupant has binoculars trained on Ros, glinting as the sun catches them.

—

Sam wonders how long before they come for him again. Word will get out that he's blabbing to the investigators. AFP–OSI, a joint agency initiative with the ongoing pressure of competing agendas, and a propensity to leak when it suits. Sam knows how easy it would be to make his testimony disappear and he knows they haven't even started questioning him fully about the actions of his comrades yet. Larissa Barclay was allowed to record his self-incriminating confession, but will she be allowed to film the next phase too or will it be deemed top secret? Sam foresees weeks, months, years before any of what he has to say will see the light of day and any consequences. Perhaps never, except for him. Anyway, he is now going on the record, he is now doing the right thing.

The quiet life is no longer an option. Maybe never was. He calls Larissa Barclay.

'You're awake,' she says. 'Feeling better?'

'Great. Wondering if you'd like to do an interview. Got a scoop for you. Do they still call it that? Scoop?'

'Sure.' There's a smile in her voice. 'Exclusive. Scoop. Always welcome. There's just one tiny problem.'

'Yep?'

'I'm no longer allowed access to you until the inquiry is completed.'

As anticipated. 'Did they give a timeline?'

'No.'

'Could be a while, a long while.'

'Yes.'

'How do you feel about that?'

A bitter snort. 'Feel? I'm not sure feelings come into it. I'm a journalist, a professional. Rules are rules.'

'But?'

'What's your big scoop, Sam? Give me a hill to die on.'

Not the best turn of phrase under recent circumstances. 'How about hitting Turnell where it really hurts?'

'Where would that be?'

'Ego and male pride.'

'I'm listening.'

'That Star of Gallantry medal isn't his. He's a fake hero. A fraud.'

'How do you know?'

'Because he stole it from me.'

She laughs. 'Miaow! A cat fight between tough guys. Even if it's not true, it's beautiful. How do we make this happen?'

Sam tells her.

—

'Swap you,' says Jill. 'Your car, wallet, computer, assorted other goodies. For my car, my gun, my computer.'

Ros feels a flush creeping up her neck. No point in lying, especially to this woman. 'Tea?' She invites Jill inside. 'How did you know to find me here?'

'Lucky guess.'

Jill's bruises are colouring nicely, just a day or two behind Ros's own slowly fading ones. They settle at the kitchen table, kettle on the boil. Mid-afternoon and the sun isn't far from dropping behind the Snug Tiers. Already the air is cooler.

'This isn't sustainable, Ros. You know that.'

'I've been looking into DTS. David Trembath.'

'So are we. It's in hand.'

'We?'

Jill outlines the regime change in her department. 'I've pretty much got the gig. I'm on the case.' She smiles. 'Just need my car and my gun and I'm off to round up those bad guys.'

'Footrot? Aaron? Whoever else with the dagger tatt waiting for the call to arms? You've rounded them up too?'

'Not exactly.'

'Thought not.'

'They'll work out you're here. Even with my gun, you wouldn't have a chance. Come back with me and we'll make sure you're safe.' Jill angles her chair away from the glare of the falling sun. 'We need to do this our way, Ros.'

'Do you even want to hear about DTS?'

'Sure.'

Ros tells Jill about the decapitated landowner on the Tasman Peninsula. About the blue-blood Derwent Valley dairy farmer driven off the land. Points out the similarities in the death of Zeb Meyer, the treatment of Stephanie Howden. Knows, even as she relates the tales, how circumstantial it seems.

'We'll look into it,' says Jill. 'It all helps build the picture.'

'You're not convinced?'

'Not yet. I deal in evidence, Ros. I want people behind bars.'

'Maybe there will be a phone or email trail connecting Zeb Meyer into this network?'

'I'll follow it up, Ros. Don't worry.'

'How do D'Entrecasteaux and DTS know each other?'

'Military and family connections. Milsom's son, Peter, served with them. We're looking into it.'

'Building that picture?'

Jill stands to rinse her cup in the sink. 'It'll be dark soon. Are you coming back with me?'

'They trashed my house. Killed my cat.' Ros supplies further details at Jill's invitation.

'All the more reason.'

'What drove them to kill Steph?'

'We'll find out.'

'Will you?'

A hand on her shoulder. 'Ros, you have been through so much in a very short time. You need to find a way forward. Let me do my job and you, you look after yourself.' Picks up the gun, laptop and car keys from the table. 'Coming?'

'No, I'm sick of running.' She meets Jill's gaze. 'Please.'

'Technically you're trespassing. This is still a crime scene.'

A sad smile. 'Arrest me then.'

Jill shakes her head. 'I filled your tank and pumped up the tyres. The gear is in the boot.' Taps her fingers on the laptop. 'This stuff, it's what's keeping you going, isn't it?'

Tears brimming, she nods.

'I'll call you in the morning, Ros. Check how you are. Keep you updated.' The sun finally dips behind that western hill. 'Another day or so, then I'm going to start insisting.'

—

It's about half an hour since Sam recorded a three-minute video bombshell on his phone and sent it to Larissa. 'TikTok that, you bastards.'

It contains information that only he could know. Larissa is now in the process of getting it copied to the AFP–OSI investigators as well as into the news cycle. There's also the danger of the video being leaked online as a fait accompli. 'You know that, don't you?'

'Pin it on me if it gets too much.'

'That's not what I'm saying, Sam. You've got yourself and your family to think of. These days, journalistic scoops don't bring down bad people.

That's a Hollywood-Age legend the boomer lecturers tell us about at journalism school. Nobody's listening anymore, too busy scoring Twitter points.'

'Cynic.'

'You nearly died out there. You've been given a second chance. Enjoy it.'

'I am,' he'd said, closing the call. Chickenshit bravado to the very end, but he knows he's not cut out for the long game. He's destined to lose those. This is another of his mad dashes at the enemy machine-gun nest. Therm the fuckers and take whatever's coming.

And it sounds like it's coming now.

Commotion in the corridor and a familiar voice.

The door flies open, bouncing off the inside wall. Grant from OSI. 'Unhook him from everything except the drip.'

One of the brutes who's been on guard outside does the honours.

A nurse. 'What's going on? You can't …'

'Can't what? You're employed by us.'

'What's this about, Grant?' says Sam.

'Shhhh.' He nods to the brute who holds Sam down. Given Sam's post-op weakness, it doesn't take much doing. 'We need to move you for your own safety.' He removes a syringe from a pouch. 'This will help keep you settled for the journey.'

'No need, mate. I'll be fine.'

The nurse is shaking her head. Insinuating herself into more trouble than she realises.

'Better safe than sorry.' Grant pushes the needle into Sam's neck.

'I can't allow this.' The nurse takes out her mobile phone but already Sam's vision is blurring, blood roaring in his ears.

The second guard takes the phone off her and leads her away down the corridor. 'You need to do what you're told, sis. Trust me.'

'Let go of my arm. That hurts. This is outrageous.'

Sam slips below the surface. Outside it's dark. Inside too.

'Okay,' he hears Grant say, echoing in the far distance. 'Let's get going.'

—

Jill gets back to the office against the flow of homebound traffic. David Trembath awaits her in one room, she is told. Kristin Baker, the other. Jill curses silently. She probably should have specified to Hughesy, no need to bring them in at exactly the same time. Bit of spacing would have been good.

'Want any help? Press the record button or something? Man the thumbscrews?' Hughesy's finishing off a kebab, expecting this to go on a bit beyond early evening. Needs to keep his strength up.

'Sure,' says Jill. 'Baker first, we'll let Trembath stew.'

'I could send him in a tea from the vending machine.'

'Big softie.'

'Have you ever tried the stuff?'

And in they go.

'This better be good.' Kristin Baker straightens in her chair like the live cross is returning to the studio presenter. 'I've requested my lawyer. Where is she?'

'Must be stuck in traffic,' says Jill. 'Happy to push on? Sooner we do this, sooner we all go home.'

'No. I'll wait for the lawyer.'

'Sure?' Hughesy shrugs. 'Your call.'

A few minutes elapse, filled with Hughesy's tuneless whistling of 'What's Going On?' Tori Amos? Somebody else? No matter, it's driving Kristin nuts.

'For goodness' sake. Let's get on with it. If I don't like something, I won't answer.'

'Happy to wait,' says Hughesy, blowing his nose and inspecting the contents of his hanky.

'Do it,' says Kristin, gritting her teeth.

Recording, cautions, introductions.

'Kristin Baker. Sustainable Business Team. What does that entail?'

She leans across the table towards Jill. 'Are you serious?'

'Yes. And curious. Corporate titles are very faddish, aren't they?'

Kristin blows out a breath. 'A combination of marketing and PR, bit of policy and strategy thrown in.'

'Give me an example.'

'We could have done this over the phone, or by email. Or I could have directed you to the website.'

'Indulge me.'

'Not feeling too indulgent right now.'

'D'Entrecasteaux is a bit under the pump lately PR-wise, eh? Big Salmon in general.'

'Big Salmon? Been hanging with the protestors? Maybe try hanging with all the people we give jobs to instead. All the support businesses we sustain.'

'Sure, fair enough. But still, challenging times, hmmm? Especially with a takeover in the wings.'

'It's what I get paid for.'

'Acting Sergeant Hughes here could identify with that. The burden of leadership. He's just been saddled with it. Finding his way.'

'Steady on, Senior Constable,' says Hughesy.

'Sorry, boss.' Jill looks suitably chastened. 'Did you come up with the spin about Sam Willard being a dud employee, unreliable, and you had to let him go?'

'It wasn't spin,' says Kristin. 'We let him go within the three-month trial period. He wasn't working out.'

'But he was taken on immediately by one of your preferred subcontractors and given an even better job.'

'We've already been down this path. D'Entrecasteaux is not involved in the recruitment decisions of our contractors and subcontractors.'

'C'mon, Kristin, we all know this is nonsense.' Photo printouts on the table, laid out one by one. 'You're in deep with David Trembath and DTS. Known each other, what, fifteen, twenty years? There's you and him in uniform back in the day. Two thousand six, seven? Comrades-in-arms, thick as thieves. You recruited Willard and pushed him Trembath's way.'

'I'll wait for the lawyer now, thanks.'

Jill isn't finished. 'You're a fixer, it says so in the puff pieces about you. Make problems go away. That's fine, every organisation needs them. But putting your neck on the chopping block for a thug like Dave Trembath? That's beginning to seem like poor judgement. Not a good look on your LinkedIn profile.'

A thin smile. 'Speaking of necks on chopping blocks.'

Hughesy leans in. 'Wouldn't issue threats if I were you, Ms Baker. With the untimely passing of Detective Cavanagh, it's no longer business as usual around here.' Sits back. 'Okay, we'll wait for your legal representative.'

23

Borrowed time. Ros knows that Jill is right, she can't stay here in a dead woman's house, and she can't find the evidence needed to bring Niamh's killers to justice. This isn't bloody Netflix. But. Beyond medication, therapy, a lobotomy, this is all she has to keep her on this right side of despair.

They killed Steph Howden here in her home. Was she that much of a threat to them? Or did she simply fit the profile of a convenient victim for other purposes? It's dark now. The floodlights around the salmon pens have been dimmed; whatever it is they do down there, they're not planning to do at least for the next few hours. Cold. The gothic Tasmanian kind that slices through your ribs and messes with your mind if you let it. Is it worth getting a fire going or maybe just flicking on the heat pump? Ros opts for the latter and microwaves one of the pre-cooked curries she stocked up on. She can see how lonely it might get here, particularly fighting a one-woman war against a ruthless corporation.

But Steph didn't seem lonely or downtrodden. Maybe she was just one of those individuals blessed with immense fortitude and spirit. Or maybe she had something up her sleeve. Curry and rice into a bowl, Ros eats on the move, idly scanning the walls and artwork, the bookshelves; whatever crosses her line of sight. If the place had been trashed during the murder, then the trashing would have been an element of the crime scene. Clearly some tidying up would have occurred once the forensic techs had finished their work. There's no sign of any blood, no stepping plates or police forensic markers like you see on the TV shows. Yes, there's that residual tang of chemicals. But there's something about the way things rest in this place that suggests they haven't been tidied by a stranger. They're as they always were. Maybe the place wasn't trashed.

So, they came in, killed her, and left. They weren't searching for anything. Some items must have been removed, surely, if only by detectives investigating the murder. Computers. Correspondence. She notices an empty hook on the wall beside the kitchen counter: calendar?

The artist's studio. Canvases stacked, facing inwards, against a wall. Many half finished, or half started. Landscapes marred by alien shapes. An abandoned portrait of a young man in profile. Angry daubs. That element of Steph's spirit, at least, strangled. A desk. Drawers ill-fitting and hard to open. Crayon, charcoal, pencils, rubber bands, paper clips, batteries. A scraping, scurrying noise. Ros jolts. A mouse running along the frame of one of the canvases. That's the extra smell she detected, the sour neglect of mouse droppings. Wind picking up outside and a gate or loose bit of tin squeaking and slapping.

A shoebox with photographs, lists, bills and magnetic letters, the type you find on many fridges. She recalls now, the fridge door was clear. Had these been taken down by police, perhaps briefly examined, then just placed to one side out of the way while they went about their work? Over here on the sideboard, a box file. The fridge-door stuff. A list of planned meals for each day of the week. A shopping list, including new mousetraps. A to-do list, some gardening chores. A bill, due to be paid last week. The photographs. Grandchildren? A dinner gathering, raised glasses. Niamh is there. A spasm tears through Ros. When was this? Short sleeves, a warm summer's eve perhaps? Ros no doubt at home in the doldrums while Niamh tries to get on with her life. Genuine happiness in Niamh's smile. A sob catches in Ros's throat. Next photo. Sun shining on the rear deck; a young man enjoying the rays. The camera loves the form of his neck and face. That same pose as in the abandoned portrait on the canvas facing the wall. Ros leans in to be sure.

Zeb Meyer.

—

Predictably the interview with Kristin Baker had ground to a halt soon after the lawyer arrived. Fair enough. She now knew they were onto her, and she had been presented with a choice: sink or swim. They weren't going to go away and D'Entrecasteaux no longer had a tame cop at their disposal, if that's indeed what Ian Cavanagh had been. Not at investigator level anyway; who knew what awaited them further up the food chain? And that's not to speak of the pet politicians and high-ranking public servants, journalists, et cetera. Jill feels hunger pangs as the evening drags on. There was the sense of the ground shifting; not seismically, barely more than a shudder. Maybe enough to send some vermin scuttling from their comfy nest into pastures new.

So, David Trembath.

'As Edmund Hillary once said, "Let's knock this bastard off." It's been a long day.' Hughesy stands taller, pulls his gut in. 'Ready?'

'Yep.'

Trembath is bearing up well for a man who has been left to stew for the best part of three hours. 'This take long? Only I should have been home two hours ago. Help my wife get the kids down for the night.'

'Hopefully not,' says Jill. 'You didn't request a lawyer?'

'Why would I?'

Why indeed. They do the formalities. 'Maybe you could start by explaining the function of DTS in relation to D'Entrecasteaux Salmon.' Jill appears to check her notes. 'Looks like you go back a bit, you and Mr Milsom.'

'And you want to know this in relation to ...?'

'The death of Stephanie Howden, the death of your employee Brett Armstrong.'

'Both of those are down to Sam Willard. Maybe you should be talking to him?'

'We are. I'm also interested in your decision to employ Willard, and his role in your company.'

'He wasn't an employee. He was an independent subcontractor. As was Mr Armstrong.'

'Sure, mate,' says Hughesy. 'The gig economy. But whatever the contractual details, what did these blokes do for you?'

'That's commercial-in-confidence.'

'Mate, you're not helping yourself. This is a murder inquiry.'

'And you have your murderer.'

'At this stage, to help build a picture, we would like from you a clear explanation of what you, these men and your company do in relation to services provided to D'Entrecasteaux Salmon.'

'Strategic risk management.'

'Which entails?'

'Strategically managing any risk.'

'How about an example?'

'Nothing comes to mind.'

'Try.'

'Sorry.'

Jill leans in. 'Maybe I can help. Do you deal with troublesome critics of the salmon farm? Bricks through the window. Threatening phone calls. Arson. Vandalism. Murder. That sort of thing?'

'A bit melodramatic for my taste. And illegal.'

'The ex-soldiers you employ. Afghan war veterans. Such stuff would be bread and butter to them. No?'

'These men are professionals. Heroes, who selflessly served their country.' A disgusted shake of the head. 'And you portray them as thugs. Shame on you.'

Hughesy. 'It's going to come tumbling down soon, buddy. People you know, people who know you. People you thought you could trust, or thought would protect you. They're going to hang you out to dry.'

'Well, nice as this has been. Family calls.'

'What was Sam Willard's job description?'

'We don't have them, as such. Very last century.'

'By all accounts he's being very cooperative with the war crimes investigators and we have every confidence he'll be helpful with us too.'

'On the mend, is he? Good to hear. Not a bad bloke at heart just – I don't know – unreliable, unpredictable. Loose cannon, as they say.' Trembath smiles. 'But he's a family man, like myself. Can't fault that, can you? Without it we're nothing.'

—

Of course, Zeb Meyer and Steph Howden would know each other. Kindred spirits in the fight against Big Salmon. There's something intimate about this photo. A moment captured without the awareness of its subject. Stolen even. Did Steph have a crush on Zeb Meyer? Why not? On the surface at least, he's crushable. This brings Ros no closer to understanding anything about any fucking thing.

The throb of a car engine out on the road. She checks the time: nearly nine. Goes to a darkened room at the front of the house to see outside what's going on. Decides to leave the light off. A ute, idling on the road, blocking the driveway. How many people in it? One, two? Hard to tell. So, Jill was right, they've found her. Defenceless. Alone. She even gave that bloody gun back.

The ute revs, turns into the driveway, headlights on full beam. Ros steps back from the window; have they seen her? Rolling forward, slowly. Oh God, they're coming in here. Phone. Phone for help. She scrolls to Jill's number. Leave a message, it says. She does.

Hide.

Where? They know she's here. Seen the lights on. Seen her outside on the deck sunning herself and chomping her fucking sandwich.

Arm herself.

With what? A knife from the kitchen drawer. Better than nothing. She heads back and finds the best there is. Returns to the window. Engine still rumbling. Nobody has exited the car yet, to the best of her knowledge. It sits there, lighting up the house. She finds herself willing them to get on with it. Finish her off. Footrot. Aaron. Here I am.

Niamh. Soon we'll be together again.

Except she doesn't believe in that stuff.

And yet hoping that they'll just go away. That it's a lost tourist, needing directions. Directions? It's not that hard; there's only the one road. The headlights go off, they cut the engine.

Jesus.

She tries Jill again. Again, no reply. Phone switched off. Triple zero? Is there a police post on Bruny? The main settlement she assumes, forty-odd Ks away at least. The car rests on the driveway. She can see now that there are two of them. Occasionally the flare of a cigarette ember. What are they waiting for? Reinforcements maybe. No need. Just little old me. Instructions? Possibly.

The car engine and lights start up again. The vehicle rolls forward. Then reverses out onto the road and heads north. After a while, Ros's trembling subsides.

24

Thursday. Jill is halfway through her first coffee of the day when she remembers she left her phone in her coat, and the coat in the car. Knackered by the end of yesterday's long day, she'd fallen straight asleep. Negligent, given everything that's happening, but she's had a good night's kip and feels all the better for it. If a little guilty now.

A screenful of missed messages. She groans. Maybe she should have left the bastard in the car. A slurp of coffee and she attends to the first message.

'Ros? Are you okay?'

'Yes.'

'Sorry my phone's been ...' What's the point in explaining? 'What happened?'

'A car turned up in the driveway last night. Stayed for a few minutes, then left.'

'They didn't get out, didn't say anything?'

'No.'

'Must have been scary.'

'Yeah. It was.'

Jill bites back an I-told-you-so. She had offered to take her somewhere safe, advised it was not a good idea to stay there. 'So, now are you ready to leave Bruny and let me put you somewhere safer?'

A pause. 'Sorry, you did offer, didn't you?' Ros sighs. 'I don't know. Of course, it makes sense, but it just feels like the answer might be here somewhere.'

'Maybe that's why you had the visitors. Let us look for the answers, Ros. All you need to do is stay safe.'

A bitter laugh. 'Easy.'

'Pack your bags. Lock up the house and get yourself back over here.' Jill refills her mug from the plunger. 'It's not a surrender. Call it a tactical retreat if you like.'

'Okay, I'll give you a call when I'm on my way. Most likely this afternoon.'

Jill decides not to push for an earlier departure. Turns instead to the matter of the second message.

Somebody has abducted Sam Willard.

—

Ending the call, Ros knows she's pushing her luck with Jill Wilkie. She'd had a crappy night's sleep, jerking awake at every sound and, with the windy weather and the salmon farm, there were many. What was Jill meant to do? Drop everything and fly over at the speed of light? Whoever it was had gone within minutes. No, it was Ros's fault for not accepting Jill's earlier offer of relocation.

The wind is still blustery this morning and, out on the water, choppy whitecaps foam around the salmon pens, sky dark with rain clouds. A thick stubborn greyness to everything. No runabouts or wellboats today. The weather might bring some peace and quiet for a while. Okay, pack your bags and turn the lights off before you leave.

Yeah, later. Another pot of coffee and a brood first. Then shower and go. This doesn't feel like a tactical retreat, it feels like surrender. A betrayal of Niamh. That canvas leaning against the wall. Sketched outline of a young man in his prime. Even in a relaxed pose, there's an energy fizzing under the surface and Steph, who must have given up on her art by then, finds herself once more inspired. Zeb Meyer – swimmer, activist, muse. Dead. Along with the woman who hosted him here and strove to capture his vibrant essence in charcoal. Dead. Niamh too. What did they all have or know that was worth killing for?

Back to the kitchen table. The pot of coffee. A bowl of muesli. The laptop. Zeb Meyer on Facebook and Insta. Wearing his causes on his sleeve. Lots of friends. And selfies. Does Ros detect a narcissistic streak in some of those poses or is she just being a bitch? About: *Zeb Meyer. Born 1982.* Older than he looked or seemed. Ros would have put him at around thirty. Not so. Nudging forty, in fact. *Education: Clements School and UTAS,* like many a well-heeled son of Hobart. So, the surfie rebel demeanour had a chunk of family money behind it. He could afford to be a wild child, or even a wild man-child. Stop it, Ros. Niamh never did like that judgmental side of you.

Never married, it seems. The photo archives show a man at ease with himself and all those around him, male or female. No smooches, intimacy or abandon in any of the photos. All have a hint of asexual reserve about them. The sexual energy that Steph strives to capture in the sketch might, in fact, be her own projection. FB friends in the hundreds. A cluster of causes pages followed, along with some uni and school reunion pages. Beyond that, his social media presence doesn't provide anything particularly revelatory.

A Google search throws up reports on the 'diving accident' but all remain vague and brief. No striking anomalies or lightbulb moments. Except. Back to Facebook and the school reunion page. An invitation to a function for the class of 1998. Zeb had clicked Going. Some photos posted to jog memories. In 1998, the Clements School swim team won the statewide championships. A picture of them with the trophy. There's Zeb, already a fine figure of a lad at just sixteen. Broad swimmer's shoulders. Enviable abs.

And hoisting the trophy beside him, according to the helpful L–R caption: Peter Milsom. Since dearly departed soldier son of Teddy Milsom.

—

'What do you mean "abducted"? Who by? When?' What Larissa is saying doesn't make sense. Or is it just that Jill doesn't want it to?

'Drugged and taken away at gunpoint. By three, maybe four people. One of them might have been part of the AFP–OSI war crimes task force. Last night, around nine, nine-thirty.' Larissa's voice tightening, sounding impatient. 'Sam had just sent me a video he'd made, claiming that Mike Turnell, the gallantry medal recipient, was a fraud.'

The weather is turning miserable, kitchen window rattling in its frame and spattered with rain. 'In what way?'

'Sam claims he did those things, not Turnell. Claims, in effect, Turnell stole his Star of Gallantry.'

'That would ruffle some feathers, I guess.'

'That was the idea.'

'Would anybody else have seen the video apart from you and Sam?'

'No, I don't think so. Not yet. I didn't get around to sending the copies on. Maybe his calls were being intercepted.'

Not impossible, particularly with the Feds. 'Drugged, you say?'

'The nurse says. She had her phone confiscated by them and she was threatened. Told to keep quiet and mind her own business.'

'But she told you.'

'She's a nurse. Her job is to look after people. She takes it seriously.'

Jill's not sure where to even start. 'I'll make some enquiries.'

'That doesn't sound very urgent. I'm assuming Sam's life is in danger given recent events. Maybe we should be raising hell.'

'That's the difference between your job and mine,' Jill says. 'What did you intend to do with Sam's video?'

'Try to have it admitted into evidence with the war crimes task force, but I suspect it's not their priority.'

'Otherwise?'

'Accidents happen. Leaks. Hackers. Stuff sometimes unexpectedly ends up in the public domain.'

'That'd be a shame.'

'I'll do my best to ensure it doesn't happen, of course.'

'I'll get on with things at my end. Talk later.'

Sam Willard abducted within a couple of hours of the interviews with Kristin Baker and David Trembath. Within minutes of sending his incendiary video to Larissa. Ros menaced by late-night callers. Things seem to be coming to a head. Jill checks the time on her phone. The working day hasn't even started.

—

'That was a dumb-arse stunt to pull. What were you thinking?'

Of course. The phone they kindly supplied to him. Monitored. They were on to the video immediately. Did he forget or did he no longer care in the heat of this new battle? Sam feels nauseous and his head is pounding. He certainly doesn't feel like justifying himself. 'What's going on? Where are we?'

'Somewhere safe,' says Grant from OSI. The bloke looks tired. Maybe feeling a bit old for this crap.

'Safe for who?'

'All these questions.'

Round in circles. His stomach and head are already doing that, he doesn't need any more. It's a house. Outside, daylight and green hills.

A touch of condensation on the inside of the window. Gusty out there. Sam has been asleep on a couch, travel rug cast over him. A pot-belly stove throws out some heat but not enough. The joint needs renovating. We're talking either abduction on a budget or expert deep cover. Still, no handcuffs or cable ties. No gun at his head. Promising.

'Let's start again. What do you want from me?'

'Your coffee order, I'm getting a large flat white. You?'

The bloke is serious. 'Same, thanks.'

Grant keys in a number and passes the orders through to his colleague. 'Some pastries as well. Surprise us.' Kills the phone. 'Banjo's,' he says to Sam. 'Can't go wrong.'

A Banjo's within cooee. So, we're not too far from civilisation. Sam really shouldn't be up and about. It's only been a few days since he was machine-gunned on a mountainside and left for dead. 'I'll ask yet again. What's this about?'

Grant frowns. 'You might not want to believe it, but this really is for your own good. Sending that video to the journalist was the last straw. Provocative. You're not only putting yourself in the firing line, but others too.'

'Like?'

'Your family, hospital staff, AFP–OSI employees.'

Point taken. Chastised pause. 'Where to from here?'

'I await further instructions.'

'If you know who is behind this, why not do something about them?'

A grim smile. 'We can't apply the same rules of engagement you might use in Uruzgan. Unfortunately.'

'What, we wait for them to come to us?'

Grant shrugs. 'One possibility.'

The penny drops. 'You've let them know where to find me. Limit the engagement to this place out in Woop Woop. Minimise the chance of civilian casualties.'

'You want this to be over, don't you?'

'After a fashion.'

Grant's phone buzzes, he checks it. 'The alternative is we have drawn-out investigations, arrests, charges, court cases, court appeals, et cetera. How long you got?'

All the time in the world, thinks Sam, but the Taliban are in a hurry, as are those Wakas and interpreters on the death list. '*Assault on Precinct 13*, huh?'

'I was thinking more *Rio Bravo*, but I guess we're on the same page.'

'It seems a bit risky.'

'Like I said before. Sending that video was a dumb-arse stunt. What were you thinking?'

'Of expediting the matter.'

'Fine, we're still on that same page. So, this is what we're gunna do.'

—

Ros has zapped the photo of Zeb Meyer and Peter Milsom through to Jill. The detective got back quickly, letting Ros know she has more immediate priorities and would forward it to the ABC journalist to look into. Ros wants more, now. Sure, rules of evidence and doing things by the book, but there's a sense of time running out. As a lawyer, Ros concedes she should know better. Nuts and bolts, painstaking research and hard yakka is what gets the results in the end. But still.

The Peter Milsom connection to Zeb has triggered a memory. The backgrounder on Teddy mentioned charitable interests and yes, there it is, The Peter Milsom Leaders of Tomorrow Foundation. More googling. Set up by Edward Milsom three years ago to honour his son's memory. Took a while, a solid decade or more after Peter died, but it's the thought that counts. An initial input of five million bucks from Edward Milsom, since matched by both federal and state governments, annually, along with certain other major donations. Now the charity is worth a little over forty million. But no annual reports, no annual accounts or tax returns, not even an office. Just a PO box number. On the website, a photo of Peter Milsom looking smart in his uniform. About us: troubled times, now more than ever we need good leaders, together we can find and support the young men and women to become the inspiring leaders of tomorrow. And so on and so forth.

Forty million or so invested in the fond memory of a dead military hero who sacrificed all for his country. Forty mil unaccounted for. Small fry these days on the scale of governmental nepotistic largesse. Forty mil, a handy slush fund to finance the political campaign of a war hero and promising candidate for national leadership, or to pay for grotesque mercenary pantomimes in the snowy Tasmanian wilderness. Another day, another rabbit hole, and time is running out.

If Ros really believes that then she should get her arse back to the Tassie mainland. She commences a tidy-up: dishes, bed. Sure, the owner is dead so who cares what state she leaves the place in, but that's not Ros, never was. Then packing. Half an hour later she's ready to go. One last glance out of the window down at the salmon pens. The runabout is there once again, bouncing through the dark choppy waters. Cutting whippies. The driver always looking this way, like the performance is for her benefit. Maybe it is. One last sweeping glance of the room. She has the snapshot of Zeb Meyer packed away safely. Wonders about that unfinished canvas. Would it be okay to steal a dead woman's painting? Probably not. How about borrowing with a view to purchase? Whoever has inherited this place will probably just clear it out and sell it anyway. Steph, Zeb, Niamh: there was a connection there. In life and in death. Okay, borrow it then.

A wry head shake, this seems an impractical, absurd, even ghoulish thing to do. For the moment she is effectively homeless, living out of an overnight bag. She can't return to her house until the threat has gone and the place has been cleaned up. So why cart a framed canvas around with her? Because if she leaves it behind, she fears it may be lost forever. And she wonders whether Steph or Niamh would ever forgive her for that.

Final check. She hasn't left anything in the bathroom. Spare bedroom, nothing. On top of the wardrobe, an old backpack. Did Steph hide something here, just as Ros herself did with the USB in the chook food bin? Can't help herself. Lifts it down, rummages inside. Nothing in the main compartments. Side pockets. Zilch. Flap zip pocket. Same. What does she think she's looking for? Slides the backpack into its resting place and dislodges something which falls down behind the wardrobe.

For goodness' sake, Ros. Stop faffing around and get a move on. Crouches down into the narrow space and squeezes her hand into the dusty gap between wardrobe and wall. It's a book, she pulls it free, catching her wrist on a splinter, drawing blood. Cursing, she clambers back to her feet. A notebook, relatively new. Ros opens it.

Statement by Zebediah Meyer, 8th February 2021, witnessed by Stephanie Howden. In the event of my death …

8th Feb. This would be about a week before he died.

Jill has come up against a brick wall in her enquiries about the missing Sam Willard. The AFP–OSI task force won't return her calls. She's asked Hughesy to shoot the request further up the food chain, see if a kind word between the powerful can sort this out. Meantime, she wants this Footrot character under lock and key. Shane somebody, did they ever get a surname for him? The name doesn't show up on the log of the search operation in the national park. They were simply Defence Department consultants. My arse. Cavanagh colluded in keeping their names out of the system. Cav's dead, Sam's missing. David Trembath will clam up. How else to trace Shane Footrot? If he was brought in from interstate during the Covid lockdown then his name would be on a register of approved workers and other personnel. He'd need legit ID to enter. Jill gets a minion to trawl for any Shanes. Could be a few. Oh, and don't forget this Aaron fella.

'About the same time and under the aegis of DTS or D'Entrecasteaux Salmon.'

'On it.'

'Great. And while you're at it, telcom records for Zeb Meyer, Stephanie Howden, David Trembath, Kristin Baker, Edward Milsom. Ian Cavanagh too.'

Her phone goes. Larissa Barclay. 'TurnelltheFraud is trending.'

'Glad to hear it. What about the official path into the AFP–OSI investigation?'

'Sure, they'll put it into the mix but it'll need corroboration and may be problematic anyway. A falling-out-amongst-war-criminals kind of thing.'

'Fair enough.' Jill is beginning to wonder what any of this has to do with her. 'That pic Ros sent through, Peter Milsom and Zeb Meyer, any developments?'

'Nothing new on Meyer. I'm looking closer at Peter Milsom's life, his army career, the manner of his death. I can only go so far with my contacts and resources. Might need the police hierarchy to nudge the Defence Department to get any detail.'

Another one for further up that food chain, thinks Jill. 'Will see what I can do.'

'No word on Sam?'

'Nothing. But something else to keep you busy.' Jill refers Larissa to that series of old army photographs. To Footrot in particular. 'Shane something. Reckon you could dredge up a surname for him through your contacts?'

'Will give it a shot. Are you planning something?'

'Pre-emptive strike, I believe they call it.'

'Sam's in real danger, isn't he?'

'Looks like he has been for quite a while.'

—

Ros is torn. Stay here, settle down and read Zeb Meyer's statement, or hit the road and hand it straight over to Jill Wilkie? A flick through the notebook. The statement is substantial, maybe fifteen to twenty pages. But she could probably read it in a quarter of an hour and be on her way. A fierce squall outside and a storm threatens. What's the harm in waiting a short while longer?

Statement by Zebediah Meyer, 8th February 2021, witnessed by Stephanie Howden. In the event of my death, I would like this statement released to all media and handed to the police.

"I would like ..." Very polite, well-mannered. And yet it hadn't happened. Instead, gathering dust on top of a wardrobe in Steph Howden's spare room.

Where to begin? I'm couch-surfing as I write this. My 6th lodgings in about 3 weeks. At first I thought I was just imagining things. Missed calls from unknown numbers in the middle of the night. Cars following me, whether I was driving, walking, or on my bike. Had somebody broken into my unit and moved stuff around or was my mind playing tricks? I can't even blame my overactive imagination on TV, books or movies. I don't really do that escapism stuff. This isn't the first time I've faced intimidation on a campaign. I've been followed and run off the road by loggers in the Tarkine. I've had beer bottles thrown at me when I was on a mine site blockade in Queensland. Shit in the mailbox, gutted wallabies on the porch. Poor bloody marsupials must be sick of being used as calling cards.

What's different this time? I can't put my finger on it, but all of a sudden I'm actually really properly scared. They've hacked my emails and social media – I know that much. Probably phone and laptop too. I tried being clever to catch them out, laying a false information trap about where I might be at a given time. I watched from a distance and saw them turn up. Scary-looking bastards. So that's why I'm writing this by hand.

Scary-looking bastards, thinks Ros. Moose? Footrot?

Is all this intimidation about the corrupt toxic salmon industry? Maybe. Probably. But I've been campaigning against it for best part of two years now. It's taken them a while to get aggro with me. Or is it to do with the company I keep? Maybe a bit of both. Imagine a Venn diagram. One circle has Big Salmon. The other has Zeb's mates. The overlap isn't about my fellow campaigners. It contains just one name. Pete Milsom.

Pete and me go back a long way.

A knock at the front door. Gentle. Timid even. Ros freezes. She never heard a car pull up. Nothing. Slips the notebook under the cushion of her armchair. Another knock, firmer this time. Should she answer?

'Hello?' A woman's voice calls out. 'Ros?'

Ros goes to see who it is.

—

Shane Hawke. Okay, thinks Jill, we now have a name for Footrot. He entered the state back in January, listed as an essential worker for DT Logistics, an offshoot of DTS. No huge attempt to disguise the paper trail. Perhaps David Trembath is feeling cocky and untouchable. Shane Hawke sharing a list with Brett Armstrong – Moose to his friends, Aaron Folau and Robert Beckett – now deceased. Three of the four believed to be ex-military and the fourth – Aaron Folau – will no doubt check out too. Shane and Aaron still in play and, probably, Trembath. Would these three old soldiers be enough to complete whatever mission they've embarked upon or have they brought in reinforcements? Jill wants to avoid a Hollywood-style shootout outside some small-town bakery in rural Tasmania. Imagine the headlines: DUEL AT BANJO'S! No. This needs to be nipped in the bud real soon. Bring Trembath back in and sweat the bastard.

'Jill?' Hughesy's popped his head round the door. 'We've got a visitor.'

'We?'

'Don't you mean *who*?'

'Go on then.'

It seems David Trembath has beaten her to it. He's waiting downstairs in the reception area. 'Interview Two is free, I checked.' They agree to take the stairs. Hughesy is embarking on a health regime as befits his new rank. He needs to set a good example. 'Trembath's brought a lawyer with him. One of those from Salamanca who like to go on the news.'

'Okay,' says Jill. 'I'll mind my p's and q's.'

Trembath is wearing a suit and tie as if he expects to be put straight in front of a magistrate. The lawyer is dressed likewise and calls himself Andrew.

'Mr Trembath has a statement he'd like to read,' says Andrew, once the recording gear is whirring and the introductions have been made. Hard copies slide across the table.

'Sure,' says Jill. 'And we have some questions we'd like to ask. Meantime, we're all ears.'

A rambling affair. If it's been scripted, then he needs to sack Andrew and get a new writer. The gist is that Trembath believes he may have committed some errors of judgement in his execution – nice choice of words – of his subcontractual obligations to D'Entrecasteaux Salmon.

Jill holds up a hand to prevent him rambling on. 'Errors of judgement? Please explain.'

Andrew taps his pencil on his notepad. 'That's the purpose of this prepared statement, Detective Wilkie.'

'I would expect a prepared statement to be more precise and focused. Bring clarity to a situation rather than obscurity.'

Andrew's first one-star review. It hurts. 'May we continue?'

Jill checks the time on her phone. Grimaces. 'You may.'

Employing Sam Willard was a bad idea but DTS thought it was doing the right thing offering opportunities to struggling military veterans. Dave also regrets associating with Shane and Brett. Their heavy-handed approach is not his way at all. Miscommunications. Misunderstandings. Et cetera.

Jill feels her temper fraying as the monotone drones on.

'The responsibility for this state of affairs rests squarely with D'Entrecasteaux Salmon and, in particular, Kristin Baker.'

What? Something big just happened. 'I'll just stop you there for a moment. Forgive my interruption. You're saying that Kristin Baker is behind all this?'

'It's all in the statement, Detective, if you'll just bear with us.'

Scanning her hard copy, Jill sees there's about a paragraph left. Light on detail but it may as well go onto the video record too as back-up. 'Let's hear it.' Thin smile. 'Then it's our turn.'

25

Sam needs to do something. Fast. These jokers are no match for Footrot and his crew. Grant from OSI might well have a military background but Sam suspects career military. The guy can probably finish an assault course and hit a target with his M15, maybe even lead a peacekeeping patrol in a soft posting, but his instincts are KPI rather than capture-kill. Loyal Labrador versus junkyard pit bull.

'You're making a mistake, Grant.'

'You reckon?'

'You said it yourself. These guys play Uruzgan rules. They'll paint us all over the walls.'

A shrug. 'We'll see.'

But Sam has to have faith in Grant's plans; his options are severely limited. He can't believe that months of pre-planning – the back channels to the Taliban, the investigations, his coercion into the cause and soft intro to D'Entrecasteaux/DTS – will boil down to this last-minute gamble and scramble. Then again, that's how the whole Afghanistan misadventure looks set to end.

The coffees arrive. Sam never even heard a car pull up.

'Sugar?' The young bloke chucks some sachets onto the kitchen table. He seems confident and capable. He introduces himself. 'Simon.'

Maybe Sam is worrying about nothing. Maybe there's a squad of commandos out there, battle-hardened, greasepaint and camos, just waiting. A protective ring of steel.

'When are the others arriving, or are they already here?'

'Others?'

Forget the ring of steel. Sam is beginning to wonder: are these guys so blasé because they're idiots or because something else is at play? Grant doesn't seem like an idiot but he could possibly be overconfident. Maybe he's mucking around, enjoying Sam's unease, controlling the information flow. Or maybe Grant is confident because there's no impending shootout. He's in on it. He'll hand Sam over and disappear back under the rock. Impossible to read the bloke, this could go either way.

Sam weighs his options. Not long out of surgery and vulnerable if things get overly physical. Grant and Simon murmuring just out of earshot, occasionally glancing his way.

'Toilet?' Sam eases himself up off the couch. Every movement a huge effort and it shows on his face.

'I'll escort you,' says Simon.

'No need.'

'I insist.'

'As long as you wait outside. I clam up under scrutiny.'

The bog is down the hall. Sam assumes there is a bathroom adjacent and perhaps a bedroom or laundry behind the other door. Just those few steps from the lounge felt like a solid uphill slog. He snicks the lock, sits and thinks. Examines his newly wound bandages and dressings. Hopes they'll do the job.

That's when the shouting starts.

—

'Where are we going?'

Ros is in the back seat of an SUV flanked by two men, one of whom she recognises as Aaron from her misadventure up north. Footrot is driving, casting the occasional amused glance her way through the rear-view. Winding along Nicholls Rivulet Road north and west, inland from Kettering. The scenery is lush, pretty. A gang of feral roosters pecking by the side of the road. Ros doesn't know the woman in the front passenger seat but could hazard a guess. She had been at Ros's, or rather Steph's, front door. Smiling, friendly, disarming.

'Hi, can I help you?'

'Rosalyn?' the woman had said, tilting her head.

'Yes, I ...' realising her mistake too late as Footrot stepped out from the side into her line of vision.

Ros could have kicked up a fuss when the SUV rolled onto the Bruny Island ferry for the short hop back to Kettering, but there was a gun jammed into her ribs and the threat of innocents getting hurt – particularly that car next to them with the happy family, cute kids. Maybe she should have called the bluff but life is full of could haves and should haves. For now, she is useful in some way. Not dead yet. If that was the sole intent, it would have happened back at Steph's place.

'Where are we going?' she says again.

The woman turns in her seat. 'I'll say this just the once. Don't talk, don't ask questions. This will all be over soon.' To the gorillas on either side of Ros: 'Make sure she understands.'

'Where are we going?'

A sharp elbow jab to the ribs takes the wind out of her. Hot breath in her ear. Aaron. 'Really wouldn't push it if I were you, Miss. We're serious people, especially her.'

Okay, she gets it.

On past the apple orchards. Through Cygnet. Isn't this where Mark Limace lives these days? A village waiting for a long overdue fete. Meandering back roads beyond Huonville, from bitumen to gravel. Places that don't see much sun in winter. Trees closing out the light, damp that never dries. A place where people come to hide or die.

'Up ahead to the right.' They slow and turn through the gate.

A weatherboard farmhouse, once-white planks faded and stained green with moss. Gutters sagging and sprouting grass. Tin roof rusted like the rocks at Bicheno. A ute and SUV parked down the far side of the house. They come to a stop but nobody gets out. The front passenger window whirrs down.

'We're here,' she shouts. 'Not looking for trouble. We have Rosalyn Chen with us. Swap you. Send Willard out.'

Footrot catches her eye in the rear-view. Unfinished business lurking there. Lots of clicking and ratcheting of guns by people supposedly not looking for trouble.

—

Jill doesn't buy it. Dave Trembath finished his prepared statement and has since gone all 'No comment' or 'You'll have to ask her that' in response to questions about Kristin Baker. He's taking the piss.

'Without any additional detail, your allegation that Kristin Baker is to blame for everything seems baseless. All that leaves me to go on is the admission in your statement of certain "errors of judgement" on your part which have culminated in at least one homicide and certain assault, criminal damage and trespass incidents. All warranting a remand in custody, I reckon.' She turns to Hughesy. 'Want me to do the honours?'

'Go for it.'

Trembath confers with his lawyer. After a few moments, Andrew clears his throat. 'My client will endeavour to answer your questions to the best of his ability.'

'Great,' says Jill. 'Let's get on with it then. Tell us all about Ms Baker.'

Trembath settles in, collects his thoughts. 'She was, is, the channel of communication between D'Entrecasteaux and DTS. She requested we up the pressure on Stephanie Howden. Burgle the property of Ms Rosalyn Chen to retrieve stolen documents.'

'How was that request made? Email? Message? Phone?'

'Verbal. Face to face.'

'When? Where? Exactly what was said?'

He provides some details for the record.

'Any witnesses? Anybody in earshot?'

'No.'

'Your word against hers then, eh?' Hughesy tuts his disapproval.

A shrug. 'You asked. I answered.'

The jobs were tasked to Sam Willard. He'd been recruited to D'Entrecasteaux and talent-spotted by Kristin. Recommended to DTS. The transfer kept at arms-length. A termination of one contract and the signing of a new one.

'Spooky coincidence him being in that same SAS unit as your other employees.'

'Contractors.'

'Whatever,' Jill looks up from laying the old army photographs on the table. 'Coincidence all the same.'

'Tasmania,' says Trembath. 'A village.'

'Threw him in the deep end, didn't you?' says Hughesy. 'One week he's mending salmon nets, the next he's a hired assassin.'

A shake of the head. 'Nobody hired him to be an assassin. Like I said, he was hired to do ...' Trembath struggles for the right phrase. Gives up. 'He was a standover man. Muscle. He was there to apply pressure. Not kill.'

'But kill he did,' says Jill.

'Kristin strongly recommended him. What could I do? I trusted her judgement.'

'Why did Kristin want the extra pressure applied to Stephanie Howden? Why the burglary on Ros Chen's house?'

'As I said, stolen documents. Leaked, hacked, whatever.'

'And with Stephanie Howden?'

'She was applying some kind of personal pressure to Edward Milsom. Blackmail if you like.'

Jill leans in. 'Kristin Baker told you that?'

'Yes.'

'Did she provide any detail on that allegation?'

'No.'

'You just took it at face value.'

'Need to know basis, I guess.'

'What about Zeb Meyer?'

'Who?'

'An associate of Niamh Cassidy.'

'Who?'

Jill breathes deeply. 'Ros Chen's partner. Deceased. The recipient of the documents you claim were stolen, leaked, hacked. Whatever.'

'Don't know anything about that.'

Seriously? A new tack. 'So, Edward Milsom had communicated his concerns about Ms Howden to Kristin Baker and she took the matter in hand.'

'It would seem.'

'He took her into his confidence.'

'Yes.'

'Any idea why?'

'No.'

'Then Sam Willard went a step further and killed Stephanie Howden.'

'Looks that way, doesn't it?'

'A grudge maybe. A brain snap. Maybe an order from Milsom via Baker that you weren't in on?'

'I had considered that possibility.'

Hughesy. 'But you chose not to share it until now.'

'An error of judgement,' Trembath concedes.

Another new tack from Jill. 'Shane Hawke. Aaron Folau. Where are they right now?'

'Search me.'

'Where do you recruit these people from?'

'Hmmm?'

'How do you know them? All of these highly trained military men, coincidentally from the same SAS unit?'

A glance at the photos on the table. 'I'm ex-military, as is Kristin. We compare notes, talent-spot.'

'You go back a bit?'

'Sure.'

'But now you've decided to throw her under the bus.'

Trembath shakes his head sadly. 'Regrettably.'

And downplay your own involvement. 'This blackmail, this thing that Steph Howden had over Edward Milsom. Salmon-related?'

'Makes sense, she had a bit of an obsession about all that, didn't she?'

Jill points to a face on one of the photos. 'Edward Milsom's son, Peter. Did you know him?'

'Not really.' Too quick.

'So, a bit then?'

'S'pose.'

'In what capacity?'

'Occasional army colleague.'

Jill points to another pic. 'Did Kristin know Peter well?'

'You'd have to ask her.'

'I'm asking you.'

'Can't help you, sorry.'

'Why are you dumping on Kristin?'

A sigh. 'I want an end to all this crap. It's got way out of hand. She doesn't know when to stop.'

'How do you mean?'

'We got a tip-off that the Chen woman was at the house on Bruny, the one that belonged to Howden.'

Jill's blood freezes. 'And?'

'Kristin left in a hurry not long after we got word.'

—

Exiting the toilet, Sam sees that Simon has taken up position at the window just along from Grant, Glock drawn and ready. Grant, meanwhile, stands in the doorway like a welcoming farmer.

'Can I help you folks?'

Sam finds a window of his own to observe things. Sees the SUV parked in the drive. Kristin Baker and Footrot in front, a crowd in the back. Is that really Ros there in the shadows?

'Send Willard out and you can have Ros Chen.'

Grant straightens, hands on hips. 'Think you might have the wrong house, Miss …?'

The front passenger door opens and Kristin steps out. Squints at the sun trying to break through the clouds. 'Don't test us, mate. We'll take Willard and be on our way.' Gives him a wintry smile. 'Chop. Chop.'

'Try the house down the road, love.'

A glance towards Footrot. The driver door opens and out he comes. Suitably armed. Grant has badly miscalculated, thinks Sam. He'd told him so. Meanwhile, Simon is twitching from his vantage point, getting ready to use his weapon. Sam foresees a bloodbath. In a few steps, he brushes past Grant at the doorway.

'Here I am. Let Ros go now, and everybody gets on with their day.'

'Willard,' growls Grant from behind. 'Keep the fuck out of this.'

A bit rich, thinks Sam, given that this is all about him.

Kristin signals behind her and the rear passenger doors open. Two big guys climb out, followed by Ros. She looks at peace, as if resigned to whatever the fates throw her way. Understandable given the past few weeks.

'Sam,' Kristin tilts her head. 'Not looking too well.' Gestures towards the car. 'Maybe take a seat, in the back.'

'Once Ros is in the house.'

'Don't, Sam,' says Ros.

It all feels a bit too late. 'It's fine, Ros. Go in the house.'

'No.'

'Please.'

'Off you go, Rosalyn. Do as he says.' Kristin nods to one of the guys to chaperone Ros away from the scene. 'Ready now, Sam?'

Grant has his smartphone up, filming everything, giving a running commentary. 'This is being livestreamed. Just so you know.'

Simon decides to join the fray. Glock in aiming position. 'Drop your weapons.'

'Mate,' says Sam. 'It's all good. Leave it.'

'Drop your weapons.'

Kristin sighs. 'Tell him, Sam. Tell him it can't end well.'

'Grant, call Simon into line. We've got this in hand.'

'Says who?' Grant signals for Simon to lower his gun. 'They just want a word with me.'

'Have it here, now. With witnesses.'

A chopper approaching. Grant has friends in high places. Sam needs to decide, needs to be convinced. 'What's it to be, Kristin? What do you want with me?'

'T-Rex would like a word. Just thought you'd be interested.'

Sam is. He gets in the car and they drive off. Just like Grant predicted.

—

Jill had tried Ros's number half a dozen times but no reply – ringing out to voicemail each time. Sent the cops from the Alonnah station on South Bruny to have a look.

'She's not here, but her phone is.' As was her car.

Shit. Make enquiries. Talk to the neighbours. Check the ferry, the aerodrome. Can TasPol spare the chopper for a flyover? Looking for what, precisely? No go. Needed for a drug raid up at Bridgewater. Next, she gets the Kingston plods to go over and check the Margate house. Twenty minutes later they call back. Empty but trashed, as Ros had reported. Bad smell from the wheelie bin; dead cat in there, not nice.

Jesus. Where are you, Ros?

Bring in Kristin Baker. So now Jill's in a mini-convoy heading down through the Channel towns towards D'Entrecasteaux Salmon, having also despatched a patrol car to Baker's Taroona hillside home. She's also requested, and is about to get, an urgent trace on Baker's phone. Beside her, in the driving seat and reliving his glory days on the Targa road race, Hughesy is in his element.

'Here's me thinking I'd be deskbound until retirement, as befits the burden of leadership.' His phone lights up in the coffee-cup hole. 'Get that for me, please, Detective.'

The caller ID on the screen says unknown number.

'Hello? Acting Sergeant Hughes' phone.'

'Who's speaking?'

'I might ask the same thing.'

They exchange names; he's Grant from OSI and he's glad to know she's Jill Wilkie. 'Got someone here who'd like a word.'

'Jill?'

'Ros, where are you?'

Some murmuring. 'Out the back of Huonville, near Ranelagh.'

Rolling hills, duelling banjos country. 'You're okay?'

'Fine.' She recounts the story of the unexpected female visitor to the house on Bruny. Kristin Baker, she had since learned. Footrot and Aaron were with her, and another bloke. Sam was at the Ranelagh place with Grant and, more murmuring, a bloke called Simon. There was a swap – Ros for Sam.

'Grant let that happen?'

Some rustling. 'Hi Jill, Grant here. You were on loudspeaker so I thought I'd best jump in to defend my honour.'

'Not accusing, just ...'

'Yeah, yeah. It was a complex situation, civilians et cetera, and Sam pretty much volunteered himself, much as I protested.' Next, the deal closer. 'T-Rex was mentioned.'

'T-Rex?'

'That was the army nickname for Michael Turnell. Know who he is? Been in the news a bit lately.'

And it turns out he flew into Tasmania last night on a private jet owned by none other than Edward Milsom. Strings pulled to allow him to sidestep Covid regs. Turnell's and Milsom's phone traffic already under surveillance by OSI.

'Small world, eh?' says Grant.

'Tasmania, mate,' says Jill. 'Any idea where they are now?'

'Weird,' says Grant. 'If our tracking tech is accurate – and we have been having some teething troubles – they're somewhere near the Iron Pot Lighthouse off South Arm. Bobbing on the ocean blue.'

And, give or take a few hundred metres, that's where the police tracers put Kristin Baker's phone too.

Ros is back on the line. 'Jill? A favour before you go?'

Sure. Not like Jill's busy or anything.

—

'Sammy J.'

T-Rex in corporate casual, he looks expensive. Smart haircut. Kept himself in good shape too although not quite up to his glory days as a patrol commander in Uruzgan. Same average height and build as Sam, although he'd always seemed bigger. 'Michael. Pleasant surprise.'

'I doubt it.'

Bumping through the chop on the powerboat has battered Sam's already traumatised insides and he's not feeling crash hot. Now transferred to a salmon farm wellboat out in the Channel, at their disposal courtesy of Teddy Milsom. The first-mate's quarters, room to swing a cat and a half. Little chance of being effectively bugged or remotely monitored through the hull and deck steel plating, and boarders or snoopers will be seen from miles off. Compressors and engines throbbing as a thousand tonnes of fish are vacuumed up out of their nets to keep them clean from amoebic gill disease before sorting them into those ready for slaughter, skinning and packaging, or the others who need to grow a little more. So noisy you almost need to shout. 'Hotels all booked up, Mike?'

'Not staying long.'

Footrot and Aaron dismissed, along with the remaining henchman. Just Sam, T-Rex and Kristin. 'You guys know each other, then?' enquires Sam.

Kristin begins to speak but Turnell butts in. 'Yeah, mate. We do.'

Down to business. 'You wanted to talk to me?'

'Looking a bit green there, Sammy. Seasick?' Turnell grins at Kristin. 'I bet he didn't mention that when he applied for the salmon farm job.'

'Say your piece, mate. Long way to come to fuck around.'

Turnell shrugs. 'An hour or so on a fast plane. But yeah, I have got a few things I'd like to get off my chest.'

'Fire away.' Sam holds up his hand. 'Any chance of a glass of water, cup of tea, whatever?'

'Sure, mate.' Turnell nods curtly at Kristin like she's the office casual. Off she goes.

Soon as she's gone, Sam tries a nudge. 'High body count for the sake of a bloke's reputation, Mike. Even yours.'

'And that's why we're here. Literally, Sammy. Why I am here and you're there.'

'Very existential.'

'You've been following developments?'

'Not closely, but I get the gist. Not going too well, I gather. Past catching up with you.'

'Appearances can be deceptive.'

'Can they?'

Kristin returns, Footrot in tow, with three plastic bottles of mineral water and three mugs of tea on a tray. Resumes her place next to Turnell. Footrot nearby. 'Hearsay,' he says. 'Blue bloods from Toorak stirring up shit because their candidate didn't get the gig. Recycling old allegations. The papers lap it up but it's not the same as evidence.'

'Yet the news seems to get worse every day. People lining up to accuse you of this and that.'

'None of it provable in a criminal court.'

'So why the long face? Why all this bloodshed? Why are you so interested in me?'

'You and Qadim. Got a thing going, have you? Bring down T-Rex and share the booty?'

'Seriously? You killed the guy's father. It's not about money.'

'It's always about money. They'll sell their daughters for a couple of hundred. Redeem the honour of their martyred son, brother, father for the price of a second-hand ute. You know how it is. You were there.'

'That's right, Mike, I was. Is that what this is all about? That one day, that one incident among many. The word of a kid in a field, and me, your brother-in-arms. Two eye-witnesses – a bit stronger than hearsay, eh?'

'I need to know, here and now, if I can depend on you, Sam.'

'I said nothing when they first interviewed me back in the day and just after I quit. I've said nothing since.'

'Not what I hear, Sammy. You've been playing games. Provoking. Hanging with OSI. I need you to be staunch like Moose and Footrot. You owe us. The Code, mate.'

'Setting me up for a murder and trying to have me killed doesn't inspire the confidence I need to have in you or the Code. In short, you started it.' Is what's being said enough for the microphone? More detail perhaps. Spell it out for the transcription. 'It's not just me that's your problem. Qadim saw and heard you murder his father in cold blood. What do you intend to do about him?'

A shrug. 'The Talibs will be back in soon. Qadim will be lost in the chaos.'

'So, just me then.'

'Just you.'

'And after all this drama I finally get the personal treatment from you. You could have phoned or messaged. Saved you the trip.'

'You know me, Sammy, I'm a hands-on kind of bloke when it comes down to it. We used to talk about you in Club Foot. Never quite fitting in. Different worldview, different sense of humour. Definitely not staunch.'

'Why did Stephanie Howden have to die?'

'Who?' He looks over at Kristin. 'Oh, the activist?'

'Yeah.'

'Two birds, one stone. Teddy and Kristin have their own history to reconcile. Kristin's very Taylorist in her approach to problem-solving. I would have just had you bumped straight off. End of story. But Kristin saw an opportunity to take both you and the activist out of the game in one move.' A stern look her way. 'The more complicated you make things, the more room for error. And now there's an even bigger mess to clean up.' Back to him. 'That right, Sammy?'

'Keep it simple, stupid?'

Turnell laughs. 'That's the one.'

Sam turns his head. 'That the way you see it, Kristin?'

'We all make mistakes,' she says. 'Best thing is to learn from them.' A grim smile and an exchange of glances with Footrot.

The boat is pitching a little in the swell. Sam feels the need to sleep, he'd like to be back in the hospital bed, recuperating with professional carers around him. 'So, what now?'

Turnell again. 'I'll always be looking over my shoulder with you, eh? Fuck, mate, you even want to take my medal away. That's a dog act.'

'Not rightfully yours, Mike. You know that.'

'Legends are more important than facts. This country, now more than ever, needs leaders, needs heroes and legends.'

'Great speech. You should go into politics.'

'Laugh a minute, Sammy.'

Sam isn't meant to get off this boat alive, just like he was never meant to get off Bruny alive the day Howden died. He sees that now. This conversation? Blocked by the sheet metal of the hull plates and drowned out by engine and compressor noise. All for nothing, Sam is sure. 'Like I said, what now?'

A smile. 'Fancy a tour of the boat? State of the art, apparently.'

—

'Are we there yet?' Hughesy doesn't travel well away from terra firma, and bouncing around in a helicopter in the swirling winds has him green around the gills.

Mid-afternoon and everybody's a bit low on blood sugar. Nobody is sure what to do about that wellboat out in Storm Bay. The top brass has been kept informed, given that there is a high-profile personage on board as well as numerous civilians and the crew. Along with one or two potential killers. The Soggies do an SAS-style landing on the poop deck? What if they're all just having a nice chat in the captain's cabin? Or what if those real ex-SAS mercenaries are waiting there in ambush? A massacre, and all Jill's fault. Or even Hughesy's, God forbid. They're in the TasPol chopper, miraculously freed up now that the situational jeopardy has upticked. Josie from Special Operations Group is there too. Around and around while the wild wind blows and, below them, the wellboat rides the choppy waves and sucks fish from a salmon pen. Circling at a five-hundred-metre radius, two high-powered RHIBs packed with ninjas awaiting instructions. One of them, at OSI's request, patched into their comms, picking up whatever's happening on the wellboat. Apparently, Willard is wearing what is colloquially called a wire. OSI Grant had fitted him up before his anticipated reunion with Turnell.

Win-win for all as far as they can make out, although Jill believes something might be being held back from her.

'We can board them,' says Josie. 'We've done the training with the navy.'

No, thinks Jill. Enough drama; it's what these people feed on. Through her headset she asks the chopper pilot to make contact with the wellboat. After a protracted exchange of call signs, she is switched through to the captain.

'You have some visitors aboard your vessel.'

'The company VIPs. Yes?'

'We'd like you to stop what you're doing at the salmon pens and head over to Margate wharf. Dock there.'

'I'm halfway through uploading a few thousand tonnes of fish. Once they've been rinsed, they'll have to be sorted and some returned to the pens. It will take a while.'

'Not my problem. This is a police directive. Stop what you're doing and head to Margate wharf.'

'We're talking several hundred thousand dollars of stock here. Are you serious?'

'Yes.'

'I'll have to talk to my superiors.'

'Advise them that the other option is an armed boarding party on open water. Perhaps with news media watching. Either way, today's operation gets closed down. What's it to be?'

'I'll get back to you.'

'No. What's it to be?'

'What's your name again?' Jill gives it. 'Weren't you in the news recently? Breaking some other poor bastard's balls?'

'Margate wharf, see you soon.'

'Yeah, yeah.'

Josie gives her a wink. Hughesy shakes his head.

26

Pete and me go back a long way.

They've found Ros a spare room at Tasmania Police HQ to while away the hours until Jill's return. Where safer than the third floor of police HQ? The office is empty, used partly as temporary storage but somebody has rustled up a folding table and a reasonably comfortable chair from the meeting room. And the cops from Alonnah have delivered the documents she requested: Zeb Meyer's brief memoirs, hidden under the cushion on Steph Howden's armchair before Ros's abduction. Another mug of tea. Ros is drowning in the stuff today. At that cottage near Ranelagh the older guy, Grant, quizzing her while Simon made them all a cuppa. How much does she know about what's going on? Very little, she'd insisted. Maybe he believed her, maybe not. They'd delivered her to HQ safely, Grant giving Ros a distracted farewell wave as he talked into his phone. A wind gust sends rain spattering against the window. Gloomy out there. Where is Jill? Where is Sam? He looked frail in that brief encounter outside the Ranelagh shack. Soldiering on, as they say. Driven by guts and glory? A powerful motivator for some. Sam prepared to sacrifice himself for her. But for others, like Michael Turnell, it seemed to be more about glory than guts.

Back to the subject of Zeb Meyer and Peter Milsom.

I suppose I must have loved him. I never realised it back then and he never knew it ever. Or maybe he did. Maybe that's why he kept writing to me all those years afterwards. After our school years. After uni. After he joined the army. After we went our separate ways. Often those emails and messages might be no more than a few lines. Rehashed jokes and catchphrases. Catch up for a drink after a tour of duty. Conversation often as abbreviated as an emoji but a connection that didn't need any useless words. Occasionally the electric brush of hands or shoulders over a beer.

2007. The year Pete died. It started off fine. He was even hinting at some chemistry between him and a colleague. Kris. Male or female? Made me jealous as hell even if I was happy for him. Kris this, Kris that. Turned out, after a few letters, Kris is a woman. Kris Baker.

The woman knocking at Steph Howden's front door.

Then contact dropped off. From a message or email a month to something maybe every two or three. Something bad had happened but he never said what. It was getting him down and people were giving him shit, blaming him. Even Kris had turned on him. She's cold, dude. Ice. His words, not mine.

Then, within a month or so, he was gone.

His last message to me was words to the effect of, those fuckers aren't going to pin this on me. I'm not taking this one for the team. We'll all swing together. I remember that last phrase particularly because it was the words of one of those foul songs the jocks at our old school used to sing.

Then he died, I mourned for a while, thought about him sometimes, often even, and gradually got on with my life.

Until I saw her name in the local press. D'Entrecasteaux Salmon's latest next big thing. Kristin Baker. Could it be the same person? The profile in the Mercury *mentioned a military background. It must be her. I tried to make contact with her. Maybe she could tell me something about Pete's last days. She wasn't interested. I suppose I should have backed off. I must have seemed like a crazed stalker. Maybe I was. She blocked me from emails, phone and social media, but whatever chink I could find, I used it.*

I went on Google, learned of a massacre of about 20 Afghan civilians around that time. A joint US–Australian operation.

Nothing on Australian news sites, just Al-Jazeera, stuff like that. Was this the bad thing Pete had been involved in? I put it to Kris Baker. Nothing. Went on chat forums, anything. Maybe I was jealous of her and what she'd meant to him. Maybe her being at the centre of this industry I detest triggered me. I began to openly speculate as to how Pete died, wonder if she was involved. Suggest he'd mentioned her name. Suggest I had proof. Of course I didn't, but I was desperate to provoke some kind of reaction.

Well, I got one.

Someone wants me dead, whether because I'm pissing off their business interests or because I've raked over their murky past. Either way, Kristin Baker ticks both boxes.

—

'Amoebic gill disease. You've heard of it?' Turnell is in expansive mode. He never tires of being the centre of attention, even when it's negative. As a TV and radio pundit with the shock jock shows he could expound on climate science, health, you name it. Just flick the switch. Now he's holding forth to everyone, a sudden expert on salmon.

'Sure, I used to be in the industry,' says Sam. 'Remember?'

'That's right, mate, of course. Jack of all trades.'

'Tassie water is too warm, not meant for Atlantic Salmon. That's why they get the disease, and why they need regular rinsing with fresh water. They don't belong here. Same as growing mangoes in the Arctic, I guess.'

'Scientist as well. My oath.'

'Darwinism. The natural order of things. Try to disrupt it and shit happens.'

'We still talking about salmon here, Sammy?'

Below them, thousands of fish swirl in a giant washing machine. The noise is deafening, rushing water, pumps, compressors, the ship's engine. Turnell's hand rests between Sam's shoulder blades. One good shove and he would end up in the swirl, sucked into one channel or another – the slaughter conveyor belt or back in the pen with the runts. Very symbolic. For witnesses he has Kristin, Footrot and Aaron. Slipped on the fish scales, mate. Gone. Tragic. Or maybe he just decided to end it all, given what he was facing. Was that circling chopper above, the cavalry come to rescue him? They better be quick.

'You know they mean to bring you down, Mikey, one way or another?'

'What's that?' Turnell steps closer, as does everybody else.

Sam repeats himself, almost shouting.

A nod from Turnell. 'Why would they want to do that? Why destroy an Aussie legend?'

'Legends, myths. Fine line.'

Something's happening. The noise has changed; the engines, the pumping and flushing stopped. A moment later, engines restarted. Kristin steps over to the radio box and has a conversation. Doesn't look happy.

'The ship has been ordered to stop operations and head for dock. Over at Margate. Police order.'

Turnell shrugs. 'We're nearly finished here anyway.'

Nearly?

Kristin is fuming. 'They can't do that. Mid-flush. It costs big money.'

'Hose them back into the pens. Come back later. No big deal.' He turns back to Sam. 'Where were we?'

'Myths and legends.'

'Right. Here's me thinking I'm too big, too well connected to fail.'

You and the salmon companies both, thinks Sam. 'Use-by dates. They're a bastard.'

'And you reckon I've reached mine?' He prods Sam in the chest, near the heart. He knows that's gunna hurt. 'You don't get it, never did. People like you – you follow. People like me lead. That's why you live in Shitsville and struggle to hold down a job. It's your manifest fucking destiny.'

'Manifest destiny? Been hanging out too long with the Yanks, Mikey. You're still headed for a fall. It's been decided.'

'Who by?' Turnell barks, cutting through the engine noise. 'What the fuck for?'

Now he has Sam turned and pressed against the safety rail which is stopping them all from tumbling into the salmon soup. The fish frothing and jumping, as if from some collective genetic memory of leaping the rapids in a Canadian river, avoiding the paws of that waiting grizzly, yet desperate to spawn and die. Sam feels the metal bar dig into his chest, tearing open sutures, the warm blood bathing his bandages. Too weak to resist. This day was always coming. Sam deserved to die back there in Afghanistan for what he did, what he was part of. This is just destiny delayed.

'Why?' Turnell barks again into his ear, genuinely perplexed as to why the world should suddenly turn against him.

'Bigger fish to fry,' says Sam, chuckling. 'You're fucked, Turnell. Hero, my arse.'

More hands on him. Lifting him over the safety rail.

—

Ros has been issued a temporary visitor's pass and swipe card which allows her, within limits, to come and go for the day at police HQ. The threat to her is deemed to be reduced. All the key players are out there somewhere chasing phantoms. Now, from the coffee shop over the road, she studies the edifice of TasPol HQ, the comings and goings at the busy pedestrian crossing, and the onward roll of quotidian existence in Hobart. The world just keeps on turning. Zeb Meyer's statement is probably worthless as evidence. It's a statement of belief and hearsay, not of proof. But yeah, a war crimes cloud over the illustrious hero Peter Milsom would taint the legacy and those taxpayer dollars locked up in the charity that bears his name. Enough to kill for, in order to keep it covered up? Who knows the minds of rich entitled folk? Even if there is now the glimmer of some kind of logic, an alternative narrative, for Zeb Meyer's death, it still doesn't explain why Niamh had to die. Surely Kristin Baker wasn't so paranoid about whatever she thought Zeb knew that she found it necessary to start killing off everybody around him? That's insane.

Where do you fit into this, Niamh? Okay, you made some connections among the anti-salmon activists, sympathisers and whistleblowers. Somebody sent you a shipload of information to do with what you will. But you never did. So why did you have to die?

The fruit juice is overly sweet, the sandwich dry. She never really wanted either anyway. A TV on the wall, ABC News 24 with sound muted, images of Taliban fighters retaking territory without resistance. All it needed was patience. Townsfolk watching on, wondering what the last few decades has been about. A fever dream of sorts and then one day you wake up and everything is back to being as it always bloody was.

Ros wants to go home. She's not in danger. If she ever was, it must have been mistaken identity. She doesn't present any threat to anyone. Kristin Baker and her goons had Ros at their mercy today and did nothing about it. She was currency for exchange, nothing more. Her overnight bag and her car, which were both back at Steph's place on Bruny, have since been delivered to her at police HQ. Ros is free to do what she likes. Hand in the visitor's pass and get somebody to note down your intentions just in case.

How is Sam? What is going on? Maybe Jill needs to know the contents of Zeb Meyer's statement. Will that help in whatever she is doing to liberate Sam and bring the bad guys to justice? Or maybe she's already kicking down doors and doesn't want to be interrupted right now. As if on cue, the TV switches from the Afghanistan badlands to an unfolding situation in Tasmania, just south of Hobart. Aerial shots of a salmon wellboat being escorted by two powerboats of paramilitary police. At a nearby wharf, more police vehicles await, lights flashing. Ros recognises the location.

Margate wharf. Just down the road from her house.

Well, as she was going to be in the area anyway.

—

'Goodness' sake. Give it a rest, boys.' Kristin looks up from her phone. 'There's a few hundred thousand dollars' worth of salmon in there and we don't want it contaminated with him.'

Sam is hauled back from his precarious dangling over the fish churner.

'Just having a laugh, Kris.' Footrot slaps him hard on the back. 'Eh, Sammy?'

'He's bleeding. Get him cleaned up before this boat docks.'

'Who's in charge here?' Turnell asks.

'Not you, mate.' Kristin frowns once more at her phone.

'What?'

Sam has heard that tone in Turnell's voice before. It spells danger. It presages a violent tantrum.

'You heard.' Kristin has given up on trying to get a phone signal down below and heads aloft. 'We do this my way from now on.'

Turnell looks from her to his mates, clownish expression on his face. 'Excuse me?'

'I did what Mr Milsom asked. Played second fiddle. Gave you a chance to redeem yourself.'

'Redeem myself?'

'People place too much faith in you, Michael. But truth is, you're a fuck-up.' She looks at Footrot from the half-open door at the top of the stairs. 'Explain it to him, Shane.' And disappears into the grey light.

T-Rex. 'Got something to say, Shane?'

Embarrassed glance at the floor. 'She's right, mate.'

Sam's not sure what's happening here but he can't help liking it, danger-ous as it might get.

'Aaron?'

'With Footrot on this one, Mikey. Sorry.'

'Mutiny on the fucken *Bounty*. How about that?'

A chuckle. 'Only you're not even Captain Bligh anymore.' Sam can't help himself. 'Just the ship's cat.'

The elbow to the chest is as swift as it is crippling. 'You're siding with this loser?'

'Not necessarily,' says Footrot. 'Not the same thing at all. Look, mate, Kristin's right. We can't go Uruzgan rules over here, much as we'd like to. Brings way too much heat down on everybody.' He gives the crouching and weakened Sam a head slap to show solidarity with T-Rex. 'We tried shooting the cunt but he wouldn't die. And now we've lost Moose. All for what?'

Cold, calm, insistent. 'For me. For what we stand for.'

'You. Yeah, it always was about you, wasn't it?' He looks Turnell up and down. 'You've done well for yourself, Mikey. Smart clothes, top new wife, billionaire friends, spots on the telly and radio. Everybody wants a piece of you. Or at least they did.' A sniff. 'Thought you were Teflon but you're fucking cheap tin, and shit sticks.'

Aaron feigns extreme interest in a pressure gauge above his head. Sam wonders when his bleeding will stop.

'Been bottling this up, eh?'

'One thing you don't lack, Mikey, is self-belief. Never have. You still use those bullshit phrases like "manifest destiny". Full of shit, mate. It's piss-easy to pop an unarmed terrified civilian. We all know that. And we all know that the SG wasn't ever yours to claim but we went along with it because all the way up the chain of command it was understood you were the chosen one. Golden Boy.' Footrot snorts. 'Moose, Aaron, me, even Sammy here – we're all better fucken soldiers than you ever were. That book you say you wrote? Fucken fairytales.' He steps close to Turnell. 'So go on, buddy, take a pop at me if you think you've got it in you.'

Turnell won't. Everybody knows that, especially him. 'What does Kristin propose we do with this one, then?'

'Remind him of his obligations.' Shane shows Sam a recent picture of

Kaz and Ollie on his phone. 'Taken this morning, Sam. You know it can happen – days, weeks, months from now. We did it with that guy's family in Kandahar, remember? Didn't even need to kill them – an acid blinding here, a maiming there. Don't even need to touch it ourselves, just contract it out.' Crouches down to Sam. 'Got it?'

'You shot me, Shane. Not easy to forgive. Try as I might.'

'Moose shot you, mate. Remember?'

'No. You shot me. And to help out Turnell?'

'Not just him, mate. Kristin too.'

Is the mic recording audible now? It's quieter; the ship's engines have slowed from a roar to a throb. But once these bloody dressings come off the game is up. Looking at Turnell. 'All those murders you, we, committed over there in Afghanistan. Innocent farmers, blameless kids. All the things they're saying about you, about us – your comrades – true. Has it been worth it?'

Turnell, pondering a riposte. 'Depends on what you mean by "worth" doesn't it?'

For fuck's sake just confess, you bastard. Loud, clear, and unequivocal for the tape. 'It's the truth. Plain and simple.'

'Reputations, who can put a price on them?'

'That posh private schooling you had didn't teach you about honour?'

'Jeez, you're a boring prick, Sammy. Always were.'

Footrot's had enough. 'Well, lovely as it's been to have this old comrades' catch-up.'

The phone rings on the wall. Aaron answers. 'Skipper wants us all up top.'

Footrot helps Sam to his feet. 'Let's get you to the first-aid room to get re-bandaged, soldier. Can't have you on parade looking like that.' An absent-minded glance at Turnell. 'Coming?'

—

Jill has been fielding calls from top brass for the last fifteen minutes. It seems like everybody on the D'Entrecasteaux board or executive management team must have their own mate in Tasmania Police. The calls really should have gone to Hughesy as her superior but he just glumly passed over his phone each time it rang.

'Another one for you.'

So much for having my back. All Jill can do with each earbashing is to cite operational imperative and brace for whatever might come in the aftermath. The wellboat is tied to moorings at Margate wharf, the ninjas are in place, ready to board. Jill has requested of the skipper to have all personnel and visitors lined up on deck for a roll call. She doesn't want to have to go searching for anybody down below. Now she has Kristin Baker on the line.

'I'm seeking some assurances, Kristin. We want to make sure this doesn't go pear-shaped.'

'How do you mean?'

'Are you or any of your colleagues armed?'

'Yes.'

Josie is listening in; she passes instructions to Jill to relay onwards to Kristin. Jill does so. 'Understood?'

'Yes.'

'You will comply?'

'Yes.'

There's something robotic and disingenuous about the replies. Jill doesn't like it. Nor does Josie. 'We want all of you to assemble on deck for roll call.'

'Yep, the skipper's already explained.'

Josie despatches one of her ninja squads to board the ship at the stern, out of immediate view from where everybody has been told to line up.

'Can I ask what this is about?'

'I think you already know, Kristin.'

'I assure you, I don't.'

'I'll explain it all when we chat later.'

'You're disrupting our operations, costing us money. If you were an environmental protestor, you could be jailed for that under Tasmanian law.'

'We'll be up to say hello in a short while. Appreciate your cooperation.'

A tap on the shoulder. One of the uniforms from the cordon. 'Lady would like to speak to you. She's pretty insistent.'

Jill follows the direction of his thumb. Ros, fifty metres away beyond the tape. Not good timing. 'Tell her I'll call her later, when this is over.'

Hughesy sidles up with a cardboard tray of coffees from the van that's appeared as if by magic. It's doing good trade what with cops, journalists, local workers and voyeurs thickening the throng. Josie doesn't want her coffee, she's got stuff to do, checking her machine-gun and pulling her balaclava on.

'Everything in hand, Jill?' asks Hughesy.

'I hope so.'

'Those soldiers playing nice?'

'So far so good.'

'That Willard bloke still alive?'

'So they tell me.'

'I'd high five you but this isn't over yet, and you've got a coffee in your hand.'

'Appreciate the sentiment, though.'

'The telcoms analyst has been in touch. Reckons there's a whole lot of possibly meaningful traffic between those names you gave him. Meaningful timings too.'

'Super,' says Jill. The coffee is tepid and tastes crap. They bin them simultaneously. 'Let's get on with this, eh?' They pat their kevlar one last time, bring out the Glocks and follow Josie and her team up the gangplank.

—

'No need, I'll be fine.'

'You're bleeding, mate. Look like a Tarantino film. We don't want them thinking we've been mistreating you.'

Heaven forbid. Sam wonders how much of the recent conversations has been captured, whether it managed to make it through those thick steel hulls and bulkheads. Whether, once the mic is discovered as the last bandage is unwound, he is about to die for no good result. 'They can sort it at the hospital.'

Footrot looks momentarily hurt. 'I was also a medic, remember?'

Yeah, a murderous one. In the background, blocking the doorway, Aaron hovers; looming relaxed menace, the build of a prop forward. The bandage clips are unhooked, the unwinding begins. The room, while clean enough, is hardly a sick bay; this is a working boat that rarely operates more than half an hour from shore. This is more an extension of the kitchen galley area with a well-equipped first-aid box. The risk of infection is not to be sneezed at. The bandages are sticky with blood, at times Footrot's ministrations seem a tad robust, drawing hisses of pain.

'Sorry, mate. You good?'

Is there a way to spin the inevitable mic discovery to Sam's advantage? 'Hope you guys are getting well paid for all this grief.'

'Don't worry your pretty little head, Sammy.'

'What's the ratio?'

'What?'

'The split. I mean, how much of the job is about T-Rex, how much Kristin?'

'It's complicated, mate. Doesn't matter in the end. Money's money.'

Sam presses his point. 'Haven't we always been at the pointy end of someone else's obscure agenda? Governments, politicians, big business, rich folk.'

A sigh. 'Goes with the job, mate. We know that when we sign up. Nearly there, just this last one to go.' Indrawing of breath at the last red ribbon. 'Jeez, you need to take better care of yourself.' A twist of the head. 'That right, Aaron? Sammy here needs to kick back and relax, give up on the causes and the fair maidens. Look after himself and his family.'

'S'right,' says Aaron. 'Do like the lady said. Mind his own business, keep his head down. Safest bet.'

Sam shifts his attention to Aaron. 'I remember you telling me you thought T-Rex was a racist. No surprise there with how he treated the Afghans. But I remember him giving you shit plenty of times too. Wasn't your grandad, or whatever, blackbirded back in the day? Once a slave ...'

Aaron steps forward. 'Watch your mouth, don't think you can talk about my family.'

'Aha!' Footrot has finally found the microphone. A little black square, barely wider than a fingertip and as thin as a credit card, coated in blood. He lifts the glistening thing. 'Sneaky. This why you've been so garrulous today, Sammy?'

'Loving your expanded vocabulary.'

Footrot turns to Aaron. 'Go and get Kristin.'

27

Ros can see she's not going to get through the cordon and that Jill is otherwise engaged. No point fighting it, what Ros has to say isn't going to change what's happening here today. Back to the Margate house. Time to return to normality and clean up after the home invasion.

She resists the temptation to turn on the radio for a running commentary on what's unfolding at the wharf. Pulling into her driveway, she smells poor Monica singing out from the wheelie bin. Maybe she should bury her instead of waiting for the next rubbish collection. The verge and front lawn need mowing and weeding. Ros doesn't want to even think about what awaits out back in the vegie garden. Upon opening the front door, she is struck by the task ahead of her. Everything trashed, just as she left it. A musty, mouldy smell. It's tempting to close up again and just call in some professionals to come and do the job. No, this thing is hers to do. Ros must be the one to get her own house in order.

Bags down. Windows and doors open, despite the brisk chilly breeze. Kettle on. A roll of garbage sacks at the ready. Next door's dogs howl at a siren in the distance.

'Yeah, yeah. Scream, you mongrels. All things pass.'

Between slurps of yet more tea, peppermint this time, sack after sack is filled and dumped in the wheelie bins out front with Monica the cat. Gradually blocking and masking her smell. Stuff is returned to cupboards and drawers. Perhaps Ros should have made a police report first and got insurance to cover some of the costs of the broken stuff, but she just wants this job done. Link the Bluetooth speaker to her phone for some music while she works. Nina Simone, an old favourite of Niamh's. Vacuum, sweep, wipe. Onward and forward. It's a new dawn, it's a new day and she's feeling ... determined.

A glance out the kitchen window. Driving rain. The mountain shrouded in cloud, the vegie garden in weeds. The now feral chooks pecking away at the dishevelled lawn, their genetic memory as jungle birds serving them well. The sound of helicopters; media maybe, or rescue or ambulance. What is happening down there? Is Sam still alive? How can she do the housework at a time like this? Simple. It's a way of not going insane. A grimy dull grip on everyday reality.

'Hi, Ros.'

She straightens from behind the kitchen counter, dustpan and brush in hand. A man, late forties maybe more, close-cropped greying hair. Looks fit. 'Who are you?'

'My name's Dave. We haven't actually met but I feel like I know you.' David Trembath. 'I let myself in, the front door was wide open.'

A sudden deep chill. 'What are you doing in my home? What do you want?'

'Just a chat.'

'You should leave. Now.' She reaches for her phone.

A staying hand. 'Don't you want to know who killed Niamh?'

—

'We're being summoned on deck.' The voice on the tannoy sounds edgy. The skipper is jack of this day. Sam knows the feeling. Kristin is holding the tiny spy mic up to the light as if it should be transparent and reveal all its secrets. Footrot and Aaron stand back, blocking the door, bracing for action.

Kristin stamps on the mike, grinding it with her heel. 'Who's been listening in?'

'Where's T-Rex? Gone home already?'

Kristin gives Footrot a nod and he steps forward, punching Sam in the face. Not a nose breaker, but unpleasant all the same.

'Who has been listening in?' she asks again.

'An AFP–OSI taskforce. Investigating Turnell. Not interested in you, as far as I know.'

'But if they get the goods on T-Rex for a criminal prosecution, that drags us in,' says Footrot. 'Clusterfuck.'

'I can't see this cheap piece of crap working out here.'

'Are you talking about me or the mic?' says Sam.

'Punch him in his wounds next time he speaks without permission.'

'I think we should top him.'

'Tempting, Shane, but that won't stop them using whatever they might have got from this mic, if anything.'

'Permission to speak?' Sam braces for the pain but it doesn't come.

'Quick learner,' says Kristin. 'What?'

'I have a proposal.'

'Go ahead.'

'Cut Turnell loose. The task force isn't interested in you and whatever you've been up to. I'm meant to be a key witness. I'll make sure Footrot and Aaron aren't in the frame.' A glance at Footrot. 'It was Moose that got a taste for it, if anybody. Right?'

No hesitation on behalf of his dear departed comrade. 'Right. Sure.'

'How do we know we can trust you?' asks Kristin.

'That photograph of my wife and kid. I get the message.'

She ponders the matter for a while. 'That's one scenario,' she concedes.

'Can you think of any others?'

A thin smile. 'Neither you nor Turnell see out this day. That takes care of everything, doesn't it?'

Sam has to admit that the idea has legs.

—

'I'll put the kettle on, eh?' Trembath fills the kettle and flicks it on. Leans against the kitchen counter, too close for comfort.

Ros gives herself some distance. 'Was it you who trashed my home?'

'Yeah, sort of. Sorry.'

'Sort of?'

'It's complicated. Some people did it for us.' He reaches for the assorted teabags. 'Builders or herbal?'

'Are you here to harm me?'

A cup slides her way. 'I'd like to think not.'

The bloke is smug, enjoying the theatre he's creating around himself. Another control freak – like Ian Cavanagh, like Mark Limace, like her former boss in the Perth law firm who bullied her into nothingness all those years ago because he just felt like it. Ros has had enough of them all. Fuck you, David Trembath, get to the point. 'Tell me, then. Who killed Niamh? You?'

'No-one you know.'

'I can't be bothered with these games. Piss off out of here before I call the police.'

He snatches her phone and puts it behind him, out of reach. 'I'm not finished.'

Good, she thinks. He's no longer as playful, enjoying himself a little less. 'Get on with it, then.'

Trembath frowns. 'It's all got way out of hand.'

It's a pity she's not recording this, he obviously wants to offload.

'That Meyer bloke,' he goes on. 'Zebedee or what the fuck. He kicked it all off. If he'd kept his nose out, he'd still be alive, Steph Howden would be, your Niamh would be. This bother with you and Willard.' Shakes his head. 'Meyer. What a tosser he was.'

'He didn't kill anybody. Can't be that bad.'

'Blackmail? No, not quite as bad, eh?'

Okay, she gets it now. 'Zeb used what he knew about Peter Milsom to try to pressure the father into cleaning up his act with the salmon farms. Daddy doesn't like being on the wrong end of pressure and intimidation, particularly in the midst of a massive takeover deal. He certainly doesn't want to hear about his boy being a war criminal. These days it might be believed, mud might stick. After all, it's all over the news, isn't it?'

Trembath sips his tea. Regards her over the rim.

Blackmail? Desperate stuff and unlikely to get the desired result. 'So Milsom Senior gets you and Kristin to deal with the matter. Which you did. Cue Zeb's boating accident. Then Stephanie Howden takes up the baton and meets her fate too.'

'That lawyer's mind of yours, hard at work.'

'And Niamh?'

'At the time of her death, firming up to be the next in line with the blackmail baton. We intercepted communications between her, Meyer and Howden.' The empty bubbles, maybe. The unsent messages. 'Plus, she had been involved in stealing information from D'Entrecasteaux. Privileged information.'

'Stealing? Or receiving leaked information?'

'Same thing,' he says. 'Receiving stolen goods. Look at WikiLeaks.'

'Three people dead for threatening to reveal a Milsom family secret?'

'Reputations, pride, hmmm? Priceless.'

Not quite priceless. Maybe forty million dollars' worth. 'Did Peter

Milsom really commit suicide out of shame, or did you and Kristin shut him up? You were both in intelligence. Needed to cover up the massacre.' Ros can see she's on target. 'Does Teddy Milsom know the truth of it? That you killed his son?'

'No. Not yet. Nor will he.'

Higher stakes for Trembath and Kristin then, maybe they were the ones who declared the death sentences on Zeb and Steph. 'He believes you and Kristin were there for Peter. He owes you. Feeding you all this work as a thank you.'

'Analytical mind like yours, and you wonder why we were worried about you?' A powerful gust sends a plant pot rolling across the deck. 'We've been following you online too. Can see where you're headed.'

'Overkill, surely. Where does it stop?'

'That's my thinking too.'

For all this confessional scenario, something doesn't add up, something is being held back. 'So, who killed Niamh?'

A shrug. 'Some bloke hired for the occasion.' Wry smile. 'You already have your revenge, though. Willard shot him, somewhere out near Derwent Bridge. Buried him in a paddock.'

Robert Beckett. So, vengeance was hers and hers alone. Even if this is the first she's heard of it. It feels like an anticlimax of sorts. But maybe that's the true nature of vengeance. 'Okay, now I know. You can leave.'

Trembath shakes his head. 'That's not going to happen.'

Outside, the incessant drone of helicopters hovering over Margate. Today, the centre of the bloody universe. Rain spattering the window and trees bending in the gusts. More passing sirens. The dogs next door kicking off again with their howling.

—

'What's going on?' Turnell had been dealing with a few phone messages, it seems. The busy life of a media pundit and aspiring political candidate. Aaron went to find him and brought him back to the first-aid post.

'Ask him,' says Kristin, nodding in Sam's direction and holding up the splintered mini-mic as illustration. 'Informing for the war crimes task force.'

He takes it from her, peers closely at it, steps closer to Sam. 'It's true. You really are a dog.'

Behind him, Kristin and Footrot exchange a look. Game on.

Sam breathes deeply, trying to master his pain. 'They're setting you up, Mike. Watch your back.'

Too late. Turnell's left hand is at Sam's throat and the right is punching him repeatedly in the chest. Reopening those barely closed wounds. Sam is weak, powerless to respond. Besides, he knows this isn't in Kristin's immediate interests.

'Mike,' she says, like a trusted confidante. 'Hold off a second. We need to think this through. There are armed police up on deck, they'll come looking for us if we don't put in an appearance.'

'So?'

'Maybe we could stall them while you do whatever you have to do with him.'

'If he's been broadcasting all this time, it might be too late.'

'Doubt it. He'll need to verify its contents in court. Without him it'll be practically worthless. A good lawyer would see to that.' Smile. 'Know any good lawyers, Mike?'

'What do you suggest? Take him into the bowels of the ship and pop him?'

'A helpless, unarmed prisoner,' concedes Sam. 'Not like it's the first time, Mikey.'

A chuckle from Footrot. 'Love your spirit, Sammy.' Hands Turnell a pistol and a muffler. 'Here, you might want this.'

'How do we account for his absence up there on deck?' asks Turnell.

Kristin is already at the doorway. 'Maybe weigh him down and chuck him in the salmon well. By the time they come looking, he'll be flushed into the Channel. Like he was never here.'

'Got it all worked out, Kris.'

'That's what they pay me the big bucks for.'

And away they go, answering the summons up top.

'Just you and me, Sammy.'

'You're really falling for it? The cops know I'm here, they'll come looking straight away. Kristin's playing you. The idea is that you kill me, and they set you up to be killed by the cops.'

'You were always good at the chat, weren't you? Talk your way off the gallows, I reckon.'

'But not this time, eh?'

A shake of the head. 'Not this time.'

—

Jill's feeling puffed after walking up the gangplank in her heavy kevlar. Josie and the ninjas scooted way ahead in no time and even Hughesy was surprisingly nimble. The ship's crew is assembled, sheltering beneath an overhang leading to the bridge. Imports from overseas on shit wages. Cold, bored, pissed off. No signs of curiosity or fear. Josie's ninjas strategically placed in a semicircle facing them. Her back-ups from the stern gang dotted here and there about the ship superstructure.

'Where are the others?'

'Others?' says the guy who looks like he might be the skipper.

'Don't mess,' says Josie. 'Tell.'

A nudge from Hughesy. 'Here they come.'

The ninjas take their positions, guns raised. Josie: 'Any weapons, throw them out ahead of you, well away, then hands on your head, kneel, then facedown on the deck. Got it?'

Kristin emerges first. 'No weapon. Unarmed.' A pause. 'Got it?'

'Me neither,' says the man she knows as Footrot. 'Unarmed.'

The next. That'd be Aaron Folau. 'Got a penknife. Want that?'

All three acting amused. Jill doesn't like it. 'Where are the other two?'

'Hmmm?' Kristin is facedown on the deck being frisked by a ninja.

'Willard. Turnell. Where are they?'

'You mean Sam Willard? Haven't a clue. Sorry.'

Jill gets the nod from Josie to approach. She crouches down near Kristin, back twinging with the effort. Blinks rain from her eyes. 'We got the list from the skipper. He confirmed Willard and Turnell were aboard. Where are they?'

'I really don't know. I've been busy doing a health and safety inspection of the vessel. Sam had expressed a wish to meet Mr Turnell; I believe they served in the army together. I left them to it. I know Mr Turnell arrived by his own means. Maybe they left together.'

Let's see how far the lie goes. 'And what was Turnell here for?'

'He's an investment consultant. I believe he's good friends with the owner, Mr Milsom. Maybe they have a project in mind.'

'And Sam Willard knew Turnell would be here?'

'It was mutual. I told him. They were both keen to catch up. Turnell in particular. I think he might have a bone to pick with Willard. Looking daggers, he was. Murderous.'

'And these goons?' says Jill, gesturing to Footrot and Aaron.

'Helping me with my health and safety assessment.'

A chortle from Footrot.

'Fucking bollocks,' says Josie. She signals the stern gang. 'Downstairs, search the vessel.'

That's when they hear the bang.

—

Rewind a few minutes. Blood courses down Sam's front. Shirtless, no replacement bandages. Wounds raw. There's a gun barrel jammed in the back of his neck, a fist scrunched in his hair. The ship hisses and throbs, echoes to their footsteps on the steel-grille decking. They're making their way back to the salmon well.

'You've lost it, Mikey. Desperate stuff. You're smarter than this.'

'Shut it.'

'You're not untouchable. This is madness.' A sharp jab of the gun barrel and it feels like a vertebra has been displaced. 'It serves their purpose that neither you nor me get off this ship alive.'

Sam knows this ship well. During his farm attendant induction, he spent a week on board getting to understand the processes and the job. After that he did the odd shift here and there to cover gaps from sickness and holiday leave. It's his only advantage over Turnell. But how to use it?

'How so?'

Engaging with the prisoner. Bad form in Uruzgan, but a positive sign for Sam. 'Footrot, Aaron,' Sam says. 'They're not on your side. Never were. Moose neither. Kristin and Teddie Milsom do the bidding now. You come in under "Any Other Business".'

'Explain.'

'You. Me. A couple of dead anti-salmon activists. Grist to the mill. Edward Milsom's got some agenda and we just slot into it.'

A grunt. 'That'd be his boy, Pete. It's why he's halfway up my arse with the funding and patronage. Wants to preserve Peter's sainthood.'

'You knew the son?' Just ahead, one of the storage lockers for the shotgun and beanbag rounds for deterring the seals. Next to it, the store of seal crackers.

'Bit like you, was Peter. Holier-than-thou when it suited him. Bitching about a recent operation where some Muzzies got killed. Some operation just before my time. My first tour out there. "Not my fault," he says. "Don't blame me." I mean, who gives a fuck? No such thing as an innocent muzzie.'

'Is that what this is all about?'

'Can't see why. He topped himself not long after. End of story.'

'Well, Milsom or Kristin or both have something to hide from back then. Dave Trembath too, you'll have heard of him?'

Turnell shakes his head in disgust. 'Kristin and Trembath think they're Mister and Missus Fix-it. Mister and Missus Fucks-it-up, more like. Supposedly hotshot intelligence analysts. Providing us with the targets. All they ever listened to was gossip from peasants with a grudge against their neighbours, or some local warlord wanting a rival out the way. Believe that shit and you may as well just pick up the first Afghan you see on the street and pop him. Just as useful.'

'Which was your MO, right?'

'Be fair. Some of them were legit insurgents. The rest served as deterrence.'

'Trembath and Baker have been running Moose, Footrot and Aaron. And a bloke called Robert Beckett?'

'Yeah? Who cares? The last few weeks they've all lurched from one tactical disaster to the next. Why couldn't you behave yourself and die when they wanted you to?'

'Why's Milsom backing you?'

'He's a crusader, mate. Maybe I'm the war hero son he always wanted. I mean, the one he had must have been a disappointment, eh? Or maybe I serve a purpose for him like he serves one for me. With his sort you can't always tell where the personal crusade ends and the business one starts.'

Takes one to know one, thinks Sam. 'If you go down, and take Footrot and Aaron with you, then whatever Milsom, Trembath and Kristin are up to starts to unravel because sure as fuck Footrot will sing if he has to. That's why it suits them if you and I die today.'

'Reckon?'

'Yes.'

Turnell smiles. He seems saddened, as if recognising the end of something. His run of good fortune maybe. 'I grew up bulletproof. I have to believe I can keep on getting away with murder.' He lifts the pistol, screws on the silencer, his face a study of concentration.

—

'Yes, David. It is going to happen. Leave now, go and tell the police everything you know. I'm not your confessor. They are.' Ros continues sweeping and cleaning.

'No.' He lays a hand on her shoulder. 'You need to understand.'

She shrugs him off. 'What's this about?' Gets in his face. 'I'm not some fucking barmaid here to listen to your late-night sob story while I polish the glasses. Or are you working yourself up to adding me to the list of the dead? If so, get on with it. I no longer give a shit.' He flinches away from her vehemence. She seizes the opportunity to snatch a knife from the magnetised strip in arm's reach. Pricks the side of his neck with it. A tiny crimson trickle. 'Why are you really here?'

He holds her gaze. As if he wants her to follow through with the knife. Willing her. 'It was an accident.'

It takes a moment. 'You,' she realises, finally. 'You killed Niamh.' Not Robert Beckett.

'I was going to wave her down. Ask her about Zeb Meyer. Warn her to keep away from him. Not get involved. Make her see sense.'

Ros still has the knife to his neck. It would be so easy to press, keep on pressing. He won't struggle. This is what he wants. After years of being hollowed out as a human being, he's collapsing in on himself. Or is he? 'Quite a turnaround. One minute you're dishing out orders to hired killers, the next you're confessing your sins to me. Why?'

'A road to Damascus moment?'

Ros reads his face. He's failing to hide the calculation there. 'No. Not you. You're looking to cover your arse, get in first. They're on to you, and you know it.' Ros breathes evenly. Feels calm. Cold. Save for the tightness in her gut and her heart. 'Tell me anyway. What happened?'

'I was waiting towards the Sandfly end, near the oval there. Facing east. I knew this was her normal route, followed her a couple of times previously from a distance.' A shaky breath. 'I saw her heading my way. I had a detachable blue strobe light and false police ID. The idea was to pull her over for a chat.'

'Why not just drop by the house and knock on the door?'

'You were here, a possible witness.'

Fair enough, but I probably would have been asleep. 'Niamh was headed your way on her bike. Then what?'

'Two things. Cresting the hill up from the oval, the sunlight at that time of day, the glare blinding. My phone went off at the same time. I lost concentration ...' He trails off. 'I didn't mean to, I just ...'

An accident. 'But you left her there to die.'

'Yes.'

One quick movement with the blade and it's all over for him. All she needs is the courage, the will. 'What do you expect from me? Forgiveness?' Presses the knife a little further, releasing more blood. 'Sweet release? Redemption? Eye for an eye? What?'

'I don't know. This endless cycle of death. It has to stop.'

He's right, though. There has already been too much killing, and she's played a part in it too. All through this she has asked herself, what would Niamh do? What would Niamh do?

Niamh wouldn't continue the killing, that's for sure. Ros chucks the knife down on the kitchen counter in disgust. She wants to cry, scream, yell at the stupid, useless waste of it all. But she'll be damned if she'll do so in front of him. 'Go to the police, kill yourself, whatever. I'm not solving this for you. Get out of my house, I'm not part of this anymore.'

And almost as suddenly as he appeared, he is gone.

—

'You know how to use these, eh Sammy?' Footrot had slipped the devices into Sam's pocket moments before Aaron returned with Turnell in tow. 'Giving you a fighting chance, mate. Only fair.'

Or will this be part of the new narrative?

He looks over Turnell's shoulder. 'You're back, then?'

Turnell turns. In the moments that he is distracted, Sam removes the seal cracker from his pocket, along with the Bic cigarette lighter. Ignites, lobs and crouches, trying to shield his head and ears from what is to come. In the confined space, the explosion is deafening, the flash disorienting. Turnell is on the floor, clutching his head, dazed. Gun still in his hand. Sam is first to react, landing a kick to Turnell's skull. Stamping on the gun hand, kicking the weapon away down some stairs. A fire extinguisher near to hand, bracketed on the wall. It serves to brain Turnell.

How long until either armed police or Footrot and Aaron come running?

Has he killed Turnell? Does it matter? Sam knows that either way he faces at least the next twenty years in jail. The bare minimum of what he deserves. You don't shoot unarmed prisoners on the battlefield because you were only obeying orders or wanting to fit in. You just don't. He hears footsteps approaching – or does he? Ears still ringing, the noises could be in his own head. He arranges Turnell in the recovery position whether or not the bastard deserves to recover.

'Fuck you and your Teflon upbringing.'

Sam lies facedown on the deck, hands behind his head. 'Unarmed,' he yells within his own mind. Hoping someone out there can hear him. 'Unarmed.'

And awaits his manifest fucking destiny.

EPILOGUE

SIX MONTHS LATER

'Are you sure you don't want the extra days?'

'Positive.' Ros smiles, feeling light. She's enjoying the part-time work with solicitor Jo Burke. From her desk by the window, summer casts a glow over kunanyi. The days are longer, she has time for exercise, walking the trails that snake up and around the mountain. The work is simple enough for a once high-flying corporate lawyer: conveyancing, wills, fence boundary mediation, family law. Admittedly, some of the family law cases still trigger the heebie-jeebies, men being what they are, but she's no longer quite so reliant on medication to keep things in check.

'Just say the word, I'm more than happy to cut my hours back.' Jo is easy to work with, easy company. Conversation flows naturally, no agendas. Silences aren't awkward. 'Heading up the mountain later?'

Ros nods. 'The Organ Pipes.' She loves the view from there out over the city, the river and Channel, the bays and islands. Every time she gazes out it's an affirmation of her decision to stay. She had toyed briefly with the idea of selling up and moving back to WA. Here or there, both places have their memories, good and bad. Except here can be, at times, indescribably beautiful in all weathers. Ros has grown to love the contrast in seasons, in landscapes. And here she can rebuild, reinvent. They say Tasmania is a village but that corner of Perth society she once inhabited, the legal fraternity, was as claustrophobic and inbred as anywhere or anything in Tassie. Niamh would approve, she thinks. She wouldn't want Ros to go backwards.

She still misses Niamh. Not a day goes by without thinking about her. A moment she would have loved to share, something funny, a commentary, an observation, a feeling, some tears, their bed. She had even pulled on Niamh's wetsuit, just the once, and joined the Kingston Beach Selkies for their Spring Fling in honour of Niamh and Zeb. Felt the Channel's icy sting on her face, breathing it away to numbness over one hundred strokes. Experienced the exaltation of prevailing. Allowed some tears to thaw her frozen cheeks. It was a more fitting farewell, though. Ros is beginning to accommodate the solitude. The despair has dissipated and, in its place, a certain peace and resolve. She doesn't hate David Trembath for running Niamh down and leaving her to die. The man is weak: Ros felt that when she held a knife to his neck. Like many men she has encountered, he will try to wriggle out of his responsibilities. Duck, weave, evade, avoid. The term 'gaslighting' has become even more prevalent of late – manipulating people to question what is real and what is not when there really isn't, and never was, any doubt. The borders are reopening and more people than ever are getting sick and dying, and those who have been in charge and failed are trying to blame everyone and everything but themselves.

Jo hovers at Ros's desk, file in hand, face unreadable.

'Something for me?'

'Conveyancing matter. Somebody selling up, moving interstate. You might recognise the name of the vendor. I'd be happy to deal with it if you like.'

Ros opens the file, sees the name. Mark Limace. Upping sticks from Cygnet and pissing right off out of Tasmania. 'Not a problem,' she says. 'Leave it with me.'

—

Over these last six months, Ollie has transformed from a tot to a little boy. He's walking with confidence now, forming words, developing a personality, thriving in the absence of his father. Sam studies Kaz; in some ways she too seems to be thriving. Maybe it's for the best, he thinks. I'm not getting out of here any time soon. This is likely the last in-person visit they will allow for a while. The border has reopened and Covid cases are on the rise just in time for Christmas. An outbreak here in prison will be no picnic. Lockdown looms.

'You going okay?' Kaz wants to know. Ollie already struggling on her lap, keen to get away.

'Yeah, babe. All good. What's been happening?'

Broken nights, some because of a restless Ollie, others down to threatening phone calls from friends, colleagues and supporters of Michael Turnell, who is going on trial for war crimes sometime in the new year. The covert mic had been practically worthless against the background noise and the steel plating of the ship. Snippets only. But they were pushing ahead anyway based on testimony of others. The tosser survived being brained with a fire extinguisher, more's the pity. Other trials in the offing for Footrot and Aaron. In each, the star witness: Samuel Willard.

Kaz studies his face, sees the new bruises there. Courtesy of associates of Turnell who, along with Footrot and Aaron, is being held in detention somewhere on the mainland. Their proxy assassins here in Risdon don't really have their hearts in it, and Sam usually sees them coming. Maybe one day his luck will run out. Karma, he guesses. Sam studies Kaz too, looking for clues, will she stick by him? Why should she? Her arms, bared for the summer outside, goosebumped by the prison chill.

'Can't you ask to be put in isolation, away from those thugs?'

'In with the child molesters?' Sam shakes his head. 'I'll manage.' He misses her. Feels her drifting away from him. Wants this all to be over, to have never happened. 'Change the phone number, is there anywhere you could go and stay for a while?'

'It's in hand.' She blinks away tears. 'Blue Wren Estate would have been nice, eh?'

'Sorry, Kaz.'

'Yeah, me too.' She lets Ollie down to the floor. Hands him a cuddly toy. 'Distract me. What's happening with your case?'

Assault and terrorising Stephanie Howden. Guilty as charged. Still a toss-up between him and Footrot as to who will be charged with her murder. Investigations ongoing. Trespass and criminal damage on Howden's property and on Ros Chen's. Terrorising and burgling Ros. Shooting Moose on the mountainside even though that was Footrot's work. Sam was claiming the shooting of Robert Beckett and illegal disposal of his body, in order to take the heat off Ros. She'd visited him a few times. After all they'd been through together they still ran out of words pretty soon. Each had their own ongoing battles to fight, alone. There was his conduct in Afghanistan, the murders and brutality he'd been part of. A Bayeux tapestry of innocence and guilt to unpick.

'A lawyer's picnic,' he says. 'I'll let them sort it out.'

'But aren't you going to get any deal for cooperating with the Turnell case? Because I'm fucked if I'll be threatened for no good reason.' A brave smile. Maybe Kaz does intend to stand by him.

'I've been advised to be optimistic.' Larissa's podcast has started airing, generating debate, outrage and some unexpected sympathy for Sam. The video he made and the tears he cried, helping his cause.

'I did get one phone call that wasn't threatening,' says Kaz.

'Yeah?'

'Bloke called Qadim? Don't know how he got my number. Just arrived on one of those evacuations from Afghanistan.' Yes, the inevitable had happened. The Taliban were fully back in charge and the evacuations were a predictably heartbreaking shambles. But Qadim must have got lucky and he'll be a handy addition to the Turnell prosecution. 'He said to thank you for doing the right thing and he hopes to visit you soon when his paperwork is arranged. Very formal way of speaking.' She smiles. 'Sexy voice.'

'He's married now, with children.'

'So are you. And I'd fuck you too,' she says through more tears.

—

'Got a moment, Jill?'

With every day that passes, Hughesy seems increasingly comfortable in that office and chair once occupied by Ian Cavanagh. Jill has no complaints. The management style is decidedly less erratic and no longer a game of playing favourites. Poor corrupt and compromised Cav. Although you wouldn't know it from the bells and whistles guard-of-honour send-off given him by Tasmania Police. Full uniform, the Commissioner spouting about the bloke's service to the community, the mental health toll, et cetera. Jill wasn't game to pursue the matter. Hughesy has turned out to be surprisingly empathic, astute and intuitive. And it's getting results. The gangland drive-bys and tit-for-tats have stopped, the culprits dead, fled or in the clink. Jill's star has risen under the new regime and she's been encouraged to reconsider her retirement plans.

'Yep. What's up?' She's hoping for an early departure today. Having dodged the many Covid bullets early in the pandemic, Dad's rest home in Austin's Ferry is on the verge of lockdown after a cases surge following the reopening of borders. As early as tomorrow, she's been led to believe. Sure, her visits don't mean a great deal to him, but she feels obliged anyway.

'The Niamh Cassidy hit-and-run file ready for the Prosecutor's office yet? They've been ringing, wondering where it's at.'

'In a hurry, are they?'

Hughesy shrugs. 'Bit antsy wondering what the new "let-it-rip" health strategy will do to schedules, budgets, personnel, whatever.'

Aren't we all, she concedes. 'A couple of loose ends, should be with them by Friday.' It's Tuesday today, that should be enough time.

'Loose ends?'

'Trembath and Baker.' The worms wriggling on the hook. Each trying to lay the blame on the other. 'Still trying to do a deal.'

'Still? Fuck them. The deal is none of our business. The D'Entrecasteaux standover tactics and suspicious deaths of opponents bear scrutiny, but I personally don't buy his little conspiracy theory about Edward Milsom, Kristin Baker and some war crimes bullshit from the Dark Ages.'

'Why not?' Jill taps a file on her desk. 'The phone records between Meyer, Howden and Milsom all back it up. And the same stuff is playing out in the news right now. Turnell is in freefall – disgraced pundit, medal retracted, dumped candidate – and facing a criminal trial soon.'

'And that one's got a fifty-fifty chance of going somewhere. This one? Another five years earlier. Was Peter Milsom a mass killer? Was he not? Did he kill himself or did somebody help him along? Murky as fuck, like the waters under Milsom's salmon pens.'

'So, your answer's "no" to any deal with Trembath and/or Baker?'

'Absolutely. If someone wants to overrule me down the track, then let them. I've had enough of this bunch of grifters.'

Grifters indeed. Milsom, as well as pocketing millions in pandemic JobKeeper subsidies, has just hit paydirt with the sale of D'Entrecasteaux Salmon to a Canadian bidder, gazumping the earlier Norwegian and Queensland bids. Thrown out of coastal waters near Vancouver by more stringent environmental rules, they are cock-a-hoop at the prospect of a regime-less free-for-all in Tasmania.

'Bin them, Jill. Flick it to the war crimes task force to worry about. Got a domestic homicide in Bridgewater for you to look at. Interested?'

'Lovely, boss. But hoping for an early finish today to go and see Dad.'

'No worries, Jill. And don't call me boss. I know you don't mean it.'

Yep, she thinks, I'll hang around for a few more years.

—

Ros stops for a moment and takes in the view from the Organ Pipes. Out over Hobart, the Channel and beyond. A breathtaking landscape, doubly so on a perfect day like today. Too far away for Ros to see, a seal washes up on a plastic-littered shore off Bruny Island with half a skull blown away, flies buzzing in anticipation of the feast. Another bay, a kid exits the water after swimming, algae coating her lower legs, the beginnings of a rash. A wellboat edges towards a salmon pen with a roar and hiss of hydraulics and engine noise. A salmon leaps, sunlight glinting off silvery scales. A silken splash as it returns to the deep. A bird's-eye view of the salmon pens spreading across the bays and inlets.

AUTHOR NOTE

The ongoing investigations of allegations of war crimes in Afghanistan, as well as the continuing debate about the pros and cons of salmon farming in Tasmania, are matters of public record and frequent news reports. Nevertheless, all characters and events portrayed in this work are fictitious and any resemblance to events or real persons, living or dead, is purely coincidental.

It was an interesting challenge to link two such apparently disparate subjects into the one narrative, but that's the great thing about writing fiction: you get to make up stories. And the further down the path I went, I did pick up threads of connection, certain themes around a sense of entitlement and untouchability which worm their way into many aspects of our society.

I am indebted to two major non-fiction reference works from which I've drawn inspiration: Mark Willacy's *Rogue Forces* and Richard Flanagan's *Toxic*. Both authors shine a bright forensic light into some very dark places and I encourage you to read their excellent books. Any credit for details which make me sound knowledgeable should go to them. Any errors I claim as my own.

Early readers Kath McGinty, Jim McGinty and Martin Shaw all provided valuable feedback along the way. Thank you.

Thank you too to Robert Beckett, who bought a raffle ticket to help raise funds for my local swim group and won the right to have his name attached to a character. Sorry the character didn't last very long, Rob, but you get that in crime fiction.

Thanks again to the fantastic team at Fremantle Press for continuing to support me, in particular, my editor, Georgia Richter, whose wisdom, grace and willingness to indulge my writing adventures is very much appreciated.

As always, a huge thank you to my partner, Kath, my muse and love, for continuing to allow me to pursue my little hobby while you bring in the real money. It is our ongoing adventure together that provides the inspiration for much that I do.

This book was written in lutruwita (Tasmania) on the land of the Melukerdee people of the South East Nation, the true custodians of this land that was never ceded.

MORE GREAT CRIME

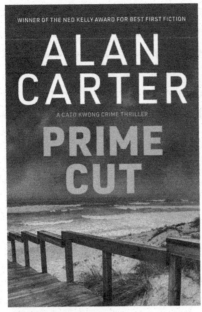
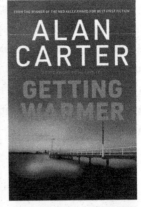

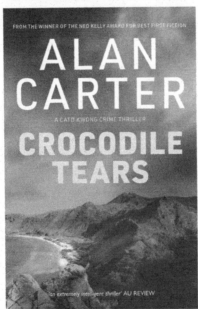
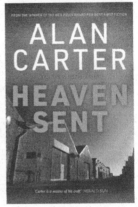
FROM FREMANTLEPRESS.COM.AU

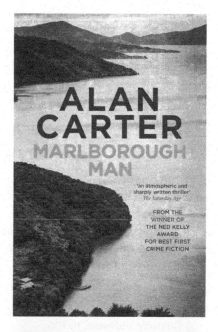
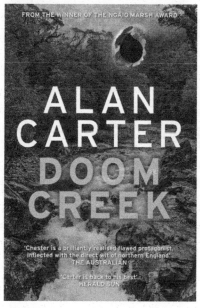

First published 2024 by
FREMANTLE PRESS

Fremantle Press Inc. trading as Fremantle Press
PO Box 158, North Fremantle, Western Australia, 6159
fremantlepress.com.au

Cover image by Zoltan Tasi, unsplash.com/photos/blue-sea-under-orange-cloudy-sky
Designed by Nada Backovic, nadabackovic.com
Printed and bound by IPG

 A catalogue record for this
book is available from the
National Library of Australia

ISBN 9781760993153 (paperback)
ISBN 9781760993160 (ebook)

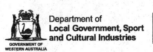

Fremantle Press is supported by the State Government through the
Department of Local Government, Sport and Cultural Industries.

Fremantle Press respectfully acknowledges the Whadjuk people of the
Noongar nation as the Traditional Owners and Custodians of the land
where we work in Walyalup.